DESPERATION'S
FURY

DAVID ANDREW TUCKER

Manufactured in the United States of America

First Printing, January 2019

1-7216109381

ISBN 978-1-7320966-3-9

David Andrew Tucker
mtwordweaver@gmail.com

This is dedicated to my beautiful wife and best friend, Tara – thank you for your love, your support, and your enduring patience.

To my children, Donovan, Brendan, and Ashley – I love you and I'm proud of you all.

CHAPTER 1

FRIDAY, APRIL 16TH

It was nearing daybreak and Seattle's rain-soaked streets were slick beneath the clearing cloud cover of the multi-colored sky. Ben Thompson steered the stolen green coupe into the city park's deserted parking lot at the foot of a sloping hillside. The spot offered seclusion; shrouded by thick stands of conifer trees and overgrown shrubs towering above the tall, untrimmed wild grass. He was safe from any prying eyes. At the edge of the woodland, a narrow two-lane road snaked between the evergreen trees making its way through the elegant neighborhood overlooking the city from the hill's crest high above.

Heavy metal music drummed in low tones from the car's speakers, muted to slightly more than whispering static. Ben couldn't afford to draw attention to himself – not with the law so intent on finding him. He lit an unfiltered cigarette and took a long drag, inhaling the heavy smoke deep into his lungs. Wariness coursed through him. The cops were closing in. His wicked exploits had raised their ire, placing him at the top of their apprehension list. Wherever he traveled, he left destruction in his wake. The victims meant nothing to him. They were merely innocent pawns in his twisted game of crime and violence, and he had nothing left to lose. With ice running through his veins and a heart of stone, he cared for no one other than himself.

He scanned the lights of the homes on the ridge. Somewhere among them, nestled in the serenity of the tall ponderosa pines, he would find Sarah, his older, long-lost sister. He couldn't even remember what she looked like – only fragmented visions of her remained in his memories. They were separated when he was but three years old. She was just a week shy of her fifth birthday at the time – when the drug enforcement agents raided their parent's ramshackle home.

Ben glimpsed at the digital clock in the car's center console. 6:42 AM showed in bright green. He rolled the window down a crack and flicked the butt of his cigarette onto the wet asphalt. The smoldering cherry sizzled on the damp earth and finally died with a few final wisps of smoke. He took a deep whiff of the clean, crisp air breezing into the coupe, instantly contrasting with the stench of stale smoke persisting in the car's interior. Cigarette butts filled the car's ashtray, threatening to spill out of the overloaded bin. The humming of tires on the glazed road passing the park signaled a vehicle was moving up the quiet street. He ducked down into the seat. Regardless of concealment, he couldn't be too cautious. He would have to ditch the stolen car soon. He'd already pushed his luck keeping it for three days.

He grasped his .45 caliber semi-automatic from the passenger seat and tucked it into the waistband of his pants, covering the gun's grip with his gray cotton t-shirt. Examining the crinkled city map, he focused on a penciled-in circle where his sister's house should be in the neighborhood looming on the hill above. *I'll wait another hour… and then, sis'… it's time for a reunion.* His research had been meticulous. The previous months, he scoured the internet, studying his sister and her husband. After Mark Taylor's picture appeared on the cover of Forbes Magazine, no doubt remained his sister and brother-in-law had amassed a sizable fortune from the internet security software Mark co-designed. The lure of easy money beckoned – a temptation too compelling to pass up. And maybe… just maybe… squeezing his lost sister for cash would be far more profitable and easier than a bank heist.

The sports coupe growled to life with a turn of the ignition. Ben steered the car toward the lake at the edge of the lot and parked at the shoreline. He opened the door and hopped out. Walking to the water's edge, he surveyed the murky pool in front of him. It was deep enough. The car would sink to the bottom – if he used the eight-foot-wide wooden pier to get out a way onto the lake. He ambled over to the dock. The varnished boards creaked beneath his black combat boots with each step, but the large diameter logs serving as pylons holding up the structure would be strong enough to support the weight of the vehicle. He slid back behind the steering wheel and shifted the car into reverse, chirping its tires while he sped backward sixty feet from the dock. Thrusting the driver's side door open, he tossed his backpack and faded green jacket onto the damp asphalt. With a quick press of the console buttons on the door's armrest, he lowered the car's two windows. The vehicle would fill with the cloudy lake water and remain submerged and out of sight long enough that he would be far from the scene before the cops ever discovered his visit to the hidden parkland.

He pulled a wooden dowel rod from the cramped backseat – cut just long enough to do the job. Keeping firm pressure on the brake pedal with his foot, he wedged the rod between the driver's seat and the accelerator. The machine groaned while the powerful engine's horsepower strained to overcome the applied brakes. Ben shifted to the edge of the seat, and then leaped from the open door, slamming it shut while the car surged away and toward the dock at high speed. It raced down the wooden planks and sailed through the air once it reached the end of the pier. His plan worked. The vehicle shot across the calm surface of the lake until its momentum could no longer overcome the pull of gravity. With a tremendous splash, water sprayed high into the dense air. After bobbing briefly on the surface, the car sank while large bubbles burped around its sleek exterior.

Ben smirked. He stood and brushed bits of leaves and dirt from his clothes. Snatching his jacket from the ground, he slipped it on and grabbed his backpack from its resting place. He glared at the elegant homes on the ridge in front of him. *Thirty-four Whispering Pines Way...* The long-awaited reunion with Sarah was just a twenty-minute hike up the quiet road. He slung the black canvas bag onto his back and trudged toward his destiny.

Sarah, what have I done? How the hell did it come to this? In a restless state of slumber, Mark Taylor struggled to clear his mind. The bus seat lacked comfort and showed years of wear from the countless number of travelers which had journeyed long and weary miles on the cracked and faded leather upholstery. Each of those unknown souls had their own stories and desires. But, none of that mattered – not with despair clutching each of his senses for the life he left behind eight hours earlier when he boarded the hulking transit bus. He opened his eyes and squinted out the window. Blazing by at sixty miles per hour, the Montana countryside bathed in the early morning light. A light fog filled the valley, and the frosted peaks of the vast Rocky Mountain range broke through the top of the gloom.

He glimpsed at his watch. The hands of the gold Rolex displayed 7:05 a.m. Yes, he made his fortune from technology. But, a digital watch wasn't his style. Some things were better from a simpler time. The events of the previous months turned his world upside-down, and hiding from the reality he created was impossible. His tryst with Stacy Kellner shattered his marriage with Sarah. After hammering out a lucrative sales agreement with Kellner Industries for the Cyber Safe security software he co-designed, a night of excessive drinking clouded his judgment. And in that clouded judgment, he surrendered to temptation. Stacy Kellner was young and beautiful. Her flirtations awakened desires within him which he never knew existed. Their affair lasted only one passionate night, but the consequences would last a lifetime.

Mark slipped on his sunglasses. He groaned and tugged at the black and gray whiskers of his beard. Before that fateful night of betrayal in Phoenix, his beard had always been trimmed short. But after his near-fatal accident and his subsequent trip to recuperate in Montana, he changed. A clean-cut appearance no longer mattered. After the sale of his interest in the software company to his longtime friend and business partner, Dan Wilson, a new life awaited. It wasn't what he wanted. He never planned on leaving Seattle's bright lights behind in a wake of trepidation. But, Montana beckoned. His father's health continued to deteriorate a little bit more each day. And, the situation with Katy Olsen lingered. Did he love her? Only time could reveal the answer. But before he left the ranch and returned to Seattle to face Sarah, Katy made it clear she loved him.

Everything is such a mess. He shielded his eyes from the bright rays of sunlight pouring through the window. His heart ached the further the bus lumbered away from Seattle – further from Sarah and the life he wasted. He pulled his cell phone from the breast pocket of his denim jacket. The display revealed a strong signal – three bars. With a long sigh, he opened a text window to Dan. He tapped out a quick message to his friend.

Dammit. What am I doing?

After a minute passed, Dan's reply buzzed on Mark's phone.

You know you didn't have to go back. You're always welcome here.

Mark leaned forward in his seat and rubbed his temple. The headaches were increasing in intensity, and they never seemed to go away. Yes, Dan would always be his friend – even after revealing he and Sarah were on the cusp of a serious romantic relationship. Mark couldn't blame anyone but himself, nor would he. Like a stone cast upon the surface of a tranquil pond, his affair sent ripples through the lives of those around him. The pit of his stomach churned with agony. Did he make the right decision to return to his father's ranch? Should he have boarded the bus the night before after listening to Sarah's heartbroken plea that he stay in Seattle and attempt to save their marriage? Was he a fool to leave? The questions pummeled his introspections, and no answers were forthcoming.

The bus lurched to a halt. Mark glanced up. The transit terminal lay just outside his window. *Now what?* He hadn't told his father or Katy he would be arriving that morning, just four days after he left in the first place. Until he climbed the entry steps into the bus the night before, he never expected to return so soon. Despite Sarah's appeal they attempt to reconcile, the notion of competing with his best friend for her affection was too much to bear. They had been separated for eight months before their brief reunion, and it seemed like a lifetime apart. Gazing at her on the footstep of their elegant home's front door upon his return, she seemed like a distant stranger. The bitterness of their split made him question every decision he had made. It seemed as though that would be the constant in his life from the moment he saw the rage burning in Sarah's eyes the night she discovered his infidelity.

Mark shrugged off his reverie and climbed out of his seat. He shuffled down the narrow aisle splitting the seats on the aging bus, down the steep steps at the exit, and onto the pavement. There would be plenty of time later to mourn his circumstances. But at that moment, more immediate problems required his attention. *How the hell am I supposed to get to dad's place? No one is expecting me back.* Being stuck in the unfamiliar city of Butte wasn't a pleasant thought.

He collected his duffel bag then plodded toward the main terminal. A lone taxi – an early model, gray minivan with a magnetic sign slapped haphazardly on the driver's side door – waited in the passenger unloading zone in front of the building. Leaning against the front fender of the disheveled vehicle, a haggard man puffed on a cigar. Dressed in faded blue jeans and a tattered denim jacket, the old fellow eyed Mark and pushed the grimy baseball cap covering the length of his shaggy white hair higher on his brow.

Mark adjusted the duffel bag on his shoulder and approached the driver. "Are you looking for a fare?"

The old man dropped his cigar to the asphalt and crushed it with the weathered tip of his tan cowboy boot. He peered up at Mark and seemed to size him up. "Yeah, how far ya goin'?"

"About fifteen miles outside of Crystal Creek – a little

town northeast of here."

Scratching at the white scruff covering his cheek, the driver hesitated. "Hmm... I know where that is... it's a might far – about eighty miles one way, I'm thinkin'."

Mark nodded. "Yes, I know it's a long way... but I'd be happy to pay for your troubles."

"How much?"

"Does four hundred dollars sound fair?"

The old man's face lit up. He cleared his throat, obviously pleased with the offer. He sniffed and rubbed the back of his neck. "Well... that sounds like it would be worth my time. Ya got cash?"

"Absolutely," Mark answered.

The old man cocked his head and squinted at Mark with steely-gray eyes. "Ya mind if I see it first?"

Mark huffed and strained to hide his agitation. He dropped his bag to the pavement and reached inside his jacket, pulling his wallet from the interior pocket. Snatching four crisp one hundred dollar bills from the billfold's soft leather, he held them out for the driver to inspect. "Satisfied?"

The driver grinned, revealing tobacco-stained teeth with a few missing from the gum line of his lower jaw. "Yessir, that'll do." He scurried to the side of the van and grasped the door handle. The door screeched with a hair-raising pitch as he slid it open. "Hop on in and make yourself comfortable."

Tossing the bag on the far edge of the rear seat, Mark scooted onto the ripped cloth bench. Discolored from age and wear, the once blue fabric appeared more of a ghastly white than its original hue. Mark wrinkled his nose and settled in. The fetor of old cigar smoke filled his nostrils and burned his throat. He rolled his window down, gasping for fresh air. *I'm going to need an hour-long shower once I get to dad's place to get rid of this stink.*

The old man plopped down into the driver's seat and turned the key in the ignition. A sickening grinding noise clattered from beneath the hood, then diminished into a series of weakening taps. He peeked over his shoulder and shot a look at Mark – his face a shade of crimson. "Might be gettin' time to take her in for some service," he chuckled. With a few more turns of the ignition, the van sputtered to life and backfired instantly, sending a choking cloud of acrid black smoke spewing into the air. The old man slapped his wrinkled hand on the dashboard. "Good girl. Good girl."

Mark slumped into his seat. He shook his head while rubbing his brow. *What I wouldn't give to have my own wheels right about now.* The doctors still urged him not to drive – not with the lingering issues from the concussion he sustained when he was mowed down by the car back in August, eight months earlier. He already felt helpless – reliving the emotional turmoil of losing Sarah. But not having the freedom to do the things he'd always taken for granted… wore him down more with each passing day.

The taxi driver peeked at Mark in the rearview mirror. "Uh, sorry 'bout the ol' girl chuggin' a bit. She's not pretty, but she gets to where she needs to go."

"No problem. As long as it can make it to my dad's place, I'll be fine." Mark reached into the side pocket of his duffel bag and pulled out his earbuds. He tucked one into each ear. *This guy seems like a talker. Some tunes will drown him out. Hopefully, he gets the hint.* With a few flips through the screens on his cell phone, the music app quickly sent soft jazz flowing to his ears. While the music offered a soothing distraction from the jostling ride compliments of the crumbling roadway beneath the tired old van's spinning tires, Mark scrolled through the image gallery on his phone. Like a chronological record of his life, the series of pictures began with image after image of Sarah – illustrations of happier times. And while his heart sank more and more with each digital memory of his lost love, he finally came to the picture of Katy standing beside her beloved white Arabian colt. He smiled. A sense of ease surged through him. His friend waited just on the other side of the rugged peaks, and he couldn't wait to see her again.

CHAPTER 2

It was just a few minutes after eight o'clock in the morning. Ben trekked through the upscale neighborhood. Clad in ripped blue jeans and a faded green army jacket, he was, without a doubt, out of place. His gaze danced warily around his surroundings. He was close to finding his ticket to freedom away from the ever-present threat of arrest. He needed cash. His sister would fill that need. Sly and cunning, Ben excelled as a master of manipulation. And if his gift of words wouldn't be enough… well, then… he would resort to other measures.

He tugged a black, knitted stocking cap from his jacket pocket and stretched it over the ragged tufts of his cropped blonde hair. All the wanted posters he had seen with his likeness displayed him with shoulder length hair and a long beard. A quick trim and shave using his folding combat knife in the truck stop's restroom back on the Oregon-Washington border altered his appearance just enough. When he bumped into the Washington State Trooper coming out of the mini-mart at the edge of Seattle's city limits, the veteran trooper didn't recognize him. Considering the extent of the manhunt directed toward his capture, it was a welcome surprise. Getting careless wasn't in his nature. One little slip... one small instance of becoming too comfortable... would be his demise. And, his mind was already made up – he was ready to go down in a hail of gunfire with his pistol drawn and barrel blazing, rather than surrender and stand trial for the heinous crimes he committed. After ten years on the run, crisscrossing the country on his deadly rampage, a death sentence waited – and he was prepared to make his last stand at any moment.

Ben advanced along the sidewalk eyeing the luxurious homes. They flaunted wealth with their grandeur and size. They reeked of money. *Big sister must be more loaded than I thought. Maybe I should modify my plan a bit. There's more in this for me than I expected.* He scanned the addresses displayed on the mailboxes. *There it is.* A red-bricked column with a silver mailbox protruding out its side facing the street advertised the number thirty-four in polished brass numerals. An expansive two-story home sat at the end of a driveway wide enough for three cars. The lush front yard boasted a sizable lawn groomed with meticulous care. Evergreen shrubs, spaced evenly between thriving beds of brightly colored daisies and petunias, lined the red bricks of the walkway leading to the home's entrance.

Ben hesitated and wiped his face with the sleeve of his jacket. He was as presentable as he could make himself considering the circumstances. Grasping the butt of his pistol, he pulled it from the front of his pants and tucked it inside the waistband at the small of his back. He strode up the walkway to the exquisite hardwood front door and pressed the doorbell.

Sarah Taylor laid curled up on the plush, white leather couch in the front living room. In front of her, on a glass coffee table with frosted beveled edges, steam wisped into the air above a fresh mug of coffee. The doorbell chimed in alternating tones and echoed throughout the home. She placed a bookmark between the pages of her romance novel and set it on the arm of the couch. Strolling to the front door, she peeked through the peephole. A stranger stood at the doorstep. Through her limited view, he appeared ragged and dirty. *What is a vagrant doing in this neighborhood?*

She quietly stepped away from the door toward where her phone lay on the couch's seat cushion. A quick call to 911 would solve the problem. Clutching the phone, she tapped the emergency number on the virtual keypad.

"Sarah? Sarah Taylor?" a voice called out from the other side of the door.

She hesitated with her thumb on the phone's call key. The voice was unfamiliar. *How does he know my name? My phone number and address are unlisted...* She tip-toed back to the peephole and scrutinized the man. A gentle knock caused her heart to skip a beat, and she jumped back. After a deep breath, she reached for the deadbolt. Her fingers lingered for a second on the brass latch. Her instincts screamed out to step away from the door, but without another thought, she impulsively released the lock and opened it. "Yes, what is it?"

The man stood in silence for a moment looking her over from head to toe. "Sarah? It's me... Ben..."

Sarah opened the door wider. The name coursed through her memories in a jumble of confusion. No. It couldn't be. It couldn't be him – not after so long. Not after so many years of searching for him without success. In the depths of his piercing blue eyes, something... something seemed familiar. She took a deep breath and tilted her head, studying him. "Benny?"

Ben grinned and nodded. "Yeah. I don't remember much... but I know you used to call me that – before they took us away."

Sarah covered her mouth with both hands. Tears trickled down her cheeks. How many hours had she spent trying to find him? How many times over the years did she search? And there he was – standing before her right then and there. "Oh my God," she muttered. She stepped to him and placed her hands on his arms while she scrutinized every feature of his face.

"Uh... sorry to just show up out of the blue, but I was so excited when I found your address... I had to come see you. I wanted to know if you even still thought about me – or even if you remembered me." Ben shuffled his feet.

Sarah barely remembered the last time she saw her younger brother. It seemed like a lifetime ago. The young siblings had spent two lonely nights and long days on their own after their parents were tipped off that a drug enforcement team was preparing to raid their forsaken home. Thinking of only themselves, their parents fled. Bringing two toddlers with them would just slow them down and they wouldn't take the risk. The front door of the small, two-bedroom home tore away from its hinges when agents burst in, their faces masked, and their bodies covered in black, bullet-proof Kevlar. The two children screamed in terror while the strangers swarmed inside, guns drawn, seeking their prey.

Wiping her cheeks with the back of her hand, Sarah yielded to the nostalgia tugging at her soul and said, "Come in. Please."

Ben shuffled inside, shifting his gaze all about when he entered the tiled foyer. "Wow. This is a really nice place."

"Would you like to set your bag down? Maybe hang up your jacket?" Sarah motioned to the couch in the adjoining living room. "We can sit and catch up."

He slipped off his backpack and set it beside the mahogany coat rack standing next to the entrance. "Yeah, that would be good. I think I'll keep my jacket on though – if you don't mind."

"No. That's fine. I just made a fresh pot of coffee. Would you like a cup?"

Ben nodded. "Sure. It's been a while since I had a good cup of coffee." He rubbed his hands together and shivered. "I'm freezing my ass off. Something warm would help get rid of the chill."

Sarah sauntered into the kitchen and took a ceramic coffee mug from the cupboard. While she poured the robust coffee into the cup, she called out, "Would you like cream or sugar?"

"Both would be awesome."

She finished preparing his drink and strolled back to the living room carrying his beverage. He paced restlessly, scanning his surroundings. She handed him the mug. "Please, sit."

He took a long sip from the mug then set it on the glass table. Wiping his palms on the seat of his pants, he sat on the white leather couch. "Good... I mean... great coffee. Thanks."

Sarah settled in at the opposite end of the couch and placed her hands on her knees. "So, I didn't see a car. Did you walk here?"

Ben cleared his throat and scratched his temple. "Uh... yeah. I took a city bus to get to the closest stop. It was only a mile or two on foot to get here."

"Where are you headed? Where have you been?" Sarah reached up and raked both her hands through the long blonde locks of her hair. She laughed in exasperation. "God, where do we start? It's been so many years."

"I know. It's been a long time. I've just been around. I go from here to there. I don't like staying in any one place too long. I'd rather drift with the breeze."

Sarah studied him carefully. His appearance revealed a man aging prematurely. She was thirty-eight. That would make him thirty-six. While she scrutinized him, her thoughts drifted back to when their bond was shattered after the police raid.

Child Protective Services took custody of the two siblings, caring for them under the guidance of stale state laws and antiquated bureaucratic policies. The dedicated professionals did what they could – feeding and bathing the two young children, rinsing away the layers of dirt and grime which covered the innocence of their tiny faces and bodies after their lifetime of neglect. Attendants were able to cleanse the adolescents' bodies, but they were helpless as to wiping away the horrid nightmares which raced through the little ones' minds in the darkest hours of the night when the hopelessness of their existence pervaded their thoughts. No amount of tender hugs –filled with warmth and love – could erase the horrors that little Ben and Sarah had witnessed.

It wasn't long before the two were separated – each sent to a different foster home while they awaited adoption. Sarah was lucky – Mike and Tammy Fisher welcomed her into their loving home. They were childless, as Tammy was barren. With their thoughts set on adopting the quiet little girl, she became the center of their universe, and she was loved.

Thankful for the saving grace of her adoptive parents, overwhelming sorrow swelled in Sarah's heart. Her brother's life hadn't been blessed like hers. "That sounds like a rough life, Ben." Her eyes welled with tears. "I tried finding you many times. I even considered hiring a private investigator… but I guess… life got in the way, and I never followed through. The last information I dug up was about you being adopted by a family on the East Coast. But that was years ago. I never learned what became of you after the adoption. I never was able to find out the family's name or where they were exactly."

Ben fidgeted on the cushioned seat. "They were just a family in Virginia. They were okay, I guess. I was more like a pet to them than anything else. They were pretty rich. I think I was more of a charity case for them than an actual member of the family."

Sarah sat for several minutes while Ben filled her in on his past. His recounting seemed contrived, and he divulged details of his life as though he sought pity. She placed her hand on his arm. "I'm so sorry things turned out so difficult for you."

"I'm doing okay. I'm not gonna cry about any of it. Everything that's happened to me has made me strong. I learned how to take care of myself a long time ago."

The tone of Ben's voice and the intensity in his eyes when he spoke sent a shiver up Sarah's spine. She didn't doubt he was her brother. Their features were similar, and he recited tiny details about their shared past no one else would know – or could know – even though they were foggy memories. But, the more he spoke, and the longer he sat there, it became increasingly clear something wasn't quite right. He swiveled about, seemingly soaking up every detail of his surroundings. Sarah's brain signaled danger while uneasiness grew within her. *Why does he seem to be getting so angry? He's really giving me the creeps.* She took a quick sip of coffee. Hopefully, he hadn't recognized her apprehension. After licking her lips, she placed her mug on the glass table. "So, what are your plans?"

A smirk broadened on his weary face. He leaned back into the couch and stretched. A vexing glint sparkled in his eyes. "I dunno. I was kinda hoping we could get to know each other better. You know – reconnect after so many years."

Sarah casually scooted her cell phone closer to her thigh. Maybe he didn't notice. With every passing second, he became increasingly restless and agitated. *I really need to get him to leave.* The hair on her neck bristled. "Um… sure… I'd like that." She snatched the phone and held it tight against her body, obscuring it from his view. She stood. "Well… I'm really glad you stopped by. But, it's getting late and… you know… I do… uh… actually, have someplace I need to be soon. If you want to leave me a number where I can reach you… or where you're staying…"

Ben lunged from the couch and faced her. He grabbed her wrist and seized the phone from her hand. Evil blazed in his once-friendly eyes. "You're shaking, sis'."

Sarah strained to free her wrist from his grip. It was no use. "Look… Ben… you're *really* scaring me." She trembled. Tears fell from her eyes, and she wiped them away with her unrestrained hand. Her voice quivered when she asked, "*Money?* Do you need some money? I think I have a few hundred dollars in my purse."

Glancing around the interior of the home, he slowly looked back at her and glared deep into her eyes. Any bit of warmth his eyes contained upon their first meeting drained away. "I think you can fix me up with more than just a few hundred dollars, sis'… a *lot* more."

She swallowed. The lump in her throat threatened to stifle her breath. Over the course of an hour, her joy of being reunited with her little brother had evolved into pure terror. *What was I thinking let him in? How could I be so stupid?* Okay. Whatever he wanted – she would pretend to go along with it. At the first opportunity, she would bolt from the house… to a neighbor's… anywhere. *Just get away!* Sarah took a few deep breaths. There was no point in exposing the amount of fear pulsing through her body like an electrical current – it would only empower him further. Relaxing her stance, she ceased her struggle to free herself from his grip. "Ben, I'll help you any way I can. I have some money… you can have it. You need to understand though, my husband and I split up… most of our finances are tied up with court proceedings…"

Ben stared at her with clenched teeth. "I *don't* believe you," he snarled. He dragged her with him to the front door, her feet kicking and sliding across the expensive cream-colored tiles covering the floor. With a quick slap, he activated the deadbolt on the door. Reaching to his backpack, he snatched it from the floor with his free hand.

"*Please*, you're *hurting* me!" Sarah pleaded while he lugged her out of the foyer and down the long, tiled hallway taking her deep into the heart of the home.

"This is an awfully fancy place you've got. It's big enough I can find a safe place to keep you from causing any trouble."

Ben glowered at his surroundings while they made their way to the den at the back of the home. Stepping inside the vast room, he flung her to the floor. While she lay on the luxurious carpet writhing in pain from the impact of her fall, Ben unzipped the front pocket of his backpack. He reached inside and pulled out several half-inch-wide zip ties. Kneeling next to her, he rolled her to her stomach.

He forced her hands together behind her back and secured them tightly at the wrists with one of the nylon zip ties. After binding her ankles together in the same manner, he completed his ensnarement by connecting the two bands with a single zip tie. Sarah lay hog-tied with her face pressed into the soft strands of the crème colored carpet. She struggled for breath while Ben jammed his knee into her back. "Please…"

He pulled his pistol from the waistband of his pants and laid the cold-blue steel of the weapon's slide against her cheek. Leaning close to her ear, he muttered, "Now, you're not gonna cause me any trouble, *are you?*" He swiped the hair from her eyes with the pistol's muzzle. "I would hate to have to hurt you… especially considering how long it's been since we've seen each other." He sneered, and added, "We've got *lots* of catching up to do."

Sarah clamped her eyes shut. His stinking breath fell against her cheek like fire. The tang of stale cigarettes churned her stomach. She was at his mercy. The pressure of his knee in her back subsided. She opened her eyes while he searched the room. *God, someone help me, please!* She struggled to regain control of her senses, but her efforts were in vain. The plastic straps binding her wrists and ankles cut into her skin with every movement. It was hopeless. She resisted the impulse to scream as loud as her lungs would permit – no one would hear. The house was too large, and the distance to the nearest neighbor was too far. Besides, it would only anger him even more – and anger seemed to grant him dominion.

Ben scurried to his backpack. He snatched a partial

roll of duct tape from within the bag's main compartment and tore off a strip seven inches long. Hauling Sarah to her knees, he supported her with his grip while slapping the length of tape over her mouth with his free hand. Once it was firmly in place, he released his hold. She fell to the floor, sobbing.

He wiped his nose with his sleeve and looked around nervously. He shifted his eyes to her. "Don't go anywhere, sis'. I'm gonna go do some looking around." Patting the grip of the pistol stuffed in the front of his pants, he said, "Remember – no causing *any* trouble."

Sarah pressed her eyelids shut, but tears still escaped and rolled down the contours of her fair-skinned cheeks and onto the long fibers of the plush carpeting. While she lay there trembling, her thoughts turned to Mark. Would she live to see him again? What would he say if he knew she had been so foolish by letting a man she didn't know into their home? The panic filling her heart slowly transformed into regret. She should have fought harder to stop Mark from getting on that bus. They agreed to separate before making the final decision regarding divorce, but what if this was it? What if the dire situation she faced prevented them ever being together again? Yes, she was terrified of the violent man she once knew as her brother. But while she wept, the notion of never having accepted Mark's heartfelt apology lingered in her mind. *I want to find a way to forgive you, Mark... more than I realized.*

Dread numbed her senses. Fate might not permit her the opportunity to grant absolution.

CHAPTER 3

The decrepit van traveled down the interstate for several miles before exiting onto the state highway. It chugged up the high mountain passes and weaved between craggy peaks towering high above the green, grass-filled valleys which lay surrounded by a tall dense forest of ponderosa pines, western larch, and Douglas fir. Mark stared out the window in awe while the stunning scenery rolled past. Seeing the beauty of the wilderness never grew tiring. Every time he was confident his eyes had beheld the grandest of view, another bend in the road would offer an even more spectacular sight. Watching the majestic firs and spruce trees dancing with the breeze was like witnessing poetry in motion.

After a couple of long hours, the approaching turnoff came into view. "Make a right just after the next mile marker. My dad's place is a little over six miles down the dirt road," Mark said. Relief filled his mind after enduring the seemingly longest stretch of seventy-plus miles he had ever traveled. The beauty of the terrain made the trip more bearable, but he ached for the journey to find its conclusion. His nerves refused to settle while he peered through the windshield of the rickety taxi. The van slowed down and veered off the paved county road onto the dirt track leading to his father's property. The vehicle bounced and jostled. The ruts were deep and plentiful, and the van's tires spun helplessly in their futile attempt to gain traction in the mix of gravel and dirt.

The driver gripped the steering wheel tight between his white-knuckled hands. "Holy smoke… I'm a'thinkin' four hundred dollars might have been a tad light for the fare, considerin' this here road… if that's what ya can call it." He swatted the grungy ball cap from his head and rubbed his sweaty brow. "It'll cost me more than four hundred bucks to fix all the breakin' this road is doin' to my poor girl," he lamented.

Four hundred dollars is more than this piece of crap-on-wheels is worth. Mark anxiously tapped his fingers on his knees and looked out at the dense timberland engulfing both sides of the road. He tucked his tablet back into his duffel bag and tugged at the zipper, closing the partially open bag. "They must have gotten a good storm or two over the past few days. I was here just four days ago, and the road was in much better condition." The condition of the road was the last thing he was paying attention to when he last traveled it. He was thinking of Sarah – of Katy – of his father – and where they all fit into his life from that moment on while his father drove him to the bus station in Butte. It was a sudden and unplanned departure. But he needed to contend with Sarah after eight months of living in exile.

And four days later, he was back where he began. He left with the hope he would find answers to several questions, but less than six miles from his journey's destination, the questions lingered. The harder he contemplated everything that was important to him, the more uncertainty ensued. Soon, he would see Katy again. He couldn't deny how much he missed her. Feelings he never experienced before filled his heart and soul when they were together. But love? There was only one woman he had ever truly loved, and they parted ways less than twenty-four hours earlier. *Could* he even love another woman? The more he considered the different possibilities, the more his head throbbed. A queasy feeling tugged at him from the pit of his stomach. Katy was in love with him. She made her feelings clear before his exodus. But, she wouldn't push him and risk the sacred bond they shared.

Twenty minutes later, the van sputtered through the open six-tiered galvanized steel gates of his father's ranch. The collection of buildings sat encircled by steep, timbered hills on three sides; with the entrance overlooking an extensive meadow just across the back country road to the south. The sprawling compound at the heart of the property's two hundred acres was a welcome sight. Mark stared out the dust-covered window at the grand log home at the center of the complex. He took a deep breath. *I'm home.*

The van backfired with a loud bang after the frazzled driver shifted the van into park. "Well, mister, I hope ya enjoyed the drive." He flicked at a grease-stained yellow lighter and tickled the flame across the end of a cigar butt he had been voraciously chewing the last several miles. Taking a long puff of the noxious-smelling stogie, he muttered, "I know I sure as heck didn't enjoy them last seven miles."

"The ride was a long one, but I'm happy to be here. Thank you for bringing me." Mark handed five one hundred dollar bills to the man. "Here's an extra hundred for your troubles."

"Why, thank ya. That's a might nice of ya."

Sliding the side door open after a brief struggle to get the stubborn latch to release, Mark stepped out onto the gravel drive. He grabbed his bag from the bench seat and then slammed the door closed. With a quick wave, he bid farewell to the quirky man. He took a few steps up the circular drive toward the main house and stopped. He closed his eyes and lifted his face to feel the warmth of the gentle rays of early afternoon sunlight falling upon his skin. With a deep breath, he inhaled the clean mountain air carrying the sweet aroma of the surrounding pine trees on the breeze while horse hooves pounded in quick succession on the distant meadow's fertile ground.

"Well, I'll be!" a familiar voice bellowed out from behind the home's screen door. It creaked as the stout old cowboy pushed through it and clomped out onto the weathered planks of the front porch, limping with each ginger step.

Mark opened his eyes and gazed at his father. "Do you allow unexpected visitors?" he called out. He strolled the remaining distance to the porch steps and paused before climbing them.

The old man chuckled with a huge grin plastered on his face. He pushed his soiled straw cowboy hat higher on his brow. "Well, it depends on who it is that comes a'callin'!"

The wooden steps groaned with each of Mark's footsteps while he climbed them. He stood in front of the old man and dropped his duffel bag to the ground. "Hello, dad."

Will Taylor reached out and embraced his son with a big bear hug. He stepped back, and his joyful expression turned serious. "I'd be lyin' if I didn't say I was happy to be seein' ya again so soon… but tell me son, are ya all right?"

Mark sighed. He wasn't going to attempt to hide his angst, but he wasn't about to discount his pleasure for returning either. "I'm still a mess. But, I'll be okay. I couldn't stay in Seattle – it just didn't feel like it was home anymore."

The old man's gray eyes filled with understanding as they fell upon his son. He nodded. "Well, let's get that bag of yours to your room – then you and me can set on the front porch for a bit and talk. Sound agreeable?"

"Yeah, I could use a few bits of your old-fashioned sage advice right now." Mark swiveled and scanned the various outbuildings and the large metal barn just across the way from the main house.

"No worries, my boy," Will said with a few pats on Mark's back. "Miss Katy is taking the colt out for a stretch right now." He glanced up at the trail winding its way up the side of one of the forest-covered hills cloistering the compound. "She'll be back soon, I'm sure. I think she'll be pretty happy you're back. She's been mopin' around since I carted you away." He plucked off his hat and scratched the top of his head through the thinning gray and white hairs covering his scalp. "In all the five years she's been here, I don't ever recall her goin' such a long stretch sayin' so little." He popped his hat back on and slapped Mark's shoulder. "C'mon, let's get ya settled."

Mark's heart raced. He was anxious to see her again – much more than he cared to admit. "Yeah. I'll go toss this in my room – then we'll talk."

Will waited until Mark entered the rustic log home, and then followed behind him after pulling the screen door shut. Mark trudged down the long hallway to his room. It was just as he left it four days earlier – except for the clean sheets covering the full-size bed. He stepped over to the lone wooden chair in the room sitting beside the four-paned window and placed his duffel bag on the seat. The room was meager at best, but he found it had been comfortable during the previous eight months. The small closet hidden behind the single door was large enough for several days' worth of clothing, and the tall five-drawer dresser standing between the cabinet and doorway was suitable for his miscellaneous apparel.

He plopped down on the edge of the mattress and surveyed the room. Eight months earlier, he stumbled into the room for the first time with his shattered leg encased in a cumbersome ceramic cast. The light-colored pine panels covering the walls seemed less than welcoming at the time. But throughout countless sleepless nights, he found their scarred surfaces soothing to his heavy conscience and aching soul while he memorized every split and every knot they embodied. Peering over to the window, he remembered his first night on the property. Through the weather-smudged glass, he had spotted Katy in her cabin forty feet away, separated only by the fresh air and the patch of wild grass covering the space between the two buildings. Her graceful figure stole his breath while he unintentionally witnessed her undress before retiring for the night.

He shook off his daydream. Reaching to the cramped stand next to the head of the bed, he scooted the burnished antique lamp a few inches off to the side. After setting his cell phone down by the lamp's base, he stood and shuffled down the hall to the front door, passing the living room to his left and the kitchen to his right. He joined his father on the porch. The old man sat on a pine bench between the front door and the living room's large picture window.

Will patted the empty seat beside him. "Take a load off, son."

Mark sat and clasped his hands in front of him. He stared at the scuffed deck beneath his feet for a moment, and then shifted his gaze to his father. "Damn, dad. I thought everything would be better once I talked to Sarah. But I'm more torn up now than before."

Will sat looking straight ahead, staring out across the compound and to the lithic mountains across the valley to the south. He seemed lost in thought. After a long pause, he took a deep breath. "Son, I know what it's like to lose the one you love the most. After the cancer took your mother, I didn't know how I could go on without her... I just knew I had to. I know it's got to be kinda how you might be feelin' right now."

Mark shook his head. "No, it's completely different. Losing mom wasn't anything you had any control over. I lost Sarah because I broke her trust. I betrayed our wedding vows."

"Yes, but the feeling of loss makes ya feel helpless – no matter what the cause. The fact is you're still apart from the one you love the most. That's not somethin' you can ever get over. You can learn to live with it… but it's a wound that don't ever heal."

Mark leaned his head back against the logs forming the home's exterior front wall. He blew a long exhale in frustration. "Sarah asked me to stay. She didn't want me to leave Seattle. I couldn't do it. The entire time I was there, all I thought about was being here." He pounded his fist on his knee. "I love Sarah so much… and yet… it seemed like we were strangers. We talked for hours, but all the hurt remained – for both of us. It's like no matter how many words were spoken between us; nothing was better. And yet, the further the bus got from Seattle, the more I wondered if I made the right decision. Should I have stayed?"

Will pushed the brim of his hat higher on his head and leaned forward. "Only *you* can answer that question, son. When I first met with Sarah before we went to the hospital to check on you after the accident, she was pretty tore up. She was feelin' a lot of the same indecision as you – just from a different angle. The poor girl was hatin' you for what you'd done and not sure if she even cared if she ever saw you again."

"She seems to be over the hate – but she said she wasn't ready to forgive me." He stroked the salt and pepper whiskers of his beard. "I don't blame her. I'm not sure what I did deserves forgiveness."

Stretching his right leg out in front of him, the old man massaged his knee. He grimaced and relaxed back against the backboard of the pine bench. "Son, if in your heart, you truly understand the wrong you did and you're truly sorry for it, then there's nothin' wrong with askin' to be forgiven. I remember you and me talkin' about this when I was first drivin' you here when you got your busted-up body out of that hospital bed. Forgiveness might come in time... but there won't ever be any forgettin'..."

"I know. Sarah and I talked about that too." Mark winced and rubbed his throbbing temple. The events of the previous months had caused deep furrows to form on his forehead. He felt much older than his thirty-nine years. In a few months – early July – he would celebrate his fortieth birthday. It would be the first time since he was a young teenager that he wouldn't be celebrating the occasion with Sarah. Their high school romance had evolved quickly into true love, and they rarely had been separated for any period longer than a few days.

"So what's your plan? Are you here to stay?"

Mark cleared his throat. "Yeah, I'd like to stay – if you were serious about the offer you made before you dropped me off at the bus terminal."

Will patted Mark's back. "Yes, my boy, I was serious. You and me spent more time apart than I wanted. Havin' you around would make this ol' codger very pleased."

"Thanks, dad. I really appreciate that. When I first got here months ago, I thought I'd hate being away from

Seattle… out here in the middle of nowhere. But you were right – once this place gets a grip on you – it doesn't let go."

"It sure don't," the old man chuckled. "Have ya made arrangements for all your belongings to make their way out here?"

Mark shook his head. "Not completely. After I boxed up all my stuff, I had the moving company take it to Butte. The truck is on hold at their terminal there. I wanted to talk to you first."

"Call 'em up. Tell them movin' boys to bring it over." Will gestured at the line of metal buildings and log cabins topped with green aluminum roofs. "Only a few of the hands live here on the property. Most are locals who drive in from town every day. Lord knows there are plenty of empty buildings to store stuff if it don't fit in the big house. Or if you're wantin' your own space, two of the cabins are furnished and vacant."

"The room I'm in will be fine. I told Sarah to keep all the furniture. It was meant for the house back in Seattle anyway. I just have miscellaneous crap. I could use some storage space – but I won't need much."

Will struggled to get to his feet. Using the armrest of the log bench, he pulled himself up. Mark rose from his seat and braced the old man's right arm until he steadied himself. "Some days I feel just a bit older than seventy-four." He stomped his cowboy boots on the porch a few times in a whimsical jig, then said, "But as long as I keep these tired old knees and feet movin', I'll keep chuggin' along. Now, get your phone call made and get your gear headed this way."

"I will. Maybe tonight at dinner we can discuss some ideas I have about the ranch."

"You just worry about gettin' settled in and comfortable again. We'll have plenty of time later for ranch talk." The thudding of hooves accompanied a few whinnies. The two men looked over to the expansive barn across the compound. A young woman with her long auburn tresses lifting on the wind emerged from the tree line atop a spirited white Arabian and trotted toward the open bay door at the southern end of the structure. Will glanced at Mark and grinned. "It's lookin' like you have a few hellos to make before you start thinkin' about anything else." He squeezed Mark's arm then shuffled through the open screen door and into the house.

Mark strolled to the edge of the porch while Katy Olsen lashed the colt's reins to a metal hitching post next to the barn. Seemingly aware of his presence, she whirled around and faced his direction. She paused. With a constrained pace, she crossed the expanse of the courtyard toward him. He rambled down the porch steps and met her halfway. She was as beautiful as ever; even garbed in her dusty, faded blue jeans and the red, long-sleeve t-shirt. They stood toe-to-toe – her well-worn cowgirl boots to his expensive sneakers. Her lovely face glowed in the brilliance of the sunshine. He gazed into her light blue eyes. They beamed with affection. "Hello, Katy," he said softly.

Katy shifted her gaze from his and looked to the ground. She reached her hand to his shoulder and gripped his flannel shirt firmly with her delicate fingers. Falling into his embrace, she clung to his six-foot frame with all her might. "I thought I'd never see you again," she said in muffled sobs.

Mark brushed the long curls of hair from her eyes and searched them for understanding. "I'm sorry I had to go. I had to face her. I couldn't go on carrying the shame anymore without telling her in person how sorry I am for what I did to her."

"I know… I guess I'm just selfish. After all the time we spent together, I didn't realize… I didn't want to accept… how much you mean to me." She pursed her lips then added. "I didn't think I would fall for you – but I *did*."

Mark's chest tightened. Words he wished to speak knotted up in his throat. Denying his feelings for her grew more difficult by the moment while he studied her. But, the time wasn't right. Conflict raged within his broken heart. Sarah remained in his thoughts, and her memory wouldn't fade no matter how hard he fought to chase her image from his mind. He cocked his head to the side and took Katy's hand in his. "I just don't know where I'm at emotionally. I'm so… so *lost*. Sarah and I have been married for nearly twenty years. I still love her, Katy. It's going to take me time to get my head and heart straight." He paused. How could he find the words to help her understand what he didn't understand himself? He drew in a deep breath and stared at the eastern slopes of the great Rocky Mountain range soaring high into the blue sky off to the west. Focusing back on her, he touched his fingers to her chin and directed her gaze to his. "Please be patient with me? I have intense feelings for you… I wish I could explain them. Please don't shut me out – I need time."

Katy wiped a tear from her cheek with the back of her hand. She smiled and nodded. "I won't shut you out. I won't rush you. I'll be happy to have any part of you – even if all you're able to give me is friendship…"

"Thank you." He cleared his throat. "Now how about we get that wild little colt of yours groomed and stabled for the night?"

"Okay," she replied.

The two meandered back to the hitching post where the colt pawed impatiently at the ground while he waited for Katy's return. They laughed and joked while they attended to the feisty young horse, trading small talk while they worked. Mark planned on presenting his idea of investing in the horse breeding operation to his father that evening. His fortune would serve him well only if it were used for something meaningful, and there wasn't anything more important than investing in the ranch – a memorial to his departed mother.

CHAPTER 4

Ben skulked about the Taylor household. Sarah was secure in her restraints – bound to a long brass footrest protruding from the base of the grand mahogany bar in the den downstairs. She wouldn't be able to hold him back from his methodical planning. Nor would she be able to flee. He pilfered through the home freely, acquiring items useful in aiding his escape.

He glided from room to room, searching for anything of significant value. While he rummaged through Sarah's personal effects, the elegance of the residence left him awestruck. Tall vaulted ceilings loomed high above the fancy tile floors of the long hallways and expansive kitchen. Plush carpet sprawled from wall to wall in the four spacious bedrooms. The walls exhibited expensive canvas oil paintings styled in colorful contemporary fashion, adding a boastful flair to the already intimate setting. Grandiose hardwood furniture trimmed in dark tones lay strategically placed amongst the posh leather couches and cozy recliners in each of the dwelling's rooms.

Ben's thorough search tendered a wall safe hidden at the back of the master bedroom's sizable walk-in closet. The initial exploration was nearly complete. *Only a few more rooms to check out – then sis' is going to open that safe. I bet there's some good loot waiting inside.* After a visit to each of the upstairs rooms and closets, he descended the hardwood steps of the staircase, frowning at the gallery of images displayed on the wall to his left. *Family pictures – the hell with that.* He glowered at each of the portraits. Hatred and jealousy smoldered in his heart. The depictions sickened him and set his blood to boil. It should have been *him* illustrated in such an array of happiness and warm memories. While he studied the pictures, his mind wandered back to his younger years.

His existence after being adopted hadn't been as blessed as Sarah's. Although his first set of foster parents tried with all their efforts to tame the energetic little boy, Ben was always angry and wild, as though a malignant spirit possessed him. With their hearts filled with sorrow, they reluctantly requested that he return to the state's custody so they could restore their home to a peaceful state, free from the acrimony which persisted with the troubled little boy's presence. Ben migrated from foster home to foster home, until he was eight and finally adopted by the Thompson family of Dixson, Virginia.

Richard and Connie Thompson were wealthy, both descendants of tobacco plantation tycoons who ruled the state of Virginia going back to the colonial days. They were well-intentioned – adopting Ben. They sought to ease their heartache when their son, Robert, fell through the ice and drowned while skating with his friends on a chilly afternoon back in the winter of 1992. Little Robert had just turned seven, and the tragedy nearly destroyed the heartbroken couple. At the time of his passing, Connie feared she was too old to have another child, and she loathed the thought of going through physical labor ever again. As their peers took delight in watching their offspring mature while gaining bragging rights for their accomplishments, the Thompsons decided they would fill the void in their hearts and social status by adopting a needy child. That would be their solution to overcome their feelings of awkwardness during their many social events when their friends would speak in hushed tones around them for fear of awakening the couple's tragic memories.

Young Ben's physical appearance was similar to their departed son. His sandy blonde hair and bright blue eyes, his slender, lanky form... all brought back fond memories of their beloved Robert. But the similarities ended there. Robert had always been loving and kind. He was gentle and thoughtful. Ben possessed none of those qualities. He was shifty and restless, continually assessing his surroundings. Regardless of the situation, he wanted to be in control and to hold the upper hand. He was always ready to fight – to prove he was the strongest and smartest. That would be his way, and the people he killed throughout his rampaging years... they were merely in the wrong place at the wrong time.

Ben choked back the bitter memories. *There's no time for this nostalgia bullshit. Got to keep moving.* He continued down the stairs. Near the bottom floor landing, one portrait stood out. He snatched it from the wall in dismay. The color photograph featured Will Taylor standing next to Katy Olsen, the reins of a white Arabian in her hand. *No… it can't be… it can't be her…* But the more he analyzed the image, the more confident he became. Yes, it *was* her – the young brunette who scorned his advances several years earlier in that dust-bowl of a town back in Nebraska. *But how? What the hell is her picture doing on sis's wall?* The reason didn't matter. All that mattered was after searching for her for over eight years, he found a solid lead. He could… he *would*… find her again.

The fire he set to her parent's farm home which sent them to their doom while they slept peacefully was no match for the inferno raging in his heart for the beautiful young woman. The photograph elicited the events of those fateful days so long ago. After a three-week love affair with the shy twenty-year-old, Ben demanded the small-town girl run away with him. Her refusal set in motion the confrontation between him and her father. It was an easy decision to burn the whole damn place to the ground while the old people slept. It was a shame the naïve young woman escaped his relentless pursuit after his act of revenge.

The first successful bank heist a few months before meeting her left him flush with cash – but he spent it quickly. Murdering three people during the robbery was just part of the game. Those were the first lives he snuffed out. But they wouldn't be the last. He stayed in the small town too long, wooing Katy. He needed to keep moving – and he wanted her by his side, for she was his sole obsession.

Ben scowled at the portrait. *If you just would have come with me... mommy and daddy might not have burned...* He gripped the gold picture frame tightly in his hand, nearly crushing the glass pane protecting the photo with his angry grasp. He dashed down the long hallway to the den where Sarah lay on the soft carpet, still bound by the hands to the elaborate bar's pipe footrest. Dropping to his knees beside her, he tore the duct tape from her mouth. Sarah shrieked in pain. He thrust the portrait at her and pointed to the young woman. "Who is she to you?" he snarled.

Tears poured from Sarah's eyes. She glimpsed at the picture. "I... I... don't know!" she huffed breathlessly.

"Think! Who is it? Who's she with?"

Sarah's body shook, and she closed her eyes. After a brief pause, her voice quivered when she answered, "It's my father-in-law. I... think... the girl is one of his employees..."

Ben leaned closer to her face. "Where was this taken?" he growled with foaming spittle flying from his lips with each enraged word.

"Montana. He lives... in Montana."

Taking a deep breath, Ben calmed himself. "How long ago was this taken?"

"Just a few months ago."

Ben rose from his knees and stepped away from his frightened sister. He pored over the picture. The revelation changed everything. Wandering over to a dark brown recliner at the far end of the dimly lit room, he plopped down into the comfort of the chair. *Montana. After sis' hooks me up with my cash haul, that's where I'll go. If that little bitch is still at the old man's place... me and her will get a chance to get back together. Canada is an easy shot away. There we can hide up for a while to let things cool down. The cops will never find us in the backwoods over the border...*

After mulling over his plan, Ben approached Sarah again. He snatched the lock-back knife from his pocket and cut the zip tie binding her wrists together. With a forceful tug, he pulled her to her feet. "C'mon. You're going to open the safe I found upstairs."

Still hobbled by the zip tie binding her ankles, Sarah asked, "What about my feet?"

"Those are gonna stay tied. I don't want you getting any ideas about trying to take off." He grabbed her arm and headed toward the door to the hallway. Sarah hopped frantically to keep up. Every time she stumbled, his grip kept her from falling all the way to the hard floor. After making it to the top landing, Sarah crumpled to the carpet in exhaustion. He yanked her to her feet. "Come on. Going down will be much easier," he sneered. Dragging her with his firm grip, they entered the master bedroom. He flung the closet door open and pushed her inside. Unable to hop fast enough, Sarah tumbled to the floor.

"*Please stop.* You're *hurting* me," Sarah sobbed breathlessly.

His nostrils flared with impatience. "I'm gonna hurt you a whole hell of a lot more if you don't get up and open the damn safe." He jerked her back to her unsteady feet and shoved her toward the wall where the safe sat exposed after the mirror veiling it was torn away. "Open it!" he demanded.

After several attempts entering the digital code on the vault's keypad, the lock clicked then disengaged. Ben pushed her to the side and whipped open the heavy steel door. He grinned with satisfaction. The safe's contents yielded a stockpile of valuables. Reaching inside the twenty-four inch by twenty-four-inch interior, he grasped a 9mm Glock 19 from the bottom shelf. Eyeballing Sarah, he scoffed. He popped the magazine from the grip of the pistol – filled to capacity with fifteen rounds of hollow points. Jacking the slide back only half an inch, he peered into the chamber. The nickel casing of a cartridge shined under the overhead light fixture. He released his hold on the slide, allowing it to slam forward and reload the live round, and then slapped the loaded magazine back into the grip. "You and your hubby don't mess around, do ya?" He stuffed the pistol in the front of his jeans next to his .45.

"Mark bought me that for protection. I hate guns," Sarah replied from her crumpled position on the floor.

"That's too bad, sis'… I love 'em." He grabbed four stacks of crisp hundred dollar bills and flipped them over, pleased with the bounty. A white band around each bundle stamped in red print declared *Ten Thousand Dollars*. "*Forty grand?* You've got *forty grand* just *sittin'* here locked up?" He scowled at her.

Sarah seemed ashamed and looked away, brushing the hair from her eyes in contempt. "We've always kept some cash around the house."

"*Some* cash?" He knelt and slapped her across the cheek with one of the bundles. "That's ten grand you just tasted, babe!" He shook his head in disbelief. Only rich people, living in their great big, perfect houses, would consider forty-thousand dollars pocket change. With further inspection, the safe contained several documents, and finally, a wooden box made of cherry wood. He stuffed all the items under one arm and dragged Sarah by the forearm out of the closet. Surveying the room, he relished its level of luxury. The king size bed, adorned with silk sheets peeking out from under the fluffy comforter, looked inviting. But, the surroundings failed to offer any suitable place to secure his hostage. Back to the bar in the den – that's where they would stay – for the time being.

Upon returning to the den's seclusion, Ben tossed the items from the safe on the glass coffee table when they stumbled into the room. "I've got a better idea how to keep you from getting away. He snatched a pair of handcuffs from the bottom of his backpack and cuffed Sarah to the footrest of the bar. The robust fixtures were well-anchored to the hardwood base. *There's no way in hell she'll be able to break free*. Her imprisonment was complete, and he chuckled. While she lay on the floor weeping, he wandered over to the sectional sofa at the far end of the room.

He dropped his pack by his feet after retrieving a map from the front pocket. The crinkled map displayed the northwestern states – all the main roadways and even ones of less traveled fare. "What's the name of the town – the one where your hubby's daddy lives?"

Sarah writhed on the floor. She sniffled. "Crystal Creek. He lives just outside Crystal Creek, Montana."

He searched the map until he found the tiny dot seemingly in the middle of nowhere. He tapped his finger at the point on the map. *There it is — Crystal Creek. That's the place*. Secluded in a valley just east of the Rockies, the town lay surrounded by lofty mountains and shrouded within the forest. *It looks like the place is far enough out in the sticks that I won't have to worry too much about anyone getting in my way.* He continued to formulate his strategy – there were many details to consider. It was a little over eight hundred miles from Seattle to where the ranch lay hidden, and such a journey would need to be well planned to evade the cops. Time was running out.

Sarah's cell phone buzzed in his back pocket. Snatching it from his jeans, he swiped at the screen. "What's your passcode to unlock this thing?"

Sarah huffed. "That's none of your business."

"I don't have time for this shit. Either tell me now, or I'll bust your skull wide open," he roared.

"Six-two-nine-nine," Sarah muttered.

After tapping in the code, Ben read the notification. "Who the hell is Dan?" he grumbled.

Sarah twisted on the floor. "He's just a friend," she whimpered.

"Well, he's damn annoying. He's sent you three texts over the past few hours." Flipping through the messages, he snickered. "He wants to know how you're doing. Should I tell him?" The lengthy text history disclosed an intimate conversation. "So... ole Danny boy is *just* a friend? This is some pretty intense stuff to be talking about with a *friend*."

Sarah strained to get comfortable. Her right hand was chained hopelessly to the brass fixture. Tugging at it made the cuff's frame, forged from cold steel, cut deeper into her wrist. Pain shot through her limbs with every movement, but she *had* to try. She laid down parallel to the bar, attempting to find some respite from her predicament. *Oh, Dan… I wish you could help…* Fear gripped her. If she didn't answer, Dan would undoubtedly swing by to check on her. And he had a key… *Please don't come, Dan… the psychopath will kill you… I know it.* There had to be some way to warn him – some way to keep him away… some way to keep him safe.

Sarah pressed her eyelids tight, reliving the many sensual nights she spent with Dan Wilson after she and Mark separated. The software engineer and business partner had been a friend of Mark and Sarah's since they were all roommates sharing a small rental home while attending Washington State University. It was during those college years Mark and Dan met in one of their courses. They were best friends ever since and worked together to design the Cyber Safe internet software which eventually brought a windfall for all of them.

A terrifying realization crept into her mind and overwhelmed her ruminations. *How does Ben know Will's ranch supervisor? For God's sake… Mark and Will are there too. Are they all in danger?* The peril to all whom she loved was obvious. Desperation swelled within in her. She took several deep breaths to calm her racing heartbeat. After a few minutes, she sat up. "Ben?" she called out to the other side of the expansive room.

"What?" Ben grumbled.

She brushed her hair back with her free hand. "Please

tell me what it is you want. How can I help you?" She puffed out a nervous breath. "What will it take to get you to leave without anybody getting hurt?" She strained to keep her tone calm and reassuring.

Ben tossed the map on the sectional sofa. He reached into his front jacket pocket and snatched a smoke from the nearly empty box and tucked it between his lips. Flicking the flint of his lighter, he leaned into the flame and lit the tip of the cigarette. He took a long drag and closed his eyes. After holding the smoke in his lungs for several seconds, he exhaled the smoke from his nostrils. He stood and wandered over to Sarah, while seemingly lost in thought. Kneeling on one knee, he glared at her and took another drag. "I need cash – lots of it." He blew the smoke into her face, causing her to gag then cough. "Now... I'm not gonna guarantee no one is gonna get hurt. Someone always gets hurt. That's just the way it works." He stood and meandered several steps across the room.

Sarah shook her head. "No, Ben. No one has to get hurt. I'll find a way to get you what you want. Just promise me you won't hurt anyone."

Ben snorted and opened his hand. He didn't wince as he extinguished the cigarette by driving the smoldering cherry into his palm while it sizzled and cooked the flesh, creating a sickening smell. "Look, sis', you're not in any position to be making requests."

Sarah cringed in disgust and resisted the urge to vomit. The sour taste of bile crept up her throat and filled her mouth.

"But... you know what? If you're good and don't cause

me any problems… I'll consider letting *you* walk away from this without too much damage." He flicked the crumpled cigarette butt at her and snickered when she swatted it away, deflecting the wad before it hit her.

"How can you be so filled with hate?" she shrieked in frustration. Dropping her face into her hand, she curled her head to her knees and bawled.

"Hate is all I know. It keeps me warm." He trudged back to the sectional and flopped onto the expensive leather seat. "Get some sleep. You're gonna need it. Now leave me alone – I have some planning to do."

Sarah dried her tears. She was angry – angry at herself for giving him the pleasure and satisfaction of seeing her cry. Seeing the maniac sort through all the important documents he seized from the safe only added to the emotions of defilement rippling like waves in her head. Soon he would know the extent of the fortune she and Mark had amassed. Most of it was in stocks and bonds. But considering how meticulous he seemed, it wouldn't be long before he discovered the couple had access to several million dollars – not counting what they held in cash accounts. She shuddered when he opened the cherry-wood box. Inside the delicate case, several pieces of jewelry Mark had given her over the years lay sorted in the felt-lined slots of the inner receptacle. Gaudy necklaces, earrings, bracelets, and occasion rings – all set in gold and embellished with valuable diamonds and other dazzling gemstones, filled the box.

Ben popped the case open and raised his eyebrows. "Holy shit!" he gasped. He plucked each piece from its resting place and stuffed them all in a felt bag lying wadded up in the corner of the container. Once filled, he tucked the pouch in the interior pocket of his jacket.

He's violating every bit of my life – what an asshole. Sarah turned away. She couldn't bear to witness any more of his callous invasion into her most precious items. Their value wasn't due to the intrinsic value of the metal and stones – but the memories of the occasions on which her husband had given them. It seemed like everything related to her love for Mark was being tarnished and stained while it was ripped away from her, bit-by-bit.

Her heart ached from the previous night's events. Mark was gone. The daunting metal bus carried him away and out of her life. Filled with regret, she was honest when she told him forgiveness for his tryst wasn't something she was able to offer yet. Would it have made a difference? If she had forgiven him, would he have gone anyway? Or would he have swept the notions about returning to Montana out of his mind and retraced his steps back home? She reclined on the carpet, trying to push the thoughts of him from her weary mind. It no longer mattered. She was on her own now. She closed her eyes, hoping for deliverance from her nightmare.

CHAPTER 5

I t was just after seven o'clock on Friday evening. Dan
Wilson sat at his office desk in downtown Seattle.
The suite was one of several owned by Cyber Safe
Incorporated, located on the twenty-second floor of the
building. The multi-million dollar company started as
Mark and Dan's pet project back when they were enrolled
in the software engineering program at Washington State
University. The two friends and classmates stumbled upon
the idea for the new form of internet security software
when they were assigned a semester project researching
the evolution and hazards of the internet. It took them
several years of writing code to keep up with the world
of ever-changing technology, but they finally found their
stride and attained success.

Dan stared at his flat screen monitor as if in a trance.
Concentration eluded him while he tapped his fingers on
the glass desktop. His best friend had been away for over
eight months, and just when he returned, he was gone

again like a whisper in the breeze. Guilt tugged at his gut. He admitted to Mark five days earlier he was interested in Sarah – romantically. The two buddies had always been honest with one another, but he couldn't push from his thoughts the idea he was at least partially responsible for chasing his longtime friend away. The two were more like brothers than friends, and he missed Mark's companionship. He tried to persuade Mark to reconsider selling his share of the company, but his attempts were futile.

Surveying all the awards hanging on the office walls – given from software review periodicals over the years – he snatched his black horn-rimmed glasses from his face and tossed them on the desk. He rubbed his eyes and leaned back in the leather executive's chair. He sighed. The place just wasn't the same without Mark around. Even the other employees felt the loss. The two partners always kept a buzz throughout the company with their practical jokes and good-natured humor – especially when it was directed between the two of them.

When Mark arrived five days earlier, Dan was thrilled. He figured after Mark's hiatus in Montana recuperating, perhaps his dear friend returned to stay. It wasn't so. Before Mark left, the two men shared a quick drink at Baker's – their favorite hangout. During their visit, Mark announced he was leaving yet again – but this time for good. Montana's call was just too powerful, and suddenly, the city seemed too crowded. Mark offered his blessing for Dan and Sarah to explore the romantic feelings between them – he expressed his wishes that the two find happiness together. But, Mark's grief was evident. The forced smile on his face when he spoke the words failed to disguise his sadness. And at that moment, Dan shared the feeling of loss which gnawed at all three of them. The single event in Phoenix nearly a year earlier had turned the world on its end.

Dan grudgingly popped his glasses on and pushed them high on the bridge of his nose. Grabbing his cell phone from his desktop, he swiped at the screen. His text messages to Sarah sat idle with no replies. *What the hell Sarah, did you put me on ignore?* He typed at the digital keyboard,

Hey, good looking! Are you ok?

Usually, Sarah would respond to his missives without delay. Considering he hadn't heard from her all day long, worry set in. The work day was over, and he hoped they could meet for a quiet dinner at one of the classy restaurants in the heart of the city. He spoke to Sarah the night before after she dropped Mark off at the transit terminal. She was obviously and understandably distraught by Mark's departure. It took almost an hour of giving her words of encouragement while listening to her quiet sobs before he was able to elicit a laugh from her with one of his quirky jokes.

Frustrated, he sent another text.

I haven't heard from you. I'm worried about you. I'm coming over.

He powered down his computer. Snagging his keys from the desktop, he hustled out of the office and headed to his SUV waiting in the building's attached parking garage several floors below.

In Seattle's downtown police precinct, Deputy Tom Hensley of the U.S. Marshall's Office sat at a paper-strewn desk in a borrowed corner office poring over new leads relating to the possible whereabouts of Ben Thompson. Sixty-three years old, his precisely-trimmed white hair hinted at his disciplined persona. His partner, Joe Chavez, sat across from him leafing through a manila folder two inches thick. The younger marshal was business-like – cut from the same cloth as his more accomplished partner. Tall and athletic, Chavez was eager to prove he was every bit as capable as the more hardened veterans composing the detail.

Hensley tossed the daily briefing on the desk. He glimpsed at his watch. It displayed 7:23 PM. "This is ridiculous, Joe. How the hell are we expected to find this scumbag with the limited resources we've got?" he asked with a gravelly voice.

Chavez peered over the top of the folder. "Tom, you know with the budget issues, resources are stretched pretty thin. Top brass says we'll have to make do with what we're allotted."

Hensley shook his head in frustration. It was bullshit. Trimming the size of their task force down to eight agents from two different bureaus with sporadic support from local law enforcement agencies wasn't going to cut it. Not with as elusive as the fugitive had proven to be. "This is getting turned into a steaming heap of bureaucratic crap. If we had even three more detectives working on this case, we could cover a hell of a lot more ground. Thompson has left a trail of bodies everywhere he's been – how long until he kills again?" He reached into the breast pocket of his white button-up shirt and retrieved a pack of gum. After popping a piece of the mint flavored gum in his mouth, he held the package out in offering to his partner.

"No thanks." Chavez scowled while he studied the daily briefing. "You know, there have been multiple sightings of that green coupe in Washington. The latest was from last night. I reviewed the tape from the parking lot security camera that caught the theft. It was definitely our boy."

"Yeah, I know. We're close. I can smell 'im. You would think having the vehicle on a hot sheet for three days would give plenty of time to catch the sonofabitch." Hensley chomped the gum with hasty determination while he contemplated the pile of leads listed in his copy of the briefing. "But one thing I've learned after chasing Thompson for the past eight years – he's like a cockroach – good at skittering away at the first sign of danger. He always seems to be one step ahead of us."

Scratching the back of his head, Chavez placed the folder on the edge of the desk. "Eight years... and you've worked the case the whole time too."

Hensley nodded. "Yep. I've been after the scum since the FBI requested assistance from the Marshall's Office after the bank robbery at the Canton Savings and Loan back in 2009. Man, that was a scene of carnage." He ceased chewing and rolled the gum in his cheek with his tongue. "Three innocent people died that day. And for no reason – they cooperated fully with Thompson. They didn't give him any trouble at all, doing everything he told them to. He had the cash he came for. I guess it wasn't enough of a thrill for him without slaughtering someone." He took a deep breath before exhaling and massaged his temple. "I'll never forget the victims. A thirty-six-year-old father with two little kids, the bank manager who was going to retire in a year – after he logged his twenty-fifth year working for the bank, and..." Hensley paused and choked back the emotion tugging at his gut. He cleared his throat. "The twenty-seven-year-old teller. She was a beautiful girl. She'd just gotten married and returned from her honeymoon a few days before the robbery."

Chavez stared at his older counterpart. "That's messed up, boss."

"Yep. It sure as hell was." He clawed at his clean-shaven face and continued. "We were hot on his trail – the Marshalls and the FBI – then he fell off the radar. After three-and-a-half weeks, a solid lead came in, and we tracked him to Noble, Nebraska – a small farming town in the southwest corner of the state. But by the time we got there, he had split. But not before setting a house on fire with a middle-aged couple inside. All the locals we interviewed raved about what fine folk they were. John and Gloria Olsen were their names – a loving husband and wife in their late fifties."

A look of dismay fell over Chavez's face. "What the hell did he have against them?"

"It was all about a girl – the couple's daughter. Seems as though she got tangled up with Thompson in a romance. She was young and probably didn't know any better. Her father had a run in with Thompson after he beat her. The scumbag was trying to get her to go with him and she refused. The bastard knew we were close, and he didn't want to leave without her. So… one night while they were sleeping, he set the house on fire – killed them both in their sleep. They never had a prayer."

"What about the girl?"

"She escaped. It took me a little over a year to track her down. The night of the arson, Thompson went to get her – her parents had sent to her to stay with the mother's friend in a town just a few miles away. After he burned the house to the ground, he headed her way. She spotted him before he got to the door and snuck out the back. She hit the road, wandering aimlessly – terrified he would find her."

"That's nuts. Why didn't she get witness protection?" Chavez asked.

Hensley stretched his arms out then leaned back and clasped his hands behind his head. "We offered it to her," he gruffly replied. "She refused… said she knew Thompson too well and that he would find her – said she was sure of it and she stood a better chance staying hidden on her own. The poor girl feared for her life. I've kept tabs on her and every now and again she'll contact me to check on the case and find out if we've nabbed him yet. She's holed up at a ranch in Montana, working as the operation's supervisor."

Chavez stroked the black whiskers of his mustache, seemingly disgusted by his partner's revelation. "I read the case profile when I was assigned to this investigation. But, hearing you tell the background details that were missing from the report… it…"

"Makes it hit a hell of a lot harder when you know the human aspects, doesn't it?" Hensley scrutinized his young partner. He was a good kid – a good detective. At thirty years of age, he was clean-cut, straight-laced, and already seasoned with the brutal aspects of the job. But, he still needed more experience before he would be ready to take the lead on any high profile investigations. He speculated once they successfully apprehended Thompson, the young marshal would get the promotion he so eagerly looked forward to and deserved.

"Yeah, it hits harder when you think of the victims."

Sadness filled the young deputy's eyes and Hensley sensed his apprentice was affected by the background of the case. He sat up and leaned his elbows on the desk while staring intently at Chavez. "We need to get this guy, Joe. We need to get him soon. We've already connected him to sixteen murders – including the ones I just told you about. I don't have any doubt there are several more just lurking out there in unsolved case files across the country. Thompson is a cold-hearted killer. There's no other way to describe him. He's evil incarnate."

Chavez slumped in his chair. "Boss, I've studied lots of cases – even ones I wasn't assigned to – I've taken several psychological analysis courses offered by the bureau… and after studying all the high profile serial killers from the past few decades, this guy gives me the creeps. He seems to be diabolical to the extreme. I mean, what the hell causes someone to be so messed up?"

"I don't know. I've investigated his background completely – been extra thorough in checking out every bit of his past." He reached for a folder buried under the stack of files on the desk. He skimmed through the collection of documents and refreshed his memory of the details they provided. "Thompson came from a broken home. He was taken into the state of Oregon's custody with his older sister when he was three. His parents were drug traffickers. They were pretty much lowlife scum… addicts who were in and out of the system all the time. The sister was adopted pretty quickly – when she was six. Thompson, on the other hand, was in foster care for several years. It seems as though he was a monster even when he was a little kid. He finally did get adopted though – by a rich couple in Virginia." He paused and flipped ahead in the case file. "and… he was just as much a handful as a teen – kicked out of three private schools for fighting and other infractions. The court ordered him into counseling for anger management."

The younger deputy snickered and rolled his eyes. "Well, we know how much good that did."

Hensley handed the folder to Chavez. "Here, take a look at his rap sheet."

Chavez scanned page after page of incidents in Thompson's record. "This is obscene. The guy should have been locked up long before he committed his first murder. Larceny, assault, extortion, assault with a deadly weapon… it goes on and on. What does it take to get someone put away?"

"That's the power of money, Joe. When I dug deep

into his past, his parents always found a way to get the deviant out of trouble. They were a pretty powerful couple in their part of the country. Cash donations go a long way in smoothing over rough edges and buying political favors." He wheeled the rolling chair away from the desk and wandered over to a large regional map tacked on the wall. After inspecting it for a few moments, he added, "I guess it was more important for Thompson's adoptive parents to save face by not having their kid locked up than allowing justice to run its course by making him pay for his behavior. Having their son in prison would have *tarnished* their reputation."

"It would have saved a lot of lives if they'd parked him in a cell and thrown away the key."

Hensley placed his hands on his hips, resting his right hand on the butt of the semi-automatic pistol holstered at his side. He nodded. "Yes, it would have. But that's one of the frustrating things you'll have to get used to – sometimes you'll work your ass off… doing everything by-the-book to make sure you have an airtight case – but in the end, it's the court system that decides how things will work out. I don't know how many times I've seen a perp – guilty beyond a doubt – walk free over a small technicality."

Closing the folder, Chavez placed it neatly on the desk and stood. After a drawn-out stretch, he asked, "Is this case the only thing holding you back from retiring?"

"Yes. I've been at this line of work too long. After all the cases I've worked on, and all the horrible things I've seen – innocent lives devastated – I'm ready to turn in my badge. It would be nice to finally be able to get a good night's sleep.

But… not until I've nailed this psychotic sonofabitch." Hensley's weariness showed in the deep lines and wrinkles on his face. Yes, he was tired – burned out. But he wouldn't rest until Ben Thompson was either dead or standing in front of a federal judge to receive his well-deserved death sentence. Aside from his youngest daughter's upcoming wedding, that was the day the marshal was most anxious to see. He sniffed and straightened the starched collar of his shirt. He turned to Chavez and raised an eyebrow. "Let me give you a solid piece of advice. Be committed to the job – give each case your full effort. But don't let it consume you. Make it home safe every night to kiss that pretty wife of yours. Be a great dad to those two little kids you're both raising. Don't waste the best things in your life while hunting down the bad. This line of work can twist the good right out of you – warp into you a shadow of who you are and who you're meant to be."

Chavez pressed his lips together. He seemed to be lost in thought while absorbing his partner's words. "I'll be all right. I understand how tough a career this is. I have a good enough handle on things to keep the bad aspects of what we deal with separate from my off-duty life."

Hensley nodded, but he was skeptical. He'd keep his thoughts on the matter to himself. It was impossible to prevent the job from entering one's home life. Young cops always seemed to think it was an attainable feat, but after being in harm's way on a constant basis long enough, they soon realize they too had become jaded. Being a cop was in the blood – it wasn't something you could limit to duty hours. In his younger years, He'd thought the same way. After two broken marriages, he finally realized the amount of stress being a cop put on a relationship. There was always the possibility of kissing a loved one before walking out the door in the morning and never surviving the shift. Death was waiting around every corner. Only wile, wisdom, and quick reflexes could prevent a routine encounter from becoming a final downfall. He worried about his partner, but he wasn't there to babysit. They had a job to do. Pointing at the regional map, he placed his index finger on the city of Seattle. "We're fairly certain Thompson is still somewhere in the city, but considering how slippery he is… there's no way to be sure."

"So what's the plan?"

"Well, we've had the State Troopers set inspection roadblocks on all the major entrances and exits to the city." He paused and rubbed his chin in thought. "The problem is our boy is too smart to use the interstate for travel. It's almost a sure thing he's ditched the car by now."

Chavez seemed somewhat befuddled. "What about roadblocks on the county roads?"

"We don't have the resources for that. There are too many." He studied the vast city's road system – a sprawling confused web of backroads offering a multitude of avenues for escape. "No… right now we're just making him feel the pressure. By limiting his choice of travel, we can try to squeeze him into a trap." He sighed in frustration. "The problem is he thinks on the fly. He adapts quickly and seems to have thought out in advance several different scenarios. My gut tells me our best opportunity to catch him is in a chance encounter. I want you to get with the composite artist and have her work up some different possible images. Everything we've released to the public through newscasts has shown Thompson with long hair and a beard. No. He's too smart not to alter his appearance. Get a clean-shaven composite made up – and ones with sunglasses, hats, and so on. Get 'em out to the public – fast. We can use all the eyes possible looking for this guy. The more desperate we make him feel, the bigger the chance he'll slip up and make a mistake. Even if it's a small one – we need to be ready."

"What about the reports he's been taking refuge in safe houses? I mean this guy has ties to the mob."

Hensley shook his head. "No. I interviewed two of the FBI's informants. This guy is so far out there on edge even the mob has shunned him. He's freelanced as an enforcer for them on occasion over the years, but he's such a psycho even they don't want to have anything to do with him. He's too high profile. And that's bad for business."

"I understand, but there are always favors traded in the underworld. We can't rule out he's getting help from somewhere."

"No, Joe. We won't rule it out. I'm just saying it's highly unlikely. He knows the heat is on. He'll keep skipping around from hiding spot to hiding spot until he sees an opening. Then he'll make a break for it."

The expression on Chavez's face hardened. "So what do you think his destination is?"

The older marshal slapped his hand on the top of the map. "Here – over the border into Canada. He's had plenty of outdoors experience. I think he's getting tired – beaten down. He wants a chance to lay low and lick his wounds."

"What problems would we have extraditing him if he makes it?"

"If he gets over the border, extradition wouldn't be a problem. We have a good working relationship with the Canadian government. The issue would be finding him. Canadian law enforcement would absolutely apprehend him if they had the chance. But, that being said, they're not going to put resources into actively searching for him – unless Thompson starts perpetrating crimes on their soil."

The young deputy puffed out a breath in exasperation. "And I'm sure Thompson knows that."

Gritting his teeth, Hensley replied, "Without a doubt. Yep, he'll be a good boy while he's there, too. He won't risk a chance to find time and a place to relax. So I figure we can expect a flurry of activity – a violent spree before he cuts and runs. He needs cash."

Chavez peeked down at his watch. "What do you say about going and grabbing a bite? I've about had it with the crap that falls out of the vending machines in the lounge."

"No, Joe. You go ahead. Take off for the night after you check in with the composite artist. I'm going to hang out here for a bit. One of the Seattle PD detectives got a tip of an individual purchasing several pre-paid cell phones from a small retailer on the edge of town."

"Burn phones?"

"Yep. The easiest way to make cell calls without having your name tied to an account. As I said, this guy is smart. Thinks of everything. We can't underestimate him. The detectives are attempting to acquire the sim codes on the phones. It'll be a bitch to do – we'll need a warrant to obtain them, and it's going to be tough to convince a judge we have solid enough evidence the buyer was our guy."

"Have you seen the security tape of the buyer?"

"Yeah, but the footage was from an outdated camera system. It was pretty grainy and didn't offer good enough details for facial recognition. It's pathetic a store selling technology relies on such an antiquated system when they sell state-of-the-art cameras on their shelves. No... it's a huge longshot we'll get the warrant. But, it's a lead. And considering how thin we are on tips at the moment... we're not going to squander any that come our way. I'll hang out here until I get the lowdown. I'll give you a call if anything comes in."

"All right, boss. I'll check in later."

The young marshal shuffled out of the office and into the bustle of the precinct's large open room crowded with a maze of desks attended by various detectives and other department personnel. Hensley stepped back to the desk and pulled out the most recent sketch of Ben Thompson from his ever-growing case file. Scrutinizing every feature of the face displayed on the wanted poster, he mumbled, "Where are you hiding, you bastard?"

CHAPTER 6

The daylight waned while evening shrouded the Montana landscape in darkness. A soft afterglow illuminated the western horizon, offering a medley of colors blazing from a hue of light orange into deep red across the broken clouds blanketing the frosted mountaintops. Mark and his father sat on the lodge's front porch. A chill hung in the air and the two men relaxed on the log bench while they sat bundled in their fleece-lined jackets. Forlorn howls from a wolf pack across the valley rang out through the dense night air and shattered the silence with their eerie cries.

Mark zipped up his denim jacket to shun the cold from his body. "Wow, this mountain air sure gets chilly once the sun goes down."

Will took a long sip from his steaming mug. He swallowed the bold coffee slowly, and then replied, "Yep, it sure do. Even springtime is pretty nippy at this elevation."

Picking up his coffee cup from the armrest at his side,

Mark cradled it in both hands, allowing the heat of the concoction to warm the nip from his fingers. "That was an awesome meal Katy made tonight. It's been a while since I've had homemade meatloaf."

The old man patted his full belly. "Yessir, she's a fine cook. Almost as good as your mom was. She knows just how to make a good pot of coffee too – strong and hearty." He pulled up his collar and stuffed his hat lower on his head. "Brr... it's gettin' kind of brisk out – especially to these old bones."

"Yeah, it is. But I like it. There's something about the air being crisp like it is tonight. It's so clean and refreshing." He scanned the gloom across the compound in the direction of the front gate. A thick fog rolled heavy in the air like a boiling soup and sank lower to the ground while it crept toward the main house.

"It seems like Miss Katy has returned to her spry ol' self now you're back. It makes me happy seein' that beautiful smile light up her face again – especially when she's lookin' at you."

Mark nodded. His face warmed with the rush of blood filling his cheeks while he thought of her. "It's good being back. Even being gone only four days, I missed her more than I thought I would." He placed his coffee back on the arm of the bench. The bite in the air had sapped most of the heat from the half-filled mug anyway. He stuffed his hands in his jacket pockets and stretched out his legs. He slumped back into his seat. "Dad, Katy told me how this place is struggling. She said you've been having a hard time keeping up with the cost of upkeep."

Will fidgeted on the cold, hard bench. He stared down at his feet seemingly embarrassed by his predicament. He cleared his throat and gazed at the advancing mist. "Oh, we're okay, son. This is a tough way to earn a livin' – but we'll make it – just like we always have."

"Katy said you're planning on selling off more of the herd than you originally planned. I'm not going to pretend I know much about horses or the breeding business, but it's common sense if you have fewer mares to breed, you're facing a reduction in foals."

"Yep. It's simple math. But sometimes it's a necessity." The old man reached over and placed his hand on Mark's shoulder and gave it a gentle squeeze. Peering at his son from under his low-lying hat brim, he said, "You don't need to be concerned about me. I do have a bit of money pack-ratted away. It ain't a lot, but it'll help some."

Mark studied his father's eyes. They twinkled with kindness even though they exposed the sadness gripping the elderly cowboy. "Dad, you don't need to struggle. I've got more money than I'll ever know what to do with. I *want* to invest in this place. I want to build it into the operation you and mom always dreamed it to be."

A few tears rolled down Will's weathered cheeks. He shifted his gaze away and wiped them without delay. He shook his head, and his voice wavered when he spoke, "No, son. That wouldn't be right. You need to save what you've worked so hard to earn for your future." He wiped his runny nose with the back of his hand. "I know it was you who paid off all the medical bills your mom rung up while she was fightin' the cancer. The insurance only paid a sliver of the total. I made arrangements to make monthly payments to all the different places we owed money to. It woulda broke me for sure if I had to pay even just the installments. I remember several years ago when I sent out the monthly round of checks to pay the vultures. All the checks came back uncashed with final statements marked "balance-paid-in-full." When I called each one of them doctors and medical offices, they wouldn't tell me who paid the bills... but I knew it was you and Sarah that done it." He pushed the brim of his hat higher on his brow. He grasped Mark's hand in his. "I never thanked ya for what you did – I want you to know it meant a lot to me." He tilted his head skyward and looked to the sea of stars peeking out between the occasional patches of clouds. "I know your mom is proud of you."

"I didn't want to ask you then if it was okay to settle your accounts. I know you would have refused. But, I'm asking you now... *let me invest in this place.* Trust me, even though I sold out my portion of the company to Dan, I'll still receive royalty payments from the software. And even without the royalties, I have a sizable fortune tucked away. I can easily afford to infuse quite a bit of cash into the ranch without having to worry about the risk. I mean it – I won't miss it at all. I have plenty of stocks and bonds – all that kind of crap. It's important to me. I want to see this place exceed the vision you and mom had for it."

Will sighed, obviously conflicted by Mark's offer. "I don't know, son... I'd have to kick it around a bit. Katy has been doin' her best to keep things on an even keel... but she's tied to the resources I have to work with – and they ain't much. We're always just scraping by."

"It doesn't have to be that way, dad. Katy keeps talking about how she's trying to get you to agree to sell that white colt she loves so much. She said it would bring you at least five thousand dollars. Forgive me for being arrogant, but five grand is a pittance."

"Yep… that gal is always thinkin' about others first. The colt is precious to her – and yet she's still needlin' me to sell him to bring in some cash."

Mark straightened on the uncomfortable bench. He was cold, but his father had finally opened up to him. He wasn't about to interrupt the flow of the conversation. He glanced over to the large aluminum barn. The halogen floodlights fixed high up on its sides cut through the ever-increasing sea of fog. "Katy only told me bits and pieces about the colt. I know he's the only Arabian on the property. You're raising quarter horses and Appaloosas – how did you wind up with him?"

"Well, it was just kind of a chance happening. Me and Miss Katy were in Helena at a stock auction. We were lookin' for a few more broodmares to add to the herd. We come across a fella desperate to sell the pregnant mare carryin' the unborn colt. He was a younger guy – around your age. He had his mind set he was gonna make a fortune raisin' Arabians." Will kicked his boot at a stone lying on the cracked planks at his feet and sent it flying off the porch. "The kid didn't know nothin' about the horse business. In fact, he didn't know nothin' about horses. He spent big money on the mare and gettin' her bred to a fancy stallion with papers and an expensive pedigree. When

Katy and I checked her over, it was pretty clear the mare was close to foaling – we could tell she wasn't doin' well. The kid who owned her had gotten some bad news from the vet caring for her – said the odds of her and the foal surviving the birth were pretty slim. He got scared, knowin' how much financial trouble he was already in. So, me and Miss Katy decided it was worth a gamble. Miss Katy never was one to walk away from an animal in need. She was pretty determined to do what she could for the poor beast. I shelled out ten thousand dollars for the mare – all while knowin' it was probably a crap shoot. And spending that amount of cash ate up our entire budget for buyin' any other mares at the auction."

"Yeah, Katy told me it's been rough around here financially since he was born. She said not having the extra mares you expected to breed from that one auction has caused an extended hardship."

Will nodded. "We knew at the time spendin' our entire budget on one horse and not sticking to our plan of adding more mares to the herd was gonna cause us some problems." He rubbed the back of his neck and rotated his head in a slow circle. "We came out of it better than I expected though. I figured we would lose both the mare and the foal. But it didn't work out that way. I guess, sometimes when you put faith in long odds and have faith in yourself; the Almighty rewards you for it." He took a sip of his coffee. Swishing the cold liquid in his mouth for a moment, he gulped and flung the remaining brew onto the ground in a splatter in front of the porch. He set the empty ceramic mug on the armrest beside him. "Miss Katy stayed with the mare for two full days and nights without any sleep. After the vet checked the poor girl out, he was pretty certain the foal would be stillborn – suffocating during birth. The colt was breeched. We knew by then we'd lose the mare and it was all out of our hands… nothing we could do for her. But Miss Katy was bound and determined to rescue the foal. She knew once the mare went into labor, she would only have a few minutes to save the poor critter. And by God, she did it." The old man's face lit up while he recounted the events.

Mark smiled. That's Katy all right. She's fierce. Anyone who underestimated the amount of passion and tenacity her five-foot-nine-inch petite body contained would be in for a surprise. The two men sat idle for a few moments without speaking. They listened while the yowl of a mountain lion on the prowl carried down from the hillside a few hundred yards away. The blood-curdling scream made Mark shiver. He glanced at his father. "I've got a tidy sum sitting in several different bank accounts right now. Let's sit down with Katy over the next few days and work up a plan to crank this place into gear. No more struggling to pay for feed and supplies – we'll pour the resources we need into the ranch. We don't have to stick to raising horses for the hunting and guide teams. We can breed Arabians, thoroughbreds… whatever is profitable and makes the most business sense. You've already got the white colt to use as a stud. His papers make him a valuable asset – especially if you breed him with purebred Arabian mares."

The home's front door swung open and Katy pushed the screen door out of the way with a loud creak. She poked her head out and said, "Are you two boys planning on freezing yourselves to death out there? Get yourselves in here and warm up! I just pulled an apple pie out of the oven."

Mark sniffed at the air. The delicious aroma of the freshly baked pie filled his senses, inducing his mouth to water. "We'll be right in," he called out before she closed the door. He sprang from his seat and helped his father up. "I sure don't want to let the pie get cold. I don't think I've ever tasted anything yummier than one of Katy's pies."

Will shuffled his feet while he strained to gain his balance. "That's no lie, my boy. We need to get in there and plop a few scoops of vanilla ice cream on top while it's still pipin' hot."

Mark collected the two empty coffee mugs then held his father's arm while he guided the old man to the door and inside the warmth of the cozy log home. The two men joined Katy in the kitchen. Scooting up to the table, they anxiously waited while Katy gathered plates from a pine cupboard at the far end of the kitchen. She opened a drawer and collected forks from a divider tray holding the silverware. After placing a white porcelain plate and a fork in front of Mark and Will, she dragged a chair away from an empty setting at the table and slid onto to it, adjusting her plate and fork once she settled herself. The pie sat in the middle of the table, steam curling in ascension above its golden crust. Both men stared at the pie and inhaled the savory aroma wafting from it, blended with the scent of melting brown sugar and a dash of cinnamon.

Will snatched the cowboy hat from his head and hung

it on the back of the empty chair beside him. His eyes glistened, craving for the delight he awaited. "C'mon, Miss Katy – get to cuttin' that confection before I die of old age!" he cackled.

Katy brushed back the curls of her long auburn locks and rolled her eyes. "William Taylor – you're so impatient sometimes!" She reached for the silver spatula sitting next to the pie and grasped it, carefully sinking its serrated edge through the crisped flaky crust. With four determined cuts, she sectioned the dessert into eight equally-sized pieces. The moment she lifted the first piece of pie from the baking tin, the sticky apple filling oozed slowly from under the crust and over the sides of the spatula, threatening to drip gooey clumps of apple slices and sweet syrup onto the yellow tablecloth.

Will snatched the pie tin from the warming pad and placed it on his plate. Grinning from ear-to-ear, he chuckled. "You youngsters can split that there piece. I'm claimin' the rest."

A look of aggravation fell across Katy's face. She quickly deposited the sagging helping of pie onto Mark's plate before the inner contents drooped free from the utensil. Seizing the pie tin from the old man's plate, she set it back on the warming pad at the center of the table. Her eyes blazed with displeasure, daring Will to attempt his antics even just once more. "You're about to lose your dessert privileges, William," she declared sternly.

The old man raised his eyebrows then winked at Mark. "You can't blame an ol' feller for tryin'."

Mark snickered and shook his head. His father's habit

of acting like an overgrown child was still intact – even in his golden years. Glancing at Katy, Mark asked, "Is there any vanilla ice cream stashed away anywhere."

"Oh, geez – of course! We can't forget the ice cream."

Before she could push her chair back from the table, Mark held up his hand. "I'll get it, Katy." He rose from his seat and stepped over to the freezer atop the aging refrigerator. After digging through the ice-encrusted appliance and then rummaging through a drawer filled with cooking gadgets, Mark returned to the table clutching the container of ice cream in one hand and a pink-handled ice cream scoop in the other. He pried the lid off the small cardboard bucket and gouged out a heaping scoop of ice cream. The moment he dolloped the frozen treat onto Katy's piece of pie, it melted into a thick, sludgy goop over the piping-hot crust. He swiveled to his father. "You always taught me ladies first, dad."

Will nodded. "I did indeed, my boy. But sometimes, we old folk forget our manners." He offered an apologetic half-smile to Katy. "Forgive me for forgettin' my manners, Miss Katy. You know I love teasin' ya!"

"Yes, William – I know." She flashed a quick look at Mark, raising one eyebrow.

They relished their dessert in silence. After clearing their plates, Mark dabbed a napkin to his face and wiped away the white drizzles of ice cream clinging to his beard. "So, Katy... I've been talking with this old guy sitting next to me, and we need to share some ideas with you." He shot a glance at his father. Will blinked slowly then nodded slightly, acquiescing to Mark's intent.

Katy stood and collected all the plates and silverware from the tabletop. "What kind of ideas?" she asked. She strolled across the kitchen and set their soiled dinnerware in the sink. Rotating the faucet handle, she waited while scalding water filled the stainless steel basin.

Mark followed each of her graceful moves. *You're staring. Get your mind back on business.* "Well, I'm going to be injecting some much-needed cash into this horse breeding operation. You and dad need to spend some time working up a plan. Anything you need – equipment, breeding stock, personnel – anything you've been dreaming about to make this place what it should be."

She paused from washing the dishes, spun around, and faced the table. The color drained from her face. She took a few deep breaths as the announcement seemed to sink into her thoughts. "Mark?"

"There's no need to be thinking about selling the white colt – ever. I've talked with dad and I'm going to invest in the ranch." He peered at Will, reassuring the old cowboy of his intentions. "This is a no-strings-attached deal. I'm not going to meddle into the details. It isn't a line of credit – there's not going to be any repayment." He shifted his gaze back to Katy and smiled. "Dad has been a pain about accepting this offer – and I've been pounding it into his head he doesn't need to feel like his pride is being stepped on. It isn't. I think I've finally made him understand this is something that's really important to me."

Will cleared his throat. "Yes, Miss Katy – it's a tough proposition for a grumpy ol' cuss like me to swallow – but my son is right. We sure could use the help." He clasped his hands on the table. After a short pause, he said, "I'm thinkin' you finally need to name that rowdy little colt you've been watchin' over."

Tears rolled down Katy's flush cheeks. She pivoted to the sink, turning her back to the two men. She dropped her head and stood in silence. The operation's dilemma obviously burdened her – no matter how hard she tried to hide it. It wouldn't be that way any longer. Mark was well aware of how much mental and emotional anguish existed while trying to keep a dream alive. He'd been there himself. He and Sarah struggled to make ends meet while he wrote the code for the security software. It was grueling – tiresome. How many nights had he and Sarah laid in bed unable to sleep due to the financial pressures they faced? How many times did he think of giving up and walking away from his goal because of seemingly insurmountable odds? No, he wouldn't stand idly by and see his father and Katy struggle any longer. He possessed the resources to help them achieve their aspirations and he wouldn't let them fail.

Katy sniffed and dried the tears from her eyes. She turned and approached the end of the table. "I've had a name for him since the day he was born – Shiloh. It's Hebrew for *His gift*. I never mentioned it… I didn't want to keep you from selling him. This place needed the money."

The kindness sparkling in the old man's eyes revealed he understood the young woman's attachment to the horse. "Miss Katy, there's never been a single moment that I forgot how much you love that wild lil' critter. He wouldn't be out there prancin' around right now if it weren't for you."

"But I know how much money you spent on his mother. It cost you everything – every last dime we needed for new broodmares. We've been pressed since that day at the auction," Katy lamented.

Pushing his chair away from the table, Will rose to his feet, standing his six-foot-two-inch frame fully upright. He plucked his cowboy hat from the chair where it hung. After plopping it on, he adjusted the hat until it was straight on his head. A wide grin crossed his face and his eyes narrowed beneath the hat's brim. "Miss Katy, some things are worth far more than money. The way the colt warmed your heart from the first second you laid eyes on him – was worth every penny we spent on his doomed mother. I've never regretted our decision – not even once. Sometimes, the difficult decisions we make in sacrifice for others... even though we know we're making things tougher for ourselves in the long run... come back to grace our lives in ways we never expected or imagined." The old man tipped his hat to Katy then ambled out of the kitchen and toward his room just off the main hallway dissecting the home.

Katy sauntered over to Mark's chair. Her blue eyes burned with longing. He stood and embraced her while she snuggled her head firmly against his chest. With soft strokes, he caressed her hair and breathed in the sweet scent of lilac emanating from her long curls. She clutched him tight and trembled in his arms. "Everything's going to be okay, Katy." He planted a tender kiss on her forehead.

"Thank you, Mark. This means so much to your father – and to me."

CHAPTER 7

SATURDAY, APRIL 17TH 12:06 AM

B en paced back and forth in the den. The long journey ahead would be perilous. Fortunately, his sister's home provided an abundance of resources. Yes, making an immediate beeline for the border would be the wisest course of action. But, the circumstances called for boldness. Taking a chance was worth the risk. The reward would be Katy Olsen – and she was *absolutely* worth the extra effort.

The most immediate threat was an unwanted encounter with Sarah's boyfriend. The situated needed to be resolved – fast. He pored over the text conversation between Sarah and Dan on her phone, paying close attention to her texting style and manners of response. Tapping out a reply to Dan's last message, he texted:

His ruse worked. Dan's reply shot back almost instantly.

Ok gorgeous. I really want to see you tonight, but I can wait until tomorrow. Get some sleep. You can

make it up to me tomorrow. Dinner maybe?

Ben was under the gun time-wise. Things were becoming more and more complicated by the minute. Staying in one place too long, especially in an urban location surrounded by a legion of cops, was a recipe for certain disaster. His police scanner had always served him well, helping him keep a step ahead of his enemy. It buzzed with cop talk and agency codes alluding to the reality the task force seeking his capture was hot on his trail. And while Sarah tussled with her shackles, he piled the tools required for his escape into her white SUV.

There wasn't time for him to complete the extortion he sought – not yet anyway. But, he controlled the ultimate prize which would lead to his windfall. *He had Sarah Taylor.* And if he relied on his cunning ways, he would receive more than just a fortune – he would be reunited with Katy as well. The house was ransacked. Anything essential or useful was already securely stuffed into the late-model SUV parked in the confines of the home's three-car garage. He had thousands in cash, two handguns, untraceable cell phones, Sarah's laptop, a vehicle which hadn't been reported stolen, *and* a hostage. But most importantly, he had his wits.

The preparations for his mission were complete. Shuffling over to Sarah, he knelt by her side. Terror shimmered in her light-green eyes as she recoiled far away from him until her restraint halted a further retreat. Her reaction caused his skin to prickle. "Sis', you and I are going to take a road trip. You need to be on your best behavior." He drew his pistol from his waistband and racked the slide, ejecting the live round from the gun's chamber and sending it sailing through the air until it landed on the carpet eight feet away with a dull thud. He stood and stepped over to the cartridge. He plucked it from the floor. Smirking, he meandered back to Sarah with the .45 ACP hollow point clenched between his thumb and index finger. He stooped down and held it before her eyes. The color drained from her face. "See this? I have plenty more of them. I'll use them if I have to. Now, I have a plan that's going to get me away safe. And you're going to help me. Do you understand?"

Sarah nodded. "Wha... what do you want from me, Ben?" she asked, her voice thin and quivering.

"Your husband and I are going to make a deal... and you're going to help make sure everything goes down smooth as glass."

"What kind of deal?" Tears clouded her eyes.

"Your husband is going to hook me up with twenty million dollars. And in return; he gets you – still breathing." The more he considered the bounty, the more excited he became. Goosebumps tingled up his arms, erupting across the surface of his skin in a miniature outbreak. "It's not going to be easy. We have some traveling to do, and there are lots of people looking for me. You're going to be on your best behavior. The way I see it, I've already done you a big favor. Your boyfriend – Danny boy – was all set to come and see you a little while ago. Fortunate for him, you texted just in time, and changed his mind." Ben paused and popped the magazine from the base of the pistol's grip. He slid the live cartridge between the component's feed lips and then slapped magazine back into the mag well of the pistol. "You just saved your boyfriend's life. But, you see... this was a one-time favor... a freebie... I know where Danny boy lives – I got his address from his contact entry on your cell phone. One slip from you and I'll go visit him – it'll be the last visit he gets from *anyone*. Got it?"

Sarah sat crumpled in a ball on the floor convulsing with fear, tucking her knees tight against her chest. "Yes."

Ben reached into his jeans and drew the handcuff key from the coin pocket. He released the cuff from the brass footrest at the bar's base and wrestled Sarah onto her stomach. After slapping the silver restraint around Sarah's free wrist, he clasped it tightly, biting the cold, metal edges into her soft skin. Once again, her hands were bound and handcuffed behind her back.

"Ow! They're too tight!" She shrieked.

"You'll be all right. If you start to fuss – I'll close them tighter," Ben sneered. He dragged her to her feet and shoved her toward the small bathroom at the far end of the den. "We're getting ready for a long drive. Go use the shitter."

With her feet still bound by zip ties, Sarah hopped toward the small half-bath, resisting Ben's every move. He blocked her just before she entered. Stepping inside, he yanked open the drawers at the vanity and rustled through each of them, searching for anything that could serve as an impromptu weapon or escape device. The drawers contained nothing of concern. He retreated to the main room then shoved Sarah inside.

"*How* am I supposed to do this?" Sarah asked, raising

her restrained hands away from her back.

Ben huffed and spun her around. He unlocked one of the cuffs then pulled her arms in front of her before re-shackling her free wrist. He flashed a menacing glare and growled, "The door stays open. Don't worry – I may be a little crazy, but I'm no pervert. Now take care of business – and be quick about it." He backed out of the tiny room, remaining vigilant to any desperate moves she made.

After a few minutes, Sarah emerged from the doorway. "So now what?"

"Turn around. Your hands stay cuffed behind your back." He whirled her around and adjusted the restraints, securing her hands behind her. Dragging her by the arm, he led her to the center of the room. He zipped up his bulging backpack, stuffed full of the items and documents he seized from the safe in her bedroom. He laced his arm through one of the bag's frayed straps and slung the rucksack over his shoulder. He tugged Sarah out of the den and down the long hallway leading to the front of the home. Just before they reached the foyer, they hung a left and moved down a short corridor to the garage. He snarled one final warning. "We're going out into the big, bad world now. If things go wrong – people get hurt. People will die. Be a good girl, and this will all be over soon."

Sarah nodded. "I know. You keep telling me," she muttered.

Ben thrust open the door leading into the garage. He groped at the wall's light switch and flipped it up. The overhead lights flickered on. He scanned the room for any signs of disturbance. Sarah's white Lexus sat in the center of the large stall – just as he'd left it when he packed the SUV with a final load of gear. His previous venture into the garage included an inspection of the vehicle – its gas tank was nearly full. He dug into his pocket and retrieved the car's FOB. With a quick press of a button, the rear hatch ascended open with a hiss from the gas struts. He shoved Sarah to the back of the vehicle. "Get in," he commanded.

Indignation glowed in Sarah's eyes. She slumped down into the rear cargo area, her body trembling.

While she settled into the confined space, Ben slipped the backpack from his shoulder, dropping it next to her. He unzipped the front pocket and reached deep into the black nylon bag, retrieving a syringe. "This is going to help you sleep. You'll just close your eyes, and when you wake up, we should be pretty close to where I want to be."

Sarah shuddered. Her eyes remain fixed on the syringe while he tugged off the plastic cap covering the long needle. He pressed on the device's plunger until tiny drops of clear fluid spurted from the needle's sharp tip. "Ben… please… no! That's not necessary," she pleaded.

Ben flicked at the top of the syringe's cylinder, and then stabbed the instrument's sharp tip into her upper arm, piercing her flesh. A tiny drop of blood encircled the circumference of the needle while a crimson trail trickled down her soft skin. "It'll just hurt for a second, sis'." The panic in her eyes dulled and her heavy eyelids closed within seconds after twitching briefly. Her flailing ceased, and she fell into a deep, drug-induced slumber. He sneered and grunted, "Nighty night!" while he withdrew the needle. Adrenaline pulsed through him. *This is all too easy. She's not going to cause any problems now.* He set the empty syringe on the SUV's bumper then arranged his gear. Sarah kicked in her unconscious state, sending the syringe tumbling to the garage's concrete floor where it ricocheted off the hard surface and rolled until finally coming to a rest underneath the vehicle. Startled, he grabbed at Sarah's limp body. She convulsed two more times and then lay utterly still.

After positioning Sarah onto her side on the back cargo mat, he secured the bindings on her hands and ankles to cargo hooks connected on each side of the vehicle's interior. *Ha! Try to get out of that, sis'. She'll hardly be able to move… when she finally wakes up. I knew those tranquilizers would come in handy at some point.* The drugs in her system would keep her unconscious for several hours. The improvised plan was flawless considering he concocted it on-the-fly. At the late hour, they could travel the side roads without incident – the cops didn't have the resources to cover every exit from the city with roadblocks. As long as he followed the speed limit and didn't do anything stupid, the cops wouldn't have any reason to pull him over.

Ben snatched the backpack from the cargo mat and closed the rear hatch. Scurrying to the driver-side door, he flung it open and hopped behind the steering wheel. He tossed his bag on the leather passenger seat then seized a crumpled roadmap from the bag's outer pocket. Green fluorescent ink highlighted several potential routes on the map, skirting the roadblocks he expected to encounter on the interstate. The sheer number of possible evasive avenues would leave the cops scrambling. Their apprehension efforts would be daunting – like trying to catch a grain of sand with a fishing net.

At the moment, he held the upper hand. The cops were looking for a green coupe – a luxury SUV that wasn't on a hot sheet would slip past their scrutiny. A multitude of scenarios blazed through his mind. Surely, the cops figured he was still in the city limits. The further he left the bright lights of Seattle in the rearview mirror, the safer he would be. Once he cleared their initial search grid, he could find a small town – something off the interstate – and resupply with fresh attire. It had been a few days since he changed clothes. He appeared grungy, and the irritating sensation of grit on his skin didn't ease the discomfort. If not for the prospect of Sarah's boyfriend popping by unexpectedly to check on her, he could have showered and cleaned up. But, there hadn't been time – not with so many details to consider.

I've got plenty of cash for now – thanks to sis'. Finding that wall safe was lucky. When we get some breathing room, it'll be time to go on a shopping spree and buy some new threads. After a supply run, the race would continue to the secluded ranch on the eastern side of the Rockies. His cargo was precious. Mark Taylor would pay for his wife's safe return – and if the software mogul wasn't willing to do what was necessary – then Sarah would suffer for her husband's lack of devotion. There would be no other way.

Ben folded the map after studying it for a few minutes. He tossed it on the seat beside him. Closing his weary eyes, he rested his forehead on the top of the soft, beige leather covering the steering wheel. *Man, I'm burned out.* How long had it been since he was able to get a full night of peaceful sleep? The cops were always close, always closing in. A sense of dread filled his cursed heart. He had seen the inside of a jail cell only once – when he was seventeen.

The cops picked him up for assault after he beat a bigger man unconscious with a three-foot length of a two-by-four. The section of splintered lumber served as a convenient weapon – snatched from the vacant lot's debris-strewn ground where the older vagrant encountered the savage teenager. The scruffy homeless man begged for a drag off Ben's smoke, but Ben spurned the request and demanded that the downtrodden soul depart immediately. The man ignored the warning. That was it. Ben showed the filthy scum size didn't matter. While he stood above the bloodied man's battered body, a street patrol happened upon the scene. The blonde-haired cop and his black partner roughed up the young offender, slamming him into the side of the police cruiser before shoving him into the rear of the unit while he cursed them.

In the county's holding cage, the cops didn't lift a finger to protect him. They stood idly by and watched while the crowd of older and more experienced inmates heckled and sodomized him in the dank coldness of the shared detention cell. He fought with ferocity. He struggled with all his might – but there were too many. The smiles and laughter from the stinking cops while they witnessed the event with glee remained etched into his memory. He hated them all – and he would never again allow himself to be caged.

Ben lifted his head and stared through the windshield without focusing on anything in particular. His mind filled with notions of freedom. It was within reach. With a little luck and a lot of determination, he would be rich. Soon, he would reunite with the only woman who made his emotions seethe with wanting. By way of the interstate, he could reach the secluded valley in Montana in less than twelve hours. But the zigzagging course he plotted out would add several hours to the journey. He would use deception to keep the heat off his trail. If his plan worked, he would slip through the snare and leave his pursuers mired in his confusing wake of subterfuge.

He pressed a button on the SUV's visor imprinted with a house icon. The garage door lurched then shook and rattled while it climbed its track, its steel wheels squeaking while they rolled upward. He pressed the ignition button and shifted the vehicle into reverse. The SUV shot backward, missing the ascending door's bottom edge by mere inches. He backed the SUV to the street then tapped again at the visor. The garage door jolted to a halt before descending closed.

After he shifted into drive, he took a final glance at the extravagant home. *The place looks nice and peaceful from the street.* They had a head start of several hours before anyone would suspect anything was awry. Sarah's boyfriend was the wildcard. As long as he stayed away until sunrise, everything would be just fine. Cruising through the neighborhood, Ben set the satellite radio to scan mode, locking in the station once the pulse of heavy metal music thumped from the upgraded sound system's speakers. He spun the volume button to a lower setting – better to avoid bringing any unwanted attention to the vehicle in the

wee morning hour. *Follow the speed limit. Drive carefully.
Don't break any laws.* By dawn, they would be hundreds
of miles away.

While he navigated the quiet, less-traveled streets,
impatience swelled within his chest. It seemed like they
were moving at a snail's pace. He repelled his anxiety. *Come
on – stay cool or you're going to do something stupid.* The sleepy
neighborhoods on the outskirts of the city passed without
incident. Within a few hours, the luxury SUV traveled far
enough from the sprawling metropolis that it was safe to
head to the interstate. Adrenaline coursed through his
veins as he steered up the on-ramp. *It's time to pick up the
pace. No more stop lights to slow us down.*

He kept the SUV in the far right lane and glanced at
the speedometer. 65 displayed in bright green numbers.
Fidgeting on the embroidered leather seat, he craved a
smoke. He patted his jacket's breast pocket. The box of
cigarettes was empty. *Shit.* Stopping to resupply was out
of the question – at least for a few more hours. Red and
blue lights flashed in the rearview mirror, sending a shiver
racing up his spine. He ducked into the seat and took a
long peek in the mirror. The cruiser gained ground at a
rapid clip. His breath stalled. *The windows are tinted pretty
dark. They won't be able to make out my face – not at night.*
The State Highway Patrol car zipped past. He puffed out
a long breath in relief.

He set the car on cruise control. Convulsing with
nervous energy, his body shook. *Come on, you idiot. Pull
your shit together. You've got this.* A few miles up the road,
three police cruisers sat parked off the right shoulder of the

asphalt. He steered into the left lane, maintaining a clear buffer between him and the scene. He surveyed the action as they passed. Two troopers stood over a man flailing in the grass, illuminated by blinding spotlights mounted on the vehicle doors. A third trooper knelt on the man, his knee pressed into the suspect's back while he cuffed the offender. Ben snickered. *Better you than me.* It was fortunate – there were only a certain number of troopers patrolling any given stretch of highway, and three of them were occupied.

Fifteen minutes passed. A large, green sign with reflective white letters stood by the roadside, "Minton 28 Miles." *It's time for a quick pit stop. I need smokes. Some munchies and a few sodas would be good too.* It was about as safe a place to stop as any other – considering there wasn't anywhere he could truly be at ease. The mile markers blew past. Finally, the off-ramp to Minton came into view. Although the small town was a quarter mile away from the interstate, a truck stop sat at the junction of roads beside the main thoroughfare. The bright neon of red and orange lights flashed like a beacon in the night.

Ben steered the SUV next to one of the many gas pumps. He dug a hundred dollar bill out of his pocket and hopped out of the vehicle. Strolling through the deserted parking lot toward the mini-mart set back from the array of gas pumps, he scanned his surroundings while he approached. Nothing seemed out of the ordinary. Several darkened semi-trucks with attached trailers sat parked side-by-side in a long row on a dirt pad at the lot's far end. *Good – it seems like everyone is asleep. There shouldn't be anything to worry about.* He pushed through the front door of the mart. A chime chirped a greeting.

A lone clerk stocking shelves laden with bags of different brands of chips and other snacks glanced over and called out, "Hey, how are ya doin'?"

Ben surveyed the store's layout. "I'm good. Just need a few munchies and some gas." He stepped to a refrigerator spanning the length of the back wall and grabbed four bottles of soda along with two bottles of water, tucking the twenty-ounce containers under his arm. Pivoting to the shelf of snacks behind him, he yanked a bag of chips from the wire display then headed toward the entrance. An open-top cooler across from the checkout counter beckoned with fresh sandwiches. He grabbed two and added them to his collection of goodies. Without looking directly at them, he noted the most likely locations for security cameras. It didn't matter. If any nosy cops showed up and checked the security video, he would be long gone.

He plopped the armload of items on the counter. The sleepy clerk – a chubby man in his mid-twenties, with long, curly, black hair puffed out into an afro, shuffled behind the counter and began ringing up the medley of items. Ben snatched a few bags of beef jerky from a display rack next to the register and tossed them onto the pile. "I also need a carton of Hemington Filterless." He scratched his neck and added, "Oh, and I need to fill up on pump seventeen – so set me up for say... thirty bucks on the pump."

The lazy clerk seemed overwhelmed by the amount of effort required by the sale. He let loose a deep exhale and replied, "Yes, sir." He finished scanning all the goods and huffed, "That'll be sixty-two dollars and thirty-eight cents for the groceries. Plus thirty on pump seventeen – your total comes to ninety-two dollars and thirty-eight cents."

Ben tossed a crisp hundred dollar bill on the countertop's red laminate. "Sweet – just barely made it with a hundred spot."

The clerk scratched at the puffy acne outbreak on his cheek before flicking the felt tip of his specialized pen across the bill.

"It's real. I just printed it this morning," Ben joked.

The clerk rolled his bloodshot eyes, obviously unamused by the jest. He tapped at the register's keyboard. As the cash drawer swung open, the man slipped the hundred dollar bill into a cash drop slot just below the console. He dug into the drawer then handed over the change. "Here ya go. Seven dollars and sixty-two cents is your change." His arms dangled loosely by his sides. "Would you like a bag?"

Ben raised his eyebrows and stared at the heap of goods he just purchased. "Um… *yeah!*" he answered sarcastically. He tapped his foot on the freshly mopped tile floor while the clerk stuffed the items into two separate bulging plastic bags. Ben grabbed them from the counter and headed to the exit.

"Have a great night," the clerk called out lethargically while Ben pushed through the front door.

"Yeah, whatever," Ben muttered under his breath. He hurried to the SUV and opened the rear side door. Tossing the grocery bags on the seat, he tore open the cigarette carton and took a fresh box of smokes and held it while he snagged the empty box from his jacket. He dumped the depleted box of smokes into a trash can next to the gas pump then stuffed the new pack into his pocket. After opening the fuel hatch at the vehicle's rear fender, he slipped the gas hose nozzle into the receptacle and flipped the pump's lever. With a press of the button on the pump, gasoline gushed into the tank. Pungent vapors billowed from the flow of fuel, and he inhaled the sweet scent. *When I get to a hardware store, I should pick up some empty fuel cans – never know when extra gas will come in handy.*

A few minutes later, the pump clicked, and the flow of fuel ceased. Ben pulled the nozzle from the tank and latched it back on the pump's cradle. He spun back around and slapped the gas tank door shut. Stepping to the partially open rear passenger door, he pressed a button by the seat's headrest. The seatback swung forward, exposing Sarah's limp body. He placed his index and middle fingers on her neck. Her pulse was slower than normal, but still strong. *Glad to know you're still breathing, sis'."* He lifted the seatback and clicked it into position. Their journey could continue. Once they crossed into Idaho, they would make another, more in-depth supply run. They still had a few hundred miles to travel until they reached the state line. By the time they reached their next stop, it would be mid-morning, and all the stores would be open for business.

Ben opened the driver-side door and settled into the seat. He reached behind him and snatched a bottle of soda from the bag. Spinning off the cap, he chugged the beverage completely then tossed the empty plastic bottle on the front passenger-side floorboard. He grabbed his pack of smokes and opened the box. After peeling the inner foil wrapper away, he wadded it up and dropped it by his feet. With a quick flick at his lighter, he lit the cigarette and took a long drag. The nicotine sent a welcome buzz through his body. He exhaled the smoke slowly then punched the ignition button on the vehicle's console. Holding the cigarette between his pursed lips, he steered away from the gas pump and back to the interstate traveling east – toward where Mark, Katy, and Will waited – unaware of the impending peril headed their way.

CHAPTER 8

D an glanced at the digital clock by his bedside. *I guess it's time to get going.* Sarah's last text the evening before convinced him to return to his condo and call it a night. She quashed his plan of treating her to a quiet dinner at a ritzy steakhouse on the water's edge with her desire for solitude. He wasn't going to press her – not while she struggled to come to terms with the apparent dissolution of her marriage to his best friend. After a sleepless night with visions of her consuming his reflections, he flung the white satin sheets aside. He sprang to the floor and hurried into the bathroom, determined to see her without further delay. He would find a way to light up her beautiful green eyes and chase away her sorrows.

Opening the shower's frosted-glass door, he rotated the faucet handles. Water cascaded from the showerhead. Within seconds, steam billowed from the enclosure and filled the bathroom with a thick mist. He stepped inside and wasted no time lathering up. Butterflies fluttered in his stomach. *Sarah, why can't I get you off my mind?* Soap suds trailed down his body while the deluge cleansed the foam from his skin. With a quick dab of shampoo to his sandy brown hair, he massaged his scalp then leaned under the stream of water and rinsed.

He pushed the glass door open and grabbed a fresh towel hanging from a brass rod fixed to the wall, hastily drying himself with its soft cotton fibers. The linen fell to the floor as he rushed to the vanity for a quick shave and to brush his teeth. He scurried out of the bathroom and into his walk-in closet. Slipping on plaid boxer shorts, followed by blue jeans and a black polo shirt, he snatched socks from his dresser and pulled them over his feet. He laced up his favorite pair of cross-trainer shoes and collected his billfold and car keys from his nightstand. He was ready.

He jogged out the front door and across the terracotta tiles forming the walkway leading from the condo through the small courtyard until the pathway ended at a wrought iron gate separating the front terrace from the street. Pressing the keypad of his blue SUV's FOB, he grasped the vehicle's door handle and swung the door open. He hopped into the driver seat and turned the ignition. The SUV growled to life, its V-8 engine rumbling loudly while he shifted into reverse and backed into the narrow street. He thrust the transmission into drive and sped off toward Sarah's home.

The light traffic drifted along at a leisurely pace – typical of an early Saturday morning. While the other commuters traveled with lethargic determination, Dan deftly zig-zagged between the mobile obstructions. He glanced at his cell phone lying on the center console between the driver and passenger seats. Sarah still hadn't sent her usual good morning message. A call letting her know he was on his way there would be the most polite thing to do, but if he just showed up unannounced, she wouldn't have the opportunity to discourage his visit. *I hope she doesn't stay in this depressed funk too long.* Mark's departure was unwanted, but he made his decision. There wasn't any sense in sulking over the way things turned out – it was time to adjust to life going forward. And hopefully, that adjustment included a romantic relationship with Sarah.

As he navigated the quiet tree-lined street winding up the hillside to Sarah's neighborhood, he glanced to his left and eased off the accelerator. The entrance to the small municipal park was cordoned off with yellow crime scene tape. A Seattle Police Department cruiser blocked the drive, its bright red and blue lights strobing in ominous silence. He slowed to a crawl to scan the scene, but the tall stands of evergreens and thick shrubs obstructed his view. *Now, what the hell is going on there?* Shaking off his curiosity, he pressed his foot to the gas pedal and continued on his way.

A few minutes later, he pulled into Sarah's long driveway on Whispering Pines Way. He popped open his door and stepped out onto the concrete. Trotting up the red brick pathway, he made his way to the front door. With a quick push to his glasses, he nudged them higher up the bridge of his nose then pressed the doorbell. Door chimes echoed within the home. Seconds passed without a response. He poked at the glowing white button again and again, tapping his foot impatiently on the concrete step. He yanked his cell phone from the back pocket of his jeans and held the number one key – the speed-dial code for Sarah's cell number. The call went straight to her voicemail. *Dammit, something's not right.*

He banged his fist on the hardwood door — no answer. After pacing back and forth on the front step for what seemed like an eternity, he huffed. Reaching into his front pocket, he yanked out his keychain. The friends had exchanged house keys years earlier – it seemed only fitting considering how intertwined the three friends' lives had been since their early college years. He unlocked the deadbolt then grasped the brass handle and opened the door. Stepping into the foyer, he looked around. Miniature rainbows danced across the floor's white tiles, cast down from the sparkling crystals adorning the chandelier overhead. His heart skipped a beat. Something was very wrong. "Sarah?" he called out, his voice echoing down the long hallway. Still, no response. He darted from the foyer and into the adjoining living room. Sarah was a creature of habit. Her latest novel lay on the glass coffee table in the center of the room, but the fancy piece of furniture was askew and no longer parallel to the sofa.

He raced up the hardwood stairs, leaping two at a time until he reached Sarah's bedroom. When he rushed through the doorway, his gut twisted. The room was in shambles. Dresser drawers lay in piles before the exquisite bureau, their contents strewn about the plush carpeting. The door to the walk-in closet hung wide open and the chamber's track lighting shined overhead. He scampered into the long room. Half of the closet sat empty – evidence of Mark's departure. Across from the bare shelves and garment rods, Sarah's clothes hung neatly in an elegant and organized display. At the far end of the room, the long rectangular mirror leaned against the wall, out of place, exposing the open wall safe. His mouth went dry, parched as the sun-beaten desert floor. He swallowed, but the lump in his throat persisted. He dialed 911 on his cell phone and held it to his ear. The call rang three times.

A woman's monotone voice answered, "911. What's your emergency?"

"I need to report a home invasion – thirty-four Whispering Pines Way!" His hand shook, and he struggled to keep the phone to his ear.

"Calm down, sir. Are you the owner of the property?"

"No… no… I'm a friend of the woman who lives here. I've been trying to reach her all morning, so I came over. The place is a wreck. Please! Send help immediately!" he pleaded.

"One moment, sir – I need to get some information. I've dispatched patrol units to the address – they'll be there shortly. Now, what is your name?"

"Dan… Dan Wilson." He continued to scan his surroundings. Panic surged through him and intensified the more he observed.

"What's the owner's name? Is she there with you?"

"Her name is Sarah Taylor – and no, I can't find her."

The dispatcher paused, then asked, "Are you in the residence right now?"

Dan clutched a clump of hair with his free hand. Exasperated, he replied, "Yes! I'm in her bedroom. I'm telling you, the place is thrashed!"

"When was the last time you spoke to Mrs. Taylor?"

Walking back into the hallway just outside the bedroom, he slowly descended the steps. "Last night, but we didn't actually talk – she just sent me a text message telling me she would talk to me this morning."

"Okay, sir. Two units are on their way. I need you to exit the home without disturbing anything," the dispatcher directed.

"All right… all right… I'm going out the front door right now." He opened the front door and sprinted down the walk to the driveway. Just as he reached the drive, two police cruisers skidded to a halt in front of the home. A burly officer, the size of the average football player, emerged from the lead car and adjusted his duty belt while he approached. "Okay, two police officers just got here."

Before ending the call, the dispatcher barked out one last set of instructions. "Sir, stay calm and answer any questions the officers ask."

"Yes, of course!" He pressed the end call button and slid the phone into his back pocket.

A second officer stood at his open car door, talking into the handset of his cruiser's radio while his cohort hustled over and asked, "Are you the one who called 911?"

"Yes. I've been inside. The house is a total wreck. The woman who lives here – she's gone." Two additional patrol cars arrived, and out of each, two more officers emerged and jogged up the driveway toward their husky comrade.

"What's your name, sir?"

"Dan Wilson. I've already told all this to the operator.

We're wasting time." Aggravation began to compete with his feelings of panic.

"Calm down. We're going to clear the scene, and we have detectives on the way.

Calm down. That's easy for these guys to say. He bit his lip. *They're just trying to do their job. Take a couple of deep breaths – you're not going to be of any help to Sarah if you're a basket case.* He paced erratically while the team of officers scurried up the walkway with their guns drawn.

The lead officer, an athletic middle-aged man with a bald head, approached him. "Please wait here with me while we investigate the residence. May I see your identification, sir?"

Puzzled, Dan scratched his head. "My ID?"

"It's routine procedure, sir," the officer replied.

Dan tugged his wallet from his left back pocket and slipped his driver's license from the billfold's plastic sleeve. He handed it to the sergeant and shuffled his feet while the policeman retreated to his patrol car, speaking into the handset clipped to his left shoulder. Lumbering to his SUV, Dan leaned against the side of the vehicle with his arms folded. His shoulders sagged in helpless defeat. Sarah was in trouble – and there was nothing he could do.

Deputy Hensley stood at the edge of the murky lake focused on the water's surface. A tow truck parked thirty feet away groaned. A steel cable protruding from the truck's crane strained and vibrated while a winch at its base retracted, spinning in slow revolutions. After a few minutes, the body of a car broke the cloudy surface. Water spilled from the coupe as the vehicle's tires rolled onto the muddy shoreline.

Chavez approached. "What's the situation, boss?"

Hensley glanced over at the younger deputy. "Morning, Joe. Local PD received a call a few hours ago from a father who came out fishing this morning with his son. They were on the dock and spotted a debris field floating on the water about fifty feet from the end of the pier – some clothing and lots of junk – paper and cigarette butts. It didn't look right, so they called it in. The patrol unit came to investigate and realized it required a more in-depth look-see. A dive team checked it out, and low-and-behold, it matches the coupe we've been looking for." He and Chavez approached the car while the tow truck driver knelt and checked the cable underneath the rear of the vehicle.

Chavez studied the waterlogged coupe. "Yep – it definitely fits the description."

Hensley nodded. "Seattle PD's forensics team should be here in just a few minutes. They'll get the VIN for confirmation, but it's just a formality."

Straightening his collar, Chavez peered at the older marshal. "Well… our suspect either stole another car or he's hoofing it."

"Knowing Thompson, he's already found another set of wheels. I've looked over the stolen vehicle reports for the past forty-eight hours. Local detectives are checking out each incident – like they normally do – but I've asked them to be a little more thorough with their investigations.

There are only seven reported thefts, so we should have an idea fairly soon if Thompson is to blame for any of them."

"Good – any news from the detectives on the mass cell phone purchase?"

"The transaction seems fishy, but the judge denied the warrant. He said there wasn't sufficient evidence to justify it." Hensley shook his head. "It would have been a big help if we got it. We'll have to do without the information. Did you get the sketches of our boy back from the forensic artist?"

"I did. I've got copies in my car for you. They've been released to the media and they're already broadcasting on every local network."

"Good. We need all the eyes we can get on the lookout for this guy. Now that we know he dumped his wheels, send those images out to every news station within five hundred miles of our search grid. The guy is a snake. There's no way of telling if he's close or if he's already made it beyond our roadblocks."

"You've got it, boss." Chavez pulled his cell phone from his jacket pocket and called the task team's command post to relay the lead deputy's order.

A flurry of activity sounded out across the parking lot where several police cruisers waited on standby. Hensley bustled over. A detective stood by one of the patrol cars talking on his handheld radio. "What's the commotion, Steve?" he called out.

The stout black man glanced at Hensley once the marshal reached his side. "Looks like we've got a home invasion in the neighborhood up on the bluff."

Without delay, Hensley spun, tucked two fingers in his mouth, and whistled. Chavez faced his direction. He waved the younger marshal over. Chavez closed the fifty-foot distance with a quick jog. "You and I need to get up to that neighborhood on the hill, pronto," he barked while he pointed to the top of the ridge.

Chavez slowed his gait once he was ten feet away. "What's up?"

"I'm not sure yet, but our boy may have broken into a residence up there. Leave your car here. We'll take mine." They dashed to the white four-door sedan and jumped in, slamming their doors before the car sped off. "Change the radio to Seattle PD's frequency," Hensley said. He eased his foot from the gas pedal. A sentry at the park's entrance lifted the yellow tape, allowing the car to slip underneath the flimsy barrier. Chavez tapped at the two-way radio's buttons and the police frequency crackled to life. An officer on scene reported the residence was secure and they had withdrawn in wait while detectives scoured the home.

Within minutes, the government sedan screeched to a halt in front of the Taylor home. The two marshals flung the car doors open and hurried from the vehicle, weaving their way through the ever-growing crowd of uniformed police officers and support personnel. They hustled up the long walkway to the front door, flashing their badges to the sergeant blocking the entrance. The stout officer nodded and stepped to the side, permitting them to pass into the foyer.

Hensley scanned the vestibule. A middle-aged woman, clad in a blue rain jacket with Seattle PD emblazoned across the back in bright yellow letters, snapped out orders to the forensics team gathered at the entrance. He approached her and said, "Tom Hensley – U.S. Marshals."

The woman seemed agitated by the two men's arrival. "I'm Detective Paulson – I've taken command of the scene. What are Marshals doing here? This situation is under local jurisdiction."

"Not anymore. We have strong reasons to believe this incident is linked to a high-value fugitive," Hensley replied.

Paulson's cell phone buzzed. The flustered woman snatched it from her coat pocket. Pressing the call button, she held it to her ear. Without hesitation, she barked into the phone, "I'll call you back." She stuffed the phone into her pocket and whirled back to him. "Look, buddy, I'm sure you're used to waltzing into crime scenes and throwing your weight around, but it's not going to work here."

"Detective, we're dealing with a time-sensitive issue — the fugitive we're seeking ditched a stolen vehicle just down the hill sometime within the last forty-eight hours. If he's taken a hostage, then this crime scene just became federal business. If you have any questions regarding my authority *or* jurisdiction – please, by *all* means, feel free to call the commissioner. I'm sure he'd *love* to hear how our investigation threatened your ego. You might even receive a citation for giving our suspect more time to get away by slowing us down."

The detective huffed. A vein bulged from her forehead while her face flushed beet red. "Until I hear otherwise, *I'm* in command of this scene."

Hensley shook his head. "If that's what you need – no

problem." He grabbed his cell phone from his belt. Tapping the screen, he held the phone to his ear. "Hello, Doug. Yes, it's Tom. Say… my partner and I just arrived at the site of a possible home invasion – we have reason to believe it might be related to Thompson. It seems as though your lead detective on scene is hesitant to cooperate." Tilting the phone away, he glanced over to the detective and asked, "It's Detective *Paulson*, right?" The woman nodded sheepishly. He swiveled the phone back to his mouth. "Yeah, Doug – Detective Paulson. Great. Hey, I appreciate your help. We'll talk soon." He dropped the phone from his ear and eyeballed the detective, flashing a wide grin while he clipped the phone back to his belt. Within seconds, Paulson's phone buzzed.

She stuffed her hand in her pocket and clutched her phone. Staring at the display, she hesitated before answering. "Detective Cindy Paulson." The color drained from her face. "Sir! Yes… uh… yes… *absolutely*, sir!" She quickly shoved the phone back into her jacket. Without looking directly at him, she muttered, "The scene is yours, deputy." She spun around and whisked out the front door.

Chavez shook his head. "That girl is a little too power hungry I would say."

Hensley nodded. "Let's get to work. Gather up the forensics team and let's make sure everyone is on the same page. I don't want anything missed – even the slightest clue. We can't afford to be sloppy. Thompson makes mistakes – but rarely obvious ones."

"You've got it, boss. I'll round up the techs."

Hensley cautiously moved into the adjoining living

room. With the number of officers out front, they wouldn't be dealing with an unpolluted crime scene. Too many people had already been in and out of the home. They would be searching for clues in a tainted environment – every detective's worst nightmare. He stood at the living room entrance with his hands on hips. Glancing at the crème-colored carpet, the faint outline of a shoe was barely visible. He knelt. The soft fibers were compressed and slightly discolored. *It's light, but it's definitely a shoeprint.* He stood. The coffee table sat at an awkward angle, offset from the luxurious leather sofa. Two ceramic mugs sat on the table's glass top. He stepped to the furniture, scanning for clues. The left seat cushion appeared smudged with traces of dirt.

Chavez emerged at the living room's arched entryway. Behind him, five technicians in blue jumpsuits waited. "Okay boss, everyone is here."

Backtracking to rejoin his partner, Hensley stepped into the foyer. The technicians gathered around him while Chavez waited at his side. "Good morning, everyone. I'm Tom Hensley of the U.S. Marshals. You've already met my partner, Joe Chavez." He cleared his throat and continued in his gravelly voice. "I understand that you all might be a tad upset the Marshal's Office has taken jurisdiction of this scene. Be aware we're working in full cooperation with both the FBI and your local precinct. The subject we're after is wanted on sixteen federal warrants. We can't let this guy get away. Any clues you discover – anything that seems out of place – document it and use proper collection procedures. Now, the suspect is already charged with several capital murder indictments – so whatever happened within this residence is in addition to what he's already facing. But, any information we discover during this investigation could prove critical in capturing him. Let's get started – we need to work quickly *and* thoroughly. Any questions?" The technicians glanced at one another, and one-by-one shook their heads. "Good. Get moving." He waved them on.

As the team split up to comb the residence, Chavez added, "Thanks, folks. We appreciate your cooperation." The two men stood alone in the elegant foyer. Chavez peered at him. "Tom, I've taken a quick look through the house. If our boy was here, he didn't stay very long."

Hensley nodded and rubbed his chin. "Knowing Thompson, it would make sense that he would book quickly. We should know soon if he's involved." Scanning the luxurious home and furnishings, he inhaled a deep breath then popped a stick of mint chewing gum in his mouth. After chewing in silence for a few moments, he continued, "Let's run the background history on the homeowners. It's in Thompson's nature to extort whatever he can when the opportunity arises. These folks are loaded. If Thompson took the lady of the house as a hostage, you and I both know what his intentions are."

Chavez nodded. "Yes, and the guy is frantic for a deep bankroll."

"If he's taken a hostage, it's going to be critical we outthink him. He doesn't have a history of leaving witnesses alive – even when there's no call to kill them. He murders for the pure pleasure of it." He sighed. The chase continued to become more and more complicated. Thompson was going out his way to muddy the water so much that innocent lives were increasingly at risk. "Make sure we get prints off the witness who made the initial 911 call. Seattle PD detectives are interviewing him out front. Forensics should be able to lift residual prints inside without trouble."

"The first responder – Sergeant Bales – said he looked in the garage. It's empty – no vehicles. He didn't complete an extensive search. He just cleared the area to secure the scene."

"All right, Joe. We'll give forensics some time to do their job. Get the VIN and plate numbers for the homeowner's vehicles. At least we can be fairly certain Thompson has a new set of wheels for the time being. While you're taking care of the vehicle info, I'm going to have a chat with the witness out front."

"I'm on it."

They stepped out the front door. While Chavez headed for their agency sedan to research the missing vehicle, Hensley approached Dan Wilson. The distraught man sat on the driver's seat of his SUV with the door wide open. "Good morning, I'm Tom Hensley – U.S. Marshal's Office."

Dan took a deep breath and hopped to the pavement. "I'm Dan Wilson. Have they found anything yet? What's going on?"

"We're still searching the premises. We don't have any information yet. But rest assured, we're doing all we can."

Raking his fingers through his well-groomed hair, Dan seemed discouraged. He gritted his teeth. After a pause, he said, "Look, you've got to find her. If anything has happened to her…"

Hensley placed his hand on Dan's shoulder. "Mr. Wilson, I completely understand your distress. But you've got to remain calm. I know you've already been interviewed and you're probably being asked the same questions over and over. We have several well-trained detectives working on this, and we're committed to finding answers."

"Are they out looking for her yet? Sarah wouldn't trash her own house and just disappear."

"We understand that, but we still have procedures to follow. We're not taking this lightly – we're gathering all the information we can at the moment. Now, do you have a recent photograph of the missing woman?"

Dan reached inside his truck and retrieved his cell phone from the center console. Scrolling to the image gallery, he pulled up a photograph of Sarah then handed over the phone. "That's her – Sarah Taylor. I took the picture last week when we met for lunch."

"Do mind if I text this to my phone?" Hensley asked.

"No, please… whatever I can do to help find her – just tell me what you need and I'll do it."

Hensley shared the image to his phone. Glancing back at Dan, he said, "Thank you. When was the last time you spoke to Mrs. Taylor?"

"Well, we traded a few text messages last night, but something didn't seem quite right."

"How so?"

"Sarah and her husband are longtime friends of mine. We were all roommates back in college. Sarah and Mark recently split up. Sarah and I have been casually dating. She's been pretty depressed since their breakup. We talk all the time – even when she's upset she stays in touch. Yesterday she wouldn't respond to my calls or messages… until last night when I texted her I was coming over to check on her," Dan replied.

Hensley scowled. "May I see the message?"

"Absolutely – exit the image gallery and scroll to the message window. It should still be open."

He swiped at the phone until the conversation window popped up on the display then scrolled through the most recent messages. "May I screen-shot the most recent texts and have a copy as well?"

"Sure." Dan stood silently while the marshal completed the screenshot transfer. Hensley handed back the phone. "You can see by our recent conversations her last text was out of the ordinary."

"I'm sure you're able to sense a difference, but there's nothing I can see that would lead me to believe with certainty that foul play was involved – if there wasn't evidence supporting it." He gestured to the horde of police cars parked in front of the home. "You said Mrs. Taylor and her husband just recently split up?"

Dan turned pale and glared at him. "You're not suggesting *Mark* had anything to do with this?"

"No, Mr. Wilson, I'm not making any insinuations. But, we need to know all the dynamics involved with the circumstances. Have you spoken to Mr. Taylor about this situation yet?"

"I haven't. He's my best friend. I was about to call him

when you walked up. He's living in Montana now. I wanted to get a little more information from you guys before I let him know what was going on. I know Mark – he would be on his way here right now if he were aware Sarah was in trouble. I don't want to upset him unnecessarily."

Hensley stopped scribbling at his notepad and eyed Dan. "That seems reasonable. I've got your cell phone number and personal information already. Why don't you head home and we'll be in touch later once we have an update." He reached into his shirt pocket and retrieved his contact card. Handing it to Dan, he said, "Here's my agency card. My cell number is at the bottom."

Dan examined the card then slid it into the back pocket of his jeans. "Thanks. I'd rather hang out here than go home."

"No, Mr. Wilson. It will take our forensics team at least a few hours to complete their initial investigation. There's nothing more you can do at the moment. I'll be in touch with you later."

With a discouraged sigh, Dan nodded. He climbed into his SUV and hesitated before turning the ignition. Slowly, he backed out of the driveway, steering between the fleet of police cruisers and other agency vehicles clogging the street.

SATURDAY, APRIL 17TH 12:18 PM

Several hours passed before the lead forensics technician met Hensley at the front walkway of the cordoned-off crime scene. The thirty-something woman adjusted her wire-rimmed glasses and greeted him. "Deputy Hensley, I'm Amanda Dietz."

Hensley nodded. For the past hour, he fielded phone calls to expand the inter-agency search grid beyond the Washington State line. The distraction was an important one, but it didn't suppress his desire for more information. The longer it took to gather the evidence, the farther away Thompson got. "Hello, Amanda." He glanced at the evidence bags in the young woman's clutches. "What have you got for me?"

Dietz handed the first poly-ethylene bag to him. "That's a cigarette butt we found in the large downstairs room at the back of the house."

He examined the remnants of rolled paper and tobacco. It was filter-less – the same style of cigarette he encountered on several occasions during his pursuit of Thompson. He returned the bag and grasped the second.

"Next, we discovered this empty syringe in the garage. It was between a set of muddy tire tracks. My theory is somehow after it was used, it rolled underneath the vehicle that was parked there."

Hensley scratched his head. "What led you to that conclusion?"

"The surface of the floor is relatively clean – except for the lone set of tire tracks in the center bay. With all the rain we've had this spring, the moisture on the vehicle's tires simply picked up debris and carried it to the parking spot. I located the syringe within the tire tracks – approximately dead center under where the vehicle was parked. I noted the tip of the needle appears to be coated with a trace of dried blood. There's still a slight amount of clear fluid in the reservoir of the syringe. We'll test it at the lab for identification."

"And DNA from the needle tip?"

Dietz nodded. "Absolutely. We'll also test the two coffee cups from the living room, along with the cigarette butt."

He handed the bagged syringe back to the technician. "Good work. What about prints?"

"We've completed a thorough examination, and as expected, we found a large number of latent prints. It will take some time to catalog them all, but we have more than enough to identify who's been in the residence."

"Excellent. Please expedite the DNA analysis. Get the items to the lab and keep me updated with the progress." He patted the young woman on the arm and offered a slight smile.

"We'll get on it immediately," the technician replied before hustling to the white evidence van parked in the driveway.

He scanned the front yard. The team of detectives and police officers dwindled to just a few bodies. Waiting for the report from the lab was secondary to the information he had already gleaned from the hours-long investigation. He glanced at the street. Chavez exited his white sedan. The young deputy darted across the lawn and approached.

"Tom, DMV has returned the VIN and plate numbers – I've forwarded each to the surrounding jurisdictions. We're looking for a white Lexus SUV – Washington plate number

P2714QZ." He peeked down at his notes and continued. "It's a 2016 model."

"Good. Make sure it gets listed on the hot sheet. Forensics should have plenty of evidence to weed through. The techs found a bloodied syringe. That, along with the missing vehicle and the empty safe up in the upstairs bedroom, leads me to believe Thompson is living up to expectations."

Chavez stared at him. He stroked his mustache and asked, "What does your gut tell you?"

Hensley puffed out a breath and rubbed his chin. "Just by what I've seen here so far, we still have a missing woman. The discovery of the syringe leads me to believe he drugged the homeowner and took her with him. Thompson doesn't like unnecessary hassles – he must have a good reason to contend with the complexities associated with carting a hostage around while he's trying to evade us." He paused and placed his hands on his hips. Swiveling around, he surveyed the lavish home and his brow furrowed. "It's pretty plain to see we're dealing with wealthy homeowners."

"That's for sure. The inside of the place is unreal."

"It should be. I ran a background search on the owners – Mark and Sarah Taylor. The husband is the software engineer who founded Cyber Safe Incorporated."

Chavez's mouth fell open. "Wow – that software is being talked about everywhere. There are advertisements constantly pushing it. The guy must be rolling in dough."

"Yes, he is. And we have to assume at this point that Thompson realized the same thing." He clenched his jaw. "Joe… our situation just got a lot more complicated. Timing is going to be critical. If we're going to save the woman's life, we need to hustle things up – but we're going to be stepping on eggshells while we do it. I think the woman is still alive – for the moment. With what we know about Thompson, he's going to use her for ransom." He scowled in frustration. "We're facing a serious dilemma – if we're lucky enough to locate him, we can't just waltz right up and expect to take him into custody. That would place the woman in a situation of certain death."

Chavez nodded. "And if he makes a ransom demand and gets what he wants?"

"Joe, the woman is living on borrowed time either way. This is all speculation, but I've been after this scumbag too long not to be able to get a feeling for his method of operation. If we get a demand from him, he'll squeeze every last bit he can get out of the opportunity. Whether it's money or safe passage he wants – most likely both – he'll get to the point where he feels safe and then kill the woman." He stared at the ground and tapped his foot on the red-bricked walkway. "It's important we try to outthink him. Let's update our vehicle search. Send out the word to locate, but not apprehend. I hate to pull back, but the last thing we need is another victim. Search for whatever credit card companies hold accounts for the victims. Let's set up surveillance on any credit cards Mrs. Taylor uses."

"Do you really think Thompson would be foolish enough to use a card, knowing we would be able to trace it almost immediately?"

"No, I don't think he's that stupid – but, desperation could force him into doing rash things he wouldn't normally do. We don't have any idea how much cash Thompson has access to. He might slip up and force the woman to grab a cash advance at an ATM. It would at least provide us a direction and narrow down the trail he's taking. He enhanced his resources by ransacking the home. We just don't know the extent to which he helped himself. He knew Mrs. Taylor's boyfriend would stop by to check on her at some point – that forced his timeline a bit. I'm sure he knows he has a limited amount of time in her vehicle before we put out an APB to look for it."

Sliding his notepad into the breast pocket of his button-up shirt, Chavez clicked the button on his ballpoint pen and stuffed it in the pocket beside his notes. "So how far should we expand our grid?"

"We don't know exactly when Thompson left this scene, but when we pinged Mrs. Taylor's cell phone, the last signal it registered was from this location – just before midnight last night. That means he has roughly a twelve-hour-or-less head start. Our inspection points on the interstate would have forced him to side streets and slowed him down considerably. By simple math – he's either still in Washington or possibly Idaho by now." He paused and glowered at his partner. "Let's expand our grid to the Idaho – Montana border. We'll be stretched thin on resources, but we need to try to slow him down. Order the State Troopers to set up periodic road inspection points. That should force him to keep traveling backroads. And by all means – let's emphasize to all the agencies involved that we suspect he's holding a hostage. If they spot him and there's any doubt whatsoever they can't perform a clean apprehension – withdraw. Now get the word out. I'm going to wrap things up here with local PD. I'll meet you at the car in a few minutes."

"You've got it, boss." Chavez scurried back toward their agency sedan.

Hensley snatched the cell phone from his belt. Flipping through his notepad with his free hand, he found the personal cell phone number for Mark Taylor that Dan Wilson provided. He blew out a long puff of breath. He hated making such calls.

CHAPTER 9

Mark sat on the edge of his bed lacing up a new pair of size twelve hiking boots. He pulled the long nylon coated strings tight. After tying the knot, he stared at the tan footwear. Digging the tips of his toes into the soft memory foam sole inserts, he mumbled, "I can get used to this." He stood and paced back and forth in the bedroom. *They're heavy and feel kind of clumsy…* Expensive Italian loafers were more to his liking – that was his style. But such luxuries weren't suitable for wading through the mud and muck covering the Montana ground. This was his new life. Luxury would be replaced by hard work and the sweat that accompanied such endeavors.

It was already midday, and the daylight continued to burn away under the brilliance of the springtime sun. His father and Katy had been up since before dawn. He skipped breakfast, much to Katy's disappointment. Tossing and turning throughout the previous night, sleep evaded him. His life had been at a crossroads for several months, but his new course lay clearly before him. Regardless, entering into the unknown wracked his nerves.

He stomped out of his room, down the long hallway's wood floor leading to the front door. He reached for the doorknob and paused. A silver mug sat on the kitchen counter. He strolled over to it and snatched the insulated thermal tumbler from the laminate. Beneath the cup a hastily written note read:

I hope this isn't too cold by the time you finally roll out of bed, sleepy head. You know where to find me!

Katy

He chuckled, and with the mug in hand, ambled out the front door. The sun neared its apex, and a light breeze made the air seem much colder than the forecasted fifty-two degrees. Signs of activity bustled all around him. A few of the ranch hands were busy unloading fresh bales of alfalfa from the back of Katy's red Chevy truck, while another led a mare across the compound to a wash rack at the far end of the barn. The sound of nickering horses shrilled through the air, muted off and on by the whooshing of tall pine trees swaying in the wind while their long needles acted like miniature strings on nature's violins.

He made his way into the barn and followed the long corridor between the stables lined against the aluminum wall to his left and the expansive arena to his right. The pathway lay covered in a mix of dirt and fresh pine sawdust. Each of his footsteps churned the bedding at his feet, causing the wood shavings to kick up into the air in little puffs of dust scented with their invigorating aroma. He passed several corrals, occupied by sassy broodmares strutting about their enclosures, stomping their hooves on the soft bedding in greeting as he walked by. Finally, he came to the stall he sought. He leaned against the four-tiered galvanized piping forming the boundary of the enclosure.

Katy placed a nylon halter over the soft muzzle of the white colt. She glanced at Mark and grinned while she buckled the strap below Shiloh's ear. "Well, mister… it's about time you decided to greet the day."

Mark slid the cover of the coffee mug's cap to the side and took a long swig of the lukewarm coffee. He swallowed then answered, "Yeah, sorry about being so lazy today." He popped the cap back onto the tumbler and gingerly rubbed his temple in slow circles.

A look of concern crossed Katy's face. "Are you feeling all right? You look a little pale."

Mark took a deep breath and held it for a moment before exhaling. His head throbbed, sending shooting pains like tiny daggers ricocheting in his skull. But there wasn't any need to get Katy worked up about a headache – it's not like they ever entirely subsided anyway. He forced a smile. "I'm okay. I'm just dragging a bit today." He held up the aluminum mug. "Thanks for the coffee. Once the caffeine kicks in, I'll be fine." He peered at the white colt. The feisty horse pranced from side to side, shaking his mane while he watched Mark with wide, blue eyes sparkling with youthful exuberance. "Shiloh looks like he's full of pep today."

Katy snickered. "He's full of pep *every* day! He's such

a little kid – always looking for some kind of trouble to get into…"

"Yes, from what I've read, Arabians are very spirited."

Stroking the colt's neck, Katy patted his front haunch. "This little boy is more than spirited – he's a full-time troublemaker." She held his snout, and the colt lifted his top lip, revealing a goofy smile. He dropped his head and lashed his tongue across Katy's face. She released her hold on his muzzle and wiped her sleeve across the tip of her nose, drying away the colt's kiss. "Shiloh, you little devil," she giggled.

Mark chuckled. "I guess there's no doubt about how much he loves you…"

"I think he's always considered me to be his momma. I bottle fed him several times a day after he was born – until he was weaned. It seemed like he waited forever until he started taking solid food. I think he just wanted the extra attention."

"So I've heard. Dad told me how your life pretty much revolved around him until he was strong enough to start fending for himself."

Katy leaned her head against the colt's neck and scratched behind his ear. "He's always been an attention hound, but he's worth it." She stepped away from the horse and approached the entrance to his stall where Mark waited on the other side. Unhooking the latch, she opened the gate and squeezed through the narrow opening while the hinges groaned from the movement of bare, unlubricated metal.

"Aren't you going to take him for some exercise now

that you've haltered him?" he asked.

"Yes, in just a little bit. I thought you and I could take a walk alone first." She glanced over at Shiloh. He eyeballed her, seemingly distraught that her attention was diverted away from him. The colt hopped partially into the air, wagging his hindquarters in protest while he nodded his head and offered a muted snort. "You just settle down, little boy. I'll be back shortly." Katy rolled her eyes. "He is *so* spoiled."

Mark walked with her down the remaining section of the corridor toward a door leading to the barn's southern side. They stepped outside into the bright sunlight. The sound of chirping songbirds fluttering happily amongst the wispy pine trees towering into the blue sky greeted them. He peeked back at the circular drive and noticed his father's truck wasn't there. "Where's dad?"

"It's Saturday. He headed into town to get his truck washed – just like he does every Saturday," Katy replied.

"It's kind of a waste – considering the darn thing will be dirty again by the time he gets back here. The seven miles of dirt road to the asphalt of the county road is pretty unforgiving."

Katy brushed the hair from her eyes and let it flow in the gusting breeze. She leaned against the railing of the outdoor arena and stared at the wooded hillside a hundred yards away. "Oh, you know your dad. He's stubborn. He heads into town to wash that old truck so he feels like he's accomplishing something on what would otherwise be a lazy day. Besides, I think he enjoys a little bit of quiet time away from it all now and then."

Mark nodded. He gazed at her while she surveyed the beauty of the surrounding countryside. Such a kind and beautiful woman deserved to be smack dab in the middle of such majestic scenery. "He sure loves it out here. And I know you do too."

Katy whirled back to him. "I do love it here. There's nowhere else I'd rather be. It's like heaven to me."

Mark reached over and plucked a piece of dried grass from Katy's thick curls that had floated into her hair while sailing on the breeze. She turned and locked eyes with him. Placing a hand on each flap of his unbuttoned shirt, she clutched them tight between her fingers and pulled him close. He reached to her cheek and cradled it in his hand. Desire burned in her eyes, and his ability to resist her any longer seemed to be fading. "You look beautiful standing here like this," he murmured. He moved his lips to hers. Just when they were a hair-width from touching, a loud buzz resonated across the compound. He glared at the tall telephone pole standing by the corner of the barn. A small speaker located at the top of the weathered log chattered the signal. A bright blue light strobed with each intermittent buzz while it defied the daylight.

"It's just an incoming phone call," Katy reminded with a whisper. She placed her hand on the back of his head and clutched his hair while she moved her lips to his.

A young man barged out the barn door. "Mark – you've got a phone call. The guy calling says it's an emergency."

Mark took a step back. He patted his breast pocket then the back pocket of his jeans. He forgot to grab his cell phone before leaving his room. "Thanks, Jimmy! I'll be right there." He focused back on Katy. "We'll pick up where we left off later, okay?"

A shy smile played at the corners of her lips. "I hope so, cowboy." She gave him a wink before he bolted to the barn and through the door.

He jogged into the barn and hung an immediate right into the tack room. Hustling to a small metal desk in the corner of the room, he snatched the cordless handset from the desktop and held it to his ear. "Hello, this is Mark Taylor."

"Mark? It's me!" Dan blurted in a tone fraught with distress.

"Hey buddy, how's life?" he asked.

"Not good – I've been trying to get ahold of you for hours. I had to dig to find your dad's number."

"Yeah, I never turned on my cell phone this morning. I'm pretty sure I left it in my room. What is it? What's wrong?"

"Mark, something's happened to Sarah…"

He jolted upright and gripped the phone tight. "What? What are you talking about?"

"She's disappeared. I went to your place early this morning because she hadn't been answering my texts or phone calls. I used the key you gave me to let myself in… the whole inside of the house was ransacked – and there wasn't any trace of her."

Tugging at the long whiskers of his beard, Mark strained to comprehend his friend's revelation. It seemed surreal. "Have you called the cops?" he asked in a shaky voice.

"Of course! There's a detective… a deputy from the U.S. Marshal's Office who's going to contact you. They've had dozens of cops and detectives crawling all over your place since I first called 911 this morning."

"Okay. Give me a bit. I'll get packed and find a flight to Seattle right away."

Dan exhaled loudly into the phone. "No, Mark – stay put for now – you're not supposed to be flying anyway. They're pretty sure whoever took her is on their way out of state. There's nothing you can do but wait. Get your cell phone and call the marshal back. His name is Hensley."

Mark kicked at the wall. Anger, frustration, and fear pulsed through his mind and body. "So, I'm just supposed to sit here and wait for the phone to ring?" he snapped.

"Dammit – I know you're frustrated. I share your frustration. I feel totally helpless right now. But, the cops are doing what they can. There isn't anything we can do. Just call the detective back."

"Okay. I'm heading to the house right now to get my phone. Stay in touch, will you?" Mark replied.

"I will. You do the same. Call me back after you talk to Hensley," Dan pleaded.

"I'll call you back in a few. We'll talk soon." He pressed the disconnect button on the cordless phone then tossed it on the dusty desktop. *No… this can't be real…* He bolted out of the tack room and down the long, sawdust-covered pathway. He shot out the barn's side door and covered the distance to the house in long strides. Bounding up the porch steps, he reached the rickety screen door at the lodge's entrance and flung it open, whacking it hard against the log wall. His footsteps fell hard upon the wood-planked floor, and within seconds, he reached his room. The cell phone lay on the small nightstand – just where he left it. He snatched it from the blemished tabletop and powered it up. The phone's display lit up, and after it fully booted, icons filled the welcome screen – eight missed calls and five text messages.

He swiped across the screen with his thumb and checked the text messages. Four were from Dan. *One was from Sarah.* He gulped and navigated to her message. His body went numb. The text read:

Greetings Taylor. Your wife and I are taking a road trip. You'll get her back in one piece IF you follow my instructions EXACTLY. If you don't, she's as good as dead. I'll be in touch soon with details. DON'T MENTION THIS TO ANYONE. NO COPS. NO FRIENDS. NO NOTHING. If I get even a hint of you involving anyone in our deal – it'll take years for you to find all the pieces of her corpse.

Mark nearly fell to his knees. He crumpled onto the edge of the bed; staring at the message while his hand shook so violently that his vision blurred reading it over and over. *Oh my God, Sarah… this can't be happening.* He took several deep breaths while his senses dulled. *Dammit, it! Focus!* If Sarah was in danger, he couldn't afford to fall apart. He scrolled to the phone's call log. Amongst the entries displaying Dan's calls, there it was – the one he sought – Tom Hensley. He pressed his thumb to the call button next to the name and held the phone to his ear.

"Hello, this is Hensley," the gruff-voiced bellowed through the speaker.

Mark closed his eyes and rubbed his temple. "Uh... yeah... Mr. Hensley, this is Mark Taylor. You've been trying to reach me."

"Yes, Mr. Taylor, I'm a deputy for the U.S. Marshal's Office. I need to speak with you regarding a situation that involves your wife."

Mark struggled to hold back the surge of questions racing through his mind. But he needed to be careful. He couldn't allude to being contacted by Sarah's abductor – not if it meant placing her in even greater peril. "What kind of situation?"

"We believe your wife has been taken hostage by a fugitive we've been pursuing for some time..."

Mark cut him off. "What fugitive?" he demanded.

"Sir, I can't get into details at the moment – it might jeopardize our investigation..."

"Bullshit! Who's taken her?" He took another deep breath.

After a long pause, Hensley responded, "Mr. Taylor, I'll be straight with you considering your wife has become a critical priority in the investigation. We have reason to believe a subject named Ben Thompson is holding your wife. He's currently wanted on murder charges in sixteen incidents."

"My God... What does he want with Sarah?"

"We haven't been in contact with the suspect yet, but considering Thompson's history, it's a pretty safe bet he took your wife captive for ransom. He also probably intends to use your wife as a shield so he can guarantee himself safe passage."

Mark clenched his jaw. If Sarah's captor knew of his successful enterprise, then it all made sense. With all the publicity and write-ups centering on him and Dan, it was public knowledge he and Sarah were very wealthy. "How can I help? What can I do to make sure Sarah makes it home safely?"

"First off, you need to be straight with me. No bullshit. Have you been in contact with the subject?"

There wasn't time to think. He paused, unsure how to respond. "I can't say."

"It's an easy question, Mr. Taylor. Has anyone contacted you regarding your wife?"

He huffed. His back was against the wall and either way, Sarah was in danger. "I'm telling you – I can't talk about this. I'll only say I'm not to speak to anyone regarding the situation or they'll kill her."

"Mr. Taylor, let me be blunt. We have surveillance on your wife's phone. We've run her contact history, and we already know a text message was sent to you – *after* we presume she was taken hostage."

"Then you know what I've been instructed to do."

Hensley's agitation increased with each of Mark's diversions, evident in the tone of his voice. "We're waiting for a warrant authorizing us to retrieve the message. We'll have it shortly. All you're doing right now is buying the scumbag who has your wife more time – and the more time he has… the less likely it is we'll find your wife alive. Look, this guy is intelligent – he has a borderline-genius

IQ. The only reason he sent a message from your wife's phone was to make a point – proof that he was in control of her. He probably knows we'll place surveillance on her cell number."

Mark stood from the bed and stared at the ceiling while he paced around the room. "Then why would he send me a message telling me not to speak with anyone if he knew you would be able to access the message?"

"His motive is to keep things as disorganized as possible on law enforcement's end. He's just trying to get inside your head and muddy the water. It'll make things much easier for him if you don't cooperate with us," Hensley replied.

Mark trembled with trepidation. "What choice do I have but to obey his demands? *He's* the one holding all the cards."

"Mr. Taylor, I fully understand your anger and frustration. But… we have a highly skilled team in place determined to stop this individual. And I can assure you we're doing and will do, everything we can to get your wife back safely when we apprehend him."

"And what if the only way Sarah is guaranteed safe release is to let him get away?"

"Then he walks. Our primary objective is your wife's well-being." Hensley paused and then sighed. "Look, Mr. Taylor… I've been on this guy's trail for a long time – a lot longer than I'd care to admit… but we're closing in on him. We're closer to him now than we've ever been…"

Exasperated, Mark interrupted. "And exactly how long have you been after this guy?"

"Eight years."

"Eight… eight years?! Are you *serious*?" He pulled the phone from his ear and fought the urge to fling it against the wall. He bit his bottom lip and shook his head in disbelief. After taking a moment to cool his anger, he placed the phone back to his ear. "You want me to go against what this guy has told me to do… and to listen to a supposed *well-qualified* team that hasn't been able to get him after *eight years*?"

"Thompson is a snake. We've been close to him several times, but he's managed to slither through our grasp. The past several months, it's become clear that his level of desperation is increasing. He's out of options, and we've placed surveillance on the locations he once considered safe. We've taken the few individuals into custody who have harbored him in the past. He's out of places to hide, and we'll get him soon."

Mark let the detective's words sink in. If Sarah's captor were anything like the way he was described – a vicious animal – then he would undoubtedly lash out in the same manner if cornered. But this time… he possessed a human shield – Sarah. "So what do you want from me?"

"Cooperate with him – but don't let him know you're in communication with law enforcement. All we need from you right now are details of your interactions. That will be our ace in the hole. He'll be suspicious of you, but he won't have solid information regarding what we know. That will help tip the balance in our favor."

"Should I respond to the text?"

Hensley cleared his throat. "No, not right now. We've pinged your wife's phone, and at the moment, it's a dead signal – we've got nothin'. We can only track a cell signal when the device is powered up. He's smart enough to know that. We suspect he'll be using additional pre-paid cell phones to text you – so be on the lookout for texts from numbers you don't recognize. Pre-paid phones take a great deal more effort to track. May I have your permission to place surveillance on your number? I can get a warrant – but I'd much rather have your voluntary cooperation – it'll save us some precious time."

"Is there any chance he'll be able to find out you're tracking my phone? I don't want to do *anything* that will make it more dangerous for Sarah."

"He's not stupid, so there's a chance he knows we might be monitoring your number. But with as much as he's scrambling right now, it might just slip his thought process. It's a common practice by law enforcement agencies – he wouldn't hold it against you because it's a situation totally beyond your control. By assuming he's aware of our surveillance, we can use his messages and your responses to feed him inaccurate information."

"Fine. Then you have my permission to place surveillance on my number." Mark sighed. He plopped back down on the edge of the mattress. The detective on the other end of the line didn't seem incompetent. The more he spoke, the more on top of the situation he seemed to be. "All right deputy, I'll stay in touch. Don't keep me out of the loop. I want to know exactly what's going on."

"Mr. Taylor, I'll keep you as close to the situation as I can. I appreciate your cooperation… and rest assured – we'll do everything we can to get Mrs. Taylor home again

– safely. Expect a ransom demand – and be ready."

"Thanks. I'll be expecting your call." Mark pressed the end call button and dropped the phone on the bed. *I have plenty of experience with cellular communication...* His former company, Cyber Safe, now under Dan Wilson's full control, also produced security software for use on mobile devices. Sarah had it installed on her phone – and when he wrote the code, he left a backdoor in the software allowing a programmer undetectable access to the device. *We could reprogram the software remotely to allow Sarah's phone to be tracked – even if the power appeared to be off! We hack the phone and place it into sleep mode whenever it's powered down!* He snatched his phone from the mattress. Pressing Dan's contact entry, the phone rang.

The familiar voice on the other end answered breathlessly, "Mark!"

"Yeah, man – it's me. I just got off the phone with Hensley."

"So what's the word? They won't share much with me. They're probably more likely to be upfront with you... considering you're both still legally married."

"Hensley said to expect a ransom demand." He scooted further onto the bed and leaned his back against the pine panels covering the wall. "It sounds like the guy holding Sarah is just a total piece of crap. He's a killer – wanted for multiple murders."

Dan groaned. "That's sickening. What can we do? I feel so freaking helpless right now."

"Yeah, me too. I have an idea – it's a long shot, but it might help."

"What? Tell me!" Dan implored.

"There's a good chance Sarah's phone is with the guy who has her. The cops placed surveillance on the line, but the scumbag sounds smart enough to keep it powered off..."

"So they can't ping its location..."

Mark slid back to the edge of the bed and stomped his boots on the floor as he leaned forward. "That's right. Remember the backdoor we left in the code for the mobile device version of Cyber Safe?"

Dan paused then replied, "Yeah?"

"The Cyber Safe application is installed on Sarah's phone. We can schedule a software update specific to her device... and program it to broadcast a signal – even when it appears to be powered off. We program it to go into sleep mode when it's shut down. The display would remain blank, and the LEDs on the phone wouldn't function. We could track her by the phone's broadcasted GPS signal."

"Hell, Mark... do you have any idea what that would entail? Besides the FTC and FCC would be crawling up our butts if they knew we left that kind of code in the software."

Tugging at his whiskers, Mark continued to formulate his plan. Yes, it would require some planning and effort. But, all they needed was for Sarah's phone to be powered up for a minute or two for the update to install itself. Considering Thompson's threatening text had been sent from her phone, it made sense at some point he would power it back up to check for a reply. They just needed to have the software update programmed and ready the second her phone was turned on. "Look, Dan... I understand what's at stake... but we're talking about Sarah. She's worth the repercussions. We keep this tight-lipped. I'm going to hop on my laptop to activate the update specific to her phone number by using the serial number associated with the application she has installed. I'll email you the file when it's complete. You'll have to upload it from your end – I don't have that capability from here."

"Okay. I'm heading for the office now."

"And Dan… one more thing – I've given permission to Hensley to place surveillance on my phone. I just gave the authorization, so it won't be long before they start monitoring anything from my cell number. No more discussion of this on my cell phone. Anything else will have to be over my dad's land line."

"You've got it. I'll talk to you soon."

Mark ended the call and placed his cell phone on the nightstand. He seized his laptop case from the floor at the foot of the bed and slung it onto the mattress. Unzipping the nylon case, he flipped open the cover and removed the computer. After swinging the laptop's seventeen-inch screen to a viewable position, he powered up the unit. It was time to get to work – Sarah's fate depended on his undertaking.

CHAPTER 10

Ben squinted through the bug-splattered windshield of the white Lexus. They were making good time on the four-lane interstate. He reclined the seat and slumped into the embroidered padding. The Idaho-Montana border waited just a few more miles ahead up the steep mountain pass. The trip through Washington and Idaho had been uneventful. A lonely truck stop alongside the highway at the eastern edge of Washington State afforded the opportunity to refuel a second time. With the fuel gauge reading nearly full, they were primed to strike deep into Montana before it would signal the need for another pit stop.

During the refueling break, a quick peek at Sarah revealed she remained unconscious, still lost in her drug-induced slumber. But while the luxury vehicle sped up the interstate's right lane climbing toward the highest point of the pass, muted groans sounded from the rear cargo area. The drugs were wearing off. Sarah's drowsiness was fading.

The tranquilizer had served its purpose well – keeping her a trouble-free passenger. His time estimate of the drug's effects was dead-on. A quick internet search provided the dosage based on a guess of her body weight. It was time to start searching for an obscure location where he could pull over and tend to her. Several hundred miles through the wilds of Montana lay in front of them before they reached their destination. A restless hostage would only make the distance more miserable.

Ben grabbed the police scanner from the passenger seat. Steering with his left hand, he pressed the power button on the device. The unit crackled then buzzed with static. He tapped at the buttons with his thumb and set the radio to scan for voice broadcasts on any channel. After adjusting both the squelch and volume knobs, he laid the scanner on his lap. A sudden burst of radio chatter cackled from its speaker. Idaho State Troopers relayed in code they had established a checkpoint fifteen miles behind the SUV's current position. Ben squeaked through just in the nick of time with his hostage in tow. He snickered. *Better luck next time, you idiots.* The unexpected text he received on the disposable cell phone during the last refueling stop proved useful. He glanced at the phone sitting in the cup holder of the center console. *I thought it was bullshit… but maybe you're on the level. We'll see.*

He snatched the wrinkled western states roadmap from the seat beside him and read it while he maneuvered the SUV around the sharp curves of the mountain pass. The road careened through high mountain ranges on both sides of the multi-lane highway. It was imperative to make it

through the next twenty-five miles without incident –
there weren't any escape routes until they cleared the pass.
An off-ramp to a two-lane state highway lay just beyond
the summit. It would have to do. Aside from a few paved
county roads and some lesser-known primitive roads, the
options for travel were slim.

Ben pressed a button on the door's armrest and lowered
the window two inches. He drew a cigarette from his pocket
and tucked the unfiltered end between his lips. Flicking
the flint on his lighter, he lit the tip of the smoke and took
a long drag. The situation was becoming dire. Traveling a
course with only a few avenues for escape was dangerous.
But to carry out his plan, he had to overcome the natural
barriers the wilderness proffered. Sweat beaded on his brow
and trickled down the rugged features of his face. Anxiety
was setting in. So far, he'd been lucky… but luck runs out.
It was only a matter of time before the cops discovered
the scene back at his sister's place. And while he was there,
he'd been sloppy. The Marshals and the FBI were nipping
at his tail. They would identify his presence anyway. No, it
didn't matter if he had been careless. Covering his tracks
would have been too time-consuming – and time wasn't an
indulgence he possessed. The cops probably already figured
out he was using Sarah's SUV for his escape.

After taking a long drag off his smoke, he exhaled and
held the cigarette to the gap in the window. Suction tore
it from his fingertips and out of the vehicle. He raised
the window and snapped up the map for another peek. A
small town sat along the state highway ten miles north
of the interstate. Hopefully, it was large enough to offer a

hardware store and somewhere to grab some fresh clothes. According to the map, several campgrounds were in the vicinity. Campers always needed supplies. He would find what he needed.

Half an hour later, Ben steered the SUV up the off-ramp to the connecting state highway. Slowing to a stop at the junction, he waited for an early model pickup, encrusted with rust overtaking its once-red factory paint job, to pass before he swung left onto the northbound asphalt. He peered out the side window while the mile markers passed. Dense thickets of trees and brush bordered the road. *Someplace along here would make a good place to park for a bit.* Up ahead, a dirt track cut off from the pavement. He checked the oncoming lane then glimpsed into the rearview mirror. No other cars were in sight. *This is probably as good of a place as any.* He veered onto the backroad. The late model SUV bounced along the rock-jutted path, snaking its way amongst looming stands of spindly conifers obscuring the wilderness trail with their vast numbers. Thriving clusters of thimbleberry bushes boasting large, green leaves the size of the average human hand, claimed sunlit gaps between the trees.

A bare patch of ground, free of vegetation, came into view. Hidden deep within the growth, it appeared satisfactory for a brief respite. Ben parked the vehicle in the shade offered by the canopy of pine trees. He tossed the police scanner onto the passenger seat, and then popped open his door. Stepping out onto the soft blanket of dried pine needles and fledgling wild strawberry plants, he placed his hands on his hips and arched his back. His tired muscles ached from inactivity after the long drive. Standing upright relieved the atrophy and numbness plaguing his limbs. He paced around the small clearing and surveyed the surroundings. He readjusted the pistol in his waistband. Only the breeze blowing through the tops of the pines, a twittering songbird, and the babbling of a lazy, meandering stream somewhere close-by, broke the stillness. There was no one around.

It's time to check on sis'. He kicked at pine cones littering the forest floor with the tip of his combat boot while he made his way to the back of the Lexus. Yanking the vehicle's FOB from his front pocket, he pressed a button on the plastic module. The rear hatch hissed open. In the cargo hold, Sarah twisted hopelessly against the anchor points of her bindings.

Ben stood before her – his hands balled in tight fists at his sides and his legs spread in a wide stance. He glared at his dazed captive. Her glossy eyes brimmed with confusion. "You look kinda sleepy, sis'." Seizing the combat knife from his jeans pocket, he flicked open the five-inch blade. Sunlight filtered through a break in the treetops and glinted off the knife's serrated edge. Sarah's eyes widened while he cut the nylon ties from the anchor point at her feet then the one at her hands.

"Where... where... am I?" She mumbled.

Ben gripped the menacing stainless steel blade's handle in his right hand and held up his palms. Glancing from side-to-side, he replied, "Why, you're on a field trip with your little brother. I thought I'd take you on a tour of the forest." He snickered and unlocked the handcuffs binding her ankles. Bending down, he moved closer to her – his nose nearly touching hers. "Now, you listen up good." He dangled the handcuffs in front of her face. "I'm gonna be nice and take these off for just a little bit so you can stretch your legs. If you cause me any problems… it'll be the end of me cutting you slack ever again." He eyed her bare feet. Pine needles and broken twigs blanketed the forest floor. If she tried to flee, she wouldn't be able to outrun him. He grasped her arm and pulled her to the bumper. She leaned against the vehicle's wheel well with her legs hanging over the rear of the cargo hold, still noticeably woozy from the tranquilizer. He stood and pointed his finger at her. "Be good. Understand?"

Sarah nodded. "Yes." She convulsed and leaned forward, retching on the ground just below the bumper.

Ben chuckled. "Now you know why I didn't tape your mouth shut. The shot of that stuff I gave you can make you sick. If I taped your mouth and you puked – you would have suffocated in your vomit. Understand though… if you cause any problems… I'll give you another shot and tape you up anyway."

Sarah wiped her mouth with the back of her hand. "Water? Please?" she pleaded.

Ben stepped to the side of the vehicle and flung the door open. Grabbing a full water bottle, he trudged back to her. He ripped off the cap and handed her the bottle. "Drink it slowly otherwise you'll just puke it all up."

Clasping the plastic bottle between her bound hands, Sarah guzzled the water. After downing most of the bottle's contents she moved it from her cracked lips and gasped for air. Her paleness faded while color slowly seeped back into her cheeks. She frowned at the anchor points in the cargo area then glared at him. "Is it *really* necessary to keep me confined like this? Every part of me aches after lying on my side for so long. How long have I been out anyway?"

"You were asleep for about eleven hours – long enough so I didn't have to worry about you making a fuss while we were driving through the city. And yes, you're going to stay locked up… just like you were before."

Sarah huffed. "Where are we?"

Ben closed his knife and tucked it back inside his front pocket. "We're in Montana," he curtly replied.

Sarah stared at him. "You're taking us to Will's, aren't you?"

Spinning away from her, he rested his hands on his hips and scanned the tree line. "Who the hell is Will?"

"He's Mark's father. It's his ranch you're heading to…"

Ben whirled and shifted his cold gaze to her. He scowled. "Maybe. We might find time to drop by for a visit. I'll know more after your husband and I have a chat. I'm curious to find out exactly how much you mean to him."

Sarah took another quick sip from the water bottle. She swallowed slowly, seemingly lost in thought. Eyeballing him, she asked, "It's ransom you're after, isn't it?"

He dashed to her and placed a hand on each of her shoulders, digging his dirty fingernails into her skin through her light t-shirt while he knelt and stared directly into her eyes. "Yeah, sis'… money. Money is what I'm after – and lots of it. I told you before we left Seattle… your husband is going to hook me up with twenty million dollars. Considering how much bank the two of you have,

I don't think that's an unreasonable amount for him to pay up to get you back in one piece."

"What makes you think we even have access to an insane amount of money like that?"

Ben stood and guffawed. "I checked out all sorts of interesting financial documents that came out of your wall safe in that great big mansion of yours… along with the forty grand in cash. You and your hubby have a lot more than twenty million packed away." Backpedaling from her, he rubbed his chin. He raised an eyebrow and continued, "As loaded as the two of you are… twenty million should be a painless amount to scrounge up in a short amount of time. And trust me – hubby's not gonna have much time to scrape it together… not if he wants to keep you breathing."

Sarah stared at the nearly empty water bottle while she spun it round and round between her bound hands. She glared at him. "What makes you think I'm even important to him anymore? We haven't been together in over eight months." She broke off eye contact and gazed at the ground. "We're getting a divorce," she muttered.

Ben pulled the pistol from his waistband and aimed it at squirrel darting partway up the trunk of a lodgepole pine ten yards away. Simulating the pistol's recoil, he mouthed, "Bang!" He stuffed the handgun back into his pants and faced Sarah. He flashed an evil grin. "Sorry to hear about your family troubles, sis'… I wouldn't know anything about them – I never really had a family." He approached her and leaned against the side of the SUV. Gazing down the rutted track they traveled to get to the secluded spot, he mumbled, "I don't care about what's going on between you and your ex-man. I just know both your names are on some pretty cash-filled accounts. I'm betting with him being so famous he'll be more than willing to part with a fraction of what you two have." He kicked away from the SUV and crossed his arms. "Just factor in the amount of money he gives me when you work up your divorce settlement," he mocked. He stepped to the open hatch and yanked Sarah to her feet. "All right… enough of this small talk… stretch your legs. Find a bush while you're at it – one close by where I can see you. We need to get back on the road."

Sarah carefully tiptoed across the debris-covered ground to a chokecherry bush. She glanced back at him while he stood guard fifteen feet away, ready to pursue her should she attempt to flee. She relieved herself then tugged at her black sweatpants, pulling them back to her waistline. She walked back to the Lexus with careful steps, but winced and shrieked in agony when she stepped on a sharp twig. Falling to the ground, she clutched her foot and yanked the offending sprig from her flesh where it embedded itself between her toes. She wiped away the blood from the wound and grimaced. Struggling to her feet, she limped back to the SUV.

Ben stood to the side and chuckled at Sarah's misfortune. "Life sucks without expensive shoes, doesn't it?" He placed a hand between her shoulder blades as she hobbled past and shoved her into the cargo hold. While he clasped a cuff around her ankle, she reeled back into the compartment, kicking at him. He deflected her blows then lunged forward and seized her by the throat. Terror flickered in her eyes while he constricted, digging his fingertips deep into her soft flesh. *Maybe I should kill her now... get it over with...* He seethed for a few long seconds. She was insurance... *and* his ticket to twenty million bucks. *No, I need her alive – for now.* He released his chokehold and slapped the second cuff around her free ankle. Once again, she was bound.

"Ben... please... *I beg you...* don't do this to me," she sobbed.

"You can beg all you want, sis'... this is the way it's going to be. Cooperate, or I'll beat the living shit out of you – it's your choice." She relented, ceasing her resistance while he reattached new zip ties to secure her hands and feet to the opposing sides of the vehicle's interior. After firmly positioning her on her side, he hurried to the SUV's open passenger door and snagged the duct tape from his pack, slamming the door shut behind him. Stepping back to her, he tore a six-inch long strip from the roll and slapped it over her mouth. The hostility in her green eyes filled him with satisfaction. Her hateful expression left no doubt she would take great joy in plunging his lock-back knife deep into his chest if given the opportunity. Yes, she eyed it intently. "Just a bit longer, sis'... then we'll be where we need to be." He repositioned the cargo shade over the top of the hold, making sure the pegs on each side of the leather awning locked into the plastic molding insets of the vehicle's interior. The rear hatch closed with a press of the FOB's button. Sarah lay imprisoned once again and out of sight.

Ben slid behind the steering wheel and tugged his door closed. He pressed the ignition button and shifted into reverse, backing up the SUV ten feet before slamming it into drive. Pine needles, twigs, and moist clumps of dirt spit from the tires while the grime-covered SUV lunged back to the highway. It was only another five miles to the small town according to the map. Two vehicles passed from the opposite direction. The lack of activity was a good sign, especially on a Saturday. It bode well for his desire to travel unnoticed.

The wooded mountains paralleling the weather-beaten pavement soon diverged and gave way to a narrow valley veiled in the green carpet of small farm fields bounded by multi-colored belts of wild grass. Small, decrepit buildings stood by the roadside, collapsing with age while their rotting wooden structures offered a view of life a century earlier. Ben surveyed the small borough as he stopped for a lone stoplight at a crossroad entering the town. *There we go. That's what I'm looking for…* A large building constructed of weathered logs sat surrounded by an asphalt parking lot just across the intersection. A long white sign with red letters advertising "Pappy's Mercantile" hung just below the roofline at the front of the building. The parking lot was nearly empty. Only three vehicles were visible. He maneuvered into the sizable lot and parked on a deserted side of the establishment.

He hopped out and scurried to the entrance. His eyes adjusted to the dim setting as he pushed through the smudged glass door. Off to his left, a series of two counters served as checkout points. A lone clerk leaned on one of the hardwood countertops next to a cash register.

"Good afternoon, how are ya today?" The elderly woman asked.

Ben sniffed and shot a wary glance at the kind old lady. "I'm good." He pored over the maze of tall shelves and displays filled with groceries. "Do you sell clothes? It seems I left a bag at home when my girlfriend and I took off on our trip."

The woman adjusted her glasses and pointed to the building's back wall. "Yes, honey. We have a selection of apparel at the back of the store. Nothing fancy – jeans, t-shirts, some flannel shirts, underwear, socks…"

"No worries. I'm not looking for anything exotic. I'll check out what you've got." He grabbed a small shopping cart from a line of ten carts by the front door. Pushing the buggy toward the back wall, he shook his head. The front right wheel wobbled, never aligning with the cart's other three wheels while it spun helplessly in slow rotation. *In a high-tech world, no one's ever been successful at making a damn shopping cart with wheels that work right.*

He moved down a side aisle, scouting the metal shelves stocked with cans and other dry goods. Upon reaching the men's clothing section, he grabbed three pairs of blue jeans in his size – 32x34 – then packs of underwear, socks, and medium-sized t-shirts. Flannel shirts hung on a four-way fixture, and he stuffed three of different colors into the cart. *All right. This should hold me over for now.* He trudged over to the women's section. Grabbing a pair of sweatpants for Sarah, along with a pack of t-shirts and another with underwear, his search for clean clothes was complete. *That ought to be enough for sis'… she doesn't need to be too comfortable.*

He backtracked to the center of the store. Traipsing

down each aisle, he loaded the plastic cart with a variety of canned fruit, soup, soda, water, and bread. On the last aisle, an assortment of camping gear and hardware items packed the shelves. He tossed two five-gallon gasoline containers on top of his overburdened buggy. On the top shelf at the end of the aisle, pistol ammunition lay stacked according to caliber. He snatched two, fifty round boxes of 9mm and two boxes of .45 Auto and tucked them in the cart. *You can never have too much ammo.*

Stepping to the checkout counter, he piled the goods in a heap while the clerk searched for price labels on each item.

Peering over the top of her glasses, the old woman seemed to struggle to see the lightly-printed black numbers on the small, white labels. "They just don't make these easy to read for old eyes."

Ben shuffled his feet impatiently while the clerk worked through the purchase, tapping at the archaic electric cash register while she entered each price. "You guys should join the modern age. They make cash registers these days where all you have to do is scan a barcode, ya know," he snapped.

The old woman ignored his snide remark and continued her task. After entering the last item, she punched the enter key on the register. "Okay, honey, your total comes to four hundred fifty-three dollars and twenty-five cents."

"Damn. It's a good thing I've got a good paying job." Ben reached into his pocket and slapped five one hundred dollar bills on the wooden counter.

Taking the bills, the clerk typed once again on the register's keyboard. She dug into the cash drawer after slipping Ben's crisp bills into their slot. "Forty-six dollars and seventy-five cents is your change, honey. You have a nice day."

Ben took the money and stuffed it in his front pant pocket. He shoved the overflowing cart toward the exit and pushed through the door. Scrutinizing his purchases through their flimsy plastic grocery bags, he collected enough supplies to get through at least three or four days. After reaching the parked SUV, he opened the rear door and tossed each bag onto the leather passenger seats. Sarah squirmed in the enclosed cargo area behind the seat's backrests – she obviously hadn't broken free of her bindings. After transferring the last bag into the vehicle, he slammed the door then rolled the shopping cart away from the car. He took one last gander at his surroundings. *This sure is a dumpy little town. At least now I'm geared-up.* He opened the driver-side door and hopped in, tugging the door closed once he settled into his seat. Taking a deep breath, he started the SUV.

Traveling the back highways and state routes would decrease the chance of encountering the State Troopers, but it would lengthen the journey considerably. Fuel would be the last remaining necessity before they reached their destination on the eastern slopes of the Rockies. Ben eyeballed the gas station sitting across the two-lane blacktop. *Time to top off the gas tank and fill these fuel cans.* And while Ben steered to the small island consisting of four gas pumps, two things consumed his thoughts – twenty million dollars and a beautiful woman with auburn hair. He would see her soon.

CHAPTER 11

SATURDAY, APRIL 17TH 3:00 PM

On the tarmac at the edge of Seattle-Tacoma International Airport, Hensley leaned against the four-door sedan's front fender. A blue hard-sided suitcase sat propped up by his side. He rubbed his eyebrow above the gold frame of his dark sunglasses then glanced at the vast hangar fifty yards away. Joe Chavez flashed his badge at a security gate next to the hulking structure. Pushing through the chain link fence, the young marshal hustled toward him. The clock was ticking, and the small six-seat single prop plane sat seventy feet away waiting for them to board.

Chavez approached lugging his suitcase behind him. "Sorry for the delay, Tom – you didn't give me much time to prepare."

Hensley gripped his bag's handle and hurried to the plane's open door. "No worries – I know all this came at the last minute. Let's head onboard and get moving."

The two deputies waited while the pilot stuffed their

luggage on the craft's rear seats. "Hop in!" the slender pilot shouted over the roaring jet engines of an airliner lifting off across the field. Both men settled into their seats and adjusted their headsets as the pilot secured his door. While he completed his pre-flight checklist, Hensley pulled an atlas from the inside pocket of his black leather jacket.

Chavez leaned over to view the notations written in black ink at several points on the map. Pointing his finger to a circled spot, he said, "That's the truck stop where we confirmed our first sighting. Mrs. Taylor's Lexus was captured on one of the security cams located above the pumps. We also got good video of Thompson inside the mini-mart."

Hensley nodded. "Good work, Joe. I had the detectives who interviewed the clerk send me copies of the security videos from all the cameras that caught him on the footage. Mrs. Taylor wasn't seen anywhere, but I'm guessing she might be in the back of the vehicle. The windows are tinted – there wasn't any way to see inside. But… we did get a few shots through the windshield at different angles."

"We caught the vehicle on a few other images further up the interstate. The last tip we received was here." The young deputy pointed to a spot on the map. "Right at the Washington-Idaho border. He stopped for fuel."

Studying the chart, Hensley pored over the spider web of roads and highways. "My gut tells me he's making a beeline into Montana. He's moving fast, but cautiously. Idaho troopers set up a checkpoint, but they were about twenty minutes too late according to the info we gathered from the clerk at Thompson's last gas stop." He gritted his teeth in frustration. They missed a golden opportunity to place a tail on their fugitive by only minutes, and it seemed like luck was always in his corner.

The pilot's voice crackled through the headset. "Gentlemen, get strapped in – we've received clearance from the tower. We're set to taxi for takeoff." The marshals crossed their harnesses over themselves and clipped the buckles in place.

Chavez wriggled on his seat and then peered back to the map. "Thompson doesn't have a lot of options for travel on main routes."

"True, but there are so many unmarked county and wilderness roads that it'll be impossible to cover every one of them." He tapped his index finger on the atlas. "Here – this is where we're going to set a trap – Crystal Creek, Montana. We haven't had any success trying to catch him by running after him, so we'll leapfrog to where we expect him to be." Hensley pushed his sunglasses onto the top of his head and scrutinized the region.

"That's still a wide-open valley – we won't have the manpower to comb the entire area."

"You're right – but, we know Thompson is looking to score a ransom from our hostage's estranged husband. We have Taylor's cell and data number under surveillance with his permission. I just got word an hour ago Mr. Taylor received a text message with a dollar amount – twenty million is what Thompson is demanding to return the woman unharmed."

Chavez's mouth dropped open. "Yikes, boss... that's a lot of money. Does Taylor have access to that kind of cash?"

Hensley nodded. "Hell, yes he does. We've dug into his financial affairs – twenty million is a drop in the bucket to this guy. He can raise it without a sweat. Our boy contacted Taylor via an unknown cell number."

"One of the suspected burn phones?"

"Yep. Now, thanks to the judge who refused to sign the surveillance warrant, we've lost the opportunity to get a head start on tracking Thompson's location. After I received the info on the initial contact from the unknown account, I had the sim code from that phone linked to the transaction at the retailer where the pre-paid phones were bulk-purchased. The evidence was sent back to the judge on a second warrant request… but who knows if or when he'll sign it. I think our chances are good he will – but, we've already lost too much time. This whole thing might be over with before the warrant can even be put into action."

The plane's propeller hummed louder while the pilot throttled up the engine and maneuvered the aircraft to the center of the runway. Speeding down the airstrip, the Cessna's tires bounded down the tarmac until they lost contact with the hardtop as the plane climbed into the air. The pilot and the two deputies pressed back into their seats while the steep ascent lasted several minutes until the craft broke through the clouds and reached its cruising altitude.

Chavez readjusted his seatbelt. He tugged at the microphone on his headset. "Thompson has to suspect we're onto his destination."

"Honestly, Joe – I don't think he cares. On a hunch, I checked out Taylor's father. And get this… the girl who Thompson was so smitten with years back… the one whose parents died in the fire he set… she's the operation supervisor on the ranch the older Taylor owns."

Chavez's jaw dropped, and his eyebrows rose. "No shit? Are you serious?"

"I'm as serious as a heart attack." Hensley rubbed his chin. After glancing out the window at the ground passing six thousand feet below, he turned back to his partner. "I haven't notified the girl yet. I'm not sure I want to – if she knows Thompson is heading her way, she could very well disappear again."

"Do you think Thompson knows she's there?"

"I don't know, but the sonofabitch has instincts like no one I've ever seen before – and he was pretty thorough in ransacking Taylor's home. There's no telling if there was any information about the girl lying about in the residence. The one thing I just can't get over is that Thompson could complete a hostage exchange anywhere of his choosing. Why Montana? Why would he risk traveling so far with the chance of getting caught? The only answer I can come up with – as far-fetched as it seems – is he's after the girl."

"Should we get surveillance on Taylor's property?"

Hensley shook his head. "No – not yet. I've alerted law enforcement in the area of the situation and requested they keep eyes out for Mrs. Taylor's vehicle, but we don't even know if he's switched his ride. Local agencies have been supplied with Thompson's profile images and asked to hold back from attempting an apprehension until we get there. If they try to stop him and things go bad… we'll have a dead woman on our hands."

Chavez grimaced. "What if they get the chance to

snare him but withdraw on our request? If we blow a single chance to get him… and he gets away… how many people will die because of us being overly cautious? Are we prioritizing Mrs. Taylor's well-being over countless others?"

Hensley let out a deep sigh. The young deputy's question was a valid one, and while attempting to answer the dilemma, the seasoned lawman had lost many hours of sleep. "Joe, nothing is certain in this line of work. We only have experience and our gut instincts to guide us. I can't tell you with confidence my plan is the best one. I only know after so many years of tracking this bastard we need to take well-thought-out risks if we intend on stopping him. We won't know if our strategy will work unless we see it through."

"And what about the girl at the ranch? Aren't we putting her in danger if she doesn't get the heads up?"

"I'll speak with her face-to-face. I want her to know she doesn't have to sacrifice the life she's found due to old nightmares. If we're present when she's notified, maybe she'll see the determination on our faces and the team we have… maybe that will give her enough assurance that she'll understand it's safer under our protection than if she was on her own and running."

Chavez seemed skeptical. He stared at the atlas then broke the silence. "It's your call. When's the rest of the team supposed to arrive?"

Hensley folded the map and tucked it back into his jacket pocket. "They'll be taking a commercial flight to Helena. They're meeting up with a few agents on loan to us from the Montana bureau. They'll drive to Crystal

Creek from Helena once they secure our gear. We'll all rendezvous at a motel inside the town. It won't be luxurious, but at least it has beds and showers. Taylor's property is roughly twelve miles southeast of Crystal Creek. We'll split into three teams – three deputies per squad. State Troopers and Sherriff's deputies from the surrounding county jurisdictions will provide backup. We'll be light on manpower, so we'll have to be ready to back each other up at a moment's notice." Hensley pulled his sunglasses back down onto his face to shield his eyes from the intense glare. With the sun at their backs, the rugged mountain peaks ahead of the plane reflected the bright daylight from their snow-frosted slopes and into the small plane's cabin.

"Why break us up into three teams? Won't that spread us too thin?"

"Until we have more information, you and I will stake out the Taylor property. Nelson and his team are responsible for the northern entrance to town. Bickley and his men will take the western entrance. Several backroads intersect with the county road cutting through Crystal Creek. I haven't gotten a firm commitment from the local jurisdictions regarding how many officers they'll provide us, so we'll have to plan with what we're bringing to the game. And when it comes to dealing with Thompson… we'll be spread thin no matter how much manpower we have. We've always pursued him with a crowd… and he's dodged us every time. He always senses the heat. Let's throw him a curveball and see if he still takes a swing." The two deputies then fell silent, contemplating their mission.

The plane jostled up and down through occasional

turbulence and drifted from side-to-side in heavy crosswinds while it glided between the towering mountains acting as nature's formidable barrier. Hensley yawned. He needed sleep, but the rough flight thwarted his ability to catch up on any shuteye. The closer the aircraft got to its destination at the private airstrip sixteen miles northeast of Crystal Creek, the more Hensley tasted success. He'd been close to apprehending Thompson before, but the sensation coursing through his veins felt different this time. Previously, the fugitive had always treated his evasion as a game – but now, Thompson seemed to have two goals in mind, and each was important to him. The veteran lawman's instincts told him Thompson was approaching his end game – and their final confrontation was near.

He closed his eyes and slumped into his uncomfortable seat. The padding of the red upholstered chair, lined with white trim, was constructed for utility, and the lightweight materials used to manufacture it sure didn't focus on comfort. Although sleep evaded him, thoughts of his youngest daughter's upcoming wedding – scheduled in mid-June – filled his notions. His years as a cop made his home life a wasted memory. He couldn't help but regret missing the most critical years of his two daughters growing up. Sure, he was home on occasion – but his time there was brief, making him feel more like a household guest than a father. It seemed like his short respites at home were just quick rest periods before embarking on his next assignment, and by the time he was assigned to apprehend Ben Thompson, the heavy burden on his second wife – acting as the head of the household – proved too much for her to bear.

He recalled the night he returned from Washington seven and a half years earlier. The interior of their home in Oregon was nearly bare. Only his possessions remained in the single-story three-bedroom house in Portland. The wood floors were littered with tiny bits of debris and dirty shoeprints, leaving evidence professional movers had emptied the home. Hensley didn't mourn, nor did he question his wife's reasons – he knew it was coming eventually. But, while the years passed, and his retirement drew closer, the loneliness he disregarded due to his career obsession began to sink in. And while details of the Thompson case dominated his waking hours and permutations, visions of spending precious moments with his grandchildren increasingly overtook his thoughts. After he took down Thompson, he would turn in his badge – never to look back on the honorable career which monopolized most of his life.

Several hours later, the Cessna's engine hummed at a lower tone, signaling the pilot had reduced the throttle. The plane descended thru the pass into a broad valley, encompassed by jagged mountain ranges. Hensley peered out his window while the valley floor crept closer. Surrounded by dense forest, the valley appeared multi-colored – carpeted with a mix of farm fields and meadows bursting with life. *There's nothing more gorgeous than springtime in the Rockies.* He took a deep breath, anxious to set his feet on the ground. The plane veered left – parallel to the opposing mountains to the west. Skimming one hundred feet above the treetops, the narrow runway of the primitive airfield came into view.

"Hang on, gentlemen, this might get a little bumpy," the pilot's voice announced through Hensley's headset. The aircraft bounced once then twice when the wheels contacted the runway, smoking while the rubber spiraled across the tarmac. The propeller whirred slower and slower until the engine revved just enough for the plane to steer closer to a large green hangar constructed with steel beams and aluminum siding. Behind two open bay doors, one bay sat vacant, while the other housed a twin-engine Piper.

Hensley glanced at his partner. Chavez dozed with his mouth open wide. Hensley grasped the younger deputy's shoulder and lightly shook him. "Wake up, sleeping beauty. We're just outside Crystal Creek."

Chavez closed his mouth, yawned, and sat up. After rubbing his eyes, he squinted out the window. "Wow, this place really is out in the sticks."

"Yeah, and stick close – your service sidearm won't do anything but piss off a bear. A .40 caliber round wasn't meant for a six hundred pound creature," Hensley warned.

The young deputy's eyes widened, and he wiped a drip of naptime drool from the corner of his mouth. "There aren't lots of bears around here are there?"

With a chuckle, the pilot replied, "Yep – quite a few actually. We've got grizzlies up here; lots of black bears, mountain lions… even wolves."

"Don't worry, Joe – Thompson is the only thing we need to be concerned about. The wildlife will try to steer clear of us. They don't want to run into us any more than we want to run into them."

Chavez stroked his mustache; seemingly vexed by the revelation the backwoods of Montana carried its own set of dangers. He glared at his partner. "So... boss... what's the protocol for a deputy defending himself against a bear that refuses to submit to commands from a law enforcement official?"

Hensley slapped Chavez's knee. "The protocol is: don't shoot the furry subject if he fails to surrender – just be backed up by someone you can outrun."

The pilot cackled through the headset, "Ha! Like I've *never* heard that one before."

"Sorry. We're city slickers – used to dealing with unruly citizens in urban areas. Dealing with wildlife isn't something we've trained for."

The plane rolled to a stop, and both men unlatched the buckles clipped by their sides. Pulling the harnesses from their bodies, they both stretched. As the propeller whirred to a halt, the pilot popped open his cockpit door and hopped out. He reached to the rear compartment hatch and moved to the side to allow the two deputies to exit.

Hensley stepped to the ground and placed his hands on his aching back. "These small planes sure as hell aren't very comfortable to fly in, but it shaved several hours off of our travel time. If we'd taken a commercial flight into Helena, it would have added at least four hours to our trip."

Chavez grabbed the two suitcases one at a time while the pilot handed them from the backseats of the Cessna. After he placed them on the ground, he held out his right hand. The pilot grasped it firmly. "Thanks for the lift. We sure do appreciate it."

The pilot nodded. "No problem – I'm glad to help the Marshals out anytime they need a lift." He pointed over to a white four-wheel-drive suburban with the telltale red and blue light bar prominently fixed to the vehicle's roof and a large gold star on the driver-side door. "I see your ride is here."

Nightfall threatened, and Hensley glanced at his digital watch – 6:14 PM. The sun drooped behind the mountains' towering peaks five miles due west of the airstrip. There was much to do before the remaining task force members arrived at the predetermined rally point in town. He snatched his suitcase from the pavement, choosing to carry it rather than relying on the bag's wheels. "Let's get rolling."

Chavez withdrew the retractable handle from his luggage and tugged it behind him while he scurried to keep up with his partner. They approached the suburban and a stout man, six-feet-four-inches tall, stepped out of the vehicle. The imposing sheriff smoothed out both sides of his long mustache with his thumb then pushed his agency ball cap slightly higher on his brow. Wearing a pair of gold-rimmed aviator's sunglasses, he offered a slight grin once the two marshals converged.

Hensley set his bag at his side and held out his hand. "Sheriff Dawes? Hensley – U.S. Marshals."

Dawes took the deputy's hand in his firm grip. "Good to meet you. We don't get many visits around here from you federal boys."

Hensley nodded. "Well, sheriff… this is a unique

situation – and we appreciate your cooperation." Gesturing to his cohort, he added, "This is my partner – Joe Chavez."

Chavez and the crusty lawman exchanged handshakes. "Pleasure, sheriff."

"Hop on in, boys. This breeze will chill your bones if you're out in it too long."

After they secured their bags in the back of the suburban, Chavez settled into one of the rear passenger seats. Hensley took shotgun up front and fastened his seatbelt. Dawes cranked over the ignition, and the massive vehicle's powerful V-8 roared. Hensley snatched the sunglasses from his face and tucked them inside his jacket's breast pocket. "So have you gotten a chance to look over the briefing we emailed you?"

The sheriff plucked a wooden toothpick from his shirt pocket and stuffed it in the corner of his mouth. "Yep – I've read it all the way through. Seems this Thompson fellow is bad news... not the type of person I take kindly to passing through my county."

"With your cooperation, we hope to make it the last time he passes through any county – as a free man."

Shifting the toothpick from one corner of his mouth to the other, Dawes cocked his head and eyed Hensley. "So what's your game plan here? Your fed boss made it clear that me and my deputies are to take orders strictly from you and no one else. Hell, I even got a call directly from the governor himself saying so." He kept one hand on the wheel while they steered southbound onto the two-lane highway and pulled his hat brim lower with his free hand. "I gotta be straight with you, marshal – I don't much like having someone sashaying into my jurisdiction and taking control."

Hensley attempted to neaten his windblown hair, combing the white strands with his fingers. "I fully understand your concerns, sheriff. Hopefully, we'll wrap this thing up quickly and be out of your way." He reached into his pocket and pulled out a piece of gum. Wadding the aluminum wrapper into a tiny ball, he stuffed it in his breast pocket and popped the slender stick of mint-flavored gum into his mouth. "Ben Thompson has been a top priority fugitive for quite some time. We have evidence that leads us to believe he's wearing down. This might be our best chance to nab him."

"You know… I've been reading the case file on this boy of yours… he must be awfully slick if he can keep slipping away from the FBI and the Marshals so easy all the time."

"He's the slickest criminal I've ever seen. And I know what you're vaguely trying to imply – we have some of the finest agents in the bureau working on apprehending Thompson and stopping his killing spree. It's not due to lack of effort or incompetence that we've failed up to this point. He's very adept at smelling a trap and sensing danger. He's like a cockroach."

The sheriff snickered. "Now, marshal… I wasn't trying to offend you – I was making an observation…"

Heat seared to Hensley's face. He rolled the gum to his cheek and cut the arrogant sheriff off. "Listen, Dawes… all pleasantries aside, this guy isn't your average perp. He's a cold-hearted killer – smart and relentless. If you underestimate him – lives will be lost. We're going to do this my way. I'm sure you're an excellent cop – but don't think for a second I'm going to put up with any egotistical bullshit from you or anyone else. My top priority is either seeing this guy in cuffs or standing over his dead body after he refuses to surrender. Keep in mind, he has a high-profile hostage – and he isn't known for leaving witnesses alive. I expect nothing less than full cooperation from you *and* your department – otherwise, I'll have feds crawling over every corner of your jurisdiction. Got it?"

Dawes seemed taken aback by Hensley's straight talk. He stared out the windshield for a second then pursed his lips while slowly nodding his head. "Yes, *sir*. You'll have our support. I didn't mean any disrespect – we're just used to doing things differently out here. You see, we handle things our own way in this kind of country setting. We don't have the bureaucracy to deal with like you do in the big cities. Even in this day and age, life is harsh in this part of the country. People rely on their neighbors in times of need – they have to for survival. Hell, last winter was so tough, and feed prices were so high the local ranchers had to resort to pooling their resources just to keep their livestock breathing through the season. The big national banks refused to help… so did the federal government. So, I'm sure you can appreciate why people here are leery of outsiders – especially ones with badges."

Hensley paused then took a deep breath. The sheriff's words came from a man with valid reasons to doubt the sincerity of strangers. "Dawes, I can appreciate the desire for people around here to be self-reliant. We're not here to make your life miserable. We're here to stop a maniac. Odds are, if we weren't so determined to catch him, he might wind up in a beautiful secluded place like this and take advantage of your back-country ways. He would thrive in a place where people didn't ask too many questions."

"Fair enough, marshal. So what's your immediate plan?"

"We've probably got four or five hours until the rest of our team arrives. Is there any place in town we can grab a quick bite? I'm not looking for a sit-down meal – just something we can get on the run."

Dawes chuckled. "We're a small community with fewer than two thousand people living in town limits. We don't have any fast food places if that's what you're looking for. But, the Mini Mart has a small market inside. They have a few different types of pre-made sandwiches."

"That'll be fine. Were you able to find us an unmarked loaner vehicle for the next few days?"

"Yep. Bob Mason – our county mechanic, has a souped-up and ready-to-go Jeep Cherokee. It's four-wheel drive and built for this kind of terrain. And knowing ol' Bob, it's probably faster than this machine." Dawes tapped the dashboard. "He'll be dropping it off at the motel for you."

Hensley forced a smile. "Thank you. I appreciate it. How far is the motel from the Mini Mart?"

Dawes laughed. "It's just across the street. Crystal Creek doesn't have much, but what it does have is all nestled in one spot. If you were to blink while passing through, you'd probably miss the whole damn town."

"That won't be an issue. Being in a small town like this will help us out – if anyone catches sight of our suspect, he'll stand out like a sore thumb."

"He will indeed. We're about three miles outside of

town right now. My office is thirty miles or so away to the east – in Mammoth Falls. The population out here is so small the county can't afford to have law enforcement permanently stationed in every community dotted across the land."

Hensley peered out the window and feasted his eyes on the purple hue of the mountains in the fading daylight. Dense timber of Quaking aspens intermingled with Douglas fir trees guarded each side of the weather-beaten highway. Seemingly endless clusters of low-lying Fleabane, boasting their delicate purple flowers, and white-bloomed daisies lined the edges of the cracking asphalt. And while the sun hid behind the tall peaks to the west, shadows swallowed the road. Untamed rocky outcroppings poked out from thick stands of trees. Chokecherry bushes and leafy Rocky Mountain Maples crept among the jutted boulders while they swayed in the evening breeze. "This place sure is wild. Beautiful – but wild. If Thompson ditches pavement to make a run for it…" He paused and scanned the thickets threatening to consume the roadway. "We'll never find him."

Dawes snatched the sunglasses from his face and set them on the dashboard. "Naw, if your suspect decides to use the woods as a means to escape, we'll just set our tracking hounds on him." He glanced over to Hensley and gave a sly grin. "Out here, our hunting dogs are our backup when it comes to pursuits off the beaten track."

"It looks like almost every track out here qualifies."

"Once you learn to read the woods, it's easier hunting someone down here than in a more civilized setting. Every footstep in this kind of terrain leaves a message. Hell, if you're good, you can tell if someone is running, if they're limping… even if they're carrying extra weight – just by the characteristics and position of their shoe print."

The marshal rolled his shoulders back and sunk into the seat's cloth upholstery, straining to shake off the lingering aches after the long flight. "Well, sheriff, there's a good chance we might have to rely on your expertise."

The suburban rounded a gentle curve and descended into a dip in the road. After ascending the slight hill, a weatherworn sign came into view. "*Crystal Creek, Population 1925.*" A single yellow caution light hung from a cable strung above the narrow two-lane road. "Welcome to Crystal Creek, gentlemen. You're witnessing our one-and-only traffic light."

Hensley scrutinized their surroundings. The sleepy little town at the base of an imposing mountain gave a glimpse back to a simpler time. A small grocery mart constructed of wooden siding and a steep asphalt-shingled roof lay situated at the town's entrance, sharing the same cramped paved parking lot with a smaller log building advertising hardware and sporting goods. On the opposite side of the road, a single-bay self-carwash stood next to a modest house, boarded up and collapsing from age and the elements. On backstreets behind the main drag, several modest homes were visible on small parcels – most surrounded by rusty barbed wire fences and overgrown with tall, green grass.

After passing through the main intersection, the Mini Mart, with a self-serve gas station, sat on the opposite side of the road from the town's only motel. "It's a quaint little place," Hensley mumbled.

Dawes steered into the motel's gravel parking lot. The single-story lodge lay nestled amongst the pines and appeared well-kept. With a blue aluminum roof and brick walls painted a deep red; the establishment offered a scant eight rooms – barely enough for the outsiders who would soon lay temporary claim to the tiny niches. Shifting the bulky four-by-four into park, Dawes announced, "It's not much, but I think you'll find it comfortable – if you're not expecting room service or a continental breakfast every morning."

Chavez popped open his door and stepped out. Gravel crunched beneath his weight. Glancing down at his laced black dress shoes, he muttered, "So much for keeping a good shine on these babies." He adjusted the pistol on his belt then collected the two bags from the backseat.

"You're already checked in. The rooms are unlocked and the keys are inside. Get yourself settled. Bob Mason should be here any minute now with your wheels. I'll chat with you boys again in a bit. I'm going to head over to the hardware store and talk to the owner before he shuts off the lights for the night. I'll swing back here to get the lowdown," Dawes said.

"Thanks for the ride, sheriff. We appreciate the hospitality." Hensley pushed open his door and hopped out before slamming it shut and joining Chavez. He grasped his suitcase's handle and headed to the motel door marked with a brass "one." They entered the modest room expecting the worst, but once inside, they were pleasantly surprised.

To the immediate left of the entrance, a doorway led to a roomy bathroom. In the main room, two neatly-made full-size beds sat side-by-side, separated by a nightstand with a single drawer. A long, four-drawer dresser sat against the far wall, perpendicular to the beds. And above the bureau, a thirty-two-inch flat screen television hung mounted on the wall.

Chavez sniffed at the air. "Wow, it's been a while since I've had a room that didn't smell stale."

Hensley nodded. *This place obviously was renovated recently.* It smelled of fresh paint, and the dark green carpet appeared new. "We've sure as hell stayed in much worse places." He peeled off his jacket and tossed it on a chair next to the long dresser. Removing his shoes, he dropped them to the floor and rubbed his tired toes through the black dress socks covering his feet. "Let's take five then hustle across the street and grab some sandwiches from the gas station."

"Don't worry about it, boss. You rest up for a few – I'll grab the food. What are you in the mood for?"

Hensley laid back on the bed and shielded his eyes with his forearm. "Ham and Swiss on rye sounds good. If they don't have that, then roast beef. Whatever you can scrounge up. I'm pretty famished, so I won't be picky. Grab me a large coffee too."

Chavez nodded and hustled out the door. "You got it. Be right back," he called out before clicking the door shut behind him.

Hensley held up his arm and glanced at his wrist. The other team driving from Helena was due to call at any time to announce they had secured their rental cars and were on the road to Crystal Creek. They were still at least three and a half hours away. He and Chavez couldn't afford to wait. Once their loaner vehicle arrived, the two men would head to Will Taylor's ranch. He still wasn't sure how he would break the news to Katy Olsen. Her ties to Sarah Taylor's captor were disturbing to say the least. Perhaps over the years, she overcame some of the emotional distress stemming from her horrific encounter with Ben Thompson years earlier – but he wasn't going to count on it. The kind of trauma the young woman had experienced was the sort that lasted a lifetime. And the fact Thompson might be roaring back into her life in such a manner would only complicate an already complex issue.

Sitting up, Hensley rubbed his eyes. Several nights had passed without him getting any decent amount of sleep. It didn't seem as though that would change any time soon. Was Thompson already nearby? If so, at least the fugitive was probably unfamiliar with the area – that put them on even ground. But, the task force did have the luxury of moving freely. Yes, they needed to keep a low profile to avoid alerting the felon of their presence, but they had access to any form of technology they required in their pursuit. Thompson had to keep a constant vigil – always careful not to use any device or form of communication which would give away his location.

He rolled off the bed and stepped to his jacket. Pulling the cell phone from the interior pocket, he scrolled through his emails and texts, searching for any updates on the surveillance of Mark Taylor's cell number. The team from

Seattle would be bringing in much-needed computer systems and surveillance hardware, but for the moment, he would have to rely on the information garnered from his smartphone. The regional map revealed the Taylor ranch was a twenty-five-minute drive away depending on the condition of the unpaved road that cut off the county road and passed by the property. It began to sink in exactly how close he was to Thompson's suspected destination. His skin crawled. Within the next few hours, he would be face-to-face with the hostage's husband along with an innocent past victim of the psychopath's furious rage.

CHAPTER 12

Mark paced back and forth in the lodge's front living room with a cordless phone clutched tight in his sweaty palm. Across the room, in front of the large picture window allowing a view of the compound, Katy and his father sat in silence. A dying fire crackled in the fireplace's bricked hearth, its lethargic flames hungering for more fuel while the glowing embers of charred wood hissed and spat periodic sparks against the black screen enclosing the space.

"C'mon, Dan," Mark mumbled with a deep sigh.

Will sat with his hands folded in his lap. He flashed a glance to Katy, then said, "Son, I understand you being all worked up, but you're gonna wear a hole in them new boots with all miles you're puttin' on 'em by walking back and forth in this here room."

Katy stood from her chair and came to Mark's side, placing her arms around him. "You're not doing yourself any good by worrying so much. You look really tired – at least sit down for a while."

Mark shook his head. "I can't sit right now. I feel so helpless…" He peered at his father. The old man drummed his fingers on his knees while nervously rocking back and forth in his favorite chair – more stress was the last thing he needed at his age.

Will stared at the waning fire, his gray eyes brimming with concern. "We need to have faith in the lawmen who are trying to rescue Sarah, son. I know it's hard to place faith in strangers, but sometimes it's all a person can do."

The phone in Mark's hand buzzed. Without hesitation, he answered it. "Hello?"

Dan's voice resounded through the speaker. "Mark, are you someplace you can talk?"

"One second." Mark hustled down the hallway to his room and shut the door behind him. "Okay. Give me an update."

"I loaded the file you emailed me to the server. I checked the file integrity, and everything was perfect. And get this – you were right about Sarah's abductor checking for a reply to the text he sent you. Sarah's phone powered up just long enough to download and install the update."

Mark pumped his fist in the air and shouted, "Yes! Great job, Dan!"

"Your estimate of needing only twenty seconds to install the file was dead on. The moment Sarah's phone fully booted, our servers connected with the app she has installed, and the update was almost immediate. There might be a slight lag in the communication between our servers and the phone though. For it to appear fully powered down, the signal it transmits will be weaker. If the phone is in an area with an erratic cell signal, the lag time will be even greater."

"That's okay, Dan. What we've got now is better than nothing." Mark strolled to the bed and plopped down on its edge.

"Mark... you do realize we've opened up a can of worms with this. The kind of technology we're using here is seriously frowned upon. It opens up all sorts of privacy issues with the general population. Government agencies would kill to get their hands on this kind of stuff – literally."

Stroking his beard, Mark answered, "We'll keep this tight-lipped. It won't hurt for us to know more than the cops or the criminal in this respect. Have you kept my old login active so I can enter the system remotely?"

"Of course I kept it active. I was hoping someday you would come to your senses and head back this way for good. If you do, leaving you access to the server saved me the five minutes it would take to issue you a new login."

Mark reached for his laptop lying at the foot of the bed. He rotated it and flipped up the screen. "Always the smart-ass. My system is already booted. Give me a sec, and I'll open the GPS software and see if we're in business." The splash screen flashed across the display. Once the program opened, he entered his password, and a map of the western United States popped up on the screen. A bright red dot pulsed on the map. "Dan, it worked! It shows a location in Montana. Hang on... let me zoom in." He tapped at the keyboard, sharpening the image. "The signal came from just outside a place called Paradise. Where the hell is Paradise, Montana?"

"I don't know. I'll see if I can find a decent map on the net," Dan replied.

"Never mind – I just found one. It looks like it's a small town just east of the Idaho-Montana border. The time stamp is from nine twenty-six this morning." Mark glimpsed at the bottom right of the computer screen. The clock icon showed 6:44 p.m. "Hell, Dan… that transmission is several hours old. If they're heading this way, then they may already be somewhere close by."

"Not necessarily. I've been watching the news, and they've been showing Thompson's sketch during every broadcast. Being out in the sticks like you are, you probably don't have cable television. Hang on a second. I'm going to email you the news links from the major stations here in Seattle."

A mail icon popped up on Mark's screen. "Okay. I got it. Let me cruise through them really quick." He opened the email and clicked on the first hyperlink. Instantly, a sketch of Ben Thompson's likeness filled the screen. He glared at the image and scowled, memorizing every feature of the wanted man. He scrolled down below the picture. The news alert caption read: "*Considered armed and very dangerous. Alert authorities immediately if you have information related to this subject.*" After clicking on the remaining links, he discovered they all relayed the same information. He exhaled a deep breath and closed the last news briefing. "You're right, man – if news stations are blasting this over the airwaves, he'll probably be extra cautious."

"That's not all of it – traffic reports on I-90 are saying

to expect delays due to inspection stops," Dan added.

Mark zoomed out on the map for a broad view of the western portion of the state. "If this guy is as smart as the marshal said, he'll avoid interstate travel." He scrutinized the main highways and interstates dissecting the vast state. "Just looking at the map, he'll be slowed to a crawl trying to take back routes here – there are only a few accessible routes through the mountains… especially with the spring snowpack at the higher elevations."

"There are probably more than you think. And so far, the cops haven't reported any success with their roadblocks. What if this guy is just making everyone think he's headed your way? What would be the point of him coming to you when he's the one who'll dictate how things go down?"

Mark took a deep breath. Dan had a valid point. It was evident at the very least, Sarah's phone was in the state. Without a stable cell signal, it might be hours before they received their next update. "You might be on to something. Maybe the marshal knows way more than he's telling us. When I talk to him again, I'll prod him for more info. He seems like a pretty stern old bastard, so I'm not sure it'll do any good – but I'll at least try."

"Good luck with that. When I met him, he seemed pretty rigid. He sure as hell didn't cut me in on any information. When I logged into the server to set the upload command, I also modified the software to automatically send an alert to my phone whenever there is a GPS location tracked from Sarah's device. The software is set to relay a GPS coordinate every fifteen minutes – so we get a maximum of four updates per hour."

"Good idea. Let's just hope the western portion of the state has better cell coverage than what I've got here on the eastern side of the divide. All these tall mountains are gorgeous, but they sure mess with cell phone signals."

Dan snickered. "I don't think the issue is with the mountains. I think it has more to do with the fact there are hardly any people where you're at."

"All right. You've got me there," Mark admitted.

"In your email earlier, you told me the second text was from a number you didn't recognize. Did you run a trace on it?"

"I did, but it came back as unknown. The marshal told me during our initial conversation to expect messages or phone calls from prepaid cell phones."

Dan groaned. "And prepaid cell phones are next to impossible to trace. They can still triangulate where the call originated between cell tower locations, but that gets messy and isn't very accurate."

"It would be time-consuming. I don't think the scumbag is interested in taking his time with this. He'll disappear once he gets his cash. His last text demanded twenty million – two in cash and eighteen in cyber currency."

"Shit, the guy *is* smart. Cyber coins are impossible to trace too."

Mark re-opened the web page displaying Ben Thompson's sketch and glared at the image. His mind raced with postulations as to what Sarah was going through at that exact moment – or even if she was still alive. "I don't care about the money, Dan. All I want is Sarah released unharmed. Nothing else matters to me."

"I feel the same way. Do you need me to wire you funds?"

"No. I've got it all taken care of. I'm waiting for another text giving instructions on how we'll complete the exchange. I don't have the slightest clue how this will go down. Just keep track of the GPS updates and call my dad's number whenever they come in. In the meantime, I'll sort through all this in my head. Once I find out what this guy's intentions are, we can come up with a plan. Until then... we're playing a guessing game."

"You've got it. I'll stay in touch," Dan replied before hanging up.

Mark tossed the phone down on the mattress beside him. It was like playing chess with a madman – except he could only see his pieces in play while his adversary's pieces were invisible, just waiting to strike. A strange feeling of emptiness swept over him. Both he and Sarah agreed to separate a few nights earlier. But there was always the possibility they could reconcile in the future. He noticed it the last moment he gazed at her. Sadness and heartbreak clouded her beautiful green eyes with tears before he stepped from her car and trudged onto the bus. But at that moment, he realized life didn't always offer second chances or the possibility of redemption. Fate would determine its grim course, indifferent to anyone's dreams or desires. A soft knock on the bedroom door caused him to jump.

"Mark? Is everything okay?" Katy asked.

He stood from the bed and stepped to the door. Turning the brass knob, he opened it. "Uh... Katy. Yeah – I'm fine. I was just talking to Dan. Please, come in."

Katy drifted into the room and peered at him. Her eyes

filled with concern. She placed her hand on his shoulder and caressed it with gentle strokes. "I know you're very worried. I can't stand seeing you like this. Please, if there's anything I can do to help… anything at all…"

Mark reached to his shoulder and grasped her hand. "Thanks, Katy. It's just a waiting game right now. I've done everything I can… but it's tough feeling so helpless. There's no choice but to wait and take things as they come. I'll do what's necessary to make sure Sarah makes it home okay."

Katy nodded and stepped back. Glancing around the room, her eyes locked on the image displayed on the laptop's screen. She moved closer to the bed, her eyes never veering from the sketch. Her jaw dropped, and she covered her mouth with her hand. Trembling, she asked, "Where… where did you get that picture?"

"That's a sketch of the scumbag who kidnapped Sarah. They identified him as a guy named Ben Thompson. Hey… are you okay?"

Fear crossed her face and she paled. She crumpled and nearly fell to the floor. Mark leaped into action and caught her in mid-fall. "Katy, look at me! What is it?" She began to hyperventilate, and he guided her to the bed while she gasped for breath. He slapped the laptop's screen closed and pushed the computer across the quilted bedspread until it teetered at the end of the bed.

Through sobbing gasps, Katy stammered, "It's him… Ben…"

"Yes, I know his name is Ben! Why does that matter to you?" After Mark spoke the last word, it dawned on him. *No, it can't be…*

Tears flooded Katy's eyes and left long trails down her sallow cheeks. "He murdered my parents, Mark," she shrieked.

Mark stared at her, uncertain if she was having a traumatic flashback or if it was true. "Are you sure it's him?"

"Yes... I'll never... ever... forget his face. I still have nightmares about it." She buried her face in her hands.

While Mark embraced her, heavy footsteps tromped ever-closer from the hallway. The door creaked fully open and the old man stood at the entrance of the room. With his face awash in worry, he asked, "What's all the ruckus?"

Mark reached with one hand and flipped up the laptop's screen. Spinning the computer so his father could see the displayed image, he shifted his gaze to the old man. "This is the guy who has Sarah. It's the same scumbag Katy had a run-in with years ago – before she started working for you."

Will limped into the room and held the edge of the computer screen with one hand while he studied Ben Thompson's face. He glowered at Mark. "Miss Katy, are you sure you know this fella?"

Katy nodded. "It's definitely him," she wailed.

Mark held her even tighter than before. The pieces were falling into place. Thompson wasn't just after money – he was coming for Katy. That's why he was willing to risk a hostage exchange in Montana. Mark seethed with anger but did his best to hide it. He wiped the tears from Katy's cheek and whispered, "You're going to be okay. No one here is going to let anything happen to you. *I swear it.*" He rose from his seat on the bed and cradled Katy's head in his hand. Reaching for the laptop, he folded the screen and snatched the computer from the bed. "Katy, I'll be right back. Dad and I are going to have a quick chat." He stood before her and lifted her chin then gazed into her eyes. "Wait for me here? I'll be back in a few minutes and we can talk, okay?"

Katy nodded.

Mark tugged at the old man's sleeve. Anguish flashed in his father's eyes, witnessing the young woman so distraught. "Dad, we need to talk."

"Sure, son."

The two men followed the hallway to the living room. Mark set the laptop on the old pine coffee table in front of the room's sofa. He whirled back to his father. "Dad, this whole situation just got a lot more intense."

The old man appeared bewildered. "Tell me what's goin' on, boy. This hoodlum that has Sarah… knows Katy? How can that be?"

Mark sighed a heavy breath. "It's a long story. But there's no doubt the scumbag is dangerous." His head throbbed. He rubbed his temple then scowled. "I couldn't figure out why he was so intent on bringing Sarah here to exchange for the ransom. But now… everything makes sense." He lowered his voice. "I think he's coming for Katy."

Will's eyes opened wide. "What do ya mean, *comin' for Katy?*"

"Eight years ago Katy had a fling with the guy. She didn't know he was a criminal. She broke up with him and he took out his revenge on her parents. He murdered them both."

The old man's knees faltered. He stumbled over to his rocking chair and flopped into it. He placed his fingers over his mouth, seemingly in shock over Mark's assertion. "In all the years she's been here… she ain't never said a word about her past… I knew it was somethin' bad, but I figured if she wanted to tell me… she would."

"She didn't want you to know, dad. She was afraid you'd think less of her for it. That's why she never spoke about it."

Sitting up straight, Will stomped his foot on the wooden planks beneath his feet. "It wouldn'ta made no difference to me…"

"I know. But she adores you. She knew you were in pain with mom's passing and she was afraid her circumstances would become an extra burden on you."

Will sat quietly for a few moments. He appeared to be mulling over the totality of events. He leaned back into his chair and huffed a deep breath. "Son, right now, the past don't mean much. The present seems to be pretty full-up with complications. Fill me in and let me know your plan. How can I help?"

Mark paced around the room, stroking his beard in contemplation. After a few moments, he stopped in his tracks. "First off, do still have your gun collection?"

The old man nodded. "Of course I do. I've got plenty of pieces stashed in my safe."

"Are you talking modern stuff, or are you talking old-fashioned six-shooters?"

Will hauled himself to his feet and approached Mark. Clutching his son's sleeve, he said, "Come here. Let me show ya somethin'." He ambled to where the home's two hallways intersected just past the entrance to the rustic kitchen. The main corridor passed a bathroom, an empty bedroom, and ended at the door to Mark's room. The second, however, was more of a niche. Stopping at the entrance to a walk-in closet a few steps away from his bedroom, the old man pushed down the door handle. The door creaked open and he flipped the light switch. A thick, maroon-colored rug covered the floor, and he rolled it up, kicking it against the wall. Hidden beneath the frayed matting, lay a rectangular hatch. The edges were barely visible in the dim light, the wooden planks of the aperture mating almost precisely with the surrounding hardwood floorboards. Only a small bronze handle inset into the wood gave away the existence of the secret chamber. Will grasped the handle and yanked the panel from its frame, revealing a narrow staircase three feet wide descending into the darkened passage.

Mark stood outside the closet. *What the hell?* "What's this, dad? Did you have a bunker installed when you bought the place?"

Will shook his head. "Nope – it came with the place. I'm thinkin' the previous owners were worried about a nuclear war or something. The place was built during the cold war." He snatched a flashlight hanging from a nail on the wall to his right and clicked it on. The small beam of the light poured into the mysterious opening while he carefully descended the rickety steps. "Be careful going down – this old staircase is showin' its years."

Mark followed the old man into the dank depths and

ducked his head to avoid bumping it on the mouth of the breach. The cramped steps continued twenty feet below the ground floor and ended at a small concrete landing where the cellar opened into a long, narrow alcove. He sniffed at the stale air. The faint smell of mildew filled his breath. Relying on the flashlight's beam to navigate, he muttered, "I sure as hell hope the designers of this modern bunker remembered the need for lighting."

Will flipped a switch on the wall a few feet from the bottom step. The room flooded with an eerie luminance from a track of fluorescent bulbs hanging the length of the ceiling looming fifteen feet above the floor. Concrete walls, smooth and devoid of any decoration formed the vault. "Are ya surprised the place came with a secret cubbyhole?"

Mark assessed the dreary room. A small rotted table sat against the far wall. A stack of wooden crates was stacked by its side, crumbling with time. He shivered. "It's pretty chilly in here, that's for sure. Why did you bring me down here?"

Pointing to a slender gun cabinet tucked in the corner, the old man replied, "That right there is why I brought ya down here." He shuffled to the vault and spun the dial back and forth until a subtle click emanated from the lock. As he pressed down on the safe's chrome handle, a loud, metallic clunk sounded within the steel structure. He tugged the door open then stepped back. "Go ahead – take a look inside."

In the dim light, four long guns stood side-by-side in the cabinet. Their black frames appeared similar to rifles

Mark had seen in the media. "Are you a closet militia-man, dad?"

"Nope. I've just always kept a few sportin' rifles on hand. After my tours in Vietnam I thought I'd never want to touch such a device again – but, considering how the world seems bent on destroyin' itself, it made sense to keep a couple of semi-automatic rifles tucked away." He reached into the safe and pulled out a handgun. After racking the slide, he peered into the empty chamber then handed it to Mark. "That there is a Sig .45 auto. It holds eight rounds in the magazine and one in the chamber. It gets cleaned and oiled once a year – it's ready to go once it's loaded." He reached back into the safe and retrieved two extra magazines. "Here, put these in your pocket. It never hurts to have some backup rounds if things get sketchy."

Mark gripped the pistol in his hand. It had been a few years since he visited the indoor shooting range back in Seattle. The occasional practice sessions were a fond reminder of the times he and his father had driven to the woods outside of Spokane for target practice. "It's got a good feel to it. I have a pistol back in Seattle – but I left it with Sarah."

"Well, these here in the safe are extras. I keep a 12 gauge riot shotgun upstairs in my bedroom, along with a .300 Winchester rifle and a 10mm pistol. With so many predators prowling the hills around here – especially the big cats and bears – having a gun handy is a necessity." He scratched his head and added, "I bought this safe to keep my collectibles. The fellas I paid to bring it down here nearly broke their necks comin' down those stairs."

Staring at the long guns in the cabinet, Mark said, "I'm no expert on guns, but I don't think those were designed for wildlife control."

Sadness filled the old man's eyes. He nodded. "You're right, son – they weren't. I still have nightmares about those horrible days back in 'Nam. I can't stand the thought of taking another human bein's life ever again – but not every soul that walks this green Earth feels the same way. I just keep sayin' my prayers those rifles rot away in that safe and never need to be used."

Mark studied his father. The old man possessed the kindest and gentlest soul he'd ever encountered. But he also knew his father understood there was a time to fight to protect those you love. And considering the recent events, his father's presence was reassuring. He glimpsed at the black pistol in his hand. "Well, dad, I hope these are unnecessary. I'm going to keep faith in law enforcement – but, two of the people I care about the most are in danger… and I'm not going to sit idly by and hope someone else can solve the problem. I'll be ready to take action if the need arises."

Will closed the safe's door and pulled up on the latch. He didn't spin the dial. "Now you know this room is here. You know there's some serious weaponry in the vault. It's still unlocked. If for some reason you're findin' yourself in need of such devices, you know where to find 'em. I have some boxes of .45 self-defense loads for that pistol I gave ya in the closet upstairs." He gestured at a stack of metal ammunition cans lining the wall next to the safe. "There's ammo and loaded magazines for everything in the safe sittin' right there. You still remember all the stuff I taught you way-back-when about how to operate 'em?"

"I do. It's been a few years, but I've done some practicing at a range in Seattle off and on. I'm not an expert, but I can manage," Mark replied.

"Good. Now, what's bouncin' around between your ears with everything that's goin' on?"

Mark tucked the pistol into his waistband after stuffing the extra magazines in his back pocket. "Katy has good reason to be scared. The guy who's at the center of all this is a serial killer. Hensley – the U.S. Marshal – has been after him for years. He sounds like he's a competent guy. But, Thompson seems to be extra good at getting away. I don't think the marshal has been completely open with me. I can understand why – cops are always reluctant to give out any more information than is necessary. The things he *has* told me are scary enough. I'm sure the information he's withholding is far more frightening. It would be best if we keep a close eye on Katy. The sonofabitch who has Sarah forced Katy to run away before – she might be thinking of taking off right now."

Will took a deep breath and rubbed the back of his neck. "I couldn't stand even the thought of Miss Katy not bein' around. This place is as much her home as it is mine. No – I'm not gonna let some two-bit thug mess with the peace we've carved out in this valley."

Mark focused his eyes on his father. "Keep your pistol handy. And if Thompson shows up around here, don't hesitate to use it if necessary. I know you don't like resorting to violence, but this guy deserves to be buried."

"Let's hope the marshal gets his job done. I'll be ready if he don't."

"You and me both. It might be a good idea to inform the hands of the situation without getting into too much detail. We'll need them on their toes and their eyes open for anything around the ranch that seems out of the ordinary. Maybe just the extra activity of a bunch of warm bodies going about their daily chores will help deter the guy from taking a chance by coming here."

"What about Sarah? Have you gotten everything lined up for the ransom exchange?" Will asked.

"I have the funds on standby, but I still haven't gotten any directions on when or how to make the exchange. There's a lot of heat on Thompson's trail and he knows it. I think he's waiting for an opening – the most opportune moment to get the cash. I'm worried he's concocting a plan to get his ransom before swinging by here to see Katy." Mark huffed. "I wish I knew what his intentions are. After hearing Katy talk about her encounter with the guy so long ago, I don't know if he wants to harm her or…"

"Son, we're not gonna give him the chance to get near her," the old man cut in. He squeezed Mark's shoulder. "Let's get back upstairs. Go to Katy and get her to understand she's safer here than anyplace else. I'll talk with her later in my own way – but I'm thinkin' it'll make more of an impact on her comin' from you."

Mark nodded. "I will."

The two men retreated up the narrow staircase, and Will flipped off the light switches as he passed each one. Once they climbed back out to the closet, Will bent down and pushed the hatch cover back into place before pulling the ragged mat over the hidden door. He eyed Mark after he shut the closet door. "Go ease that poor gal's mind."

Moving the pistol to the small of his back, Mark covered the butt of the gun with his shirttail. He marched into his bedroom and sat close to Katy's side. *What can I possibly say that'll make any of this seem better than it is after what you've been through?*

CHAPTER 13

The SUV sped east along the secluded two-lane highway. In the distance, the western slopes of the mountains beckoned ahead, their unforgiving peaks looming above the treetops and towering over the valley. The Taylor ranch waited less than two hundred miles away, and soon, the cover of night would cloak the landscape. Ben sighed in frustration. After leaving the sleepy town of Paradise, their progress stalled. The decaying roadway he selected for their trek underwent a temporary closure while state road crews resurfaced the weatherworn asphalt. They were stuck. Ben made the most of it, parking the vehicle in a clump of trees shielded from the highway's view. He slept for hours not realizing the extent of his fatigue until his heavy eyelids closed. After his respite, he awakened and steered Sarah's Lexus back onto the renewed blacktop and up the highway. The road was passable once again, and the construction crew was nowhere in sight, the only evidence of their earlier presence found in the bright-orange warning signs pushed to the edge of the fresh asphalt. A trip that should have taken six hours was still ongoing, and they had only traveled a fraction of the distance he hoped.

Ben rolled down his window and breathed in a whiff of the crisp mountain air. The sun dipped low in the sky as dusk approached. The cover of night would be both his friend and his enemy. It was time to switch vehicles, and he scoured the surroundings. Every few miles, the occasional glow of campfires on both sides of the blacktop alluded to makeshift campsites. He remained focused on seizing the opportunity to find a new set of wheels. In shadows cast from the majestic pines in the fading daylight, a brown sign with large, white letters declared from the road's edge a primitive campground waited just around the bend. *Time to go car shopping.* He maneuvered the luxury vehicle onto the beaten road and continued down the rockbound path for a mile. He glanced to his right. A lone car, with no others in sight, sat parked in a small turnout tucked at the entrance to a small meadow.

He eased his foot from the accelerator and coasted the SUV into the bare patch beside the road. With wary eyes, he scanned the spot. A heavy-set man guzzling a can of beer rested on a folding chair next to a small campfire, his legs stretched out in front of him. The man's vehicle suited Ben's requirements. An older model, small, four-wheel drive, it displayed 4WD on the rear hatch. *The thing is an ugly-ass green color, but it's four-wheel drive and as long as it runs…* Shifting the Lexus into park, he hopped out.

The camper struggled to his feet out of the ragged

blue chair and lumbered toward Ben. Long curls of black hair furled from beneath his grease-stained ball cap. He finished chugging the beer and tossed it back toward the campfire where a heap of crushed cans sat in a cluttered pile. Staggering on his wobbly legs, he scratched at the scruff on his neck. He held up his hand in greeting. "How're ya doin'?" he slurred.

Ben eyed him cautiously. *Ha! This dude is so wasted...* "I'm good. You?"

The man rubbed his bare belly, peeking out from under the cotton shirt straining to cover his plump stomach. "Oh... I'm just... fantastic."

"Are you here camping all by yourself?"

The man let out a loud burp. "Oh... 'scuse me. Um... yeah. My buddy was 'sposed to meet me here so we could do some shootin' tomorrow... but, he hadta... cancel. Ya know... I was gonna pitch my tent, but... I think I'll just sleep in my chair."

Reaching for the small of his back, Ben grasped the pistol's grip. "That's too bad about your friend."

The intoxicated camper nodded. "Yeah... he's been havin'..." he paused and appeared to fight back the urge to vomit. After he swallowed a large gulp, he puffed out a long breath. "He's been havin'... wife troubles recently."

Ben advanced closer until he was ten feet away. "Hmm... that's sad. Women can sure be a pain sometimes."

"Yeah... they can be..." The man tilted his head and nodded, seemingly pleased to have found a new friend.

"So... you like guns and stuff?"

Pointing his finger at Ben, he replied, "Mister... I am...

a true American. Of… course I love…" His chatter was cut short by a loud hiccup. He wiped slobber from his lips and completed his thought. "Guns." Seemingly confused by his own nearly intelligible speech, he scratched his rump.

His head on a swivel, Ben searched the woods, looking for any hint of another person. His eyes narrowed. He glared back at the man. In a flash, he drew his pistol and fired four quick shots. The empty bullet casings spat rapidly from the pistol's ejection port and sprinkled to the ground while the bullets ripped through the stranger's stained, yellow t-shirt, announcing their impact with sickening dull thuds. With an expression of complete shock, the man's eyes opened wide from the bullets' wallop as he tumbled backward onto a bed of wild grass. Ben approached the camper's jittering body and inspected the ghastly wounds soaking his t-shirt with blood in tiny spurts until the man's chest rose then fell one final time. The grievously injured man let out a ghoulish heave with a last breath while his legs twitched and his hands flopped on the blood-stained soil. Ben studied his victim's open eyes. They were glazed and fixed in an eternal stare. *Well, that's about as dead as I've ever seen anybody.*

Sizing up the man's six-foot-two body, Ben guessed he was at least three-hundred pounds – there wasn't any way he could move the body. He sauntered to the green SUV. The rear hatch was ajar, and he lifted it, eager to sort through his spoils. Sure enough, two hard-sided rifle cases lay stacked in the cargo compartment, half-buried under the man's camping equipment. Yanking the two cases from beneath the pile of supplies, Ben placed them on the ground. He flipped up the latches of the first black case and smiled once he opened the lid. *Nice... now that is one decked out AR-15!* He lifted the rifle from the foam insert and shouldered it. After rotating a knob at the base of the carbine's scope, a bright red reticle illuminated inside the scope's eyepiece. He chuckled and leaned the rifle against the vehicle. Sorting through the case, six thirty-round magazines – all loaded to capacity – lay packed in a corner compartment. *Finally, some real firepower. Awesome. This has been a good day.* He turned his attention to the second case and opened it. Inside, a 12 gauge riot shotgun lay nestled next to a bolt action rifle. After inspecting each long gun, he was satisfied they were ready for operation.

He returned to the rear of the SUV and dug through the treasure trove. Cardboard boxes filled with ammunition burst at their seams. A sleeping bag and tent were still tucked in their nylon carry bags atop a plastic milk crate loaded with canned food. After sorting through the provisions, he tossed unwanted items on the ground, off to the side of the vehicle. The small SUV wasn't as roomy as Sarah's luxury vehicle. Keeping his captive out of sight for the rest of their journey would be challenging. For twenty minutes, he shifted items from the cargo area to the back passenger seats – taking extra care to keep the long guns hidden, but within reach.

Once he was satisfied with the organization of his new-found supplies, he hustled to the Lexus. Snatching everything of use from inside, he stowed it in the new getaway vehicle. Finally, it was time to relocate Sarah. He pressed the hatch button on the Lexus's keypad and waited until the door opened completely. Sarah glared at him with terror-filled eyes. He grasped his folding knife and whipped open the blade. "Time to move, sis'." He placed the blade under the zip tie securing her in place at her ankles and slashed her free from the side of the cargo hold's anchor point. Cutting the second tie at her hands, he sneered. "Sorry about the noise. I needed to catch up on my target practice." He grabbed her arm and yanked her upright. Ripping the duct tape from her mouth, he tossed the strip to the ground. "You remember what I said about behaving... I'll give you a few minutes to walk around – then we're back on the road." After un-cuffing her ankles, he doubled back to the open passenger door and combed the compartment for anything of value he might have overlooked.

Sarah brushed the unkempt tangles of hair from her eyes and scooted to the edge of the cargo compartment. She reached to her head and tried to revitalize her matted locks, but to no avail. Placing her bare feet on the ground, she groaned. Dull aches throbbed throughout every muscle of her sore body – the confinement taking its toll after the long journey.

Night approached and the daylight tempered to a soft afterglow from the west, bathing the sky in a muted red amongst a few scattered clouds. Walking cautiously over the uneven ground, she avoided sharp rocks covering her path and placed her delicate feet on sporadic tufts of grass poking through the rocky soil like tiny green islands. She glanced back at Ben while he proceeded to scour the vehicle. Assessing her surroundings, she gaped at the poor man's body lying next to the lazy campfire, his yellow t-shirt drenched with blood. The conversation between Ben and the unfortunate camper was muffled, but still audible. Clearly, she was in the clutches of a crazed lunatic. Survival hinged on her ability to escape.

A dirt track passed the makeshift campsite. Sarah gazed up and down the road in both directions. *The highway has to be to the left – I'm sure of it.* The vehicle never turned after veering off the asphalt and onto the bumpy backroad. Her dust-coated Lexus, once bright white, had transformed to a light brown, and still aimed in their direction of travel – into a dense forest so thick it obscured anything behind its wall of leafy shrubs weaved between the pines. She strained her ears and listened, tuning out the crackling campfire. The babble of rushing water sounded through the trees just beyond the edge of the small clearing in front of her. *A stream! If I can get there, maybe I can find a way back to the highway...*

With her heart thumping against her ribs, she knelt and dug her long, pink fingernails into the earth, breaking them while she scraped up a handful of dirt and rocks. Her bindings squeezed painfully against her wrists, but she managed to fill her hands with the only weapon within reach. Ben stooped halfway in the vehicle, just ten feet away. She stood with her back to him and asked, "Please may I have some water?"

"Just a second – I'm busy," he snarled.

She took a sturdy breath and exhaled slowly. *Stay calm. Slow breaths. Keep it together.*

Ben snatched a bottle of water from the back seat. He huffed as he walked behind her and thrust it toward her back. "Here, dammit."

Without hesitation, she spun around and flung the handfuls of debris into Ben's eyes. He howled in pain, dropping the plastic bottle to the ground while he attempted to clear his eyes of the stinging dirt. "You bitch!" he screamed.

She leaped forward and barreled into him, using every last ounce of her one hundred and twenty pounds of body weight to force him through the open car door and onto his back against the seat. Still blinded by her assault, he lashed out with rage, trying to land a blow with his flailing punches. Thrashing on the rear passenger seat, he kicked at her while he pressed his fingers to his teary eyes. She slammed the door with all her might, catching his shin between the door and frame of the vehicle, causing him to recoil inside the passenger compartment. She thrust the door shut and bounded over the dead man's body, past the campfire, and toward the tree line.

Tiny twigs and sharp stones slashed at the soft pads of her feet as she fled, but she ignored their afflictions, desperate to escape the madman. Sprinting through spindly waist-high saplings, she zigzagged between them for thirty yards until she entered the forest at the edge of the small meadow. The chattering brook's melody grew louder and louder with each of her footfalls. She jostled into low-lying limbs and dead branches protruding from the trunks of the scrawny pine trees obstructing her escape, covering her eyes with her hands to protect them from the clawing sprigs. She pushed through the growth to a steep embankment above the meandering stream cutting through the gully below.

Pausing to catch her breath, she glimpsed down at her hands and arms. Long abrasions and cuts covered her exposed skin, seeping fresh droplets of blood in chaotic patterns across her fair skin. Sticks snapped behind her. Low thumps signaled rapid footfalls. Ben drew closer. She swallowed, choking back her thirst. She dropped to her buttocks and slid down the layer of dried pine needles blanketing the slope until she reached the water's edge. Countless needles pierced the back of her black cotton leggings and stabbed at her like slender spikes. Scrambling to her feet, she leaped into the eight-foot-wide stream, falling onto all fours. Only a foot deep, the frigid water's bite caused her to gasp. She scurried to the other side and struggled to her feet, stumbling across the forest floor.

Ben emerged from the trees behind her at the top of the slope. Jerking the pistol from his waistband, he aimed. "I'm gonna make you bleed, sis'," he screamed over the gushing brook as he fired a shot. A thundering clap roared across the chasm a split second before the bullet impacted with a dull thump against the trunk of a lodgepole pine ten feet away from her.

"Oh, God... oh, God...," Sarah mumbled. She glanced back. Ben hurtled down the hillside toward her. She staggered to her feet, running as fast as her aching legs would carry her into the thick brush. *I can't outrun him... I need to find someplace to hide!* Focusing on a dense cluster of thimbleberry bushes twenty feet ahead of her, she scurried to the thicket and dove headfirst into the foliage. In the dim light, she rustled through the vegetation, crawling on her hands and knees parallel to the stream. *There's nowhere to go! I'm trapped!* Just beyond the thirty-foot-wide patch of thimbleberry bushes, a rugged escarpment rose twenty feet above her, its walls formed with smooth granite and too steep to climb. Ben's footsteps crashed through the water. Wiggling slowly, she eased herself into a niche at the base of a rocky outcropping shrouded in the forest growth. She froze then took a deep breath and held it.

"I know you're here, sis'… I can smell your fear," Ben scoffed while he worked through the brush using his pistol to part the branches one-by-one.

Sarah snapped her eyes open. She cupped her mouth to cover her panting breaths. With her heart racing, surely, the sound of its beating would give her away. Her eyes strained in the failing light to pierce the thick stalks of the berry bushes camouflaging her hiding spot. The rustling came closer and closer. She pressed her body to the earth, and lay utterly still, struggling to overcome the shivers from her dousing in the creek.

Ben mumbled and grumbled obscenities in a long rant, obviously incensed she had managed to elude him. He waded through the five-foot-tall patch of berry bushes until he paused four feet from the base of the boulder – his scuffed combat boots just inches away from Sarah's face. With heavy breaths, he swatted at the brush surrounding him until he retreated toward the stream. "I know you're in here somewhere! If I have to, I'll sit and wait until you decide to come out. And when you do… it's bleedin' time," he warned.

Sarah jostled closer to the outcropping. Tiny black flies buzzed around her in a swarm like a miniature tornado bent on increasing her misery. The forest floor chilled her even more with its bleak dampness. It would grow much colder with night upon them. She tucked her knees to her chest, trying to conserve her body heat. Perhaps someone would happen upon the grizzly scene at the primitive campsite on the bluff. Maybe then she would be rescued from her nightmare. She carefully plucked a large green leaf from the bush sheltering her and held it to a bleeding cut above her right eye. The coolness of the petal slightly soothed the pain. And for the moment, there was hope. Her parched mouth craved water. Her swollen tongue thirsted for moisture, tormented by the constant gushing of the creek just yards from where she burrowed. A refreshing drink was so close – and yet so far away. She wrestled the excruciating temptation to sneak out of hiding to quench her thirst, but a maniac waited for her to make such a foolish move.

An hour passed and a full moon crept above the treetops, bathing the forest floor in a ghostly light broken by haunting shadows cast by the lanky pines standing as the only witnesses to the moment. Shivering uncontrollably, she huddled close to the outcropping. The granite boulders still retained heat from the day's sunlight, but it wasn't enough to overcome the chill of the night air. From a snaggy branch of a dying fir, an owl pierced the solitude with its ominous hoots echoing across the narrow chasm.

Sarah listened intently for any sign her captor lingered. The roar of the creek muffled any slight sounds. It was useless. She would have to make a break for it – there would be no other way. Once the sun rose the next morning, she would lose the cover of darkness and find herself at Ben's mercy. She inspected the pads of her battered feet in the bright moonlight. Deep cuts and abrasions showed through the muddied smears of blood mixed with the dark soil. Every step would be painful, but she would have to fight through the searing pain to reach the highway. *It can't be too far... a mile at most... I can make it. I can make it...* She mulled over her plan – follow the stream for a while before crossing it then head back into the trees on the other side. Somewhere beyond the thicket, the primitive road led to the blacktop.

She took a few deep breaths and summoned the courage to leave the safety of the rocky outcropping. Lying low to the ground, she inched through the berry patch, fighting the urge to swat away the ravenous mosquitos and black-winged fleas assailing her without mercy, flying into her nostrils with each breath. She strained to stay quiet, pausing whenever her movement caused even the slightest stir. After twenty minutes, she reached the fringe of the growth. She had crawled a mere thirty feet. It was another forty feet to the bank of the lively stream. Between the berry patch and the water, nothing but low-lying wild grass carpeted the ground – nowhere near tall enough to provide cover. The rushing spring beckoned like a siren's song. She licked her cracked lips. *I'm so thirsty. What I wouldn't give for a long drink...*

She scanned her surroundings in the moonlight's glow. The outcropping granting her refuge ended in an abrupt point, just ten feet beyond her position of cover. If she skirted along its edge, perhaps another thicket of berry bushes waited on the other side. Crawling inch-by-inch, she made her way until she reached the brink of the rock face. Fully exposed, she held her breath and peeked around the rock formation. Her heart sank. The steep chasm wall continued as far as she could see. Scant growth lay at its base. Only small patches of vegetation sprang up from the fertile soil, and the gully narrowed while it edged closer to the meandering stream. *Damn. I can't see a way out. I'll have to follow the stream... and there's nowhere to hide...*

She crouched against the rock wall and followed it in slow, measured steps. The cold, smooth stone soothed her stinging feet, and she advanced quicker and quicker with each step. She paused. Eyeing the meadow and the creek's bank, Ben was nowhere in sight. Had he given up and gone back to the campsite? Or did he lurk in the shadows just waiting to strike? A steady breeze swished the trees, causing them to creak and groan while their boughs wavered in the wind.

After half an hour, she had traveled over one hundred yards. The gorge spanned twenty feet wide in front of her. Unable to contain her thirst any longer, she bolted to the stream. Tumbling at its bank, she thrust her bound hands into the frigid water and cupped them to nab refreshment. She gulped handful after handful, but finally surrendered to her thirst and plunged face-first into the torrent for more.

Gasping for breath, she sat up. Her stomach grumbled for food, but the stream partially sated her hunger and filled her belly with much need water. She rested for a few minutes allowing the water to rehydrate her. *Okay, I feel better now. Got to keep moving...*

Staring down the creek bed from where she had trekked, she searched for any trace of Ben. *I don't see anything. Maybe he finally gave up.* She stumbled to her feet. The highway was somewhere in front of her – she had to be getting close. Hopping from rock to rock along the stream's bank, she scurried along its course. The gorge opened up once again and the slopes on each side gradually tapered into gentle gradients sheltered by scattered stands of scrawny pines. She brushed her tangled bangs from her eyes and stared up the creek. Bright glints of moonlight shimmered from the surface of the churning water, blinding her as she pranced across the stream. She scampered along the hillside parallel to where the dirt road should be, just beyond the narrow strip of trees. She limped while she hustled over the unforgiving terrain, but with each painful step, the taste of freedom grew stronger, and she pushed the discomfort from her thoughts.

Finally, after several minutes, a culvert came into view upstream. *The highway! It's got to be the highway!!* Her heart pounded with joy. The two-lane blacktop lay just ahead, passing over the meandering creek. Freedom was within sight. A rush of adrenaline filled her veins, and her uncoordinated jog broke out into a full-fledged run while she headed for the narrow bridge just yards away. Gasping for breath, she lunged against the grass-covered slope, clutching the soft blades with her fingers. She glanced up at the guardrails lining the asphalt. Bright light poured through the empty spaces between the guardrails' wooden support posts and tires hummed on the pavement. *A car!* She crawled up the steep embankment, grabbing at the dew covered clumps of grass for handholds while she dug her toes into the soil for traction.

With the crest of the hill only two feet above, she reached with all her might to grasp the asphalt's edge. The car was close, nearly upon her. With one final kick, she propelled herself to the top. Just as her fingertips tickled the wooden post of the guardrail, something latched onto her ankle with a vice-like grip. "*Oh, God!* Someone help me! Please! *Someone!*" She screamed. But her pleas were in vain. The headlights blew past and disappeared into the night while a forceful yank pulled her down the bank, causing her to tumble over and over while she rolled down the thirty feet to the slope's base.

She lay still in dizzied confusion, trying to make sense of what happened. Lifting herself from the ground, she looked up as a hard blow impacted her jaw. Her head fell to the ground, and she crumpled, out cold.

Ben kicked her side in frustration. He knelt beside her still body and growled, "You little bitch. You cost us almost two hours." Grabbing a handful of her matted hair, he raised her blemished face from the grass and forced her to meet his gaze. Her eyelids fluttered. He huffed. Yanking her up by her arms, he slung her over his shoulder and carried her limp body through the trees. He faltered along until they reached the spot where the green SUV waited tucked away among the trees. He thrust the rear hatch open and dropped her in the cargo area.

He clamped a set of handcuff around her ankles. The pain of the metal jaws pinching her skin caused her to stir. She opened her eyes and touched her bruised jaw. Ben stood at the open door, glaring at her with fire burning in his eyes. He pulled the pistol from his pants and cocked it. Placing the barrel to her forehead, he pressed the cold steel hard against her flesh.

"*Just do it!* Get it over with you sick bastard!" Sarah screeched.

Ben's eyelids twitched and his face swelled red with fury. His index finger quivered over the pistol's trigger. "Don't tempt me," he barked. Breathing heavy, he huffed and puffed, seemingly conflicted with the notion of executing her right there on the spot. Finally, he jerked the pistol away. "No… not yet. You're lucky I still need you… or you'd be breakfast for the worms."

Sarah rubbed her temple, massaging the circular imprint left in her flesh from the pistol's barrel. She sobbed. Freedom had been so close, and it was torn from her grasp just when she tasted its sweet flavor. While tears cut trails through the filth covering her lacerated cheeks, despair filled her heart. Ben was careless once – but he wouldn't make the same mistake again. "How much longer? When will I get to go home?"

Ben flipped her to her side and shackled the handcuffs on her wrists to the pair at her ankles. He disappeared from her view while he rummaged around in the passenger compartment. Within moments, he reappeared with a syringe in his hand. "Whether or not you ever get home depends on your hubby. Your little adventure ate up some precious time."

Eyeing the syringe, Sarah shuddered. "You know they're looking for you. The body of the man you murdered will alert the police you've been here… and they'll catch you before you make it to my father-in-law's."

A smug grin lit up Ben's face. His teeth seemed to glow under the light of the full moon. "I cleaned up the mess back at that hayseed's campsite before I came and got you. I knew you were hiding in the bushes somewhere on the other side of the creek. There wasn't any place for you to go except back down the canyon toward the road." He popped the cap off the syringe's needle and flicked at its plastic body. "And don't worry about them finding me… I've recently come into some handy information that guarantees we'll get to our destination hassle-free." He stabbed the two-inch-long needle into Sarah's thigh and pressed the plunger on the base of the syringe.

A warm, tingling sensation raced through Sarah's body. She fought against the drug shooting into her veins. Her eyelids fell heavy in an instant. *Mark… I love you…* Unconsciousness fell upon her and darkness swallowed all.

Ben rummaged through the doomed man's camping gear and yanked a grungy, blue sleeping bag from the pile of newly acquired supplies. He unzipped the sleep sack and tucked it around Sarah's listless body, carefully leaving her face uncovered. *You won't do me any good if you suffocate while we're on the road.* He scrutinized the setup. Although the vehicle's interior wasn't as spacious as Sarah's Lexus, his captive lay settled and confined. The older model SUV would suffice for the remaining portion of their journey.

He strolled to the driver-side door and slid onto the ripped cloth upholstery covering the seat. After tugging the door closed, he reached for the roadmap sticking out of his backpack's front pocket. Under the glow from SUV's faint dome light, he reviewed his planned route. The lonely two-lane highway – a hundred yards from their present location – continued for another forty-five miles until it intersected with another road. They would turn at the junction and travel twenty miles to the busy interstate cutting through the mountains.

He tapped his finger on a mile marker displayed on the map. *The cops will have an inspection point somewhere around here on the other side of the pass.* There were several options for dodging the trap – paved county roads and forest roads. He singled one out. It would only require a detour of ten to fifteen miles – and wouldn't consume a great deal of time. The mountain pass was too steep for the Highway Patrol to create an impediment for commuters – especially considering eighteen-wheelers relied on momentum to carry their heavy vehicles up the severe grade. Once they cleared the pass, isolated backroads would take them to Crystal Creek. Yes, the end of their long excursion was within sight – five hours away at the most if everything proceeded as planned.

The tranquilizer wouldn't wear off for at least six to

eight hours. Sarah wouldn't be a problem. He glimpsed at the fuel gauge. It showed more than enough fuel to make it without another pit stop. The two filled fuel containers held an additional ten gallons of gas between them – they were in good shape. Ben folded the atlas and tossed it on the seat beside him. He turned the key in the ignition and steered the SUV through the trees and back to the bumpy track. After veering left, he maneuvered toward the pock-marked asphalt. The vehicle's tires bounced onto the state highway's surface, bottoming out the shocks with a loud clunk as each tire rolled over the blacktop's edge.

Before leaving Seattle, he had researched the real estate listings near Crystal Creek. There were several unoccupied cabins and homes in the area, and many offered just the seclusion he needed to complete his quest. *In just a day or two, I'll be rolling in cash and on my way to Canada. And Katy… I look forward to seeing you again…*

CHAPTER 14

Mark sat beside Katy while she lay on the bed, her hand clasped tightly in his firm grip. For hours, his attempts to console her had failed. Her tears fell without end, like a stubborn storm that refused to dissipate. Finally, her weeping diminished, and she appeared somewhat comforted by his determined reassurances that neither he nor his father would permit anyone to harm her. "You're going to be okay, Katy. This will all be over with soon," he said. Desperately, he wanted to believe it – but there was so much at stake, and nothing seemed to be within his control.

Katy gazed into his brown eyes, massaging his palm with her thumb while they held hands. "I want to believe that, Mark. I'm just so scared. Ben is a monster. I'm afraid someone is going to get hurt, and I couldn't take it if something happened to you or Will – or even Sarah. Ben won't think twice about killing anyone who gets in his way." She closed her eyes and sighed. "I don't know if I'm even scared for myself anymore, but I know my being here puts all of you in danger." She opened her eyes and blinked. A tear rolled down her cheek and onto Mark's pillow.

Mark wiped a second tear from her face before it dripped onto her fluffy headrest. "It's our choice, Katy. We know what we're up against, and we understand the risk." He cupped her cheek with his free hand. "Everyone who's important to me is threatened by this punk… I'm not about to shrivel up and hide from him. Stick close to my dad if I'm not around – he'll protect you."

Katy sprang upright on the bed. "You're leaving?"

"I don't know what the rat bastard's plan is yet. But I'm sure at some point I'll have to meet him to get Sarah. I'm not handing over the ransom until I see with my own eyes she's safe. He's not going to get a dime until she's far away from his reach. And I'm sure as hell not going to take you with me when this all goes down – it's too dangerous. I don't want the puke to get a chance to lay his eyes on you." Mark shifted his gaze from hers and stared at the floor. He'd spent many hours trying to come up with a plan. The thought of leaving Katy's side while Thompson lurked nearby turned his stomach, but he couldn't leave Sarah's life hanging by a thread either. He was damned regardless. *At least dad will be around. Thompson won't know what hit him if he screws with my father.* A strange sense of peace came over him while the restless notions of what would come bounced around his mind.

Katy seemed to realize the angst vexed him. She placed her hand on his back and laid her head on his shoulder.

"Please promise me, whatever happens, you'll come back safe," she whispered.

Mark nodded. "I promise. But don't worry about me – just take care of yourself and my dad. I'm going to be fine." A loud knock thumped on the lodge's front door. A few seconds later, the familiar squeal as it creaked open echoed down the long hallway and into his room. Voices he didn't recognize resonated in hushed tones. Glancing at Katy, he muttered, "Stay here. I'll be right back." He hustled out of the bedroom and down the corridor, grasping the pistol at the small of his back. *Dammit! I never loaded the gun.*

The front door hung wide open. The old man stood just beyond the threshold. Mark approached cautiously, removing his hand from the pistol. It didn't appear as though there was an immediate threat. "What's going on, dad?" He stepped out onto the porch into the cold night air and eyed the two strangers standing beside his father. Studying the men, he glanced at the gold badge clipped to the older man's belt and the pistol holstered on his hip.

"Son, these two fellas are U.S. Marshals."

The older man held out his hand. "Mr. Taylor, I presume? I'm Deputy Tom Hensley."

Mark shook his hand. "It's good to meet you finally. Please – call me Mark. Although you didn't mention when – I expected you'd be here at some point."

A grave expression clouded Hensley's features, and his flinty gray eyes seemed to survey both Mark and his father, all while assessing his surroundings at the same time. "Yes, we weren't sure of our timeline getting here. Circumstances led us to believe it was important to head this way immediately." Gesturing to the well-groomed younger man with black hair next to him, he said, "This is my partner, Joe Chavez."

Mark nodded at the younger marshal. He seemed somber, like Hensley, but somewhat uneasy. "All right, deputy. I don't mean to be rude, but what's the situation? We're all on edge here."

Hensley's eyes narrowed. "Mark, we've been cooperating with State Troopers from Washington, Idaho, and Montana. None of our inspection roadblocks thus far have yielded anything related to Ben Thompson. We were hoping we might get lucky, but the outcome isn't a surprise."

Will shuffled his feet and crossed his arms. "So what do ya 'spose is goin' through this criminal's head? What do ya think his intentions are once he gets the cash he's demandin'?"

"I wish I had a crystal ball and could tell you, Mr. Taylor. All I can rely on is my history with Thompson. He likes to surprise us. We expect him to do one thing and he winds up doing the exact opposite."

Mark scowled and stroked his beard. "Do you think he'll harm Sarah if I pay the ransom exactly as he demands?"

After taking a deep breath, Hensley replied, "Mark, I wish I could guarantee he'll let her go unharmed once you meet his demands. The truth is – I can't be sure. What I am sure of though, is we'll be on him quicker than lightning once this goes down. We'll do everything within our power to protect your wife."

Mark glared at the two marshals. Even though their demeanor boasted confidence, their words sang a different tune. "That doesn't sound very reassuring, deputy."

"I'm not going to give you a false sense of security. We're doing everything we can to make certain this has a positive outcome," Hensley snapped back.

Will squeezed Mark's shoulder and muttered, "Son, these boys are here to help. Just simmer down some. Gettin' all worked up ain't gonna help a thing."

With a sharp exhale, Mark bit his lip. His father was right. There wasn't anything to be gained by insulting the officials working the case. "I apologize, deputy. I'm just frustrated. There's nothing worse than feeling helpless."

The older marshal pursed his lips and nodded. "No offense taken. I fully understand your irritation. Have you received any new messages from Thompson?"

"No. The last message I received included the demand – two million in cash and eighteen million to be transferred in cryptocurrency."

Chavez shifted his feet and asked, "Has he given you any account information regarding where to deposit the funds?"

"No… look, you guys are supposed to be monitoring my cell number. Why are you constantly asking me questions you probably already know the answers to?" Mark's blood boiled. It seemed as if the deputies were compensating for their lack of information by rehashing the same questions over and over.

"Mark, we only have your phone and your wife's cell phone under surveillance. It wouldn't be out of the bounds of reason for Thompson to look up your father's landline number and use that as an additional means of contact. We're ninety-nine percent certain Thompson is already in the area. If he's not here yet, he will be soon. It's a reasonable assumption he'll contact you with delivery instructions at any moment," Hensley grumbled. Chavez leaned close to Hensley's ear and whispered. The older marshal nodded. Peering back at Mark, he asked, "I do have another question… something we haven't discussed. Is there a Katy Olsen living on the premises?"

Mark locked eyes with his father. The old man faced Hensley and squinted. "Yes, there is. She's been workin' for me for over five years now."

"We already know her connection to Ben Thompson. She's aware of his involvement in this," Mark chimed in.

"There's a chance he knows Miss Olsen is on this property. If he does, then she very well could be in danger." Hensley pivoted and scanned the compound, the grounds illuminated by the halogen lights atop the tall poles next to the barn and stables. "It would be a cinch for him to get close without being seen until it was too late."

Mark cocked his head and studied Hensley. "We're well aware of the possibility. I've already had a long talk with Katy. She'll stick close to home with everything that's going on." Mark left it at that – there was no need to share with the detectives he already surmised Thompson planned to seek out Katy. The expression on Hensley's face alluded to the fact the deputy shared his assumption.

Hensley scratched the back of his head and took one last sweeping look of the compound. "Would you mind if I spoke with her? She and I have talked in the past. I'd like to check in on her."

"Yeah, sure – I'll run inside and see if she wants to talk." Mark backed away and hurried to his bedroom where Katy rested on his bed.

She looked up when he entered. "Who's out there, Mark?"

Mark sighed and raked his fingers through his hair. He wanted nothing more than to keep Katy detached from the situation. But it was impossible, considering the danger she was in. "Two U.S. Marshals. The deputy in charge is named Hensley. He said he knows you."

Katy sat up on the bed and swung her legs over the side. She seemed stunned. "Hensley... Tom Hensley... yes – I know him. He investigated the murder of my parents. It's been several years since I've spoken with him directly though."

"Well, he's here now. He's waiting on the porch if you're up to talking to him."

"Yes. I'll be fine." She stood and shuffled to the door. Mark followed close behind until they reached the front of the home.

"Katy, feel free to have Hensley come inside if you'd like to talk privately. My dad and I can keep Hensley's partner occupied in the meantime."

Katy nodded and gave him a half smile. "Thank you."

They stepped outside onto the porch. Mark tapped his father on the shoulder. "Dad, how about you and I give Deputy Chavez a quick tour while Katy and Deputy Hensley get caught up?"

Chavez perked up. "Yeah, that would be great." Peering out across the brightly lit courtyard, he glanced back at Mark. "It would be a big help if we became familiar with the property's layout. If Thompson shows up here, we need to know the terrain."

Mark glimpsed at Katy. She paled, and her eyes widened. He took her hand and gave it a reassuring squeeze before letting it go. He glared at the younger marshal. *So much for putting Katy at ease, you dipshit.*

The expression on Hensley's face suggested he recognized his partner's blunder by uttering the ill-advised statement. He approached Katy and put a hand on her shoulder. "Miss Olsen, I'm pleased to see you're well. I regret I'm always speaking to you under less-than-pleasant circumstances."

Katy nodded then gestured to the open front door. "Please come inside so we can chat. It's a little too chilly to stay outside."

Hensley followed behind her but paused before stepping inside. He called out to Chavez over his shoulder, "I'll join you in a bit, Joe. I have some things to discuss with Miss Olsen."

Chavez gave him a thumbs-up and headed across the compound toward the barn with Will and Mark. "This sure is a nice setup you have, Mr. Taylor. You raise horses, right?"

"Yes sir, we do. Been at it for several years now," Will replied. He kicked at stones while he walked and scrutinized Chavez's fancy black loafers. He chuckled. "Ya know, you boys from the big city sure do like them Italian-style slippers, don't ya?"

Katy drifted to the couch and sat down. She eyed Hensley cautiously while he settled into the seat next to her. Their occasional phone conversations over the previous years were brief – she only cared whether or not Ben Thompson remained on the loose. Nothing else mattered. She wasn't interested in pleasantries or speaking about her secluded life – she only wanted justice for her parents and to be free of the persistent mental anguish resulting from the ever-constant fear Ben Thompson would find her again. She folded her hands on her lap and cleared her throat. "Do you really think he's going to risk coming here, deputy?"

Hensley glanced at the fire, seemingly lost in thought. The red embers glowed bright and popped a trail of sparks against the black mesh covering the hearth's opening. He took a deep breath then looked at her. "I'm going to be straight with you, Katy. I think you're the reason he's in Montana. Yes, I'd bet my paycheck he plans on coming."

Katy trembled and stared out the living room's large picture window. "How did he find me?"

"I wish I knew. When he abducted Mrs. Taylor back in Seattle, he ransacked her residence. It's possible he came across something there linking your presence to this place. The speed of this entire situation is mind-numbing. Our investigation team is coming up with more questions than answers the more we dig through the evidence." Hensley exhaled another deep breath. Peering at her, he asked, "How are you holding up through all this?"

"I'm scared. I've spent years trying to get over my fear... but it's impossible, knowing he's still out there... trying to find me." She glanced around the cozy living room. The new life she discovered on Will Taylor's ranch had been nothing short of a blessing after spending two years on the road living out of a tattered backpack. The solitude in the secluded valley seemed unbreakable for so long. But suddenly, the horrors of her past had broken the invisible walls protecting her and reality was at the doorstep. She stood and walked to the front window, searching for Mark and the old man across the vast courtyard. They were nowhere in sight.

"I understand the way you're feeling, Katy. And I want you to know I've never gone a day without thinking about your parents and what he did to you... what he took away from you. I'm sorry after so many years I'm here to warn you, rather than being here to tell you we finally got him."

She turned and faced the marshal. "It's not your fault. I don't blame you for any of this. I know you've worked tirelessly to find him."

Hensley stood and stepped to the window alongside her. "I've spent the last big chunk of my career hunting Thompson. I would have retired a few years ago from the agency if he was already dead or behind bars. This case has become an obsession for me. I won't quit until I've apprehended the sick bastard – or one of us is dead." He locked eyes with her. "You have my word on that."

She studied the marshal's eyes. They brimmed with

determination, but weariness as well. Placing her hand on his shoulder, she said, "Thank you, deputy. I know you're doing everything you can."

The marshal nodded. "I am – but somehow it doesn't feel like it's enough. Thompson is still free… murdering whenever the mood suits him." He paused and stared out the window. A few silent moments passed, and then he announced, "Just as we were pulling up here tonight, I received a call from the rest of our team. They're in Crystal Creek. I'm going to speak with the elder Mr. Taylor and ask his permission to assign a few deputies to remain on the property – they'll help keep you safe. If possible, I'd like you to remain out of sight until this is all over. Stay in the house and lay low. Thompson might be less inclined to step foot around the buildings here if there isn't any clear sign you're present."

Katy considered Hensley's words carefully. Earlier, Mark disclosed Ben's threat to kill Sarah if there was any indication of police activity. She bit her tongue. Maybe Mark was holding something back from the marshal. "That's up to William to decide. I'll be fine – Mark and his father have made it clear they'll watch over me."

Hensley shook his head. "I'm sure they're well-intentioned, Katy. But they're no match for the likes of Thompson. Hell, even with eight well-trained deputies on my team, I feel outgunned," he barked in his gravelly voice.

A muscle in Katy's jaw twitched. Anger seethed deep within her. How long had she lived in fear? How many precious moments in her life were tainted since she fled the suffering left in the ashes of her parent's burned-out home back in Nebraska? The desire to break the psychological shackles Ben Thompson used to imprison her overshadowed the panic gripping her for so long. Her world was in danger. The madman who had already taken so much from her threatened everything and everyone she held dear. He murdered her beloved parents and stole her innocence. And at that moment, she vowed to herself she would no longer be a victim. *You'll never hold power over me again, Ben.* She would fight for the life she had built and the cherished ones who showered her with love and kindness. "I won't hide from Ben anymore," she declared. With a determined gait, she marched to the wrought iron coat rack next to the front door and snatched her denim jacket from its hook. She slipped into it then added, "I've got a few chores left to do before calling it a night." She paused. *That was awfully abrupt. It's not his fault.* She turned to Hensley and offered the old lawman a slight smile. Softening her tone, she said, "Thank you, Deputy Hensley – for everything. If you'd like, I'll take you to William. I'm pretty sure they're still checking out the arena and stables."

Hensley seemed somewhat taken aback by the once-demoralized young woman who transformed before his eyes into a determined soul over the course of a few minutes. He nodded. "Very well, Katy. Please, lead the way."

The two set out the front door, headed toward the immense structure across the compound from the stately log home, their breath billowing out before them while they walked in the crisp night air.

An hour later, Mark, Katy, and the old man strolled through the lodge's front door. They took turns slinging their jackets on the coat rack. Will stepped over to his rocking chair by the front window and placed his cowboy hat on its backrest. He sat in the chair and grimaced while he rubbed his knee.

Mark flashed a look at his father. "Is the knee bugging you again, dad?"

The old man stretched his leg out straight while he sat and rested his heel on the woven area rug beneath his feet. "Oh, it's okay. These old bones seem to feel the cold more and more as time goes on."

Katy winked at Mark. "I'll fix a pot of coffee. Maybe that'll settle him down."

"Don't bother, Miss Katy. It's gettin' pretty late. I might call it a night so I can get up with the sunrise," the old man grumbled.

"I'll still take a cup – if you're going to have some too," Mark said. He peered at his father. "I pretty much stay up all night anyway, dad. I'll keep watch." He stepped into the kitchen while Katy set a pot of water to boil. "Katy, why don't you crash in my room tonight?"

Will shot a surprised look at Mark. "That's kinda forward, ain't it son?"

Mark's cheeks warmed and flushed red. He glanced

at Katy. Her mouth curved up into a sly smile. "That's *not* what I meant, dad. Katy, take my room. I'll hang out here in the living room tonight to keep watch – just to be safe."

Katy sauntered from the stove to his side and whispered in his ear. "I know what you meant… but it doesn't mean a girl can't keep hoping…"

With a shy smile, Mark chuckled. "Sometimes it's like the two of you are bent on turning my hair gray. There's some awfully serious stuff going on, and yet, *certain* members of this household still find the ability to be… *frisky*." He leered at Katy while she fluttered her lashes at him.

She slapped her hand on his butt and replied, "Don't take it personally, mister. We're just trying to keep you on your toes. William and I are fully prepared to handle the seriousness of the current situation."

Mark planted a quick smooch on Katy's forehead. He ambled back into the living room. "Dad, where's the ammo for the .45 you gave me? I'd feel a lot better if it was loaded."

The old man leaned forward in his rocking chair and hauled himself to his feet. "I'll go grab it, son. Be right back."

Mark pulled the pistol from the small of his back and set it on the wooden coffee table along with two extra magazines. He settled back into the couch, resting his head on the padded backrest while he stared at the pistol. Cabinet doors clattered in the kitchen and he glanced up. Katy approached and handed him a ceramic mug, steam furling into the air above the hearty brew. "Thanks," he said.

Katy plopped down beside him. She eyed the pistol

on the pine table in front of them. "I hope you never have to use that."

Leaning forward, Mark took a long sip from his mug. He swallowed slowly and licked the drips of bold coffee from his lips. "It's just a precaution, Katy. If Thompson shows up here, we'll make sure he regrets it."

"Just remember he doesn't value life, Mark. He takes pleasure in violence." She set down her cup and snuggled up next to him, resting her head on his shoulder. "I'll be so glad when this is all over."

"Me too."

The familiar clomping of the old man's boots falling hard on the planked floor echoed from the hallway. He lumbered into the living room and set two small cardboard boxes on the wooden table before retreating to his rocking chair. The chair creaked as he eased back into the rickety old rocker, stretching his legs out and crossing his feet. He pointed at the ammunition and said, "There's two boxes of defense loads – all hollow points and deadly powerful. I've run a bunch of those same rounds through that very same pistol. They function flawlessly – no need to worry about feedin' malfunctions."

Mark snatched the top box from the stack and opened it. He plucked one of the fat cartridges from the inner tray and spun the nickel plated case between his fingers. He examined the gaping cavity in the nose of the bullet. Deep striations lined the bullet's outer copper jacket at even intervals around the cone. "Yeah, these look like they'd be pretty nasty on impact."

The old man nodded with a grim expression on his

face. "They weren't made for makin' friends – that's for sure."

Sliding the tray from the box, Mark placed the plastic insert filled with twenty rounds of ammunition on the table. He picked up the first empty magazine and pushed the round beneath its feed lips. Loading the magazine to capacity, he filled it with eight cartridges and then repeated the process with the second empty magazine. After loading it, he grasped the pistol from the coffee table and depressed the magazine release on the handgun's grip. The magazine sprang from the butt of the gun and he caught it with his free hand. While he loaded the last magazine, he eyeballed his father. "I sure wish there was some time to get a little bit of practice. It's been a while since I squeezed off a few rounds."

Will rocked back and forth in his chair, supervising while his son pushed the final round into the third magazine. "Pop the magazine in the pistol, son. Rack the slide and then put another round in the mag – that way you'll start out with nine rounds instead of eight. It's always a good idea to have one in the pipe."

Mark racked the slide, loading a live cartridge in the pistol's chamber. Pressing on the de-cocking lever on the pistol's frame, he dropped the hammer safely without firing the gun. He popped the magazine from the mag well and inserted another round, and then smacked it back into the gun's grip. Katy huddled close to his side. She shivered as he set the loaded handgun back onto the scarred tabletop. Putting his arm around her, he whispered, "It's going to be all right."

She dropped her head and nodded. "I know. But that

doesn't mean I'm not going to worry."

He squeezed her shoulder a few times for reassurance. "Dad, you've got your riot shotgun ready to go, right?"

"Yep – it's always ready to go. – and if anyone needs it, it's settin' just inside my bedroom against the wall next to my rifle." He peered at Katy. "And I already know you're trained on how to use a shotgun, Miss Katy. I remember last year when you chased off a pack of wily coyotes that come stirrin' around here that one night," he chuckled.

Katy forced a grin and flipped her hair back. "They were upsetting the horses. They needed a little persuasion to move on."

"And persuade them, you did, miss. I ain't never seen a set of four-legged critters run so fast for their lives like they did. They were pretty surprised seeing such a dainty and lovely young gal come after them with a barrel blazin' away…"

Mark snickered. "Remind me never to get you ticked off at me, Katy." He shared in the light-hearted moment with Katy and his father, laughing and enjoying the momentary reprieve from the gravity of the recent events. Suddenly, his cell phone chimed in the breast pocket of his flannel shirt. He tugged it from his pocket and looked at the display. Across the screen flashed,

Incoming call from Sarah.

His heart skipped a beat, and his thumb quivered as he swiped it across the screen. "Hello?"

A cold and low voice grumbled through the speaker, "Hello, Mark. It's about time we had an actual discussion."

"How's Sarah? Is she okay?" Mark shot looks to both Katy and the old man. The playful expressions drained from their faces and a somber mood drowned the cozy room.

"Oh, she's a little scraped up – but for the moment, there's nothing that won't heal – in time."

Mark rose to his feet and clutched the phone tight in his grasp. Anger smoldered inside him. "I swear... if you lay a hand on her... I'll..."

"*You'll what?*" Ben snarled back. He huffed into the phone, "You better not forget your place, asshole. *I'm* the one who decides what will happen to her... and how many scars she gets to keep forever as souvenirs. If you want to keep her breathing, you better follow my instructions *exactly.*"

"I have the twenty million you asked for. You need to know the cops have both these phones under surveillance. Don't punish Sarah for something I can't control. I haven't involved anyone in this... the cops came to me, but I haven't given them any information."

"I know they're listening. And while everyone is participating in this little discussion, I'll make it clear – if I see anyone... *anyone*... besides you, Marky... I'll slit this little girl's throat before you even make it to within one hundred yards of me. Got it? Have I made myself clear?" Ben roared.

Mark's mouth filled with the bitter taste of bile. *What I wouldn't give to be in the same room with you right now, you son-of-a-bitch.* He struggled to catch his breath. "I understand. When will we make the exchange?"

"Sometime within the next few days."

"Why so long? I have the money ready now."

"Let's just say I have a few things to get wrapped up first. I want to make sure your pig buddies don't have a trap set up for me. I'm in no hurry…" Ben replied.

Mark paced across the living room floor. How could he convince his adversary to release Sarah sooner? "Look, tell me where to meet you – tonight – right now. I give you my word there won't be any police involvement. I just want Sarah – unharmed."

After several seconds of silence, Ben answered. "No. We're doing things my way. I know the cops are listening. You better make sure they understand to keep their distance – unless they want to be on camera with every reporter from every major news station around the country explaining why they decided to ignore my demands and ended up getting a woman killed because of it."

"Fine. I already told you I would do exactly as you say. Please… let me speak with Sarah – right now. I need to know she's safe," Mark implored.

"Sure, no problem." The sounds of rustling crackled through the speaker. Suddenly, a groggy voice mumbled, "Hello? Mark?"

Tears welled up in Mark's eyes. She sounded weak and frightened. "Sarah? Are you all right?" he asked in a cracking voice.

"I'm really scared. Please get me out of this… *please*…"

Mark's chest tightened. The thought of Sarah being in danger was torture in itself, but the trepidation in her voice wracked his stomach with excruciating pain. "You're going to be fine, babe. I have everything ready and I'll do anything he asks. *I love you Sarah.*" A lump swelled in his throat. More rustling noises rattled through the speaker.

"There... now you know your sweetheart is still kicking. Remember what I said. I'll be in touch soon," Ben rasped.

The call ended abruptly. Mark moved the phone from his ear and dropped his arms by his sides in dejection. He glanced at Katy then his father. Choking back the confused jumble of emotions swirling within him, he muttered, "Sarah doesn't sound good. I've never heard her so terrified."

CHAPTER 15

Mark puffed a breath in exasperation. He stared at his father. The old man's complexion appeared sallow, colorless as sun-bleached concrete. He too obviously fretted about Sarah's plight. "I'm going to head to my bedroom for a few minutes. I need to touch base with Dan," Mark said while he hurried out of the living room and to the kitchen counter. Wresting the cordless phone from the laminate, he hastened down the long hallway to his bedroom. He closed the door and lumbered to the bed. Sitting at the edge of the mattress, he punched Dan's number into the handset.

After two rings, Dan answered. "Mark?"

"Yeah, it's me. I just heard from the scumbag. He called me on my cell."

"How's Sarah? What did he say?"

Mark slumped back onto the bed, leaning against the pine-paneled wall. "She sounded weak... really frightened. Thompson is a sadistic bastard – I heard the evil in his voice. I don't have any doubt he'd hurt Sarah without even thinking twice."

Dan sighed into the phone, his heavy breath huffing through the speaker. "This whole thing is a nightmare. Right before you called, I received a notification from the server – Sarah's phone transmitted a GPS location just a few minutes ago. The phone pinged less than twelve miles away from your location. Thompson and Sarah are just outside of Crystal Creek."

"I figured they were close by – just a gut feeling." Mark rubbed his eyes. The lack of sleep he'd been fighting was taking its toll. "Email me the GPS coordinates."

"I don't know if they'll do you a lot of good. I just pinged the phone again and there isn't any response. They must be at the fringe of cellular coverage."

"Dammit. I wish there were a way to overcome the weak signal. Thompson knows what he's doing. I checked online for approximate cellular coverage in the region, and you're right – just a few miles north of town, there's a huge dead zone in cell signals. He could be hiding Sarah anywhere within a radius consisting of several hundred square miles. It wouldn't take him very long to drive from his hiding spot to where he could capture a signal."

"Mark, are you sure we shouldn't let the marshals in on this? They might be able to coordinate it with their other technology and make use of it."

Mark groaned. The thought had crossed his mind to make Hensley privy to their clandestine endeavor, but something gnawed at him, telling him to keep their efforts hidden. "No, Dan. I can't explain it; we need to keep this between you and me. My opinion hasn't changed. Thompson made it clear he knows the cops have my cell number tapped. He threatened to kill Sarah if he runs across anyone but me once I pay the ransom. I believe he'll do it. I don't want to do anything to put her in more danger." He massaged his temple while he mulled over what to do next. "I think Thompson has a good insight into how the marshals think and operate. If we hand over our tracking methods and data to Hensley, there's more than just a good chance they'll do something to tip him off."

"Whatever you say. I just emailed you the set of GPS coordinates."

"All right – I'll jump on my laptop in a few minutes. While I'm waiting for the next contact from Thompson, let's both run a thorough search of the area. First, let's start digging for any cabins, houses… any buildings close by he could use to hole up."

Dan scoffed. "Mark, do you have any idea how many properties that would entail? You're out in the sticks, but there have to be hundreds of places he could be hiding just outside of town. It's going to be like trying to find a needle in a haystack. It's impossible."

Dan was right. The odds of pinpointing Thompson's hiding place were next to nil. But he couldn't just sit idly by, doing nothing. "I know it's a longshot, but do you have any better ideas? Sitting here waiting for the phone to ring isn't doing Sarah any good. I mean, what the hell good is the new technology we came up with if we can't even use it unless conditions are ideal?"

"We can't generate a cell signal out of thin air. We have

to rely on the network that's in place. Keep in mind though; cellular coverage fluctuates with atmospheric conditions. If Thompson is huddled up somewhere at the fringe of coverage, there's still the possibility we could receive a transmission. It's the only real hope we have," Dan replied.

Mark sat in silence, working through the details in his mind. There wasn't any way he would leave Katy unguarded to take off on a wild goose chase without solid information of Sarah's whereabouts. At least the GPS updates from the server would give him a heads up if Thompson was near the ranch – *if* Sarah's cell phone was in his immediate possession and the weak signal in the area cooperated. "Ugh! I can't stand feeling this helpless," he blurted.

"I know you're seriously on edge – I am too. We need to keep it together. We'll keep our eyes and ears open for any solid leads. But, even if we do get a hit as to where Thompson is – then what? Are you going to take off on your own and try to take him on all by yourself?"

"I don't know, Dan… I really don't know. I wish I had faith in the cops – but I don't. They have a horrid track record of dealing with this bastard. They haven't done anything to show me they're capable of taking him down. My biggest worry is paying Thompson… doing everything he asks… and him killing Sarah anyway."

"Take a few deep breaths. We need to try to be positive," Dan implored.

"Just keep me up to speed whenever you get a location transmission. I'll stay in touch."

"Try to catch some sleep, bud. You won't be doing anybody any good if you're walking around sleep deprived like a zombie. We'll talk again soon."

Mark pressed the end call button on the handset and dropped it on the bed beside him. He would stick to his plan: Katy would take his room for the night while he stood guard. Sleep would evade him anyway. He would pass the lonely hours browsing regional maps and real estate listings throughout the night – seeking that needle in the haystack. At least he would feel as though he was actively searching for Sarah.

B en shuffled back into the dilapidated cabin, its roof sagging precariously over the single room. *This place sure is a dump.* The neglected old cottage, seemingly lost in time and forgotten to the outside world, lay nestled in the woods seven miles northwest of Crystal Creek. Although the accommodations were lacking, the location suited his intentions. Getting to the old mining shack involved a half-mile drive down a rock-jutted backroad from the highway leading to town, and the place had been abandoned for so many years it was doubtful it would even be listed on any map or registry as ever existing. The place huddled between tall hills, and a cell phone signal was weak to non-existent. He could continue his careful method of relaying calls and messages to Mark by traveling short distances to use a signal. By making his contacts from different locations, he could throw off the heat closing in.

Ben scuffed his boots across the spongy bedding of pine needles while he carried in supplies from the stolen

SUV. He placed them in strategic locations – the riot shotgun by the front door, and the well-equipped AR-15 with several extra magazines, close to his bedroll by the shattered window. He plopped down onto his sleeping bag and reached to his battery-powered camp lantern. Clicking a rubber-covered button on its base, he reduced the brightness while the bulb cast out a blinding glow. It was late and his eyelids drooped with the heaviness of exhaustion. He glanced over to Sarah where she lay shackled to the foot of a rusted potbelly stove at the center of the structure's back wall. She snored in faint snorts while lying curled in a tiny ball; still gripped by the tranquilizer he injected her with earlier in the evening. Settling into his sleeping bag, he contemplated the situation. They made it to the sleepy little town unabated. No one could guess their exact location. But, the crafty veteran marshal stalked ever-closer. His instincts were dangerous and could derail the plan. It was time to be rid of him – before he was able to interfere with the upcoming ransom payment. Ben smirked and closed his eyes. *Yes… that will work… one less cop to worry about. With the sucker out of the way, the other cops will be running around like chickens with their heads cut off.*

SUNDAY, APRIL 18TH

Dawn broke peacefully, and subdued sunlight poured in through the broken glass panes of the cabin's front window. Chilly air permeated countless cracks and holes in the weathered log walls, flooding the small room with frigid bleakness. Sarah stirred restlessly while the tranquilizer wore off. Covered with only a single wool blanket, she pulled it over her head and snuggled under its protection from the morning's bite.

Ben tossed the sleeping bag's flap open. He rubbed the sleep from his eyes and scanned the small room in the dim light. Sarah wiggled under her army blanket. "Hey, it's time to wake up." He sat up and grabbed a bottle of water from a crate of provisions lying next to him. After twisting off the cap, he took a long swig from the bottle and gulped down a quarter of the plastic container's contents. Sarah ignored his command. He aimed the water bottle at her and squeezed it, sending a jet of water cascading across her blanket.

She hurled the blanket from her body and shrieked, "You jerk!"

Ben snickered. She may have ignored him, but the frigid blast of water had gotten her attention. "I said it's time to get up."

Daylight filtered through the pines and into the window. She sat up and moaned. "I'm so tired," she muttered.

"Good. You'll cause less trouble then." He snatched a second bottle from the faded green milk crate and tossed it by her feet. "Have a drink. Then get your ass up."

Sarah's stomach growled. She hadn't eaten in over twenty-four hours, and the lack of sustenance combined with her ordeal left her pale and anemic. "Please… I'm starving."

Ben paced around the cabin, digging through the various bags containing their foodstuffs. He grabbed a pack of freeze-dried fruit and tossed it on her lap. "You're lucky you're still breathing after that shit you pulled last night. I should have put a bullet between your eyes and left you to rot in the woods," he growled.

Struggling to tear open the package of fruit, Sarah avoided eye contact. "I had to try…" She finally succeeded at opening the plastic bag and grasped a dehydrated apricot. Placing the fruit to her mouth, she nibbled on the rubbery bit and chewed it slowly.

He glared at her. She was nothing but trouble, but her tenacity added to the thrill. He studied her while she ate, seemingly still affected by the beating he inflicted upon her back at the bridge on the lonely highway. A gruesome bruise the size of his fist covered her swollen jaw on the left side of her face in a sickly palette of purple and yellow. She stopped chewing and gingerly touched the blemish. "You're lucky you didn't lose any teeth from that little pop I gave you," he snickered.

Anger blazed in her eyes. "You're a monster," she snapped.

He stepped over to her side and knelt. Clutching a handful of hair at the back of her head, he forced her to share his gaze. "That's right, sis'… I *am* a monster and don't you forget it. We're almost at crunch time – it would be a shame for you to die now with the end being so close."

She squeezed her eyes shut, apparently in pain from his firm grip pulling her tangled tresses. "Ow…"

He released his grasp and stood. "Today is gonna be an important day – your hubby is gonna make me a rich man." He grinned.

"They're going to kill you, Ben. They'll never let you get away with this."

Ben pulled a pistol magazine from his pocket and inspected it – loaded to full capacity. He slid it into his jeans and slumped against the wall opposite to Sarah. Reaching to his shin, he rolled up his pant leg and massaged the contusion he received when she slammed his leg in the car door during her failed escape attempt. He grimaced and muttered, "Why the hell do you care what happens to me? After everything I've done to you – you'd love to see me burn."

Sarah scooted her legs out in front of her. She had reason to hate him for what he had done. She witnessed firsthand the evil controlling his heart. He killed without hesitation before her eyes. She glared at him, seemingly confounded by what would have led him to such a dark place. "What happened to you? How can you be so cold? How can take someone's life without it destroying you?"

"I was destroyed a long time ago. Anything that happens to me is pointless anyway. I just want to get away – to get these animals off my back."

"You're the animal – the one responsible for all this," she shot back, her eyes filled with loathing. "You've taken innocent lives. How many families are broken because of you? How many children are left without fathers or mothers because of your hatred?"

"I don't keep track… and I don't care." He rolled down his pant leg and drummed his fingers on the dirt-covered planks serving as the cabin's floor. "Anybody I've ever offed had it coming in some way or another – even if they never did anything to me."

She shook her head. "I can't believe you're so warped." She looked away, disgust written on her hardened face. "You make me sick," she grumbled.

"You better watch your mouth, sis' – keep it up, and I might not be so nice to your hubby when we complete our little business deal."

Sarah cut her eyes at him. "Don't you *dare* hurt Mark!"

"Well… it seems that got your attention. I thought you and your hubby were getting divorced. I would think I'd be doing you a favor if I took care of him."

"It's not like that, Ben. Nothing about our situation makes me want anything bad to happen to him. Just take the money and let me go. And leave him alone… there's no reason for you to do anything violent once you get what you want."

Ben scrambled to his feet. He strolled over to Sarah and unlocked the handcuffs from her wrists. "Come on. I'll let you stretch your legs and take care of any business. When you're done, you're going to get locked back up and be real good. I need to take off for a little bit and take care of a few things." He yanked her to her feet. "From now on, your ankles stay cuffed. We're not going to have a repeat of last night." He grabbed her hair and stared deep into her eyes. His hot breath spilled across her face causing her to flinch. "You're lucky I still need you. You're worth twenty million to me – but don't think I won't figure out a way to still get it – even if you're dead." He released her hair and slapped the handcuffs on her wrists. With a forceful push, he prodded her out the rickety door, barely clinging to the rotted wood by its rusted-out hinges.

Sarah stumbled and fell onto the rocky soil. "Please! It's bad enough you keep me chained like this. I can barely walk with these stupid things around my ankles."

"If you can't walk, you can't run. Deal with it," he sneered. He tugged her to her feet and stood guard while she hobbled across the forest floor. Anxiously tapping his foot while he waited, he weighed his next move. It was time to head a few miles down the highway to a cell signal. Several hours had passed since he last spoke to his contact the night before. Only a few loose ends needed to be tied up before he would be ready to complete the exchange and acquire his ransom.

Hensley sat in the small diner and chugged his coffee. Peering at his partner, he grumbled, "Hurry up and scarf that food. We've got a lot of work to do today. Thompson won't linger too long before making his move."

Chavez crammed the last bite of his breakfast into his mouth and gulped down the egg without chewing. He grasped his cup and chugged his coffee. "What's the plan today?"

"Until we get notification Taylor has gotten the ransom instructions, we'll be canvassing the area for Thompson's hideout."

The younger marshal rolled his eyes. "Tom, the guy could be *anywhere*. How do you expect to find him?"

"We've gotten a few tips from the locals. We'll start

close in and see if we can get lucky and stumble across him. We got word early this morning a camper's body was found – murdered on the west side of the mountains. Mrs. Taylor's vehicle was discovered in a ravine close to the location. Thompson changed vehicles. Montana Highway Patrol identified the victim's body and pulled up the vehicles registered to him." Hensley took his cell phone from his jacket pocket and scrolled through his text messages. "The vehicle we're looking for is a green 2011 Jeep Liberty. That's the only vehicle missing from the victim's property – some poor sap named Chet Newton. Detectives interviewed his next door neighbor just an hour ago. The neighbor said Newton was headed for an overnight camping trip." He paused and scowled at Chavez. "And we have some more bad news – the victim was a pretty big gun enthusiast. Before he left on his trip, he drank a few beers with his neighbor – the witness who was interviewed. Seems Newton planned on a shooting expedition.... but, no guns were found at the crime scene."

"So, now Thompson might have an arsenal. Did the neighbor have any idea what kind of firearms the victim had on him at the time?"

Hensley shook his head. "No, but the witness related Newton was rather fond of modern military-style rifles. It sounds like he might have been a real gun nut."

Chavez sighed. "Great. Now we're facing even more firepower."

"I don't think it makes any difference with this guy. He could be armed with a pellet gun and still be deadly." Hensley tucked his phone back in his pocket and eyed

Chavez. "Anyway it comes about, when we encounter Thompson, be prepared to shoot to kill."

A series of chimes bleated from the younger marshal's jacket. He reached his hand in the pocket and grabbed his cell phone. He looked at the display and frowned. Hurrying from the booth, he muttered, "I'll be right back. I have to make a call real quick."

"Is everything okay?" Hensley asked.

"Uh... yeah – just some issues at home. Everything is fine." Chavez bustled out the entrance and disappeared out of sight.

The marshal glanced at the bill laying on the tabletop. He pulled his wallet from his trousers and snatched a worn twenty dollar bill from inside. Tossing it on the green ticket, he took one last gulp from his coffee cup. After setting down the mug, he stood and shuffled toward the door, nodding at the young waitress before he pushed it open and stepped out into the cold morning air. He scanned the small dirt lot. Chavez was nowhere in sight. Glimpsing at his watch, he huffed in exasperation. "Now where the hell have you gone, Joe?" he grumbled. As he lifted the door handle on the borrowed four-wheel drive vehicle, the young marshal rounded the corner of the small restaurant and scrambled to the passenger door.

"Sorry, boss – wife issues." He rolled his eyes and hopped inside the SUV.

Hensley slid into the driver's seat and turned the ignition. Reaching over the steering wheel, he snagged a regional map from the dashboard. He opened it and studied the geography for a moment. "Get on the radio and have Nelson and his team head east down County Road 160. Tell them to cruise as many side roads within five miles of town as they can. They've received the description of the stolen Jeep. Bickley and his men are getting set up at the Taylor ranch. They'll keep an eye out there for the time being."

Chavez shook his head. "I still think this is a waste of time. With all the private parcels lying on the outskirts of town, it would take weeks to cover them all."

"Joe, right now we're out of options. We were supposed to get support from the State Trooper's chopper – but it's grounded due to mechanical issues." He peered around at the forested slopes rising behind the small diner and the surrounding woodland. "I really don't know an eye-in-the-sky would do us all that much good anyway. These woods are too damn thick to see through." He folded up the map and plopped it on the dash. After shifting the SUV into reverse, he backed out of the gravel lot and steered onto the two-lane blacktop dissecting the small town.

"So where are we headed?"

"We'll head toward an isolated stretch south of town – Black Tail Road. I had a chat with the manager who runs the service station next to the motel, and he confirmed there are several abandoned homes and cabins around there. He also said the cellular signals are pretty strong in that area."

For hours, the two marshals scoured vacant properties along the dusty side road. Their search turned up nothing. Despite the abundance of curious deer, elk, and foxes, any recent signs of human activity had been wiped away by the recent spring rainfall. By early afternoon, the sun sank below its apex and the warmth of the day settled in, bringing frenzied swarms of mosquitos and hungry deer flies that harassed the two marshals every time they left the confines of the borrowed SUV.

All right, enough of this bullshit. Hensley swatted at his face while he stumbled over piles of debris littering the ground beneath the crumbling shed's sagging roof. Apparently, raccoons and field mice were the only recent occupants in the old outbuilding. He stepped out the remnants of what once used to be the structure's side door and gazed across the empty field at the jeep parked sixty feet away. Chavez leaned against the SUV's grill, engrossed with his phone. *Damn young people are obsessed with technology these days. The kid is always playing with his damn cell phone.* He traipsed toward the jeep and called out, "Any news?"

The young marshal peered up from his phone and slipped it into his pocket. "No, nothing yet – but there's a decent signal here." He pushed away from the grill and stepped to the open passenger door. After they hopped in the vehicle, Chavez swatted at one of the dime-sized insects as it landed on his forearm, sinking its mandibles into his flesh and drawing blood with an eager bite. The deputy yelled out in pain. "Ouch! I hate these things!" He slammed the car door shut and crouched into his seat.

"Yeah, they sure are bloodsucking little devils." Hensley adjusted his sunglasses after wiping the sweat from his brow. "It's amazing how the day starts out so cold but gets so warm once the sun has been out a bit."

"It's got to be the altitude," Chavez replied. He reached for a half-empty bottle of water from a drink holder in the door and guzzled it down. He wiped his lips with the back of his hand and crumpled the empty plastic container into a tiny ball. "Man, we should have brought more water."

Hensley turned the ignition and took one final glance at the rotted-out structure they had just explored. He shook his head in frustration. "I'm starting to agree with you – this is pointless. We're just wasting our time. There must be hundreds of places just like this."

Chavez huffed. A smirk blazoned across his face. Casting a quick look at his partner, he mumbled, "I told you that this morning, boss – but you wouldn't listen."

"Okay. I admit it – you were right." Hensley scowled at the young marshal. "There, are you satisfied?" he growled. He took a deep breath and slapped his hand on the cracked leather covering the steering wheel. There was nothing worse than feeling helpless. Clearly, their hunt was at a standstill until Thompson made his next move. They were in unfamiliar terrain, far from the bustling city surroundings they normally safeguarded. Time moved at a much slower pace out in the open air of the rugged wilderness. It was unsettling. "Let's head back to the motel for a bit. We'll touch base with the other teams and see if they've managed to stir up anything."

"Whatever you say, boss," Chavez replied. Reaching alongside the seat, he tugged the console's lever and reclined the backrest.

They rumbled along the four-mile stretch of dirt road with a cloud of billowing dust churning out from beneath the Cherokee's all-terrain tires. As they reached the intersection with the weather-beaten asphalt leading back into town, Hensley's cell phone buzzed. He braked to a stop and pulled the vibrating device from his shirt pocket. After perusing the text message, he peered at his partner. The younger marshal was sound asleep. *How the hell can the kid crash so fast?* Hensley gently smacked him across the chest with the back of his right hand. "Wake up. We just got an anonymous tip from a pay phone. The murdered camper's jeep might have been sighted a few miles north of town. You and I will check it out. It's off a forest service road. There's nothing but private property on both sides of it. When I spoke with Sherriff Dawes before breakfast, he said there are several old mining structures scattered through that part of the forest. He and his men are tied up on the other side of the county, and they won't be able to help us out until later this evening."

Chavez yawned and twisted in his seat. "Don't you think we should wait for back up? I mean… if Thompson is there, we could find ourselves in a jam."

"What's the matter? Did the call from your wife this morning spook you or something?"

"No. I just think we should be cautious."

Hensley scratched his head. "Nelson is out of cell and radio range… and I'm not about to pull Bickley and his team from the Taylor property. The tip is worth checking out – but not at the expense of leaving the ranch unsupervised. Thompson could be trying to lure us all in one spot. If we catch sight of our guy, we'll radio Bickley our location and tell him to high-tail it on over."

"It's your call, boss. But – I want to go on record that I think we should wait for at least *some* backup. Let's at least swing by the motel and gear up first. I want to hop on my laptop and get some satellite imagery of where we're going. It'll only take about half an hour, and I think it would be time well spent – it might give us the extra edge we need."

With a nod, Hensley grumbled, "Duly noted." Shifting his foot from the brake pedal to the accelerator, he stomped on the gas. The SUV's tires spit out rocks and debris while the vehicle sped onto the blacktop toward the remote town's outskirts where the motel lay nestled in the pines.

CHAPTER 16

Mark stood at the wooden fence across the beaten dirt road from the ranch compound's main entrance. Directly behind him, the gravel drive passed through an open four-tiered gate and ended in a loop at the front of his father's log home. While the sun dipped lower on the western horizon, he stared out across the pasture. His emotions churned in a state of turmoil and waiting to hear from Sarah's captor only made it worse. It had been three days since her abduction from the luxury of the home they once shared. Up until that point, the emotional distance separating the two high school sweethearts seemed farther than he ever thought possible. Every one of his nerves twitched. She was close – he felt it in his gut.

Staying up all night to pore over regional satellite maps on the internet hadn't helped. It merely served as a diversion while he stood guard over Katy and his father while they slept. If anything, the search deepened his sense of gloom. Unless Thompson showed himself, the fugitive and his captive would remain elusive. They were at the madman's mercy. Earlier in the day, after pulling strings and calling in a few favors, a courier with a heavily armed escort arrived and delivered an aluminum-sided case containing bundles of one hundred dollar bills. Two million dollars in cash – part of Thompson's demand. The case lay tucked away under his bed, waiting as a partial payment to buy Sarah's freedom. It had taken twenty-four hours for him to arrange the withdrawal and delivery, and the cooperation of the U.S. Marshals to cut through the federal red tape. Large sums of cash rarely transferred with such haste.

While he gazed across the grass-laden meadow at the lush valley beyond, his anxiety wasn't the least bit quelled by the team of three marshals strategically positioned around the perimeter of his father's home. Sure, the three federal officers – Bickley, Munson, and Krueger, seemed like dedicated professionals ready for the situation. But, they were still strangers without an emotional link or attachment to Sarah serving as extra motivation to successfully secure her release. If anything went sour and she didn't survive the ordeal, it would only be a tarnished memory for them – a comment in their case file history. For Mark, Dan, Katy, and the old man, it would alter their lives forever. Never again would there be a day when they could wake up and enjoy the warmth of the sun on their faces and be truly happy. They would remain shattered victims forever – trapped in the horrific nightmare. Footsteps thumped behind him. He flashed a look over his shoulder. His father trudged across the dirt road toward him.

"How are ya doin', son?"

Mark rested his hands on his hips and stared at the ground. "Just killing time, dad. I can't stand this waiting."

The old man stepped beside him and leaned on the fence. He pushed his hat higher on his brow and gazed at the towering mountain peaks far across the valley. "I know, son. It's gut-wrenching. We're all in the same boat. There ain't nothin' good about it… but you got the chance to talk to her. We gotta keep hope this thing turns out okay."

Pounding his fist on the splintered top rail, Mark gritted his teeth. "Hope doesn't mean much to me these days." He huffed and kicked at the dirt. "I can't stop thinking if I hadn't been the one who screwed up our relationship in the first place, I would have been there to protect her."

"That's not the kind of thinkin' I would expect from you. There's no way of knowin' how things woulda turned out if you and that dear girl didn't have troubles to deal with. It's a waste of time thinkin' about what coulda been." The old man shook his head. "We're in the here and now. It'd be best if you saved your energy for dealin' with what's comin' up. Sarah *and* Miss Katy are both relyin' on you."

Mark pushed away from the fence and shifted his eyes back to his father. As always, the old cowboy's words made sense. Feeling sorry for himself and clinging to a mistake he couldn't change was pointless. The situation was too precarious for wallowing in self-pity. "You're right. I need to stay focused on what's happening right now." He glanced across the road at the lodge where Krueger patrolled the front porch. Mark shook his head. "I just don't see how having these guys parading around is going to help anything. They should be looking for Sarah. You and I can watch over Katy."

Will peeked over his shoulder to the main house then looked back to the meadow. "Well, they're the experts at this sorta thing. Havin' a few extra warm bodies makin' the place seem lively ain't necessarily a bad thing considerin' the circumstances. Of all the ranch hands we have workin' here, only Jimmy and Nate live on the property. Everyone else is gone until tomorrow. It gets kinda sleepy around here on weekends. I'm thinkin' I'll send Jimmy and Nate to Butte for the night. There ain't no sense in them gettin' mixed up in all this. The hoodlum holdin' Sarah might take advantage of our slim crew and come callin' on Katy."

Mark adjusted the pistol in his waistband. "Part of me hopes he *does* come. I'm about done with all this sneaking around he's doing. I'd like to meet him face-to-face."

"Careful what you wish for, son. The man is a cold-blooded killer. When people lose their sense of right and wrong, they become less than human. You don't know what it's like to hafta kill a man. You're never the same afterward. It don't matter the reason why you had to do it – a part of you dies afterward."

"I guess I'm willing to take that chance, dad. After what he's done to both Katy and Sarah… he has it coming."

A sad expression fell upon the old man's face. His eyes filled with a glint of understanding, but the solemnness remained. He nodded. "Well, maybe he does have it comin'… and I ain't gonna think nothin' less of you for wantin' to protect the ones you love." He patted Mark on the shoulder. "Let's head inside. All the chores are done for the day. Miss Katy will be startin' supper soon and she's got three extra mouths to feed tonight. What do ya say we go give her a hand?"

"Yeah. She's probably even more stressed out than we are."

The two men shuffled across the road toward the main house, walking in silence while they made their way.

Hensley steered the borrowed Cherokee to the side of the forest service road and parked. He scanned their surroundings and pointed out Chavez's side window toward a densely wooded area. "The place we're looking for should be back beyond the tree line a hundred yards or so. It's much higher ground up there and the way the ground is sloped, I doubt anyone would have seen us come in – especially with that sharp bend in the road just before we got here."

Chavez peered around nervously. "Where exactly did this tip come in from?" he asked in a wavering voice.

"The bureau in Helena traced it to a pay phone in town. The man wouldn't give his name when he called the County Sherriff's Office this morning and said there was some suspicious activity going on here just after dawn... said he and his friend were riding their horses down this road and heard a woman screaming. He also said they were too scared to check it out themselves. Considering our lack of leads lately, this is the best hit we've gotten."

"I still say we'd be better off waiting for backup."

The older marshal shook his head in dismay. "*What backup, Joe?* We're so thin with manpower on this case it's disgusting. Everyone else the bureau decided to grace us with is tied up right now. If we have to, we'll pull back. Now let's ease up there as quietly as we can. The satellite imagery showed a single building. If he's there, we'll know right away."

Chavez puffed out a breath and opened his door. Hensley followed close behind. The two marshals scurried up a slight embankment to the edge of the trees ten feet from their parking spot. Slipping through the dense foliage, they continued cautiously for several yards, diverging from one another until they were twenty feet apart. As they crested the hill, the roof of a structure came into view. The older marshal motioned to his partner to take cover while he ducked behind the trunk of a large ponderosa pine.

Hensley peeked around the pine tree's massive trunk. Less than fifty feet away, Ben Thompson stashed gear into the stolen all-wheel-drive vehicle. He signaled to Chavez and mouthed, "Thompson – outside by the car." Moving back behind the cover provided by the noble ponderosa pine, he wrestled the cell phone from his back pocket. No signal. *Damn. We're going to have to take him down ourselves.* He retreated to Chavez's position. Crouched low to the ground, he pushed the overgrowth aside and moved, stepping carefully to avoid small twigs and branches strewn about the forest floor. A mellow breeze blew through the treetops, stirring them back and forth. *The wind will at least give us some cover if we make any sound on our approach.* But, he wasn't about to make a careless mistake – not with Thompson so close and within his grasp.

Chavez scooted next to Hensley. "What's the plan?" he whispered.

Hensley took another quick peek around the trunk then settled with his back pressed against its flaking bark. "We're going to take him down now." His pulse quickened. Beads of sweat formed on his brow and a bitter taste filled his mouth. For a moment, his stomach twisted. He resisted the impulse to vomit. Years of tracking the ruthless fugitive dominated his life – and he was moments away from finally achieving a resolution to his quest.

"What about backup? We only have side arms – unless you want to run back to the jeep for the rifles."

The veteran lawman shook his head. "No backup. There's no cell signal. And the radios won't do us any good out here. The mountains will kill any hopes of that." He wiped the sweat from his forehead. Pressing the magazine release on the grip of his pistol, he inspected his ammunition reserves. The magazine was loaded to capacity. He popped it back into the pistol's magazine well and glanced at Chavez. "There's no time to get back to the jeep. Thompson might be gone by the time we get back. We're on our own. Are you up for this?"

The younger marshal seemed nervous. He nodded. "Yeah – I'm good," he puffed breathlessly.

Hensley studied him. For nearly two years, the men had relied on each other. Chavez had never let him down. The surly deputy trusted the eager kid with his life. He took a deep breath. Their options were slim. "Okay. I'll skirt to the left. The vegetation is pretty thick over there." He pointed to a natural depression running at an angle along the right side of the cabin. "You head along this ravine toward the building. Try to get in position at the back of the cabin. If you're careful, you can get behind him undetected." He took another glance around the tree. Thompson disappeared into the small shack. "Okay – he's inside. Go now. When he comes out, we'll take him after he steps away from the vehicle." Chavez sat on his haunches ready to bolt up the ravine. Hensley grabbed his shoulder and whispered, "Watch out for crossfire."

Chavez nodded and scurried away up the long gully. Hensley paused then headed for the thick patch of leafy chokecherry bushes offering cover thirty feet away. He swiftly advanced over the rocky ground until he reached his vantage point. He crouched and peered out from the foliage as Ben ambled out the front door onto the covered porch carrying a black backpack. The fugitive scanned his surroundings, visibly wary and searching for any potential signs of unseen danger. His head swiveled while he made his way to the green SUV and tucked the knapsack on the backseat. Hensley eyeballed the side of the building. Chavez peeked around the corner. *It's time to move.*

Ben pivoted and faced the cabin's doorway. When he took his third step away from the vehicle's open passenger door, Hensley crashed through the brush from his hiding spot with his pistol aimed squarely at Ben's chest – just twenty feet away. "U.S. Marshals! Show me your hands!" he shouted. Ben dropped his right hand to the waistband of his jeans but balked when Chavez bolted from behind the broken-down building and took a wide stance fifteen feet to his left.

"Drop the gun!" Chavez yelled. "Drop it now, or I'll shoot!"

Ben smiled. The evil grin stretched wide across his face while he locked eyes with the young marshal. He winked then snatched the pistol from his waistline. Gun in hand, he spun around to Hensley, his finger on the trigger of the .45. The older marshal hesitated for a split second then fired as the fugitive's aim came to bear upon him. The marshal's bullet grazed Ben's left shoulder, and he crumpled to the dirt, dropping the pistol on the ground beside him.

Chavez raced to the injured fugitive's side and kicked the pistol across the rocky ground beyond his reach. Hensley advanced, closing his distance to Ben to ten feet. With his gun trained on the fugitive's chest, he commanded, "Now lie all the way on the ground, face down, with your hands out and palms up." Glancing at Chavez, he commanded, "Search him, Joe."

Chavez dashed to where Ben's pistol lay on a bed of dried pine needles. He reached down and grabbed it from the forest floor. He tucked the pistol in the back of his pants with his left hand while he firmly clutched his service pistol in his right. Stepping to Ben, he patted the fugitive down while the man lay with the side of his face pressed into the dirt. Chavez shuffled backward. "He's clean, boss. You cuff him – it's your bust. You do the honors."

Hensley grinned. He holstered his pistol and plucked the handcuffs from their leather case on his belt. Standing triumphantly over Ben, he breathed a deep sigh of satisfaction while he eyed the wound on the fugitive's arm spilling a thick trail of crimson into a sickly pool across the ground. "Well, Thompson… you sure as hell were a bitch to snare – but I got ya. It took a while, but I got ya." A warm feeling flowed through Hensley's body – jubilation coupled with relief. Peering at his partner, he boasted, "Look here, Joe. Our boy isn't so scary now, is…" A quick blur of motion flashed in the corner of his eye, but it was too late. Before he could utter another word, a forceful blow struck the back of his head. Tremendous pain shot through his cranium. In an instant, everything went black. He slumped to the ground, unconscious.

He opened his eyes, unsure of how much time had passed. Writhing on the ground, he struggled to a sitting position. He touched the back of his head then looked at his hand. Warm blood dripped from his fingers. With blurred vision, he blinked several times, attempting to regain his ability to focus. Swiftly reaching to his holster, it was empty. He glanced up at the two figures hovering over him – Thompson and Chavez, standing side-by-side. He scowled. "Why, Joe? *Why?*

Chavez looked away, his expression replete with shame. "It's simple, Tom – money."

"*Money?* What the hell are you talking about?"

Ben snickered and knelt on one knee next to Hensley. "It's easy old man – your partner and I cut a deal a few days ago. It was a bargain too – only two million bucks for him to feed me information about what you stinking pigs are up to." He pressed the barrel of his .45 to the marshal's temple. "Don't take it so personally. I've done business with some of your work buddies before. Some of them are more than willing to earn a little side cash here and there."

Hensley stared in befuddlement at Chavez. "You would turn on *me* – on your *oath* for a *bribe*?" And at that moment, after he muttered the words, the answer was obvious. His partner was corrupt – dirty and rotten to the core.

Arrogance poured over the young marshal. He glared at Hensley. "Look at you." His voice cracked as he kicked a stone past the older man. "You've given your whole life to the job. And what do you have to show for it – broken marriages and kids who will hardly talk to you." He paced back and forth, his right hand clutching his pistol while his index finger lightly tapped the trigger. "I have a beautiful wife. I have kids. Do you think I'm going to be able to give them everything they need and want on the piss salary we get paid? Do you think I want to see my wife run off with some high-paid business hotshot because I'm never home and he can buy her the expensive things she wants and deserves that I can't afford? No. Not me. Not if I can help it."

Hensley shifted on the ground and again touched the painful gash on the back of his head. "The job isn't about *money*, Joe. *It's about doing the right thing.*" He glared at Ben and grimaced. "It's about putting scum like this away for good."

Ben stood and spat at Hensley's feet. "Screw you, lawman. You're just pissed at your partner because he showed initiative. He did in a few days what you've been trying to do for years – find a means to contact me."

"I trusted you with my *life*, Joe. I've always been good at sizing people up – but with you... I was way off. You could have made your way to the top ranks of the Marshals. But after this... you've chosen your path. Once you're dirty, you'll never be clean again." Hensley took a deep breath. He knew too much. His last moments would be spent there under the late afternoon sun. He gazed at the tall trees surrounding the old cabin. They shimmered in the breeze. The melody of the wind passing through their long green needles covering their heavy boughs was as soothing as gentle waves ebbing against the soft sands on Oregon's coast. And with the warmth of the sunshine on his face, he surrendered to his destiny.

Ben's lips drew back in a snarl. "Take care of your partner, Chavez. His stench is making me sick."

The young marshal shuffled to a stop and turned away, avoiding eye contact with Hensley. "No. That wasn't part of the deal. I'll provide you with information and help throw off the investigation... but I'm not a cold-blooded murderer."

"Your partner is just as dangerous to you now as he is to me," Ben growled. "But, whatever. I'll see you in hell, marshal." Without hesitation, he leveled his pistol at the veteran marshal's forehead and fired a single round. Hensley toppled to the ground, dead. Ben stared at the man's lifeless body and smiled. "One less dog on the hunt," he muttered.

Chavez's head drooped. He seemed to be in shock. Holstering his weapon, he mumbled, "It wasn't supposed to go down like this." He shook his head in disbelief. "I tried to steer him away from here... but he was dead-set on checking this place out."

"Yeah, well now he's just plain dead." Ben glared at Chavez. "Quit your bawling like a pussy. You're coming out of this with two million bucks. Did you make arrangements with your contact to set up and secure the cyber coin account?"

"Yes. He expects one-hundred grand once the transfer is complete." Chavez reached into his pocket and pulled out a flash drive. Tossing it to Ben, he said, "All the information is on the drive."

"Good. I have an overseas contact who's handling things on my end. You'll get two million once Taylor makes the transfer. The rest will go into my *retirement* account." He eyed Chavez cautiously and clutched his pistol tight. "That was a ballsy move sending a text to my disposable cell phone."

"It was a risk, but it's a prepaid phone, and we haven't gotten authorization to monitor it yet. We figured you were the one who made the bulk phone purchase in Seattle. I got the numbers from the detectives who interviewed the retailer. I used a prepaid phone too – when I first texted you. They'll never link me to the message. I'm just glad you replied to my offer."

"I almost didn't. I thought it was a trap. But letting me know in advance where the roadblocks were made me wonder how you could help me out in other ways to get this little transaction wrapped up successfully. And what if your authorization finally comes through and they do link the phone to you? What then?" Ben asked.

Chavez huffed. "I'll report I was attempting a means to establish direct contact with you in the hopes negotiating the hostage's release. They'll never suspect me of any wrongdoing – not with the way we set this up."

Ben inspected the wound on his left arm. It bled, but he surmised the damage was superficial. "Well, this will all be over soon, and I consider this to be a mutually beneficial business arrangement." He approached Chavez and held out his hand. "Give me your piece." The marshal's face twitched with uneasiness. "Don't stress. If I wanted you dead, I would have taken care of it already. Now, *give me your piece.*"

Handing his pistol to Ben, Chavez trembled. "What do you need it for?"

Without answering, Ben snatched the pistol with his left hand and pointed it at the cabin. He fired six shots, spraying bullets at the rotted front wall. He handed the pistol back. "There, now when you report to your cronies, you'll have a better alibi. You and your now-dead partner tried to take me on... but you lost. Oh, and one more thing..." Backing up a few steps, he aimed his pistol at Chavez and fired three quick rounds at his chest. The bullets ripped through the cotton fibers of the lawman's button-up shirt and revealed an agency-issued bullet-proof vest, the mushroomed slugs visible through the torn fabric.

Chavez tumbled to the ground from the violent and unexpected impact. He rolled in the dirt, clutching his torso while he squirmed in pain. "*Sonofabitch!*" he cried out.

Ben snickered. "Sorry… but it wouldn't look good if you went back to meet up with your pig buddies without some form of damage." He leveled his pistol and fired again, grazing Chavez's outer thigh. "And a little bit of blood loss makes it look even better." He dangled the pistol at his side, waiting for the barrel to cool before sliding it back into his waistband.

"*Are you freaking insane?*" Chavez shouted. He clutched at the laceration on his upper leg and pressed his hand against the exposed flesh showing through the hole in his blood-soaked trousers.

"Maybe." Ben surveyed the dense forest around them, scouting for activity. A few squirrels chittered distress calls from the treetops, but nothing seemed out of order after the gunfire. He peered at Chavez. "Give me forty-five minutes then get your ass back to your buddies. Tell them your modified version of what went down here. You'll have to travel a few miles on the highway back toward town before you'll get a cell signal. As far as anyone is concerned, I set up an ambush and caught you off guard. Lead the search away from Taylor's ranch. That will open things up for me."

Chavez struggled to his feet and limped in a compressed circle, dragging his scuffed dress shoes through the mix of dirt and dried pine needles with labored steps before hobbling to an unsettled stance. "What about the girl?"

"You mean my sister? She's in a safe place… and for the moment, still breathing," Ben replied.

"Your sister? What the hell are you talking about?"

Chavez scowled. The bewilderment was plain in his expression.

Ben glared at him. "What? You dumb bastards didn't know? After all this time you never checked out her background?" He snickered. "Yeah, the illustrious Mrs. Sarah Taylor is my sister."

"No, we didn't know. We didn't have any cause to dig that deep into her background. It seemed like a cut-and-dry kidnapping-for-ransom plot." Chavez paused and stroked his mustache. "The little girl Hensley told me about… when Child Protective Services took you into their custody during the drug raid at your parents' place," he mumbled.

"Yeah. Let's cut this reminiscing about happy-old-times bullshit."

Chavez shifted his weight onto his wounded leg and winced. He staggered for a moment, nearly falling to the ground. Once he regained his balance, he asked, "When are you making the exchange?"

"Soon. I have a few details to work through before I'm ready. It's important you keep the heat as far away from me as possible in the meantime." Satisfied the pistol was cool enough, he shoved it in his pants. He stepped over to Hensley's body and rolled the contorted figure to his side. Digging through the dead man's pockets, he found what he was searching for – his cell phone. He powered it off and tucked it in his back pocket, and then handed Chavez a small handwritten list. "Memorize those numbers then burn the paper. The phone numbers are listed in the order which I'll use them one-by-one as needed. None of them appear on your warrant – I took care of that little problem the moment you messaged me they were on a watch list."

Chavez peeked at the crumpled paper then tucked it in his pocket. "You know, I'm risking an awful lot by helping you out."

"Helping me out? You're making some serious bank for your troubles." Ben studied the young marshal. The guy seemed nervous. *I better give him a little bit of motivation to get his head out of his ass.* Trudging to the rear of the green SUV, he pointed to a small black box mounted to the side rail on the roof's luggage rack. "You see this? It's an Adventure Cam." He whirled and faced Chavez; his palms held up in an emphatic gesture. "This whole little execution show we put on… I recorded it all on video – with sound." He stepped to the camera and pressed a button on its side, popping the flash memory card from the camera's plastic body. Holding up the flash card between his thumb and index finger, he said, "Our conversation… you popping your buddy on the head with your piece so I could off him… it's all on this here little card." He nodded toward a tall pine tree to his left. "And on that tree… there's another cam – it'll show a different angle… wide view even." The marshal paled and appeared ready to faint. With a smirk, Ben ambled toward the queasy lawman. "Now here's what I'm gonna do… I'm gonna download this video onto my phone, compress the file, and send it in a time-delayed email to the FBI's website." He paused and rubbed his chin. "I'm gonna schedule it for delivery tomorrow evening. Now… if anything happens to me… I won't be able to cancel the email before it's transmitted. That would make you… should I say… *screwed*?" He bared his teeth in a brilliant melodramatic smile.

Chavez went limp. He gulped. "That won't be necessary," he uttered.

"Let's just consider it extra insurance you do everything in your power to make sure things work out exactly as I plan. Got it?"

"Yeah… of course…" Chavez nodded then asked, "When do I get my two million?"

"You'll get your cut soon. When the time comes, it'll be obvious it's payday. Stay in touch and keep me updated. When I give you directions, you follow them exactly as I say. Get out of here – *now*," Ben demanded. Chavez glowered at him then limped away on the narrow dirt track down the hill, peeking back one last time before he disappeared from view.

Ben scurried back to the cabin and pushed open the front door. Shackled to the rusted-out pot-belly stove, Sarah lay on the grime-covered floor. He peered into her terror-filled eyes and grinned. He plucked the handcuff key from his jean's coin pocket and unlocked the handcuff from the stove leg then lugged her to her feet. "C'mon, sis', we're moving to a different spot." With her ankles still bound, Sarah hopped across the floor to the doorway. She mumbled unintelligibly behind the strip of duct tape covering her mouth. Ben stopped and huffed. He partially ripped the tape from her mouth. "*What*?" he snarled in annoyance.

"My God, what's happening? What was all the shooting and who were those men you were talking to?"

"Just some unexpected visitors. Don't worry – I took care of it. The shots were aimed high, and you were low enough on the ground nothing was gonna hit you." He slapped the tape back across her mouth and tugged her out of the crumbling structure. Sarah tumbled to the ground upon catching sight of the dead marshal's body. Her eyes dilated with fear. Ben yanked her to her feet and pushed her to the SUV's open front passenger door. He shoved her onto the seat. "We're far enough out in the sticks – I don't think anyone will recognize you. Just behave, and you'll save yourself a lot of pain." After slamming the door, he took a wary look around. Any evidence left behind from the encounter didn't matter. The lawmen chasing him already had more than enough reason to send him the electric chair. *Time to get moving. It's going to be a long night.*

CHAPTER 17

SUNDAY, APRIL 18TH 10:22 PM

Silence smothered the living room. No one felt like speaking. Only the sound of an old antique clock, with its methodical ticks and tocks, broke the stillness of the late hour. Dread hung heavy around them like a suffocating oppressor, purging the air from the room with its choking guise. Mark's cell phone lay on the coffee table before him, waiting. Without warning, it vibrated across the wooden surface for half a second and chimed. A text notification flashed across the once-dormant display. Mark snatched the device from its resting place. He swiped across the screen and read the message.

Transfer the cyber coin now. I'll be checking to see if it's in the account. Five miles northeast of town there's a road intersecting county road 142. Name of the road is Talbot. Turn there and travel 2 miles east. Stop when you get to the house on the north side of the road. Only place nearby. You can't miss it.

Bring the rest of the cash. One hour. No cops. Come alone or I'll put a bullet between your wife's eyes. I'll be waiting.

Mark glanced at Katy then his father. They both sat frozen, their eyes locked on him. He rose from the couch. "It's time. I have to go." Angst moiled in his gut while he forwarded a screenshot of the text to Chavez. He peered up from his phone. Unease radiated from Katy and his father. "He said to meet him at a place on Talbot Road – in one hour."

The old man clambered out of his rocking chair. "That's a pretty wild area out there. The woods are thick and there are lots of forest service roads – a good place to bushwhack someone if ya got a mind to."

"I wouldn't expect anything less from this piece of scum, dad. He knows the marshals will be around. He'll make sure he has plenty of escape routes so he can slither away." Mark glanced back at his phone. Another text notification shot across the display. "Chavez says he's nearly here. He's just about to turn off the paved road from town." He glimpsed at Katy. She huddled close to the arm of the sofa, her gaze riveted on the floor. "Well, I need to make the transfer and get my stuff together. I'll be back in a few minutes." He hurried down the long hallway to his room, his mind racing in multiple directions. *I swore not to give him any cash until I saw Sarah… but, he made it clear there wouldn't be any negotiating…What if I send the money, but Sarah isn't around when I get there? What if I get there and find Sarah's lifeless body? How can I even trust this psychopath?* The questions vexed him, but the conclusion was clear – he didn't have a choice – otherwise, Sarah was as good as dead. A lump hardened in his throat, threatening to stifle his ability to breathe.

He darted into his room. He snagged his computer case from the pale wooden floorboards next to the nightstand and flung it on the bed. After unzipping the black nylon bag, he plucked the computer from inside and set it atop the mattress. With a quick flip of its screen, he pressed the power button on the laptop's bezel. The screen flickered to life. Plopping down on the edge of the bed, he waited. Seconds seemed to slog by at a snail's pace, but finally, the machine completed its booting process. He opened a web browser and navigated to the online payment site. He typed at the keyboard with a rapid clip, entering the account information sent in an earlier text from Thompson. With a final stroke, all that remained to complete the transfer of eighteen million dollars was a punch of the "enter" key. He wavered. The money didn't matter. It meant nothing to him. But once he deposited the currency in the clandestine account, any leverage he possessed to keep Sarah safe would be gone.

Mark pressed his eyes shut. Visions of Sarah swelled within his mind. The shy and awkward teenager he met years earlier in high school, the young girl who matured into an alluring woman, the love of his life whom he betrayed during a lustful and drunken encounter – her life was at stake, and only he could save her. Without another thought, he opened his eyes and pressed the key. There was no turning back. A confirmation of the completed transaction zipped onto the screen. *Well, I've done what you asked – you better keep your end of the deal, you son-of-a-bitch.*

Fumbling for the cordless house phone, he took it from his nightstand and punched in Dan's cell number on the keypad. He held the device to his ear. It droned twice before his friend's voice resonated through the speaker.

"Hello?" Dan answered.

"It's me. I just transferred the money. I'm supposed to meet Thompson in a little under an hour." Mark stood from the bed and stepped to the bedroom window. He stared at Katy's darkened cabin across the way.

"Mark… what the hell? I've been waiting all day for you to call." Dan paused then asked, "How's this all supposed to go down? What's the plan?"

"I have the additional two million in cash. I'll take it with me when I go to get Sarah." He raked his fingers through his muss of hair and heaved a deep breath. "As far as I know, the cops will be tailing me. I figure they'll try to take down Thompson once I have her. Keep an eye out for any transmissions from her phone – any updates it provides might prove useful."

"You know I will. There haven't been any additional broadcasts though."

"Yeah, just like we already talked about, the cell service is pretty spotty out here. They're most likely in an area with weak coverage and the reduced power from the phone is probably hindering its ability to relay its location." Whirling from the window, he strolled back to the center of the room. The day's events unfolded with such swift momentum he hadn't filled in his friend with the grisly details. "Dan… Hensley is dead," he blurted out.

"*What?*" Dan gasped. "What the hell happened?"

"He and Chavez were checking out a lead at an old mining property. Thompson jumped them. There was a shootout, and Hensley took a bullet when the lead was flying – killed him instantly."

"Damn... and Chavez?"

"Chavez got winged – but he's okay. They patched him up in town. In fact, he should be here any minute." Mark glimpsed at his Rolex. Precious seconds were ticking away. Time was running out. "I've got to get going. Things will probably go down fast – so stick by your phone."

"I'll be ready. And Mark – watch your ass. The guy is nuts."

"I know. I'll be in touch." He dropped the phone from his ear and depressed the call button with his thumb. He tossed the handset on the nightstand then knelt to the floor. Underneath the bed, a silver attaché holding the remainder of Sarah's ransom lay stashed out of sight. Gripping the sides of the container, he dragged the case from its hiding place and climbed to his feet.

He hurried to the foyer with the aluminum briefcase containing two million dollars in cash, its leather-wrapped handle clutched firmly in his grip. Approaching the front door, he locked eyes with his father – the old man's gray eyes charged with steely resolve. News of the ambush and Hensley's death was devastating. At least Chavez survived, escaping the brutal encounter with only a superficial wound to his upper thigh. But, the incident pronounced the gravity of the situation, and at that moment, the chill in the air didn't flow from the cloak of night in the

Montana wilderness – it arose from the horrific reality they all opposed a vicious killer.

Mark patted the bulge at the small of his back. His denim jacket concealed the pistol tucked in the waistband of his jeans. He was prepared to face his nemesis. The hours of restless waiting were over, and his body tingled with apprehension. Soon, he would meet his gravest challenge. The burden of the moment bore down on him like the weight of the surrounding mountains placed upon his shoulders, for all whom he loved were in danger. Yes, he would end the threat that very night – or die trying.

Katy bounded from the couch. Throwing her arms around him, she held him in a snug embrace and nuzzled her cheek against his chest. He lowered his head, resting his chin atop the lush curls of her hair. Her locks smelled of lilac, and he inhaled the sweet fragrance, uncertain if it would be for the last time.

"Please be careful. And come back safe," she sighed. Releasing Mark from her clutches, she shared his gaze.

Concern glinted in her blue eyes as they clouded with tears. "It's going to be okay, Katy. Stay here in the house with dad. This will all be over with soon." She paused before turning away, seemingly hesitant to leave his side, and then dashed down the corridor to his room. He stared down the empty hallway, a queasiness churning in his belly.

"Don't you worry, son – I'll be watchin' over her." The old man cleared his throat then puffed a deep breath. "You just be takin' care of yourself."

Mark glanced at his father. The old cowboy's expression

softened, and worry showed through the deep lines and wrinkles marking his rugged features. He struggled for words to quell his father's trepidation. He clenched his jaw and nodded. "I'll be careful."

"Now, I mean it – don't be takin' any crazy chances." The old man's voice broke. "You let the marshals do their job. Get in there and get out with that poor gal."

"I'll bring her home. You can count on it." He ambled over to his father. "I'm going to need some wheels. May I use your truck?"

Will dug his fingers into the front pocket of his faded blue jeans and yanked out a set of keys. "You bet. The ole girl has about three-quarters of a tank. She's got plenty of get-up-and-go. Don't be afraid to step on the gas and hightail it outta there once you take care of what needs to be done." He extended his hand toward Mark, the set of keys laying on his open palm in offering.

Mark took the keys from the old man's grasp. He brushed his father's shoulder with his own while he stepped to the door. "Keep your eyes peeled, dad. I'll be back shortly." Pushing through the front door, he stopped on the porch. Deputy Chavez and five other marshals waited in silence on the circular driveway. He eyeballed the line of lawmen, standing side-by-side. Long shadows cast forth from their stances across the courtyard under the glow of the halogen lights fixed to the sides of the compound's buildings. Chavez limped forward and waited six feet short of the bottom step. "You okay, deputy?" Mark asked.

Chavez stared at the gravel beneath his scuffed dress

shoes. "Yeah, I'm okay. The bullet just grazed me. My chest hurts like hell though."

Mark scrambled down the wooden staircase and approached the marshal. "It's a good thing you were wearing that vest." He paused then added, "Hey... I'm sorry about Hensley. I know you two were partners for a long time."

Chavez rubbed the back of his neck and appeared lost in thought. "We were. Tom died doing what he loved. I guess I can find some solace in that."

Mark surveyed the group of marshals. Indignation and conviction exuded from their demeanor. "So, what's the plan, deputy?"

"We'll follow you – five minutes behind – then wait less than a mile from the property where Thompson told you to make the exchange. We'll be far enough away – hopefully, we won't tip off our presence. But we'll be close enough to be there fast – within a minute or two. We want you to wear a wire. At the first sign of trouble, we'll move," Chavez replied. He stepped forward and fastened the electronic listening device under the front corner of Mark's shirt collar.

"How much back up will be around once this goes down?" he asked while the marshal fixed the microphone in place.

"Three of my fellow deputies will be staying here to keep watch on your dad's place. I spoke to Dawes, and he and his men are in the process of setting up roadblocks on both ends of town. Me, Nelson, and Hackett – along with two county deputies who are waiting right now at the turnoff to join us – will be on hand to make the bust."

Mark groaned. *Five cops. That's it.* He glared at the deputy. "Sounds pretty thin, marshal."

"That's it. That's what we can spare." Chavez sniffed then puffed out his chest. "Look, there's a big political rally taking place in Helena tomorrow. Even the Vice President is going to be there. It's not only sapped the local agencies' resources, but the federal agencies too – and, we still have a team working the scene where Tom and I were ambushed. We didn't have a lot of manpower to start with. Top brass ordered it this way." He shook his head, defiance written on his face. "It's not *my* call, Mark."

Eyeing each of the lawmen, Mark struggled to contain his annoyance. Inside, he fumed. "A serial killer has been holding my wife hostage for three days, sets a meeting to release her for ransom, and this…" He nodded at the group. "*This* is all we have to work with? *Seriously?* I mean no disrespect to any of you – but this is total bullshit." Mark glanced past Chavez and at the other older, obviously more experienced deputies. He flashed a look back at the young marshal. "So, you're in charge now?"

"Yes, I'm in temporary command of this operation. Tom was the lead agent. I was directly involved in his decision making. For tonight at least, I'm in charge. Look, I understand your frustration. I really do. But we're all professionals. And we'll be able to handle the situation."

Like you handled the situation earlier today… when Hensley was gunned down in front of you? Mark bit his tongue. It wasn't the time to make enemies of his only allies. He switched the briefcase to his other hand. "Well, deputy... I hope you and your men are ready... because it's obvious Thompson doesn't give a shit about who he murders along the way. You know that firsthand."

"Yes, I do." Chavez's attention seemed diverted toward the briefcase, and his eyes widened. "I take it that's the ransom payment?"

"Yeah, two million – in cash. Just like he demanded," Mark grumbled.

"Have you transferred the other currency?"

"I sent it over about ten minutes ago. I've done everything he's asked – except for the part about not talking to you. I don't want this to go bad. If Thompson gets even a whiff you guys are around, he's going to kill my wife. He's made that very clear every time he's contacted me." Mark's body numbed and his skull throbbed as if it was ready to explode at any moment from all the disquiet. Hopefully, he hadn't made a mistake by cooperating with the lawmen – even if there wasn't any other choice. Despite their unflinching eagerness and relentless sense of urgency, he couldn't help but feel the marshals had consistently bungled the pursuit.

Chavez glowered with agitation distinct in his inflection. "I'm *fully* aware of what's at stake. We'll be on standby, but we won't move in until you and Mrs. Taylor are safely on your way. If things start to go bad before you're both on the road out of there..." He peered at his fellow deputies then back at Mark. "Then we'll be on him before he has a chance to realize what hit him."

"I hope so, deputy," Mark shot back. He wheeled away from the group and took two steps toward the white truck parked at the center of the drive – right where his father parked it earlier. He peeked over his shoulder. With one last review, he scrutinized the men whom he would rely on to safeguard his wife's freedom. The federal marshals stood steadfast like statues, with only the mist of their breath billowing in the chill of the night exposing their sentience. Finally, he broke the silence. "Let's get this over with. My wife is waiting."

Chavez clapped his hands. "You heard him, gentlemen! Nelson… Hackett… with me. Bickley, Lutz, and Gibbons take up positions around the property. Stay sharp!"

The lawmen scattered away, two of them to the four-wheel drive Cherokee, the other toward his agency sedan. The remaining three marshals spread out in different directions around the lodge. Mark proceeded to his father's mud-covered truck. He opened the door and plopped down on the worn driver's seat, setting the briefcase on the passenger-side floorboard. Reaching to his seat's adjustment controls on its bottom console, he grimaced while he wriggled against the backrest. The pistol in his waistband gouged into his back, sending a sharp pain rippling up his spine. He leaned forward and drew the gun from his jeans. The heft of the handgun balanced well in his grip. While he studied its design, memorizing its every detail, his father's voice resounded in his notions.

"Taking another life is something that'll change you forever. You're stealing something away you can never give back – no matter how justified you were in taking it."

The old man never talked about his days in the service

much, but the occasional comments regarding his three tours in Vietnam, and the sadness filling his eyes when he spoke of those times left no doubt he saw hell firsthand. And it was apparent the gentle soul killed men while performing his duty during the war. The collection of medals, cached away in a dusty and battered trunk, stuffed off to a far corner in the attic of Mark's childhood home, led the young boy's imagination on wild adventures. But even as a child, with youthful enthusiasm and the romanticism of war common to young, unruly boys his age, he knew their true meaning.

Years had flown by since he last saw the symbols of valor and heroism awarded to his father. The excitement of fighting and the glory of war had long since faded. But at that moment, loathing coursed through his body like a river of fire. Embers of contempt smoldered in his soul. He hated Ben Thompson. The previous few nights had been suffused with restless and dark fantasies of training the pistol's sights on the criminal's forehead, staring into the man's fearful eyes before squeezing the trigger with all his enmity – payback for even daring to threaten those he loved. Nausea twisted his stomach and a sour taste saturated his saliva. He swallowed hard and took one last glimpse of the pistol before shoving it under the seat. *I won't need this for the drive.* Gripping the steering wheel, he took a deep breath.

Months had come and gone since he'd driven anything. The doctors were overly cautious after the accident. Sure, there were occasions when he felt woozy and lightheaded – but he'd never actually blacked out. The doctors' precautionary words echoed in his head – *brain injuries, no matter how insignificant they may seem, were always cause for concern.* But with his attention focused on Sarah, his health was the least of his worries. The previous few days proved to be a whirlwind of emotions, churning with uncertainty. And just when it appeared as though he was embarking on a new chapter in his life, fate took a drastic turn, jolting him back to the old life he abandoned. Four nights earlier, he boarded the bus. He departed, pelted by raindrops while he walked to its metal steps as if the heavens shed tears for the broken hearts left in the wake of his self-imposed exile away from the only love he had ever known. But once again, Sarah dominated his thoughts and motivations.

He cranked over the ignition. The truck's headlights activated automatically, piercing through the night and beaming on the magnificent log home. Would he ever see it again? But until Sarah was safe, nothing else mattered. Shifting the gear lever into drive, he steered hard left and stepped on the gas. The truck spun in a half fishtail while he gunned it down the driveway toward the compound's front gate. Gravel launched from the tread of the massive off-road tires while the powerful engine growled with angry horsepower and vicious torque. He glanced at the digital clock on the dashboard. Only twenty-five minutes remained of his sixty-minute deadline. *I can make it.*

The truck raced down the rutted road, sailing through the air with each bump, and skidding sideways on every turn. Occasional beams of moonlight sliced through the gloom of the bulging clouds undulating across the night sky, bathing the surrounding forest in a haunting aura. He peeked in the rearview mirror, a glint of headlights shown back in the distance barely visible through the choking cloud of dust churning in the vehicle's track. *I sure as hell hope you guys are ready for this.*

CHAPTER 18

Mark glanced at the odometer. *I've gone two miles… it's got to be close.* His head swiveled from left to right while he probed the darkness through speckles of dust clinging to the truck's windshield and side windows in powdered layers resembling miniature dunes. On both sides of the narrow paved road, the forest thinned into intermittent slight meadows, overgrown with wild grass. Sporadic turnoffs alluded to the existence of the vacation homes scattered along the way.

It was only mid-spring, many of the out-of-state property owners in the area wouldn't be arriving for the summer season for another month, once the threat of lingering snowstorms diminished. *Thompson must have done his homework – this place is definitely out of the way.* With one hand on the steering wheel, he plucked the cellphone from his shirt pocket and peeked at the display. *The cell signal is fluctuating between no signal and a single bar. Dan and I were right… the signal is probably too spotty for Sarah's phone to transmit.* He slipped the phone back into his pocket then hunched over the steering wheel and glanced at the heavens. The cloud cover began to surrender to a clear sky, allowing patches of twinkling stars to emerge from the gloom. He sighed. *So much for atmospheric conditions helping to boost the cell coverage.*

Mark eased his foot from the accelerator, slowing the truck. In the glare of the headlights, off to the left side of the asphalt ahead, a break in the trees revealed a narrow drive. *This has got to be it. There haven't been any side roads for nearly a mile.* He eyed the rearview mirror before veering off the road and onto the secluded path. Nothing shone in the dimness – no headlights from the convoy of vehicles carrying the marshals and deputies. *Good. You and your boys are holding back. I just hope you didn't find a way to get lost on your way here.* The truck rolled up the long unpaved drive at a reluctant pace. Once he cleared a thick stand of pines shielding the house from the road, the dwelling came into view. Moonlight cascaded across the ground and drenched the terrain in a spectral glow, allowing him to size up his surroundings. Light filtered through a front window of the single-story building, the sole beacon in the otherwise tenebrous structure.

He took a deep breath then shut off the engine. He snatched the briefcase from the floorboard. *This is it. Keep it together.* Pulling the door latch, he pushed the door open and hopped out onto the drive, leaving the truck door ajar. Caution pulsated through his mind and circulated like ice in his veins. The briefcase quaked in his trembling grip with each of his muddled steps toward the cottage's front entrance. "I hope you guys can hear me. I'm here," he mumbled into the concealed microphone.

He paused and examined the modest chalet. It appeared to be of newer construction. In the pale light, the vinyl siding's shade of light blue seemed drab in the afterglow. *The place must only have one bedroom, considering its size.* "Hello?" he called out. "Thompson?" No answer. Only the hoot of an owl, perched somewhere in the treetops, fractured the peace. He advanced closer, shuffling his feet in the gravel. "Thompson!" he yelled out again – still nothing. With vigilant footfalls, he climbed onto the synthetic decking of the cramped porch and halted at the front door. His ears strained to detect any sound. *You son-of-a-bitch… you better not be setting me up.* He rapped at the door with the knuckle of his right index finger then stepped off to the side – standing directly in front of the door would present an easy target should Thompson greet him with a hail of gunfire. He knocked again, but nothing stirred behind the door. With a frustrated exhale, he glanced over his shoulder. *Is this an ambush? Now what?*

The hell with this. All I want is Sarah back safe. He complied with Thompson's demands, and he wasn't in the mood to play games. The hairs on his neck prickled and stood on end. What if his worst fears were true? What if Sarah was lying on the floor behind that door, dead? Insufferable panic throbbed in his aching heart. Without a second thought, he grasped the door handle and pressed the thumb latch. He flung the door open and stepped inside. "Thompson? Sarah?" he shouted, the feeling of dread sucking the air from his lungs.

He looked about, seeking any signs of life. Sparse of furniture, the interior appeared well kept. The hardwood floor glistened under the luminance from a single incandescent lamp sitting on a small stand beside a love seat under the front window. A white dust cover draped over the sofa exposed an impression amongst its wrinkles. He set the briefcase down and tugged at the corner of the cotton sheet. Muffled rustling rattled from across the den. He glanced at a closed door opposite to the confined sitting room. "Hello?" A loud thump resonated from the other side – then another, and another. He tiptoed to the door with short, tentative steps. Placing his hand on the doorknob, he slowly rotated the brass handle. He held his breath and pushed the door open, its hinges squealing at a whispered, drawn-out pitch.

A sliver of light carved through the darkness obscuring the small room. He flipped the light switch on the wall. His jaw dropped. Sarah lay huddled on the floor in the corner, at the foot of a queen size bed. Bound by her hands and feet, a strip of silver duct tape covered her mouth – but she was alive. "Sarah!" he exclaimed in joy. He darted over and knelt by her side. Tears streamed from her eyes. The fear they held upon his initial appearance transformed into warmth and relief. He tore the tape from her face and held her bruised cheek in his palm while he brushed through the tangles of her hair with his other hand.

"Mark," she sobbed with rapid breath. "You came for me."

"Of course I did. *I love you.*" He planted a gentle kiss on her cracked lips. Inspecting her face, he wiped away at the layer of grime covering her cheek with his thumb while he cradled it in his hand. A sickening yellowish-purple bruise emerged in the semi-clean trail left by his touch. "My God, what did he do to you?" he seethed.

Sarah reached for his hand, her own still bound by the handcuffs shackling her wrists. "It's okay. I'm fine." She pulled his hand to her lips and kissed it.

Mark continued his frantic examination, searching for any other injuries hidden beneath the torn rags clothing her. Satisfied there weren't any life-threatening wounds, he gazed into her eyes. "Where is he?"

She moved her hands to her face and wiped her runny nose. "I don't know... he's been gone for hours... Mark... he's after the girl at your dad's place."

Mark clenched his jaw. Suddenly, it hit him, and everything became clear. His body tingled. The sensation of cold sapped his skin while the blood drained from his cheeks and a shiver raced up his spine like an electric shock. *This was Thompson's plan all along... he's using Sarah to lure us away so he can get to Katy.* He tugged at his shirt collar. "Chavez, get here *now!*" he growled into the microphone.

"Mark, what is it?" Sarah asked.

"I've got to get to the ranch, Sarah. That's why Thompson isn't here. He's on his way to my dad's place..." He eyed Sarah's feet. The handcuffs at her ankles threaded around the bed's heavy wooden leg. Leaping to his feet, he shoved the mattress and box spring to the side. He strained to lift the corner of the frame, raising it half an inch. "Come on, slide your feet out." Sarah yanked her feet from under the hardwood post and rolled to her side. Mark dropped the cumbersome frame back to the floor with a thud then helped her up. "The cops are on their way. When they get here, I need you to trust me."

Fear returned to Sarah's eyes. "What? What… are you talking about?"

"I don't have time to explain. Just go with the marshals – they'll keep you safe until I get back." He looked her up and down, focusing on the set of handcuffs binding her ankles. "Can you walk?"

Sarah nodded. "Yes. I'm all right."

"Okay. We'll go slow – into the front room. We'll get those damn things off of you in just a few minutes." He wrapped his arm around her and led her out of the bedroom while she hobbled in short steps. He scanned all around them while they made their way, the sense of desperation building with each second. Guiding her to the love seat, she collapsed onto the furniture and moaned. He snatched the coverlet from the couch and tucked it around her shivering body. "Here, this will help keep you warm."

She grasped his arm and pulled him close. Staring into his eyes, she wailed, "I'm sorry, Mark. I wish I had tried harder to work things out between us." She clutched his face in her hands. "I love you…"

Mark swallowed. He'd spent countless sleepless hours in imaginary conversations with her; uttering words he would say if given just one more opportunity. But, suddenly, his mind went blank. "You're going to be okay. We'll have time to talk later." Outside the window at their backs, the roar of car engines accompanied the sound of skidding tires on loose gravel. He sprang from the couch and pushed the white curtain from the corner of the window. Peeking outside, he breathed a sigh of relief. He glanced back at Sarah. "It's the cops. You're safe now."

Darting to the entrance, he pushed past the partially open front door and slid to an abrupt halt on the porch. Two sheriff's department cruisers angled in the driveway in defensive positions, the deputies poised behind their open driver's doors with shotguns aimed squarely at his chest. "Hands up!" the female trooper bellowed.

Chavez emerged from the dimness beyond the patrol cars. Jogging with a gimp in his stride through the gap between them, he gestured toward the lead deputy. "It's all right. He's with me. Put your weapons down." He staggered onto the porch and squinted at Mark. "Mrs. Taylor?"

"Inside. She's scraped up, but I think she's okay." Mark moved aside and allowed the marshal to pass. Following behind Chavez into the cramped room, he pointed at Sarah's wrists. "Get those damn things off her, please."

Chavez knelt in front of Sarah and reached into his jacket. "Mrs. Taylor, I'm Joe Chavez with the U.S. Marshal's Office. I'm glad to see you." Plucking a small key ring from his pocket, he slipped the key into the handcuff's metal frame and one-by-one released Sarah's bindings.

The handcuffs fell to the floor with a clunk. Sarah rubbed her wrists and winced, the raw blemishes from the shackles impressed into her delicate skin in bright red circles. "Oh, you have *no* idea how good it feels to finally get those things off," she groaned.

Mark leered at Chavez as the marshal stood. "We need to get back to the ranch *now*."

"We have to secure the scene here, first," the deputy replied in a matter-of-fact tone.

"Look, we don't have time to argue. Thompson set up this exchange to lure us away… he's after Katy," Mark implored.

Chavez shook his head. "No. We have three men there on watch. There are certain procedures we have to follow. Thompson could still be hiding here – somewhere close by."

Throwing his hands in the air, Mark growled, "Are you kidding me? You seriously think he's going to hang out here and wait for you guys to show up?" He flashed a look at Nelson and Hackett as they bustled through the doorway.

Nelson approached Chavez. "We walked the perimeter of the house. We've got nothing."

"Do a search and clear the building," Chavez ordered. Nelson and Hackett drew their sidearms and disappeared into the other room. He glared at Mark. "I'm in charge of this operation. We do things by-the-book. I spoke to Lutz over the radio when we were pulling up. He reported everything was quiet at his location."

Mark sneered at the young marshal in disbelief. He fumed. *How the hell can this guy ignore the obvious?* Taking a deep breath, he huffed and spun away for a moment to contain the outrage clawing at his core. He whirled back to Chavez and scowled. "At least send the deputies with me to get her and my dad out of there."

"*Once* I'm confident this location is secure, we'll head back there – but, not *until* it's confirmed Thompson isn't holed up somewhere nearby."

Shaking his head in disgust, Mark bustled to Sarah's side. "I have to go. Stay with the marshals. You'll be safe with them. I have to get back to dad's place and make sure he and Katy are okay."

Sarah reached out and took Mark's hand, giving it a gentle squeeze. "Be careful, please. Don't underestimate how dangerous Ben is."

"I'll watch myself." He leaned over and gave her a quick peck on the cheek. "I'll see you soon, okay?"

Sarah nodded. "Promise me?"

"I promise." He flashed a look of exasperation at Chavez then hurried out the door.

Sarah ogled at the empty doorway. Nelson rounded the corner into the room with Hackett close on his heels, startling her. "He's not here," she announced.

Nelson seemed to ignore her comment and eyed Chavez. "The place is clear, Joe."

Chavez placed his hands on his hips and swiveled toward his cohorts. "Did you find anything?"

Nelson handed a white cell phone to Chavez. "Just this... and there's some garbage left in the kitchen – empty food wrappers and other junk. Looks like he had something to eat before he took off."

"That's mine," Sarah declared, eyeing the phone.

Slipping the device into the breast pocket of his jacket, Chavez said, "We'll have to hold this for evidence, for the time being, Mrs. Taylor." He shot her a hollow smile, and then added, "We'll get it back to you when we can." He focused on the two marshals. "Get outside with the deputies and make a sweep of the property. Stay within sight of one another. Check every depression, behind every tree – any place he could be holed up. Be thorough."

The heavyset, middle-aged marshal pivoted away. "You got it, Joe."

Sarah scrutinized the young marshal after the two men hustled out the door. Beads of sweat trickled down the young marshal's brow. *It's awfully cold to be sweating.* "Are you okay?" she asked, huddling under the cotton dust cover for the small amount of warmth it provided.

Chavez rubbed his nose with his thumb and index finger. He seemed nervous. With his gaze fixed on the floor, he mumbled, "It wasn't supposed to go down like this."

Sarah's blood ran cold. The hair on her neck bristled. *Wait! That voice... I know those words... he's the one... from the cabin earlier today...* She searched his expression. His eyes clouded with suspicion. *Does he know I'm onto him?*

Jitters and nerves prevailed in his body language. He snatched the handheld radio from his waist. "Hackett, Nelson, give me a report," he barked into the microphone.

Static crackled from the speaker before Nelson's voice snapped back, "Uh... we're approaching the back property line – about fifty yards behind the residence. Nothing yet."

Chavez clicked the button on the side of the handset. "I'm headed to the regional medical facility with Mrs. Taylor to get her looked over. I'll check back in a bit for an update. Keep up with your search."

After a pause, Nelson's voice rang back. "Acknowledged."

Chavez clipped the radio on his belt. Forcing a smile, he grasped Sarah's arm. "Come on; let's get you to a medic to get you checked out." He guided her from the couch, snatching the briefcase from the floor while he lugged her toward the door.

His fingers pressed into her flesh. "You're hurting me, marshal," she groaned.

He loosened his grip. "I'm sorry. It's been a tense day. I'm sure you can understand me being a little edgy." Chavez led her onto the porch, his head swiveling while they advanced toward the jeep parked behind the deputies' cruisers. "They have it under control here. We need to get you to a more secure location."

"Stop!" Sarah shrieked. Her bare feet staggered across the gravel until they reached the vehicle. "I want to wait for Mark. Let me go," she demanded.

"Out of the question. You'll see him soon enough," Chavez replied, veiled agitation quivering in his tone. He flung the front passenger-side door open and prodded her onto the fabric upholstery. Weaving the aluminum briefcase between the two seats, he tossed it on the backseat before slamming the door. He skittered to the driver's door and opened it then hopped behind the steering wheel. Without delay, he yanked the door shut and fumbled for the keys, his hands shaking. He started the jeep and groped for the gear shift, jerking the transmission into reverse. The jeep surged backward while he weaved through the cluster of vehicles and down the shrub-lined drive. Tree limbs and small bushes brushed across the passenger side of the four-by-four in high pitched screeches like fingernails on a chalkboard until the vehicle bounced, announcing the asphalt's rough edge.

Sarah glowered at him. The curtness of his behavior confirmed her fears. *He knows... play it cool...* She cleared her throat. "So... where exactly are you taking me?"

Chavez wheeled the car onto the road facing east and jammed his foot on the accelerator. "There's an urgent care facility down the road. It's open twenty-four hours, so they'll be able to examine you even this late at night."

This is the same direction Ben drove to get here... we're heading away from town! Sarah glanced back out the rear window, then through the windshield. Pointing over her shoulder, she asked, "Isn't town back the other way?"

"Yeah, it is... Crystal Creek doesn't have a medical clinic..." He paused then let out a loud huff. He pounded on the steering wheel with his open palm. Glaring at her, he blurted, "Let's cut the shit. You recognized me the second you saw me. I don't know how... but you recognized me. You were there this morning – at the old mining shack, weren't you?"

Sarah hesitated. Her ruse wasn't working. With every passing second, he became more panic-stricken. *He's losing it. I have to calm him down... find a way to buy some time.* She drew in a shallow breath and mumbled, "Yes, I was there."

"Aw, dammit," he whimpered. Drawing his pistol from its holster, he aimed it at her temple. The gun trembled in his hand while the jeep's engine revved faster and faster with his foot mashing the pedal to the floor.

"Calm down, deputy. Please... just take a minute to think about what you're doing." The calm and reassurance in her voice belied the terror chilling her to the bone. She glanced to his left hand gripping the steering wheel. Moonlight glinted off the gold wedding band on his ring finger. "You're married, Joe? It's Joe, right?"

"Shut up!" he whimpered.

"You want to see your wife again, don't you?" She glimpsed out the window. *We're moving too fast. If I try to jump, I'll never make it.* "Take me back to town. I won't say a word to anyone."

Chavez pulled the pistol from her temple and pressed its handgrip against the side of his head, clutching his hair with the tips of his fingers while they remained wrapped around the pistol's grip. Tears swam from the corners of his eyes. "I just need time... time to think about how to get out of this," he sobbed to himself in short breaths.

"All the cops back at the cottage know I'm with you. You can't hurt me without them knowing you were responsible." She thought for a moment. "There's ransom in the briefcase, isn't there?" She waited for him to respond, but he said nothing. "Do you really think you can just make me disappear and walk away with the money? Go back to your wife with millions in cash with no questions asked?"

"I said shut up!" he screamed. The veins in his forehead bulged out and threatened to burst at any moment. Glaring at her, he snapped, "Thompson set me up! This was supposed to be easy... and no one was supposed to get hurt." He rested his right hand in his lap, the pistol still in his grasp. "It wasn't supposed to go down like this," he whined.

Sarah shrank into her seat. The man was going over the edge. With every passing mile, rescue faded further behind them while the SUV raced onward down the deserted forest road. Once again, freedom eluded her.

CHAPTER 19

Ben sat in the driver's seat and inhaled a long drag from his cigarette. The smoke rolled off his tongue into a flawed halo after he exhaled, disintegrating while the warped ring expanded over the steering wheel then ricocheted off the windshield into a chaotic fog. Will Taylor's ranch was within sight through the trees – less than two hundred yards away. Below his secluded perch on the timbered hillside, Katy waited.

For years, he anticipated the moment when he would once again reunite with the beautiful young woman. His thoughts drifted back to the three weeks of their whirlwind romance in that dust bowl of town in Nebraska. She was much younger then. But, a day hadn't passed in the eight years since she wasn't in his sentiments. Amongst all the strain and tension while evading the lawmen hell-bent on his destruction, he obsessed about her with relentless devotion. The recollection of her was the only memory he cherished, for she was the only one who had ever understood him. The affection in her light blue eyes belonged only to him, of that he was sure. Corrupted by those who claimed to care about her, she turned on him, spurning his love and casting him out into the hostile world on his own without her by his side. He would change that. He would make her understand she was meant only for him. Sinking back into the driver's seat, he cocked his head back against the headrest. *I've waited a long time for this, Katy… a long, long time…*

He scanned out the windows at the darkened woodland then glanced at the cell phone's screen. The text from Chavez read:

Heading to the drop point after my team hooks up with Taylor. Leaving as soon as you send him the text with your instructions. Three marshals staying on watch at his place. I've order the remaining teams to hold in locations several miles away. Roadblocks on the state highway north and south of town. Eastern routes clear. Not sure how long I'll be the one calling the shots on this operation. HQ sending senior agent and additional teams after political rally in Helena tomorrow night. Given you as much time as I can. Don't forget my cut. Stop the damn email from being sent.

He scrolled to the smartphone's picture gallery. A satellite image of Will Taylor's property flashed onto the display. He zoomed in and studied the layout. Peering out the window, he got his bearings. *Yeah, this spot will do. Plenty of cover and this piece of shit is parked close enough once I grab the little bitch we can get out of here in a hurry.* Tugging at the door latch, he eased the car door open and hopped out. He leaned against the side of the muddied SUV and scrutinized the ranch compound just beyond the base of the slope below. *Lots of buildings... doesn't look like anything has changed since the satellite images were uploaded to the net. Gotta love MapNet for the pictures.*

He shuffled to the rear passenger door and lifted the handle, inching the door open to muffle the squeal from its unlubricated hinges. *Easy, now. Gotta be quiet.* Reaching to the back seat, he snatched the two five-gallon containers of gasoline and set them on the ground. He sniffed at the clean air and sneered. *Gonna be a great night for a bonfire. Nothing like a good fire to create a distraction.* He ducked back inside the passenger compartment and rummaged through the heap of gear piled high on the bench seat. The synthetic stock of the semi-auto rifle emerged from the layers of equipment as he shoved the jumble off to the side. He grabbed the rifle and looped the sling over his shoulder. *Hopefully, I won't need this... but... better safe than sorry.* With the .45 pistol stashed in his front waistband and the Glock 9mm at the small of his back, he was ready.

Scampering from tree to tree, he descended the eastern facing slope toward the compound. With deliberate steps, he toted a red fuel can in each hand, the volatile liquid sloshing back and forth inside the plastic containers while he hiked. *The damn moonlight is awfully bright... too bad those clouds didn't stick around. I need to keep to the shadows. I don't want any of those law dogs to catch sight of me before I get the jump on them.* He rambled down the decline, his breathing quickened while he stumbled over half-buried rocks jutting from the bedding of dry pine needles and broken twigs littered across the forest floor.

At the base of the hill, the tall pines yielded to dense, shoulder-high shrubs clustered in profuse bunches parallel to a broad, fenced-in pasture. Boring through the thin spindles of leaf-covered branches, he paused once he arrived at the hedgerow's edge. A thirty-foot-wide clearing separated the vegetation from the fence line, denying him any further concealment. He poked his head from the shrubs and assessed his options for a stealthy approach. Behind the barrier and across the paddock, the imposing barn obstructed his view of the compound hidden on the other side of the metal building. A herd of fourteen horses sauntered along the pipe railing far across the pasture, their bright coats glistening in the moonlight while they pranced about one another breaking the quietude with their occasional snorts and nickers. *Well, shit. I need to find a different way. If anyone has eyes this direction, I'll be spotted for sure if I try to cross that field – and I sure as hell don't want to deal with those old nags.*

He retreated into the hedge and veered north, relying on the wild shrubs to provide cover for his advance lateral to the open-air arena. A light breeze swept across the valley, overtaking the hush of night with the whooshing of pines and the rustling of leaves in the thicket while he pushed on. Boughs grazed his face and he cursed them in agitation while they clawed at his flesh with their dogged tendrils. After a few minutes, he arrived at the rear boundary of the compound and emerged from the foliage. He breathed a sigh of relief. The path was clear. A glade separated the buildings from the northern tree line, a trail well-worn with frequent travel etched into the earth. He proceeded unfettered to the corner of the barn, crouching while he hurried along. A wide gap, over one hundred feet in expanse, separated the large arena from the magnificent log home nestled at the heart of the complex. A series of small cabins and outbuildings dotted the space in between in a staggered row, offering an intermittent veil from sight.

He stashed the fuel tanks along the barn's aluminum wall, slipping them into the blended bed of sawdust and dirt amassed against the panel in miniature drifted dunes. He peeked around the corner. No more than twenty feet away, in the foreground of the illumination cast from a light affixed to the building's rafter, a figure loomed in the moonlight facing away, an eerie shadow stretching long and gaunt from the physique's feet across the shimmering loam.

The man shuffled his feet, kicking up stunted puffs of dust with each stomp. "Damn it's cold out," he muttered to himself.

Well, look at that – one of Chavez's buddies… out here all by his lonesome. You picked the wrong place for a midnight stroll, sucker. Retreating out of view, Ben unslung the rifle from his shoulder. Grasping the handguard with his left hand, he clutched the stock in his right and glimpsed around the corner again before rounding it. His boot steps fell silently upon the ground with his deliberate pace. Slinking, slow and determined, he tiptoed closer. His prey stood within range. He poised to his full height then raised the rifle over his head, its barrel gliding above his shoulder. With a swift and forceful stroke, he thrust the butt of the rifle forward, striking the base of the man's skull with the metal butt plate on the stock. The man heaved a muffled groan and toppled to the ground face first.

Ben knelt and rolled the motionless man onto his back. *Looks like you're out of the game for good. You won't need this anymore.* Snatching the marshal's sidearm from its holster, he dropped the magazine from the pistol's grip then hurled the gun toward the tree line at the mouth of the alley, where the pistol skipped into the low-lying brush. He poked his hand inside the open flap of the marshal's jacket and yanked the two-way radio from the dead man's belt. After stuffing the receiver in his jacket pocket, he stood and slipped his rifle's black nylon sling back over his shoulder. He grabbed the dead marshal's ankles and dragged the body to the end of the alley, safely out of sight from the main compound and obscured by a small equipment shed separated from the barn by a narrow tract. Peeping to his left around the corner of the lean-to, he studied the log home across the expanse. Light poured from the windows on its western side. The figure of a woman passed behind the four-paned glass at the back of the lodge. His jaw went slack. There she was – the prize he sought. Taking a step forward, he froze in his tracks. Two men strolled into view at the front of the home, side-by-side. *Come on… get your head out of your ass… you still have some work to do first.*

He slithered back into the shadows, keeping his eyes locked on the two marshals while they chatted ninety feet away. He glanced at the crumpled body lying beside the shed and smirked. Creeping to the rear of the small structure, he eased his way along its back wall to the far corner then yanked the two-way radio from his jacket pocket. With a quick adjustment of the volume knob, he clicked the radio's transmit button several times in rapid succession. A voice crackled in muted response.

"Lutz, I didn't read you. Say again?" The radio fell silent. Ten seconds passed. Then, another call sputtered from the radio, "Lutz, copy?"

Ben poked around the corner. The two marshals appeared on edge, their heads swiveling from side-to-side while they moved about in a vigilant dance.

"Go find him. I'll keep watch here," the first man barked to the second before he disappeared from view.

Ben focused on the second marshal as the lawman drew a pistol from his waist and advanced toward the barn's closed bay door. Ben slipped the rifle from his shoulder and leaned it against the weathered panel forming the shed's rear wall. He slinked toward the structure's corner closest to the barn and waited. The intensity of rapid footsteps increased while the marshal advanced along the barn and up the narrow alley. He drew closer. Ben plucked the folding knife from his front pocket and flipped open the blade.

"Shit! Lutz!" the marshal cried out, skidding to a halt next to the shed.

Ben peeked around the corner. While the marshal leaned down to check on his fallen colleague, Ben wheeled from the rear of the building and leaped from the shadows. He gritted his teeth and grabbed the marshal from behind, forcing him to his feet while he cupped the man's mouth with his left hand. He plunged the serrated five-inch blade below the hem of the marshal's jacket and underlying Kevlar vest, shanking it deep into the victim's kidney. The deputy struggled, groaning into Ben's hand with muffled shouts of agony. Ben twisted the blade and wrested it from the marshal's flesh then thrust it again and again with savage determination until the man's flailing ceased. He released his hold, and the listless man crumpled to the ground, his lifeblood spewing upon the gravel in a thick pool of crimson. Ben snickered and wiped the gore from his bloodstained hand and knife across the man's jacket. *Two down, one more to go.* Folding the blade, he tucked the knife back into the front pocket of his blood-splattered jeans.

He darted behind the shed and snagged the rifle from the back wall. Forging ahead, he plodded behind the row of buildings leading to the main house. Once he reached the far wall of the final cabin, he paused. The magnificent lodge stood just fifty feet away around the corner to his right. He clutched the rifle in both hands. Retracting the bolt's charging handle, he glimpsed into the long gun's chamber for one final check. *Locked and loaded.* He eased the carrier forward and rechambered the cartridge. Taking a step forward, he clung to the shadows and scanned for the third marshal. The man was nowhere in sight. *The other cop must still be out front.*

He dashed to the rear of the southward facing home. Barely visible in the dim light, the building's main electrical breaker box hung at the center of the log wall. He stepped closer and analyzed the system, his eyes straining in the shade of the roof's overhang. Below the breaker load center, a section of conduit ascended from the ground and up the exterior wall to the base of a small plastic receptacle alongside the central compartment. *That's got to be the phone line. They won't need it.* Switching the rifle to his left hand, he snatched the knife from his pocket and whipped open the blade. After fumbling to open the relay box, he slashed the wires inside. *Now I don't need to worry about you using a landline to call for help.* Their only hope for contacting anyone would be by way of cell phone or two-way radio. But, cell coverage at the location was sketchy at best, confirmed when he tested the signal before leaving the hillside. Shifting his attention to the breaker box, he lifted the cover. At the base of the console, four double breaker switches lay situated side-by-side. He flipped the switches one at a time, pitching the home into darkness.

Better move fast. Now they know something's up. He sprinted around the corner and proceeded along the eastern side of the home, crouching beneath the base of the windows while he skittered past them. Approaching the front of the lodge, he paused and listened. Muffled voices chattered back and forth inside. Advancing to the front wall, he hunched and peered through the log rails bordering the porch. In the courtyard, the third marshal stood at a white, four-door sedan, parked in the center of the drive facing the home's entrance, its passenger-side door open.

Clutching a radio in his hand, the marshal hollered into the device's microphone. "Lutz, Bickley, I need a status report *now*! Over." He paused. Trepidation quivered in his tone when he called out again, "Bickley! Report!"

He's distracted. It's now or never. Ben raised the rifle to his shoulder and rotated the safety with his thumb while he clutched the weapon's pistol grip in his right hand. Using the porch rail to steady his aim, he squeezed the trigger. The loud report echoed across the compound and reverberated from the barn's corrugated metal wall like a clap of thunder. The sedan's passenger window shattered as the high-velocity round pierced the glass and tore into the marshal, penetrating his bullet-resistant vest. Ben fired again and again, the empty shell casings sailing into the air and landing on the gravel with hollow metallic chinks. The marshal groaned and slumped out of view halfway into the vehicle, his motionless legs visible beneath the open door. *Too bad those vests don't stop a .223 round...*

Ben grinned with satisfaction. Lowering the rifle from his shoulder, he rounded the porch and stepped into the courtyard to survey his handiwork. Holding the rifle's handguard in his right hand with its barrel pointed straight up and its butt plate resting on his hip, he cackled with glee. His celebration was short-lived. The front door of the lodge burst open. Will Taylor stood in the shadows, wielding his reliable bolt action rifle. The old man fired without hesitation. The .300 Winchester Magnum roared and spouted a foot-long flame from its muzzle as the bullet exploded from the bore. The projectile impacted against the aluminum receiver of the rifle in Ben's hand, sending the long gun flying from his grip and skittering onto the drive ten feet away, demolished and inoperable. Ben spun to the ground reeling from the concussion, landing hard against the gravel.

Rolling to his side, he drew the .45 pistol from his waistband and sat up. Without aiming, he pointed the gun toward the obscure figure positioned in the doorway and fired four rapid shots. "You sonofabitch! I'll kill you!" he screamed with froths of spittle sputtering from his lips. He glanced at the mangled remains of the rifle. It lay in the gravel, wrecked and useless. He vaulted to his feet while the figure in the doorway retreated into the home and slammed the door. A loud click signaled the door was locked. *That asshole is probably waiting on the other side just hoping I try to open the door so he can blow me away.*

Clutching the .45 tight in his grip, he bolted from the ground and darted up the steps onto the porch. Without faltering, he leaped onto the pine bench positioned beside the large picture window. His left boot stomped hard on the bench's seat as he propelled himself into the window pane with a forceful push-off. Smashing through the glass with a thunderous crash, he slammed hard on the living room floor. The bright halogen lights scattered across the compound filtered in through the home's windows, affording hampered visibility. He sprang from the debris of glass shards and toward the silhouette huddled at the entrance to a hallway leading from the living room.

In the dim light, terror overtook the old man's face, and bewilderment glinted in his eyes — Ben dove on Will, knocking the rifle from his quaking hands. The old man tumbled to his back, hitting his head against the hardwood floor. Will lay unconscious in a crumpled heap.

Ben snatched the rifle from the wooden planks and raised it high in the air. As he thrust the rifle's butt toward Will's head, a figure hurtled from the darkened hallway. A sharp pain shot through Ben's head as an object whacked his temple causing him to drop the rifle. He fell to the floor in agony.

Katy emerged from the shadows, the antique lamp from Mark's room clinched tight in her hands. She knelt by Will's side and lifted his head from the floor. "William! William, wake up!" she shrieked.

Ben writhed on the floor and wiped away a trickle of blood seeping from a two-inch long gash above his right eye. Stumbling to his knees, he blinked several times then squinted. "Well, well, well… look who showed up to the party." He stood and shook his head. A smug smile blazed on his face. "You and I need to have a long talk about old times."

Katy darted to her feet and pushed past him. Reaching the door, she fumbled with the brass deadbolt until it disengaged. Glancing over her shoulder as Ben staggered toward her, she flung the door open. "You stay away from me, Ben," she wailed. She bolted out the front door and flew off the porch, whipping an immediate right toward the barn once she cleared the entryway.

"Ah… it seems like old times," he muttered. Stepping back to the debris-littered about the front living room, he snatched his .45 from the jumble of broken glass and tucked it in his waistband. He dabbed at the wound on his forehead while he walked out the door and climbed down the porch steps. Taking a deep breath, he scanned the deserted compound. *Shit. I really didn't want to have to go looking for her.* He focused on the barn. A standard sized door next to the large bay door located at the building's center appeared to be ajar. *Well, crap. The place is huge. I'm sure she's got plenty of places to hide in there. Maybe she just needs a little bit of motivation to be more cooperative.* He strolled toward the massive building and paused at the bay door. "You know, you don't have to make things so difficult," he shouted. "This is no way to be treating the number one man in your life." He continued, parallel to the building and up the narrow alley to the barn's north end. Rounding the corner, he snatched the two fuel containers from the muck of sawdust then whirled around and retraced his steps. Once he arrived back in front of the bay door, he continued his diatribe while he ambled back to the lodge. Raising his voice even more as he left the barn behind him; he called out, "It's pretty damn cold out. You should be ashamed for subjecting me to this kind of weather." He laughed. "There's nothing like a big fire to warm things up…"

He paused at the corner of the main house. Spinning the caps off the plastic fuel jugs one at a time, he snatched the first and walked the perimeter of the grand home, splashing the combustible liquid along the sides and high up the log walls. Three-quarters of the way around the building, the fuel in the first container ran out. Tossing the empty can away; he sauntered back for the other filled container. Grabbing its handle, he hesitated and yelled out one final warning toward the barn. "Katherine, come out now, or I'm torching this place." He stared at the barn.

No response. *All right have it your way. You could use a little reminder of what happens when you're disobedient...* He traipsed around the front of the lodge, sloshing the fuel around the remainder of the perimeter. He shook the jug. *Still about a quarter left. That should do fine.* Climbing the porch steps, he poured a trail to just inside the open front door where he laid the container on its side, allowing the remaining gasoline to chug out into a large puddle. Before he spun away, he eyed the floor. The dazed old man floundered on the hardwood in the hallway, attempting to regain his footing. "I bet you wish right now you'd taken a little more time to aim," Ben sneered while he strolled out the front door and halted at the end of the gas trail. Plucking a cigarette from his jacket's breast pocket, he lit the smoke and inhaled. "Grandpa's about to get barbequed, Katherine..." he shouted.

Katy flung open the barn door and raced across the courtyard toward him. "Ben! Noooooo!" she screamed, tripping and landing on all fours.

Ben smirked and tossed the cigarette to the spilled fuel at his feet. A multicolored flame exploded across the puddle's surface and raced into the home. Flames snaked around the building's perimeter, encircling it with fire. "Oops."

Struggling to her feet, Katy howled as tears cascaded down her cheeks. "*William...*"

Ben faced the barn and marched toward her, flames lashing out high above the lodge's roofline behind him. He clenched his jaw. The anger inside him seethed hotter than the fire consuming the home. *You should have come with me eight years ago…You shouldn't have left me…*

Katy stared at the burning lodge. Covering her mouth while she choked back sobs, she sprinted back into the barn, slamming the door shut behind her.

Ben restrained himself no longer. He broke out in a full run, dashing toward the barn door. Reaching to the doorknob, he tried to rotate it – locked. His blood boiled. Tugging the pistol from his belt, he aimed at the handle and fired a single round. The stainless steel fixture shattered from the bullet's impact. Yanking the door open, he stood in the entryway and glared into the building. *The little bitch is gonna pay for this…*

CHAPTER 20

The white truck raced down the county back road, rattling with each bump jutting from the beaten track. Mark held his cell phone in one hand while he steered with the other. *Come on… give me a signal.* His father's property lay only another mile ahead, and there was no time to waste. Glancing at the cell phone's display, finally, a second bar materialized – enough of a signal to initiate a call. He tapped the virtual call button and held the phone to his ear. After a single ringtone, a robotic message resounded through the speaker:

"We're sorry, the number you dialed is no longer in service or is out of order. If you feel you have received this message in error, please hang up and try your call again."

Mark tossed the phone on the cloth seat. "Dammit!" He pushed his foot to the accelerator, coaxing the bulky four-by-four to surge even faster. Entering a sharp turn, the truck slid sideways, threatening to send it into a wild spin. He eased off the gas and spun the steering wheel in the opposite direction, regaining control of the vehicle. Rounding the last corner before leaving the thicket of pines crowding the road, he leaned forward and peered out the windshield. An ominous orange glow hovered over the treetops in the direction of the ranch. *What the...*

The compound came into view as the truck emerged from the thicket. He gasped. Flames engulfed the main lodge in twisting spires of fire, dancing angrily while they devoured the once magnificent log structure with their fury. He gunned the accelerator, pushing the truck to its limits while the engine groaned under the strain. The vehicle charged through the open gate at the compound's entrance, skidding to a stop in the center of the courtyard. He wrenched the gear shift into park and flung the truck's door open. Leaping onto to the gravel drive, he dashed toward the lodge. Searing heat pummeled him like an invisible wall, singeing the tips of his hair and beard, halting his advance. Acrid smoke burned his nostrils and filled his lungs with each stinging breath. The gritty taste of charcoal saturated his mouth. Above the roar of the flames and the crackles and pops, while the building surrendered to the frenzied inferno, a muffled groan called out from his right. He glanced in the direction of the sound. Crawling away from the white sedan parked twenty feet away, the injured marshal sprawled on gravel. He darted to the man's side and knelt, gently placing a hand on his shoulder. "Gibbons!" Easing the marshal onto his back, he opened the flaps of the gravely injured lawman's jacket. His inner vest revealed three small punctures in the black material, and blood streamed from beneath its hem.

Gibbons blinked several times and gawked at him with a blank stare, the deputy marshal's eyes glazed and dull. Blood seeped from the corners of his mouth in sickly trails of froth. "Thompson…" he mumbled.

Mark tore off his denim jacket then folded it into a disheveled square. Slipping it under the deputy's head, he replied, "Shh… don't talk. Help will be here soon. Just hang in there." He zipped up the injured man's jacket. "We've got to keep you warm. You're in shock."

Reaching to Mark's shoulder with a bloodied hand, Gibbons groped at the plaid fabric of Mark's shirt. He strained to lift himself but flopped back to the ground in defeat, too weak to move. He hacked, spewing droplets of blood with his exhale. "Old man… still inside…" He gagged again then struggled to continue, "Girl… barn… Thompson…" He wheezed and closed his eyes.

Mark glared in horror at Gibbons' ashen face. He glanced at the log home, a lump crawling into his throat and dread wracking his gut. *No, it can't be! Dad…* The doomed structure withered before his eyes in the conflagration and he was powerless to stem the blaze's cruel intentions. He forced thoughts of his father from his mind. There were others in danger – others he could still save. He scampered to the marshal's sedan. Stooping inside through the open passenger door, he seized the mic from the two-way radio mounted below the dashboard. In desperation, he fumbled with the knobs on the radio's console then held the handset to his lips. "Hello? Hello? Can anyone hear me?" He released the microphone's transmit button and waited. Static crackled back through the speaker. Raking his fingers through his hair, he glowered at the hellish spectacle before him. He tried again. "This is Mark Taylor. There's an officer down at my father's place. Send the fire department and ambulance... *now!* We need help here!" he hollered into the microphone.

Static crackled again from the radio. After a delay, a familiar voice answered his frantic plea. "Taylor? This is Dawes. We're on our way. Just hang tight until we get there."

Nearly inaudible, a shrill scream rang out across the compound, muted by the fire's clamor. Mark glanced at the barn. *Katy!* Pressing the transmit button again, he barked, "Sheriff, I don't have time to talk. Thompson is *here – now.* Just send help *ASAP!*" He dropped the handset to the seat and ducked out of the car. He sprinted across the courtyard as fast as his legs would carry him, skidding to a halt once he came to the unlatched barn door.

Pushing the door open, he resisted the urge to barrel through it, leaping headlong into the fray. *Remember who you're dealing with. Be smart. Katy is depending on you...* He peeked inside, wary of squandering the element of surprise – his sole ally. The immediate path appeared clear. Stepping through the doorway, he scanned the long alley separating the stalls along the length of the eastern wall from the arena at the building's heart. Horses snorted and whinnied, pawing at the sawdust blanketing their enclosures while they fussed in dismay at the commotion commencing from the center of the rink.

Mark crouched, slinking low along the stables, close to the pipe rails forming their barrier. When he reached the fifth stall, he paused. The white colt pranced from side-to-side within the enclosure in distress, rearing up and kicking his front hooves in the air, sending clods of dirt melded with sawdust flying across the pen. The young horse bounded to the stockade's gate and pressed his front haunches against it, causing the latch to groan under his weight. Mark reached up and stroked the colt's muzzle. "It's okay, Shiloh. Easy, boy," Mark whispered while he locked eyes with the horse. Fury blazed in Shiloh's crystal-blue eyes, and his nostrils flared with each snort he huffed.

Mark peered across the passage and through the railing forming the perimeter of the arena. Katy cowered at the rink's center on her knees with her hands pressed to her face while Ben circled her with a pistol in his grasp like a predator sizing up its prey. Glancing to his left, the entrance gate to the vast enclosure hung open. He scurried to the opening and stepped from cover and into plain sight. He reached under his shirt to the small of his back for the pistol. A chill shot up his spine. The gun wasn't there. *I left the gun under the front seat of the truck!* In all the harried confusion, he forgot to retrieve it. He froze, standing just inside the enclosure, no more than fifty feet from his nemesis.

Ben hovered over Katy. Shuffling to a stop, he stood behind her and grabbed her by the hair, clutching her long locks in his angry grip. He dropped to his knees and snarled, "Why can't you see how much I love you?"

Mark's cheeks burned. The rage inside him smoldered, ready to explode. *Enough of this shit!* Marching toward Ben, he clenched his teeth and balled his hands into tight fists; his trimmed fingernails wedged into the flesh of his palms.

"Get your stinking hands off her, you sick sonofabitch!" he growled.

Leaping to his feet, Ben shoved Katy to the turf and took a menacing stance. He cocked his head and glared at Mark, seemingly incensed by the intrusion. "Well... if it isn't the famous Mark Taylor..."

Mark flashed a look at Katy. "Are you all right?" She nodded and wiped the tears from her eyes.

Ben's lip curled up and he bared his teeth. "You've got a lot of balls coming here – especially considering I was nice enough to leave my sister still breathing."

"Your *sister*? What the hell are you talking about?" Mark asked in disbelief, halting just fifteen feet away from the lunatic.

Ben let out a whoop and bent down, slapping his hands against his knees, the pistol still clutched in his right hand. "Why the hell doesn't anybody know?" he muttered while shaking his head. He snickered then exhaled with a loud heave. He stood erect, his eyes narrowing while he glowered at Mark. "You heard it right. Sarah is my sister... long-lost sister to be exact. That's how this all came about – I was passing by your place in Seattle and figured I'd stop by and catch up on old times with her." A smug expression lit up his face. "Of course... I planned on hitting her up for some cash in the process. I wasn't expecting she would turn into a winning lottery ticket." He kicked at the ground in Katy's direction, showering her with a hail of sawdust as his boot tip shoveled into the bedding layered across the arena's floor and flung the matter into the air. "And to find out Katherine was here at your old man's place the whole time…" Again, he shook his head and grinned. "Ah… the odds… it was like a gift."

Mark gulped. It didn't matter. Regardless as to how or why, Thompson's evil path crossed theirs. "I don't care who you are. You got your money. You should have left us alone." Indignation overtook his senses. Notions of vengeance seethed within his mind. He took a step toward Ben, aching to wrap his hands around the scumbag's neck, throttling the life out of the bastard while he squeezed with every last bit of his strength.

Aiming his pistol at Mark's face, Ben's eyes narrowed, his index finger resting on the pistol's trigger. "You'll never make it." Slowly, he squeezed. Just as he fired the shot, and flame erupted from the pistol's muzzle, Katy lunged at Ben, wrapping her arms around his legs and toppling him to the ground.

Mark ignored the searing pain as the bullet strayed right; grazing his left temple with Ben's faltered aim. Pouncing, Mark scrambled on top of his stunned adversary and pressed his knee into Ben's right wrist while he tore the pistol from Ben's grasp. With a flailing left hook, Ben countered, his fist clobbering Mark's right cheek and sending the pistol sailing from his hand into the sawdust bedding several feet away. Blood gushed from Mark's split lip while he adjusted his weight on Ben and pinned him to the ground with a barrage of punches, driving his knuckles into Ben's jaws with each frenzied blow. "You piece of shit! I'm going to kill you!" Mark roared. Belting Ben again and again, fury swelled inside Mark, threatening to suffocate him in anger. "For what you did to my family…" he puffed breathlessly.

Ben raised his arms, shielding himself from Mark's relentless onslaught. Seizing Mark's fist before he could land another blow, Ben twisted from beneath his attacker. He planted his left hand squarely into Mark's chest and shoved him to the dirt. Mark reeled, lunging on his stomach toward the half-buried pistol ten feet away. Groping through the mire, his fingers desperately probed for the handgun as Ben yanked the folding knife from his pocket and flipped open the blade. Scuttling across the ground on his hands and knees, Ben grunted and slashed at him, slicing across the back of Mark's right leg. Mark groaned as the serrated edge shredded his faded blue jeans and gashed into his calf, the burn of the blade sending agony rippling up his limb. Ben clambered to his feet for another attack. Mark's fingers clasped the .45 just as Ben hunched over, poised to leap for a killing blow. Clutching the pistol, Mark rolled to his back and fired a single shot, the gun's report booming through the metal building and reverberating from wall to wall. The bullet struck Ben in the left shoulder with a dull thud, sending a puff of crimson mist spattering into the air while his eyes widened and he dropped to his knees.

Mark scrambled to his feet and leveled the pistol at Ben's forehead. Limping toward the wounded foe, he turned his head slightly away without breaking focus and spit a froth of blood on the muddled ground. He halted three feet away from Ben, the pistol shaking in his trembling hand. "Look at me!" he growled.

Wavering on his knees, Ben glimpsed at the hole in his

shoulder, blood spurting from the wound in a rhythmic pulse while his drab-green jacket saturated with ruddy fluid. "Lucky shot, asshole," Ben grumbled, shifting his eyes to Mark.

Mark clenched the pistol's grip tight and his fingers tingled with numbness. His index finger massaged the trigger. Desire tugged at his core. He wanted to pull the trigger. A tear streamed down his bruised cheek. *This bastard killed dad. He deserves to die. Sarah... Katy... for what he's done to all of us...* While the tumult swelled in his mind, the old man's words echoed louder and louder in his thoughts, "*Taking another man's life is something that'll change you forever. You're stealing something away you can never give back – no matter how much you might want to after the moment has passed.*" He glared at Ben, memorizing his hateful features while the gravely injured man's complexion grayed with each passing second. "Argh!" Mark bellowed as he hurled the pistol over Ben's head, far across the arena. He took a deep breath and glanced back at Ben. "You're going to fry in the electric chair... if you don't bleed to death first."

Ben snickered. A stream of blood trickled from his lips. "Pussy."

Mark thrust his foot against Ben's wound, pushing him to his back against the arena's floor. He eyeballed the assassin. Ben's eyes rolled up as he seemingly slipped deeper into death's clutches. Mark spun around and staggered to Katy. Kneeling by her side, he brushed the tangled hair from her eyes and gaped at her bruised face. "Are you sure you're okay?" he asked.

Katy nodded but burst into tears. Burying her face in her hands, she wailed, "Mark... your dad..."

Mark choked on his sorrow, for he hadn't allowed himself the freedom to lament. He embraced Katy, holding her close. "I know, Katy."

"It all happened so fast. I tried to draw Ben away, but he went back... set the fire..." She gasped for breath through her sobs. "Oh, God..."

Mark squeezed her tighter. "It's not your fault. It's not your fault."

Ben writhed in the dirt. Easing his hand beneath him, he grasped the 9mm Glock from his back waistband. He rolled to his side and floundered to his knees. His evil cackle seized Mark and Katy's attention. Leveling the pistol, he grunted in a raspy breath, "My turn." As he aimed at Katy's head and fingered the trigger, thundering hooves pounded through the open arena gate and across the paddock from behind him. Startled, he glanced over his shoulder. The white colt reared up. Shaking his head with flattened ears, the horse flared his nostrils while his eyes smoldered with venom. Ben recoiled in desperation, but it was too late. Shiloh's hooves fell upon him with fury, pawing and stomping until Ben's frantic shrieks ceased and his mangled body lay in a crumpled, blood-soaked heap.

While the dust settled, the white colt trotted over to Mark and Katy. Nuzzling them both, he nickered, the furor in his eyes softening to adoration. Mark stood and helped Katy to her feet. He stroked the colt's neck. "Good boy, Shiloh. Good boy."

Katy wrapped her arms around the colt's neck. Resting

her cheek against his haunch, she whispered, "Thank you, little man."

Gazing at Ben's lifeless body, Mark breathed a sigh of relief. He eyed Katy. "Come on; let's get you out of here."

Katy nodded. With her head hung low, she shuffled between Shiloh and Mark while they headed toward the open arena gate. Clutching Mark's sleeve, she asked, "Sarah?"

Mark placed his hand on her shoulder while they walked. "She's okay, Katy. She's with the marshals."

They made their way back to the colt's stall where the enclosure's gate lay on the ground, warped and torn from its hinges. Katy brushed back her hair then helped Mark lift the gate. After leaning the twisted metal against the corral's railing, Katy pointed to an empty stall further down the alley. "Let's put him in there for now." She patted the colt's rump, urging him forward. "Come, little man."

Mark stepped to the empty stall and unlatched the gate, swinging it open so Shiloh could enter. He moved aside while the colt plodded into the new enclosure then closed the gate after the horse trotted through. The colt whirled around and placed his mouth to Mark's hair, offering a playful smooch while he lipped the black tufts. Mark chuckled. "I love you too, boy." From outside, the wailing of multiple sirens rang out, increasing in amplitude as they drew closer. "Dawes and his men are here."

Katy plucked at bits of sawdust clinging to the chestnut-colored curls hanging across her brow, her gaze lost and unfocused. "We should go meet them," she mumbled.

Moving to her, Mark touched her shoulder and gave

it a light squeeze. "Hey, it's over now. You're safe." He studied her. The ordeal obviously traumatized her. *She looks like she might be going into shock.* "Let's take you outside for some fresh air."

She nodded. "Yes, fresh air."

The options weren't good. Outside, Katy would see the still-raging inferno. But, there was no other choice. Placing his arm around Katy's shoulder, Mark led her to the exit. When they stepped through the door, he surveyed the courtyard. Three Sheriff's Department cruisers sat parked in the compound, angled alongside one another in a haphazard array. A helicopter hovered overhead. It circled twice before descending to a clearing at the courtyard's entrance. Sheriff Dawes hopped out from the copter's front passenger seat, securing his baseball cap with one hand and crouching until he cleared the perimeter of the aircraft's blades. Hustling toward Mark and Katy, he met them at the front of the compound. A deputy stood at his open cruiser's door speaking into his handset while two others knelt by the injured marshal, tending to his wounds.

The helicopter's blades slowed, whirring to a sluggish rotation. Only the roaring flames engulfing the lodge broke the night's stillness. A halo of red and blue beams strobed from the cruisers' light bars and cut through the cloak of thick smoke as if the entire complex was a haunting merry-go-round. Mark clutched Katy tight, his arm around her shoulder. *This is the last thing she needs to see right now.*

Dawes looked them over. Focusing on Mark, he asked, "Thompson?"

"He's in the barn... what's left of him," Mark replied.

The sheriff nodded. Glancing from side-to-side, he scanned the compound. "Where's Will?"

Mark sniffed and pressed his eyes shut for a moment. Glancing over his shoulder at the blaze behind him, he stared at the hateful flames then eyed Dawes. With a loud sigh, he uttered, "He didn't make it."

Dawes grabbed the ball cap from his head and slapped it hard against his thigh, rasping his hair with his other hand. He huffed and glanced away. A muscle in his jaw twitched. Peering back at Mark, he said, "I'm truly sorry to hear that. He was a good friend." The shrill of sirens grew louder and louder from the direction of the road. The sheriff took a deep breath. "Sounds like the fire tanker and ambulance are here." He walked over to Katy. "Hang on, Katy, we'll get you looked at right away." Snagging the two-way radio from his leather duty belt, he held it to his mouth. "Dispatch, this is Dawes. Get an additional team of paramedics in their bird and over here to the Taylor property pronto." Eyeballing the blood pooling around Mark's right boot then the gash on his temple, he added, "We've got multiple injured victims on scene."

"Understood, sheriff. Dispatching Life Flight," a voice crackled over the handset.

Dawes gestured for one of the deputies. The female officer scurried over. While she approached, the sheriff called out, "Get Ms. Olsen in your patrol car and out of this chill."

The deputy nodded. Placing her hand on Katy's shoulder, she said, "This way, miss."

Mark flashed a look at Katy. She trudged to the front

passenger side of the cruiser and slid onto the seat. "She's pretty shaken."

Dawes stroked his mustache and frowned. "I'm afraid I've got some more bad news, Mark."

Mark scowled. "What is it?"

Dawes folded his arms and bit his upper lip. "We checked into the anonymous caller who tipped us off about the place where Chavez and Hensley were ambushed this morning." He heaved a sigh then continued. "When we traced the call, it came in from a pay phone in front of the Mini-Mart in Crystal Creek."

"And?"

"Seems the caller didn't count on the business having as many surveillance cameras as they do. When my deputies reviewed the video recording, we recognized him right away. Mark, it was Joe Chavez."

Mark cocked his head. His mouth hung open while he attempted to put together what the sheriff insinuated. Staring at Dawes, he asked, "Why the hell would Chavez call in a tip on his own investigation? That makes no sense..." Once he spoke the last word, it dawned on him. "You mean... Chavez was helping Thompson?"

Dawes shuffled his feet. "I can't say for sure – yet. Let's just say the marshal has a lot of explaining to do."

A shudder shook Mark to the bone. "I left Sarah with him..."

"Yes. I radioed the two deputies at the vacant cottage where you found her. Chavez left the scene with your wife – and the briefcase full of cash – shortly after you headed here. He said he was transporting her to the medical facility on Highway 238." After a brief pause, he added, "Mark… they never showed up… and Chavez isn't responding to radio calls."

There was a weak cell signal at the vacation house… and Chavez had Sarah's phone! Mark eyeballed Dawes. "Hang on, sheriff… I have an idea." He sprinted to his father's truck and reached inside, snatching his cell phone from the seat. Glancing at the display, it revealed a signal. He scrolled to the virtual keyboard and entered Dan's speed dial code. He held the phone to his ear.

After two rings, Dan answered. "Mark, give me good news!"

"Dan, I don't have time to chat. Have there been any recent transmissions from Sarah's phone?"

"Yeah, one just came over right before you called. I called you when the first notification came in, but you didn't answer. There have been a total of two over the past half hour. They've both been from the same location," Dan replied.

"I didn't have my phone with me. The signal here is pretty spotty." The call dropped. "Dammit!" Mark groaned. He redialed.

Dan answered again. "Lost you."

Mark rubbed the back of his neck. "Whoever has the phone isn't moving." He took a deep breath. "Text me the GPS coordinates – now – before I lose my signal again."

"Sending them. Why, what's going on?"

"I'll fill you in later. Can you run those coordinates on the net and tell me whereabouts it is."

"One second… okay… it's a spot on Talbot Road. Looks

like the road travels at least another twelve miles before it ends at an intersection."

Mark thought for a second. *Twelve miles from the intersection with the county road? She must have been sitting on the edge of coverage the entire time.* "I've got to go. I'll fill you in when I get the chance." Without waiting for Dan's response, he ended the call. Scrolling to Dan's text, he checked the coordinates. He hurried toward the sheriff, ignoring the throbbing pain in his calf.

Dawes glared at him with a perplexed expression. "What exactly is going on?"

Mark glanced at his phone then at the sheriff. "Fire up the chopper and get us over to this location right now." He handed the cell phone to Dawes.

"I don't understand. Why here?" Dawes replied while glimpsing at the device's screen.

"Get us in the air. I'll explain on the way," Mark huffed.

CHAPTER 21

The chopper buzzed one hundred feet above the narrow two-lane road, its spotlight lighting up the bleached asphalt in a lucent orb while the aircraft zipped east along Talbot Road. Mark fidgeted in the second-row seat, readjusting his harness. Peering out the side window, intermittent lights in the distance beamed from homes scattered about the darkened landscape. The seconds crawled by, and with every chuff of the aircraft's blades, the restlessness within him deepened.

Just when the tension coursing through Mark's veins seemed ready to cause them to burst, Dawes pointed out the windshield. "That! Down there!" his voice called out through the headset over the buzz of the whirring helicopter blades.

Mark unclipped his safety harness and wedged himself in the gap between the pilot's and the sheriff's seats. He squinted out the canopy. A figure appeared in the middle of the road bathed in the searchlight's beam. "It's Sarah!

Put us down!"

The pilot nodded in Dawes' direction then banked the chopper hard-right. "There's a clearing there. It'll do."

Swooping into the meadow, the pilot tapered back the throttle and eased the helicopter onto the grassland. Before the aircraft's skids touched down and compressed the tall grass to the earth, Mark flung open his door. Hopping into the knee-high vegetation, he didn't wait for Dawes and sprinted across the field toward the road. The fifty yards seemed like miles, his breath clouding before him in a long mist while he ran. He broke through a small growth of fledgling pines separating the glade from the roadway. On the other side, Sarah shivered on the blacktop. Embracing her as she collapsed into his arms, he panted, "Are you all right?"

She trembled in his clutch but nodded. "Yes, I'm fine. Thank God, you're okay."

Glancing down the road, Mark asked, "Where's Chavez?"

"He took off. He snapped… I convinced him I would only slow him down. I thought he was going to kill me… but… he let me go."

Mark hoisted her up, cradling her in his arms to shield her bare feet from the frigid asphalt. As he whirled back in the direction of the helicopter, Dawes emerged from the brush. "She's okay!"

The sheriff straightened his ball cap. "And the marshal?"

"He bolted," Mark replied.

Dawes flashed a look down the moonlit road then back at Mark. "He won't get far. I dispatched units to set up a roadblock at the junction. There are only two ways he can go if he beats us there – and we've got them both covered." Patting Mark on the back, he added, "Let's get this lady to the bird where she can warm up. We'll head back to the ranch and get the paramedics to look her over." He pushed the boughs of the trees aside and held them, forging a path for Mark and Sarah to pass unhindered.

Sarah snuggled against Mark's chest, her hands laced behind his neck while he carried her. Searching his face, she focused on the gash at his temple. "What happened? Are your dad and Katy safe?"

Mark pressed on, pushing through the last few trees before entering the clearing. He hesitated then swallowed. "Katy is safe."

"And Will?"

Coming to an abrupt halt, Mark puffed a deep breath then shook his head. He tried to speak, but the words refused to leave his tongue.

"Oh, no… please, Mark… tell me he's okay," she pleaded.

Mark cleared his throat. It wasn't the time to talk about the horrors he left back at the ranch. Sarah clung safely in his arms. Basking in the moment's fleeting sliver of triumph served as a good diversion from thinking about his dear father's fate. But soon, she would see the nightmare's aftermath with her own eyes. "I didn't get there in time," he muttered. Sarah cuddled even closer to him, her sobs muffled by the squeal of his rubber-soled boots slipping across the blades of dew-covered grass.

Stepping to the open hatchway, Mark lifted Sarah to an empty seat in the helicopter's cabin. Dawes leaned in from the opposing door and supervised while Mark helped her get settled. The sheriff reached below the seat and snatched a headset from the storage compartment. Handing it to Sarah, he shouted over the whirring blades, "It gets pretty loud in here. Put these on to muffle the noise." Sarah took the headset and brushed her hair behind her ears before positioning the device on her head.

Mark buckled her harness. "Is that too tight?" He asked.

She shook her head and mouthed, "No."

Mark stepped back and secured the hatch. Darting around the front of the helicopter, he clambered into his seat then closed the cabin door while Dawes climbed into the front and reclaimed the co-pilot's chair.

The sheriff glanced over his shoulder, giving Mark and Sarah the once-over. He flipped the headset's microphone to his mouth. Turning to the pilot, he commanded, "Okay, Jim, get this bird in the air and get us back to Taylor's place."

Before the pilot turned off the cabin lights, Sarah glimpsed at the floor, glowering at the fresh droplets of blood speckled on the rubber matting's tan surface. Her gaze shifted to the makeshift bandage bound tight around Mark's right calf. Grasping his left forearm, she cried out, "Mark, you're hurt!"

The cabin fell dark. The helicopter blades gyrated faster and faster while the aircraft surged high above the meadow. In the moon's afterglow, Mark peered at Sarah, her eyes glistening with concern. He took her hand and gave it a gentle squeeze. "I'm all right. It's not that bad." Sarah gripped his hand, refusing to let it go.

The helicopter streaked over the forest toward Will

Taylor's property. No one spoke. Within minutes, the craft hovered above the ranch. The compound bustled with activity. Mark craned his neck to look out the window while the chopper banked to the right and descended to the southeastern end of the complex where a landing zone remained cordoned-off amongst the chaos. Three fire tankers clogged the north end of the courtyard, hoses snaking from their massive structures while they blasted the stubborn inferno with jets of water from their nozzles.

While the helicopter's rotors whirled to a stop, Dawes yanked off his headset. Swiveling in his seat, he said, "Just so you both are prepared – the media will be crawling all over this place at any time. The political rally in Helena has them tied up with their ongoing coverage. But, this is a pretty big story – so expect them to start circling – soon. My deputies have orders to keep them off the property and at a distance… but, reporters are… shall I say… *persistent*." He eyed Sarah. "The paramedics are waiting to check you over. I'll get with you after you're settled and we'll have a talk, okay?"

Sarah placed her headset on the seat and nodded. "Okay. But, I'm fine… really."

"Just the same – we're going to get you looked at. You've been through a lot and we're not going to take any chances." He glanced at Mark then eyed the blood-soaked scrap of cloth swathed around his lower leg. "You need to get that looked after."

Mark unclipped his harness and held Sarah's hand while she scrambled out. He propped open his door. "I've got other things to worry about right now. It can wait," he grumbled before stepping to the ground and closing the hatch behind him.

The sheriff huffed and shook his head. He popped open his door and slipped out of the cabin. Wheeling back to the pilot, he barked, "Hold tight. Once I get a handle on what's happening here, I might need a lift."

The pilot flipped a few toggle switches on the overhead console "You got it, sheriff. On standby."

Mark circled to Sarah and looked her over from head-to-toe. "Shall I carry you?" he asked.

"No, I'll walk."

He placed his hand on her shoulder while he led her toward an ambulance across the courtyard. He glared at the smoldering lodge while they lumbered, steam hissing from the drenched and charred outer walls as the deluge continued from the fire hoses.

Sarah shuffled to a stop, her mouth agape at the horrific display. "Oh, my God," she gasped, pressing her fingertips to her lips. She spun and faced Mark. Locking eyes with him, she asked, "What happened here?"

Mark took a deep breath. "Thompson is dead. I'll tell you the rest later." Placing his hand at the small of her back, he urged her toward the ambulance at a slow pace. Her bare feet had already experienced enough agony.

As they approached the waiting ambulance, two paramedics hustled from the rear compartment and hurried to Sarah's side, eyeing her up and down while they directed her to a gurney in the back of the rescue vehicle. Mark stepped aside and gave Sarah a forced smile. "I'll see you soon," he reassured.

The morning air nipped at Mark's exposed skin while the sun crept higher on the eastern horizon. He stood in the courtyard with his hands stuffed in the front pockets of his jeans, looking on while a construction crane lifted the lodge's warped aluminum roof panels from the charred rubble. Katy leaned against the side of Will's truck twenty feet behind, sobbing with a blanket draped around her shoulders.

Mark glanced over to the barn. Sheriff Dawes stood at the far end of the compound with a group of detectives who had arrived hours earlier in the pre-dawn darkness. After nodding a few times while the men conversed, the sheriff spun away from the assemblage. Adjusting his agency ball cap, he marched across the courtyard toward Mark. The sheriff ambled up and glanced at Mark's pant leg. A slit up its side from the cuff to his knee revealed a bright-white gauze bandage around his wound. "I see the EMTs got you patched up."

"Yeah, they cleaned it and stitched me up."

Dawes peered over at Katy then to the gravel at his boots. He folded his arms. In a hushed tone, he asked, "The medics told me Ms. Olsen only has a few bumps and bruises. But... she's pretty traumatized. Has she talked to you about what happened before you got here?"

Mark stared at the remnants of his father's burned-out home. After a few seconds of silence, he eyed the sheriff. "She's had a pretty rough time. She blames herself for what happened to my dad… said she should have stayed with him when Ben busted into the house." He gripped a tuft of his hair then scratched his scalp. The lack of sleep over the previous few days had finally caught up to him. Once the adrenaline wore off, exhaustion set in. His weary mind fogged with jumbled thoughts. Fighting the dreaded realization that his father was gone proved to be futile. Evidence of the nightmare's reality surrounded him, causing the tightness in his chest to intensify with every sight his eyes beheld.

The sheriff seemed well aware of Mark and Katy's fatigue. "Why don't you go get some rest in one of your dad's vacant guest cabins? You sure as hell look like you could use some shut-eye."

"Not now," Mark mumbled. "Not until they find dad."

"I understand. We've got just about everything wrapped up here. The coroner has already retrieved the marshals' bodies. They dragged Thompson's remains out of the barn about an hour ago… once they finished taking all their pictures and collected all the evidence."

"How is Gibbons?" Mark asked, trying to focus on anything but his father.

Dawes let out a big sigh then rubbed the back of his neck. "He didn't make it. He died on the helicopter while it was on its way to the trauma center. He lost too much blood they said."

Mark grimaced. "Damn. He seemed like a really good guy."

"Yes, he did, indeed." The sheriff glanced at the fire crew still working on the lodge then back at Mark. "I hear your wife is doing well despite her ordeal."

"Yes. The EMTs transported her to the county medical center. They're going to keep her overnight for observation. She tried to argue her way out of going, but it's probably best she's not here... when they finally find dad..." Mark pressed his fingertips to his bloodshot eyes. They burned from lack of sleep and every time he blinked it felt like sandpaper etching his corneas. "Whatever happened with Chavez?"

"We nabbed him about eight miles further up the road from the spot we found your wife. After he ordered her out of the car, he made it a few miles before he ran smack dab into a big buck crossing the road. The jeep he was driving was pretty much wrapped around a tree." Dawes chuckled then continued. "He was such a panicked mess he took off running through the woods carrying that briefcase full of money. Those black dress shoes he loves so much didn't do him any favors. He slipped climbing a slope and broke his ankle. It wasn't difficult for my deputies to find him. They said he was curled up beneath a tree bawling like a baby."

"So what's going to happen to him?"

Dawes blew out a deep breath. "Well, I only interviewed him for about half an hour before the feds stepped in and said they were taking jurisdiction of the matter. But, I'm guessing they'll be charging him as an accessory to murder. The little bit I squeezed out of him, seems he figured by channeling information to Thompson, he could make some easy cash – said he was in financial trouble at home and he needed the money. He contacted Thompson before he'd even left Washington when this whole fiasco started... said he had a lead on a bunch of pre-paid cells phones that were bulk-purchased. He sent text messages to all the numbers hoping for a response. He got one. The marshal was in cahoots with the scumbag just about the entire time. He swears he never intended on anyone getting hurt though."

"That's just plain stupid. How could a professional, knowing the background on someone like Thompson, think it was possible to get away with some kind of deal?"

"Your guess is as good as mine, Mark. Greed does strange things to people. Money can take a normally good person and twist them into something completely different," the sheriff replied. He shuffled his feet then added, "I really don't think Deputy Chavez thought anything through. He probably stumbled on an opportunity and figured he could make some quick cash. He didn't realize the bag of worms he was opening."

Mark glared at the tumultuous scene surrounding him. The once serene compound appeared more like a war zone than a ranch. He spat at the ground in disgust. "And if Chavez would have used that contact to trap Thompson... none of this would have happened."

While Mark bristled at the marshal's betrayal, a shout rang out from inside the lodge's floundering walls. Clad in a bright yellow jacket, smeared with soot and grime, a firefighter stumbled out the structure's front door and waved over to his cohorts inspecting the integrity of the building's still-standing outer walls. Readjusting his hard hat after it slipped forward and covered his eyes in his excited state; he called out, "Hey! Give me a hand in here! I've got something!"

While three men scrambled inside, Mark bolted toward the lodge only to be halted by a musclebound firefighter as he made his approach. With both arms extended and his palms pressed against Mark's chest, the tall man asserted, "Hang on there, buddy. It's not safe to go inside. Those walls could give way at any time, and the roof is already collapsing into the building."

Undeterred, Mark tried to push past the strapping firefighter. "My dad is still in there!" he growled.

Dawes trotted to Mark's side and clutched his arm. "Easy, Mark. Just let the rescue team do their job. You won't be doing anyone any good by going in there and possibly getting yourself hurt."

Mark sighed in frustration, his eyes locked in a duel of determination with those of the fireman blocking his advance. He yielded and took a step back. The young man gave Mark a sympathetic slap on the upper arm then spun away and disappeared into the lodge. The sheriff relaxed his grip as Mark muttered, "All right... all right..." his eyes fixated on the lodge's entrance and toward the ruckus obscured from view behind the blackened front wall. His pulse raced, the suspense palpitating in his blood with each successive heartbeat. The clamor of rustling debris continued for what seemed like a lifetime. *Come on! What's happening?* Was he ready? Could he handle the sight of his father's lifeless body being carried from the wreckage of the once majestic lodge? His eyes swam with tears while he tried to swallow the lump in his throat, hampering his breath.

Minutes later, a firefighter emerged from the doorway. Crab-walking sideways, he stepped onto the porch's blackened planks. The rescuer turned and faced the courtyard. Draped around his left shoulder for support, the old man staggered into the morning sunshine, hacking with each breath, his clothes and skin streaked with soot.

"Dad!" Mark exclaimed. He bounded the thirty feet separating them and grasped his father's hand while the fireman guided him to a sitting position on the gravel.

Dawes spun and signaled to the EMTs waiting in their ambulance across the compound. "Get a move on! We've got an injured man here!" he bellowed.

The blanket wrapped around Katy crumpled to the ground in a heap, slipping from her fingers while she darted from the truck to the old man's side. She dropped to her knees and threw her arms around his neck, nearly pushing him to the ground. "William!" she shrieked through broken sobs. Will embraced her and gave her a few pats on the back while he steadied himself with his other hand.

Mark knelt and placed his hand on his father's shoulder. He stared at the remains of the lodge, his mouth open in disbelief. Glancing back at the old man, he stammered, "I… I… don't understand… *how?*"

"There was a trapdoor in the closet just off the main hallway. The whole inside of the place is burned out. While we were combing through the debris, we saw his hand sticking out from a crack between the hatch and the floor," the burly firefighter explained.

"Ha!" Mark blurted. Searching his father's eyes, they were weary, but sparkling with relief.

The old man hacked a few times then wiped his mouth with the back of his grime-covered hand. Glancing at Mark, he grinned. "And you were givin' me grief about my little, hidden vault."

"*The bunker!*" Mark chuckled, "I guess there *was* a use for it besides a place to hide your weaponry." He stood and shuffled out of the way while the paramedics jogged up and slipped an oxygen mask over Will's face.

The old man gave a thumbs-up. He wheezed a few breaths from the mask then tugged it away from his face. "I just barely had time to crawl to the closet. It was like hellfire fallin' all around me."

While one of the EMTs pulled a gurney from the ambulance's rear compartment, the other, a young woman dressed in a blue jumpsuit with her hair pulled back into a bun, completed a hasty examination of the old cowboy. She flashed a reassuring look at Mark. "He's probably suffering from a good dose of smoke inhalation. His vitals are good though. He should be fine being transported by ground to County. They'll give him a thorough examination." The woman and her partner eased Will onto the litter.

Will again slipped the mask from his face. He scowled, causing the mixture of sweat and ash to crease on his forehead into jagged ridges of sludge. Eyeballing Mark, he asked, "Is that pretty gal of yours safe?"

Mark nodded. "She's fine, dad. You'll probably see her shortly. They're keeping her overnight at the county hospital just to be on the safe side."

Katy stayed close to the old man's side, gripping the gurney's aluminum side rail while the paramedics dragged the cart through the gravel. Will eyed her. "And the thug that caused all this mess?"

"He's dead. It's all over. Katy won't ever have to worry about him again," Mark replied. The old man pressed his lips together. He reached for Katy's hand and squeezed it before collapsing back onto the cart in a coughing fit. While the paramedics slid the gurney into the ambulance, Mark turned to Katy. "Go ahead and ride with him. I'll catch up with all of you in a bit." He swept the curls from her eyes and offered her a smile.

Leaning into him, she gave Mark a quick hug then climbed into the ambulance, taking a seat alongside the EMT stationed beside the old man. Once they settled into their seats, Mark slammed the emergency vehicle's rear doors. He stepped back as the driver fired up the van and drove away down the long drive to the entrance gate.

Mark exhaled a long breath. The previous few days were hellish. But, all those whom he loved were safe. The nightmare was finally over. They would find strength in one another to pick up the shattered pieces of their lives and move on from the strife.

CHAPTER 22

WEDNESDAY, APRIL 21ST

Three days had passed since the savage showdown with Ben. Home once again, Mark's father recovered in one of the vacant one-bedroom cabins on his property. His beloved lodge lay in ruins, ravaged by the fire. With nearly all his possessions and personal effects destroyed by the unforgiving flames, Sarah and Katy set off for Helena to purchase clothing and necessities for both Mark and the old man. The day-long trip persisted of occasional small talk followed by long lapses of uncomfortable silence.

Sarah sat in the passenger seat of Katy's old Chevy while the red truck rumbled down the weatherworn blacktop toward Crystal Creek, its bed packed with multi-colored shopping bags full of clothing and assorted essentials. The sun sank lower in the sky and long shadows stretched out from the tall pines thriving beside the asphalt. The methodical drone of the truck's tires humming along the pavement and the rush of wind outside the vehicle offered the only respite from total quiet.

Sarah brushed her hair back. *Well, this is awkward.* Clearing her throat, she broke the reticence. "So… Katy… thanks for the ride. I appreciate you hauling me all the way to civilization and back."

Katy fidgeted in her seat. "Oh, it's no problem," she replied with a smile, keeping her eyes on the two-lane road. "It's been a while since I've been up to Helena."

"I'm sure you had lots of other, more important things to handle back at Will's – especially with everything that's happened."

"It's okay. Really," Katy chuckled. "I think William needed a break from me being around. How did he put it?" She wrinkled her face and bellowed her best imitation of the old man's voice. "*Miss Katy, you're dotin' on me worse than an ol' mother hen.*"

Sarah giggled. "That definitely sounds like Will."

"I'm just grateful he's all right." Katy's lighthearted expression sobered. "I was worried once he had a chance to think about losing the house… and all the memories it held… it would break his heart."

Sarah paused and took a deep breath. She peered out her side window at the sprawling wilderness while it streaked by. After a moment, she glanced at Katy. "You're really something special – the way you've watched over Will all these years."

"He's been like a father to me. I adore him," Katy replied.

"Will is a rare kind of man. I thought when Mark's mom passed he would give in… let himself die of loneliness. He's a lot stronger than I gave him credit for. I think you've helped keep him going." She bit her lip, and then added, "And… you've been there for Mark over the past several months… I think you've been a big part of them reconciling."

Katy flashed a look at Sarah before focusing back on the road. "No… even when Mark first got here – late last summer – he and William seemed pretty close. Of course, that was the first time I'd ever met Mark… but, there wasn't any friction between them – at least none I noticed." She blushed. "And Mark… has been there for me too."

Glimpsing at her left hand, Sarah stroked her bare ring finger, lacking the wedding band Mark placed on it years earlier. So many unexpected events led to that very moment – ones that turned her world upside-down. The night she held Mark's cell phone when Stacy Kellner's text message to him flashed across the screen, exposing their drunken tryst during the presentation in Phoenix the previous summer, remained forever etched in her consciousness. The bitter taste of betrayal still lingered on her tongue. Scathing words she spoke the night she demanded he leave still echoed in her head. And just when things seemed at their worst, Seattle Police officers showed up on her doorstep hours later at sunrise, informing her Mark had been critically injured after leaving his favorite tavern. News of the accident deepened the sinking, empty sensation in the pit of her stomach – a void that persisted and hardly subsided even with the passage of time.

With Mark so far away, in Montana, seeking comfort in Dan's arms turned out to be a futile aspiration. Nothing quelled her anguish. The distance from Mark only deepened her despair. Seething with anger festering in her core hadn't brought about any sense of closure. It was a mistake – not attempting earlier to reconcile their once-happy marriage. She loved him despite his sin. Only a week had passed since he left Seattle after breaking her heart yet again. And after months of sadness followed by terror-filled days and nights as Ben's hostage, she prevailed only to find herself sitting beside Katy – the woman vying for Mark's attention.

Sarah's mouth went dry. She *had* to ask, clear the air. The periodic episodes of idle chatter throughout the day were wearisome – especially considering Katy seemed to be wrestling the same restive emotions. "You're in love him, aren't you?" she blurted.

Katy's shoulders sagged and she pushed back in her seat. After a moment, she exhaled a deep breath and nodded. "Yes, I am," she confessed softly.

Although Katy's feelings toward Mark were obvious beforehand, the admission still stung, striking like a bolt of lightning. Sarah's body tingled with tinges of jealousy. "I could tell... the first time I saw you look at him."

Shifting nervously on the bench seat, Katy held the steering wheel with one hand. She touched her fingertips to her lips, seemingly at a loss as to how to respond. After a moment, she gripped the steering wheel with both hands and glanced at Sarah before looking back to the road. A forced, sad smile crossed her face. "I love him very much. But... his heart has always belonged to you," she replied with sorrow distinct in her tone. "Since he first showed up at the ranch, I think you've always been on his mind... no matter what he's doing – or how hard he's tried to forget you. There hasn't been a day that's gone by he hasn't talked about you… the places the two of you traveled together… happy times you shared." Katy hesitated and swept the curls from her brow. "I don't know how many times I thought he'd finally gotten over you, only to look into his eyes and see how heartbroken he was. I don't think he's ever slept more than a few hours at a time since he got here. He told me about what happened – how he cheated on you. The guilt has been eating him up." She sighed. "I guess I've always known you were the only one he could ever truly love."

Sarah stared at the floorboard. Katy's discourse rang in her ears. The few times she had spoken with Mark since their separation, the shame and remorse was evident in the depths of his brown eyes and unmistakable in the quivering inflection of his voice. Her unbridled anger rebuffed any willingness to allow him to attempt redemption. The pain was too much to bear. But, during their eight months apart, her ire cooled. Their marriage was worth saving despite his unfaithful encounter, for he was the one.

Sarah reached over and placed her left hand on Katy's shoulder. "Thank you for confiding in me. I'm sorry if I seemed brash. I know this whole situation is awkward – for both of us."

The two women exchanged wistful smiles, sharing the bond of loving the same man. They traveled the remaining miles back to the ranch in silence, taking in nature's splendor while they journeyed home.

M ark treasured the late afternoon, witnessing the ever-changing hues of the forest and mountains transform under the radiance of the sun while it soared across the blue never ceased from keeping him captivated. He stood at the meadow with his arms draped over the top rail of the weathered fence surrounding the vast grassland. Half an hour earlier, the familiar grumbling of Katy's truck sounded from the road to the west, signaling the women had returned from their shopping expedition.

Sarah sauntered up next to him, her long blonde locks flowing with the gentle breeze gusting in from the west. She brushed the hair from her face. "I thought I'd find you out here. What are you thinking about?" she asked softly.

His gaze remained fixed on the vistas bordering the southern end of the valley. "Everything. How much I screwed things up. How much I hurt you."

"What did you see in her?" Sarah asked after a few moments of silence. With a feigned half-hearted laugh, she spun around and leaned back against the ragged fence, folding her arms. "I mean... I've spent months asking myself what it was she had that I didn't. Before you left, I wanted to ask you..." She huffed and wiped a tear from her cheek. "But, I was afraid of hearing the answer."

Mark sighed. For months, he tried to answer that question. *Stacy Kellner. Why? What could I have seen in you to make me forsake Sarah? Why would I risk hurting the only woman I've ever wanted to love?* Night after night, tossing and turning in an unfamiliar bed so far away from the home they once shared, he suffocated in guilt. He gripped the splintered railing and glanced at his feet in repentance. Kicking his boot at a clump of grass under the bottom plank, he shook his head. "I don't know. I really don't. I don't know what the hell I was thinking. I only remember bits and pieces of that night. It's almost like watching a movie through a foggy window. She was young and beautiful… maybe it was just the excitement of something new… something forbidden." He drew a deep breath and studied Sarah. Her expression revealed the pain and heartbreak she still carried since that fateful night. "I took you for granted. I got so caught up in someone else taking an interest in me I didn't think about anything but the moment. I cast aside everything important… for something meaningless."

Sarah nodded. "When we talked before you left Seattle, I told you I didn't know if I could ever forgive you." She tilted her head and looked away for a moment. Biting her lip, she turned back to him. Tears flooded her eyes. "*All* I've thought about since you left was watching you get on that bus… watching you walk out on any chance of us being together again. The entire time Ben kept me hostage, the only thing on my mind was *I might never see you again.*" Her voice shuddered, and she pressed her fingertips to her eyes while tears cascaded forth in a torrent.

Mark threw his arms around her and pulled her close in a firm embrace. Nuzzling his forehead against hers, he said, "Sarah, I never should have gotten on that bus. I shouldn't have left... and I'm *so sorry* I hurt you."

She encircled her arms around his waist and snuggled into his chest, her cheek pressed against the cotton fibers of his plaid shirt. "Promise me you'll *never* leave me again. Promise me I can trust you'll *never* be unfaithful again."

Mark touched her chin and directed her gaze to his. "I promise, Sarah. With every fiber of my being, *I swear it*." He searched the depths of her light-green eyes. They confessed her true feelings, scintillating with the love she still felt for him – a love that eclipsed the pain and hurt arising from his liaison nearly a year earlier. He pressed his lips to hers. Time seemed to stand still while he tasted the sweetness of raspberry lip gloss on her kiss. Butterflies fluttered in his stomach with a light flurry of nervous emotion – a sensation he hadn't experienced in years, as if they were reliving their first kiss all over again.

Their lip lock endured until they could take no more and left them both gasping for air. Sarah rested her forehead against his. "So where do we go from here?" she whispered breathlessly.

Mark took a step back and held out his hand. "How about we take a walk? We can think things through – together."

Sarah blushed. She flashed him a shy smile and grasped his hand. "Okay."

Walking along the fence line, they waded through the knee-high blades of wild grass, surrounding them in a shimmering sea of green. They swung their arms while they held hands, their steps slow and steady. No sense of urgency befell them. Silence persisted for several minutes while they simply cherished the warmth of each other's touch and companionship. They neared the end of the meadow's fence when Mark broke the lull. "Dad's doing a lot better now. The doctor said he should be back to his old, spry self with a few more days rest."

"That's great news. He wouldn't talk to me about what's on his mind. He always sticks to cheerful conversation with me."

Mark chuckled. "Yeah, you know dad. He never wants to be an imposition. He doesn't want anyone worrying about him." They strolled to the end of the barricade, where it shot away from them at a ninety-degree angle to form the eastern barrier of the pasture. He led her to the final section of fencing. Resting his elbow on the top rail, he cradled her waist with his right arm. He stared out across the grassland and at the tree-lined slopes rising from the forest floor on the other end of the valley. "We're going to rebuild the old house. We'll replace it with modern construction. It's about time dad started living in a place that's more up-to-date."

"Then what?" She gazed at him, her eyes filled with hopeful uncertainty.

"I want you to stay… here, with me."

Sarah seemed bewildered. "You mean… move *here*? To *Montana*?" Her eyes widened.

Mark leered at her. "Yes. Leave the city behind. Stay here with me." He faced her and placed a hand on each of her shoulders. "I *know* it would be a huge change. But, you'll love it up here… I promise. It would give us a chance

to start over. New scenery... a new sense of adventure..."
He held his breath while he struggled to find the words
to persuade her.

Gazing at him for a moment, she turned and gripped
the fence rail. After a long sigh, she appeared lost in the
very notion of his suggestion. She scanned the surrounding
wilderness and admitted, "Well... it *is* beautiful country...
I don't know. Maybe I can get used to this."

"It'll be a change, for sure – this type of setting. There
aren't any big shopping malls... no twenty-four-hour coffee
shops... But, there are big cities only a few hours away.
You've already seen Helena... and Butte isn't too far away.
They might not be quite as refined or as large as Seattle,
but they have anything you could want."

Sarah pivoted and faced him. "If you're here, that's
all I need."

An overwhelming sense of elation surged through
Mark's body. He cupped his hands on her buttocks and
picked her up. Wrapping her legs around his waist and
interlacing her fingers behind his neck, Sarah giggled while
he twirled her around in a playful pirouette. After a few
spins, he slowed his rotation until they staggered to a stop.
She plunged her fingers into his hair and combed the
black tufts, purposely lousing it up. He cocked his head
and let out a cheerful chuckle. "You're still gorgeous, you
know." His smirk faded, and once again their lips met for
a passionate smooch. Setting her down, he caressed her
cheek with a gentle stroke of his fingertips. "I love you,
Sarah. I can't tell you how many times over the past months
I've thought about holding you again."

She clutched the breasts of his shirt and nestled her face against his chest. "Your heart is pounding," she whispered.

He eased her away and laid his palm above her left breast. "So is yours." She trembled beneath his touch. Sensing the gravity of the moment, he grasped her hand. "Come on; let's head back to the cabin. We have a lot of details to work through."

Trudging alongside him, she tugged at his hand. "Don't walk so fast. Let's take our time getting back." The lightheartedness in her tone diminished. Something obviously troubled her.

"Okay. Something on your mind?"

Sarah's pace lagged even more. After a few steps, she shuffled to a halt. "Mark, it's Katy. She's in love with you."

Mark took a long-winded breath and glanced at the drifting clouds overhead. He nodded. "I know."

"What are you going to do? With me being here, it's going to make it an awkward situation for everyone." She proceeded to stroll, leading him by the hand at a reluctant pace.

He shrugged. Katy remained at the back of his thoughts. The jubilation he felt since rescuing Sarah at the vacant cottage overshadowed the spark he shared with Katy. Up until that moment, all the excitement from the previous few days made it easy for him to ignore the impending plight. Over and over, it pulsed through his mind, how he left Katy hanging onto the possibility they could share more than a friendship. Rubbing the back of his neck while they wandered ever closer to the ranch compound, he said,

"She means a lot to me, Sarah. She's a friend... someone I can talk to. She helped me get through some difficult days and nights."

"I know, Mark. She and I talked on our way back from Helena... about you."

He glimpsed at Sarah, a nib of uneasiness rumbled in his stomach. "About me?"

"Yes. She told me how hard it's been for you. She's a beautiful girl. I like her. I really do." Sarah gripped his hand tighter. "And... she told me how you couldn't get your mind off me... that you've spent the past eight months living on next to no sleep... moping about our separation."

"Every day you and I have been apart has been torture. I hate going to sleep because you're all I see when I close my eyes."

"It's been difficult for me too, Mark," she huffed in exasperation. "I've spent months hating you for what you did... but... at the same time... staying madly in love with you." She gazed into his eyes. "And knowing another woman wants a future with you... a woman you care about..."

Mark stopped dead in his tracks and faced her. He massaged his brow, trying to make sense of the confused mess of notions bouncing around in his heart and mind. "Yes, I care about Katy. I hated leaving you back at that place with the cops, even though I thought you'd be safe. It killed me after finally getting you away from Thompson that I had to go... but I knew he was on his way here. His plan from the start was to find her." He groaned and shook his head. "I couldn't leave her to face him alone."

Sarah reached out and cradled his face in her hands. Peering into his eyes, she said, "Hey! I don't blame you for going. I'm not upset you went after her. You did the right thing. You were thinking of both her *and* your dad. If you hadn't come back here when you did, they both might be dead. Ben was evil… sick and twisted… I spent three days wondering when he was going to kill me. It got to the point where I just wanted the nightmare to end." She stroked the grizzle of his beard with her thumb. "But you saved me. Whenever I thought of you, it gave me strength. I knew I had to keep fighting… no matter how scared I was… otherwise, I'd never see you again." She sighed then added, "I've had nothing but time to think about things. And I don't think I ever wanted to give up on us."

"I've never given up, Sarah. There were moments over the past few months when I thought I'd moved on… moments when Katy and I were alone… I almost put what you and I had in the past. But, those moments felt hollow – because it wasn't *you* I was with."

"I understand. I don't know how many times I ran to Dan's open arms searching for the same emotions I experienced with you." She stared at the ground then confessed, "It never felt the same."

Mark tugged at her hand and they continued their slow procession. "So what do we do? I think Katy will be fine. I've always been honest with her… about my feelings for you. But, Dan will be here in two days. The guy is so enamored with you it'll crush him once he finds out we're back together."

Sarah tucked her fingers into her thick mane and

tugged at a clutch of hair. "I'll just tell him the truth. He's always been a good friend – to both of us. I'm sure he'll be hurt... but, we both know the kind of man he is. He'll be happy for us even if he's disappointed for himself."

"Do you want me to talk to him first?" Mark asked.

"No. I think it would be easier on him if it came from me," Sarah replied. "After all, I'm the one he's had to keep from falling apart on a daily basis."

Mark nodded. "Okay. I'll have the best friend talk with him *after* you say your piece." They strolled through the front gate of the compound and began the long walk up the gravel drive. "We're kind of short on supplies here after the fire. Let's grab my dad and Katy and head into town for dinner."

Sarah smiled. "Sounds good. You go get Katy and I'll head to your dad's cabin and tell him to get ready."

Katy stood at her cabin's kitchen window gazing out the four-paned glass. Mark and Sarah strolled across the courtyard, laughing and smiling while they held hands. They paused and latched onto one another in a loving embrace. Katy's stomach sank while the couple pressed their lips together in a long, passionate kiss before they reluctantly parted ways. Mark headed in the direction of her cottage. She scurried from the window and retreated to her bedroom. Just as she plopped down on the edge of her bed, a knock sounded on the front door.

"Katy?" Mark called out.

Katy hesitated then slipped off the bed and trudged to the entrance. Nervous energy jittered within her and intensified with her every step. The rusted hinges of the weathered door squealed as she pulled it open. "Oh, hi. What's up?" she asked while attempting to bury her distress.

"We're all going to head into town to grab a bite to eat. Would you care to join us?" Mark's brow furrowed. "Hey, you look upset. Is everything okay?"

"Yeah… yeah, I'm fine. I'm just a little tired today." She forced a smile. "Thanks for the offer, but I think I'm going to soak in a hot bath before hitting the hay early."

"Okay. Can we bring something back for you?"

Katy shook her head. "No thanks. I'm going to pass on dinner tonight."

Mark seemed to realize something was amiss. He cocked his head. "Are you *sure* you're okay?"

"Yes, I'm good – really. I'm just a little wiped. After a full night's rest, I'll be back to my chipper, old self."

"All right. I'll catch you tomorrow then. Sleep well."

"Thanks," Katy replied before pushing the door shut. She rested her forehead against the heavy wooden door, losing the battle to hold back the tide of tears welling up in her eyes. With her palms pressed against the door and her fingertips tracing the wood's uneven grain, she wept. After a few deep breaths, she regained her composure and plodded back to her bedroom. Stepping to her closet, she opened the pine panel and reached to the top shelf for an old, blue suitcase. Lamentation pumped through her veins with each beat of her heart, but leaving was the right thing to do. *Mark seems so happy now. I'll only be a distraction by being around. Maybe if I'm out of sight... out of mind... he and Sarah can find a way back to each other.*

Hours passed while Katy shuffled through each of the modest cabin's three rooms, collecting her things and packing them while she mourned. The groan of the old man's truck boomed out from across the courtyard. *It's almost time... I'll wait until everyone is asleep – otherwise, they'll try to talk me out of leaving.* During her years on the ranch, she lived a meager existence, focusing on tucking most of her wages away while keeping her purchases to a bare minimum. She didn't have much, and for that, she was thankful. Her simple trove of belongings sat bundled up on the floor in a few tattered cardboard boxes – scrounged up from the barn.

She sat on the edge of her mattress for another two hours, staring at the scant pile of possessions. *It's going to be hard to leave this place. This has been home for so long.* Glancing at the digital clock on a small table beside the bed, it was just past one o'clock in the morning. She stood and made her way to the cabin's front room. After she slipped on her jacket, she stepped outside and lumbered toward the barn. All the cottages were plunged in darkness – a sign everyone had turned in for the night.

Passing through the metal door and into the barn, horses whinnied and snorted with delight as Katy ambled past their stalls. She shuffled to a halt at one particular enclosure. The white colt shook his head and pranced around the stall, kicking his heels up in joy before lunging to the pipe railing to greet Katy with a gummed kiss to her hair.

Katy stroked the colt's neck. "Hello, handsome." Shiloh nuzzled her cheek, wiping the stream of tears from her fair skin. "I'm going to miss you, little man. But… Mark and William are going to take great care of you." She rested her forehead on the colt's muzzle and patted his haunch through the railing. The colt huffed in deep breaths, sending ripples quivering down his white coat to his rump while she hugged him through the barrier. She held on for a few minutes before stepping back. The sorrow in her heart increased with each passing second. "I've never been able to handle goodbyes, so I better go. I love you, Shiloh." She kissed the colt's muzzle then spun away, covering her mouth with her hand. As she fled down the sawdust-covered alley toward the door, Shiloh cried out his objections by stomping his hoof and sounding out with snorts followed by a drawn-out whinny.

Katy dashed to back to her cabin and flopped onto the love seat in the cramped front room. She took a few minutes to calm herself before clambering to her feet. Snatching a box from her bedroom, she hauled it out of the cabin and tucked it in the bed of her truck. Within minutes, all her worldly possessions lay packed in the vehicle. She wandered back into the cottage and plucked two yellow envelopes from the kitchen counter – missives she wrote earlier in the evening after she and Sarah returned from Helena. Tiptoeing to Will's cabin, she slipped the first envelope under his front door before continuing to the one-bedroom lodge where Mark and Sarah slumbered. Touching the last envelope to her lips, she paused. *Goodbye, cowboy.* She slipped the note under the front door then traipsed back to her truck. Easing the door open, she slid onto the driver's seat and turned the ignition. With a deep breath, she steered the truck around the circular drive and toward the compound's front gate.

The old truck braked to a stop. Katy glanced over her shoulder, burning the compound's image into her memory with one final look. Tears rolled down her cheeks. She let out a long sigh then pressed her foot to the accelerator and drove off into the night.

The new day announced its arrival, sending slivers of light through gaps in the white-laced curtains covering the bedroom window. Mark opened his eyes and yawned. Sarah's head lay on his bare chest, her left hand on his breast. *Ugh. It's too early to be awake. I need coffee.* Sarah moaned as he scooted out from beneath her. He rolled off the bed. The hardwood planks chilled his feet while he trudged out of the bedroom to the front of the cottage where the cramped kitchen lay nestled in a corner. He stepped toward the counter where the coffee maker waited. He paused and eyed the front door. Ambling to the entrance, he peered at the threshold. A bright yellow envelope lay stuffed halfway under the door. *What's this?* He bent down and snatched it from the floor. On one side, his name appeared in eloquent cursive strokes. He plucked the letter from within and unfolded the white stationery.

Hello Cowboy,

I can't tell you how difficult it is for me to write these words. Months ago, you walked into my life unexpectedly. I was broken then. But your friendship helped to heal my wounded heart and make things more bearable. All the talks we had, all the moments we shared, will always be precious and remain in my memories. You truly saved me. But I look at you and Sarah together and I know without a doubt you two were meant to be. I see how she lights up when you're near her. I see how her eyes are always focused on you and how they shine with affection whenever she looks at you. She loves you, Mark. She's a kind and beautiful woman. Hold her close and never let her go. The two of you deserve your happiness together.

My heart is broken knowing I can never feel the warmth of your love in the same way you love her. After thinking this over for the past few days, I know it's important I move on. William has been like a father to me for the past six years, and I love him dearly, as I loved my own father. The two of you picked up the shattered pieces of my heart and helped to make me whole again. I can never thank you enough. I'll miss *this place. I'll miss my darling little Shiloh. But, I know you'll take good care of him while you rebuild from the ashes. I'll head back to Nebraska. Now that Ben is gone, I'm free. It's time I visit my family and old friends. It's time I learned how to live again without fear. It's time I went home.*

I love you, Mark. You'll always be in my thoughts and close to my heart. I'll never forget you.

All my love,

Katy

Mark choked up. He opened the front door and stepped out onto the porch, warding off the shivers from the morning chill while it nipped at his bare skin. Clutching the letter tight, he stroked his beard and gazed west at the long, rugged road that carried Katy away. Ache tugged at his heart with bittersweetness. His dear friend was gone. Surely, he would miss her. The floorboards in the cabin creaked behind him. He glanced over his shoulder. Sarah sauntered up to him, clad in a sheer, white nightgown, the thin veil flowing with the morning's light breeze.

Wrapping her arms around his waist, she burrowed her cheek between his shoulder blades. "Come back to bed, baby. It's cold out. Come keep me warm."

Placing his hand on hers, he replied, "Sure, just give me a minute." He slipped free of her embrace and spun around, touching his lips to hers. She offered him a sly simper and then strolled back into the cabin.

His gaze remained fixed on her while she retreated into the comfort of the small lodge until she disappeared from view through the open doorway and into the back bedroom. He eyed the empty spot in the courtyard where Katy always parked. Drawing in a deep breath, he held it before exhaling slowly. He turned and faced the sunrise. Soft rays of sunlight beamed over the horizon, setting the landscape aglow as they fell upon him and warmed his cheeks.

The new dawn brought hope.

The End

ABOUT THE AUTHOR

David Tucker spent his youth in Phoenix, Arizona, combing every corner of the state's wilderness on horseback and on foot in search of adventure. In time, the city grew too large, and David traded life in the arid southwest for a life in the mountains. When he wasn't out exploring, he spent his time reading and writing. After working for years in the corporate world, as well as experiencing several entrepreneurial ventures, he decided to walk away from the regular grind to focus on his love for writing fiction. With a vivid imagination, he enjoys bringing his characters to life in relatable circumstances. David now resides in Kalispell, Montana with his wife, three children, three spoiled dogs, and their cat. He and his family continue to pursue their love of the outdoors and are now exploring the wilds of Montana.

www.ingramcontent.com/pod-product-compliance
Lightning Source LLC
Chambersburg PA
CBHW020519260626
47156CB00006B/2060